THE UMBRA KING

VINCULA REALM BOOK I

JAMIE APPLEGATE HUNTER

MG PUBLISHING LLC

BOOK COVER DESIGN: *Books and Moods*

The Umbra King
Vincula Realm Book I

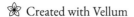 Created with Vellum

DEDICATION

Keith Brown,

I have not forgotten the time you sang Mississippi Girl instead of telling me there was a panther in the woods with us, nor have I forgotten that you never returned my favorite pen.

Count your fucking days.

WORLD GUIDE

Realms

Erdikoa ·

- The light realm
- Ruled by the Lux King
- Consists of a sprawling city and The Capital
- The Capital contains the Lux Palace
- The Capital was enchanted by the Seraphim so that any mystic other than the royals would lose their memory upon leaving; once they return, their memory of their time in The Capital is returned for the duration of their stay
- Normal days and nights
- Powered by the **essence**, or magical power that gives mystics their abilities, of the inmates in Vincula

Vincula

- The dark realm (or prison realm)
- Ruled by the Umbra King
- Has no essence
- When inmates arrive, they lose their abilities, as their essence is used to power Erdikoa
- Inmates are immortal and unchanging while in Vincula
- A large town with normal things imported from Erdikoa
- Inmates not residing in the palace live in a large apartment building with their own apartments
- Vincula's "days" are the equivalent to dusk in Erdikoa
- During Vincula's night, there is no moon and no stars – Once a month on the Plenilune (the full moon in Erdikoa) they can see the moon and stars
- Enchanted by the Seraphim so that when inmates leave, they lose all memories of their time spent in the prison realm

Aether

- Where the Seraphim live, and where good souls go when they die

Hell

- Created by different Seraphim
- Open to all realms regardless of who created them
- Ruled by Orcus

- Where wicked souls go when they die

Mystics

Mystic type and abilities are not hereditary
For example:
The heroine is a *Fey*, her sister is a *Shifter*, her mother is a *Sibyl*, and her father is a *Sylph*.

Aatxe

- Gentle souls
- Big in stature with small, bull-like horns on top of their heads
- The only mystics allowed to be enforcers, due to their pure nature

Alchemists

- The only mystics able to create potions and perform spells

Angels

- Wings
- Can shapeshift between several forms
- Have been in the two realms for an unknown amount of time

Eidolons

- Also known as phantoms
- Can walk through any non-living object except iron

Fey

- Have regular-sized ears with a slight point

- Stronger and faster than other mystics
- Graceful and light on their feet
- Can see the souls of others by skin-to-skin contact

Merrow

- Soul stealers
- When someone dies, they capture their souls in a jar
- They absorb the souls to heal injury or prolong their lives
- All merrows must take a potion monthly to bind their abilities
- The potion lasts two months, but they are required to take it every month in the event they try to skip, giving enforcers time to find them

Munin

- Can manipulate memories
- Anti-social, and do not like to spend time with other mystics other than fellow *Munin*
- Most live on a compound on the outskirts of the city (by choice)

Royal

- Rulers of the realms
- Do not possess mystic marks
- *The Lux King/Queen* – rules Erdikoa and controls light
- *The Umbra King/Queen* – rules Vincula and controls darkness/shadows

- *The Scales of Justice* – the final judge. Possesses the ability to see the souls of lesser mystics and the accused. When the Scales of Justice looks upon a criminal, they know the perfect punishment for their crime.

Seraphim *(singular: Seraph)*

- Creators of the realms
- Do not possess mystic marks
- Reside in the aether
- Celestial beings with large wings, feathers on their face revealing only their eyes and mouths, and feathers covering their legs

Shifter

- Every shifter can shift into one specific animal
- They do not have any animalistic qualities, even when shifted, other than their physical body when it shifts
- Shifts are fast, and when they shift back to their mystic form, they still have their clothes

Sibyl

- Oracles
- Once their abilities manifest, they see every potential future
- Their abilities begin to manifest in their 40s, and by 60, they take over fully

Sylph

- They manipulate air

Visitant

- Control the moods with skin-to-skin contact

NOTE:

There is an **Aeternum**, but it is a spoiler if explained.

Key Terms

- **enforcer** – police officer
- **essence** – magical power that gives mystics their abilities. It is the "essence" of their abilities.
- **essenet** – internet
- **ES/essence screen** - television
- **legion** – the law enforcement of Vincula, made up of enforcers and two *angels*
- **netsite** – website

PRONUNCIATION GUIDE

REALMS

ERDIKOA
ER- DI-KO-UH
VINCULA
VING-KOO-LUH
AETHER
Ā-THUR

MYSTICS

AATXE
(SOUNDS LIKE ATTIX)
ALCHEMIST
'ALKƏMƏST
EIDOLON
EE-DUH-LON
FEY
FĀ
MERROW
M-EH-R-OH
MUNIN
MOO-NIN
SIBYL
SIB-UHL
SERAPHIM (PLURAL)
SEH-RUH-FM
SHIFTER
'SHIFTƏR
SYLPH
SILF
VISITANT
VIZƏDƏNT

NAMES

AURORA (RORY)
AH-ROR-UH (ROR-EE)
DUME
DŌOM
KORDELIA (KORDIE)
KOR-DILL-YAH (KOR-DEE)
LENORA
LEH-NOOR-AH
CORA
KOR-UH
CAIUS
KAI-US
GEDEON
ɡID-EE-UHN
ATARAH
AET-AH-RAH
ADILA
AH-DEE-UH
TALLENT
TALƏNT
SAMYAZA
SAM-YAH-ZUH
ANASTASIA (STASSI)
AN-UH-STAH-SEE-UH (STAH-SEE)
JOPHIEL
JAH-FEEL
SERA
SEHR-UH
AEMAS
EE-MUS
LORA
LOR-UH

NOTE

CHAPTER 1

The sound of blood dripping was a beautiful thing when heard by the right person. In Rory's case, it only pleased her when the blood belonged to those with black souls. Souls had colors of all different shades, and being a *Fey* meant she could see them if her skin touched theirs.

It was her favorite thing about being a *Fey* because it allowed her to actually *see* colors. She and her fraternal twin sister, Cora, were born with grey-scale sight, and everything around them was in black, white, and greys. It was a rare condition, but not unheard of.

When Rory started seeing souls as a child, her soul would whisper the names of the colors in her mind until she learned them all. It didn't help with the rest of the realm, of course, but the burst of colors from those with good souls was a reprieve from her normal day to day.

She watched the blood drip from the man hanging upside down as she mindlessly touched the top of her ear. It was a nervous habit, stemming from her self-consciousness of looking differently from her parents and sister, who were different types of mystics.

Fey had pointed ears, and even though the point was so slight that if you weren't paying attention you wouldn't notice it, she still hated it.

She looked down at her enforcer boots with a groan. Blood covered the black leather and laces, and she knew she would scrub them all night. Lifting her boot, she peered at the soles. *At least the bottoms were clean.*

Stepping back, she made sure everything was perfect. The man's feet were held up by chains connected to a meat hook, his arms were crossed over his chest and sewn in place with fishing line, and his throat was slashed deeply enough for most of the blood to drain from his body into a nice pool on the floor.

She hoped the woman he tried to assault was okay. There was no telling what he would have done had Rory not been following them. She surveyed the man one last time, gave a nod of approval, and picked up her backpack to head home.

As Rory trudged down the sidewalk in the early morning hours, she felt the guilt settle in. It always did after one of her kills, and even though she knew she did the right thing, taking a life was never easy. She willed herself to remember why she did it.

Cora giggled as Rory elbowed her in the ribs. "Stop, or he's going to hear you," Rory hissed.

Cora laughed louder, and Rory slapped her hand over her sister's mouth. "I will shave your wool next time you shift," she threatened. Cora was a lamb Shifter, and Rory never let her forget that fact.

"*Go talk to him,*" *Cora whispered back.* "*You're acting like you're ten years old instead of thirteen.*"

"*What am I supposed to say?*" *Rory huffed.* "'*Oh, hey Judd, I think you're hot. Want to make out?*'"

"*Yes,*" *Cora asserted with a nod.* "*He likes you too. I've seen the way he looks at you when we're together.*"

Rory stared at Judd. He was a Fey *the same age as the twins, and Rory'd had a crush on him for at least three months.*

Cora stood from the picnic table and yelled, "*Judd!*"

"*Cora!*" *Rory whisper-yelled as she tried to pull her sister down.* "*What the hell?*"

Judd turned and waved, and Cora motioned for him to come over. "*You'll thank me later,*" *she said out of the corner of her mouth.*

Rory shook her head tightly. "*I'm going to murder you.*"

"*Hey, Cora,*" *Judd said with a wide smile.* "*Hey, Rory.*"

"*Hi,*" *they said in unison.*

Rory saw Dume, their oldest friend, crossing the school courtyard and groaned. She would never hear the end of this.

"*What are you doing after school on Friday?*" *Cora asked Judd.*

Rory's stomach dropped to her butt as she waited for his answer. She, Cora, and Dume were going to the movies on Friday, and she knew where this was going.

Judd stuck his hands in his pockets and rocked back on his heels. "*I'm free,*" *he replied, but before Cora could invite him out with them, he added,* "*Do you want to come over and watch a movie?*"

Rory's ears rang, and Cora's face scrunched. She looked at Rory with confused, apologetic eyes and turned back to Judd. "*No.*" *She gave no explanation.*

His cheeks turned pink, and Rory stood from the table abruptly. "You should go, Cora. It'll be fun." She threw her backpack over her shoulder and met Dume across the yard.

"What's wrong?" Dume asked when she stopped in front of him.

"Nothing. Can we go?"

He stopped her from walking around him. "Not without Cora. Tell me what's wrong."

"Rory, I'm so sorry," Cora said, out of breath from running. "I swear, I thought he liked you."

"It's fine," Rory clipped. "I'll see you at home."

She maneuvered around Dume, and Cora's protests followed her. Her sister grabbed her arm and turned her around. "I said I'm sorry."

Rory fought the tears pricking her eyes, refusing to cry at school. "I begged you not to do it."

Cora looked back at Judd, who was still staring at her, and lifted her middle finger. His eyes widened as he looked behind him, and when he confirmed the gesture was meant for him, he shook his head and stomped off.

Rory grabbed her sister's arm and pulled it down. "What is wrong with you?"

Cora shrugged. "He doesn't like me anymore." She motioned for Dume to join them. "Screw him."

Rory pinched her lips together. "He did nothing wrong."

Cora turned to her fully. "Everyone in our grade knows you like Judd, even him."

Rory's face burned hotter than a thousand suns. "No, they don't."

"Yes, they do," Dume agreed.

Cora lifted a brow at Rory. "If someone asks your sister

out in front of you, knowing you like them, they're a prick.
Even if you didn't like him, I don't date idiots."
    She threaded her arm through Rory's. "He looks like he
doesn't brush his teeth, anyway. I sit next to him in period one,
and his breath always stinks."
    Rory giggled despite herself. "That's not true."
    "She's right," Dume chimed in. "That means he doesn't
wash his balls either."
    Both girls grabbed on to each other in a fit of laughter as
they headed back inside the school. Rory rested her head on her
sister's shoulder as they walked, and Cora squeezed her hand
and whispered, "Fuck him."

Rory shook herself from the memory and whispered to
herself, "For Cora."
    Ten years ago Rory watched through a window as her
sister was brutally murdered, setting in motion Rory's path
to becoming one of the most prolific serial killers in all of
Erdikoa.
    Her guilt disappeared, and she continued home to sleep
like a baby.

∾

Rory toed off her boots and snuck into the apartment she
shared with her mother, Lenora. Most people thought it odd
that a twenty-five-year-old still lived with their parents, but
once they learned her mother was a *Sibyl*, they understood.
    Sibyls saw every potential future around them, and it
caused them to go insane. Fortunately, their abilities didn't

begin to manifest until they were around forty-five years old, giving them time to enjoy some of their life.

Every mystic was born with a mark behind their left ear, identifying their abilities, and to be born with the mark of a *Sibyl* was to be given a finite timestamp on life. Because of this, her mother had lived her life to the fullest, but now she spent her days staring out the window, speaking in riddles no one understood.

After easing open the door, Rory slipped inside, holding her boots, and crept to the bathroom. *Fey* had the gift of being light on their toes, and she could usually walk around without waking her mother.

She stared at herself in the mirror and sighed. Her straight dark hair was still in a tight bun, but flyaway strands stuck up in every direction around her face. The mascara she'd put on before her lunch with Kordie, one of her best friends, was smudged across her skin, and she looked like a drowned rat.

She wished she could see herself in color, but having grey-scale sight meant she couldn't even see the color of her own hair. Her mother said she had brunette hair and an olive skin tone, whatever that meant.

She peeled off her black hoodie, black leggings, and undergarments before turning on the shower to scalding hot. It would be more fitting if she wore a badass leather outfit like the actors in the supermystic movies, but leather was too hard to move in; it didn't have the same range of motion good old-fashioned cotton possessed.

Most of her clothes were black, white, or grey, because they matched each other no matter what, and because of that, it made owning a dozen black hoodies and leggings seem normal. She either had Kordie shop with her to confirm her selections were in black, white, or grey, or she shopped on the *essenet*. Then she labeled the tags and put them away according to color. It was a pain in the ass.

The hot water melted away the knots in her shoulders, and she let out a long moan. A good fuck would ease her tension better than the water pelting her muscles, but showing up at a bar covered in blood was frowned upon. After scrubbing herself clean, she padded to her room and threw on a pair of sweatpants and an old, ratty t-shirt.

Gathering her clothes from the bathroom floor, she threw them into the laundering machine, dumped an insane amount of detergent into the barrel, and pressed start. With a scrub brush, cleaning spray, and her boots in hand, she stepped onto the balcony. Even though the boots were black, she never left evidence behind.

Cleaning was tedious, but it was also soothing. It was familiar, which she liked. She'd hated change since the day her realm was tilted on its axis, and as it always did on nights like these, her mind replayed the worst day of her life.

Rory didn't feel well and stayed home from school that morning—at least, that's what she told her family. Truthfully, she didn't do the reading assignment for period five and didn't want to fail the test that day.

Before leaving for school, Cora promised they would watch Rory's favorite movie that night.

Rory sat on the couch by the window, bored after being alone all day. She knew Cora would be home soon and stared out the window, waiting for her as she huffed hot air on the glass to draw a smiley face.

She wiped the drawing away with the sleeve of her shirt

and saw Cora turn on their street. "Thank the Seraphim*." She pushed herself off the couch and pulled the window up to yell, but stopped when Bane, an older guy Cora met earlier that week, approached her. Did Cora forget about their movie date?*

Bane summoned her sister into an alley across from their apartment, and before Rory realized what was happening, he pinned her to the wall, clamped his hand over her mouth, and stabbed her in the heart.

Rory screamed Cora's name and clawed at the screen on the open window. She watched helplessly as Bane motioned to another man Rory hadn't seen. The new man held up a clear jar to Cora's mouth, and when she took her last breath, the inside of the jar filled with a bright pink light.

"No!" Rory screamed, the guttural cry burning her throat. The man with the jar was a Merrow, *and he'd just captured her sister's soul.*

Merrows *were soul stealers, and their abilities were supposed to be bound by the Crown, but somehow, his weren't.*

She ran for the door, sobbing in agony at what she'd seen, and her mother rushed into the room, asking what was wrong. All she could do was scream Cora's name and point at the window as she fought to unlock the deadbolt. When her mother saw Cora lying in the alley, she pulled Rory back.

"Stay here." She threw open the door and looked over her shoulder. "Do not leave the apartment."

Ignoring her mother's instructions, Rory pounded down the stairs after her. When they reached her sister's body, her mother fell to her knees and tried to staunch the bleeding, but Rory knew it was too late.

She'd seen Cora's soul leave. When mystics died, Rory saw their souls leave their bodies and disappear without having to touch them, something she learned in Fey history class last year. She never thought she'd have to see it.

Her mother stood and screamed for help as she fumbled her phone out of her back pocket. Rory fell to the ground next to Cora, pulled her into her lap, and rocked her back and forth as she cried.

Blood coated Rory's shirt from holding Cora to her chest, and when the enforcers arrived, she held her tighter and twisted side to side as they tried to pry her sister's lifeless body from her arms. She kicked and fought as she screamed her sister's name until her throat was raw.

Her mother pulled her back and into her arms, and they stood, crying together, as their realm crumbled apart.

Rory scrubbed harder, clenching her jaw to fight down the tears. From that day on, she became obsessed with hunting down her sister's killer and the *Merrow* who stole Cora's soul.

*Merrow*s used souls to heal themselves if they were hurt or to extend their lives as they aged. She could only hope she found the two men in time before Cora's soul was gone forever.

When Rory was twenty-two, she took justice into her own hands, because too many times, innocent people were found dead in the streets with no one to blame.

She needed the practice for when she finally found Bane, anyway. If only she knew something, *anything*, about him.

Her sister only mentioned him once and showed Rory a picture she'd snuck across the room of the café where they'd met. Cora asked Rory to skip first period with her that day to get coffee, but Rory refused, too afraid to get in trouble.

The picture was blurry, but still clear enough to recognize him in the alley.

When she asked Cora why she'd taken the picture in the first place, her sister replied, *"There was something different about him."*

She and her twin shared everything, and when Cora didn't voluntarily offer information, Rory peppered her with questions. Her sister gave vague answers, saying they only spoke for a few minutes, and despite the uneasy feeling in Rory's stomach, she afforded her sister privacy.

Cora never said she liked him in *that* way, just that they were going to meet up for lunch later that week. He was older than her, and it seemed weird, but again, Rory didn't want to step on her sister's toes.

That was the extent of knowledge Rory had of the man who killed her sister, and she knew absolutely nothing of the man who captured her soul.

For years, she asked around about Bane and any known unbound *Merrows,* and while she had a few leads, they were all dead ends.

When she finally found Bane, she would watch him swing as his blood played the sweetest melody she would ever hear.

CHAPTER 2

Rory struggled to hook up a new beer keg at Whiplash, the dive bar she worked at five days a week.

"I would have helped if you'd asked," Dume said from the other side of the bar.

She shot her oldest friend a glare, and he stared right back.

Dume became her best friend the moment she and Cora met him in grade one. Before long, the three were attached at the hip, including after school and weekends. They might as well have been siblings.

"I've told you a million times I will not ask you to work on your nights off," Rory called from her position on the floor. "You worry too much about everyone else."

Dume's short, dark hair, and small, light horns appeared in her line of sight. "And I have told you—helping you is not working."

He was a handsome man with a muscular build, dark skin, and big, innocent eyes. His good looks might have swayed the other women, but not her.

She stood and wiped her hands on her jeans before testing the tap. "Sit back down. Your next drink is on me."

He shook his head. "You know I don't drink."

"One day you'll say yes," she quipped as she looked over Dume's shoulder and rolled her eyes at the man approaching the bar. "Hey, Keith."

Keith flashed his perfect teeth and winked. "If it isn't my favorite bartender."

Her eyes took in his finely tailored suit, and she shook her head. Keith was a *Shifter* and one of the biggest playboys in Erdikoa. His tall, fit build, hair Kordie called sandy blonde, and light eyes Kordie said were blue, had men and women from across the realm flocking to him in packs.

Rory wiped down the bar in front of her. "Whatever you say, wolf."

He frowned. "Why do you always say that like it's a bad thing? I could be a squirrel instead of the magnificent beast I am."

Dume grumbled something under his breath, and Rory twisted her mouth to the side to keep from laughing. Keith drove Dume crazy, but she knew he would drop everything to help the wolf if he ever needed it.

If Keith was off work from the bank, then that meant Kordie would be here soon. Rory had known Keith and Kordie for about five years; the two would come into the bar after work, as would Dume, and it wasn't long before Kordie forced them all to be friends.

Kordie was three years older than Rory and Dume, one year older than Keith, and had always been the peppy one of the group despite being the oldest.

"Hey, bitches!" Kordie's loud voice came from across the

room as she bounded through the door. Rory had no idea how that loud of a voice came out of such a small body. Rory waved to her friend. Kordie's hair was a different color today than yesterday and cut off at her shoulders. It changed often.

"What color is your hair today?" Rory called across the bar.

Kordie picked through the after-work crowd. "Purple. It looks fabulous." She waved her hand in Rory's general direction. "It would go great with your eyes."

Rory shook her head as her mouth suppressed a grin. "Never going to happen."

Kordie was an *Alchemist*, and since *Alchemists* were the only mystics able to perform spells and create potions, she had an affluent beauty salon across the street.

Her spells could make a bridge troll look like a *Royal*. Not that bridge trolls were real; they were creatures from children's bedtime stories Rory had been convinced lived under her bed as a child.

Her friend huffed and planted her hands on her hips. She had a petite frame, and her light skin flushed from head to toe when she was angry, and it took all Rory's strength not to laugh. She was as far from intimidating as one could get.

Kordie was the exact opposite of Rory, who was five-foot-eight with a lean, rectangular body shape. Her boobs were small, and she had to work hard in the gym for what little ass she had.

"I should do it anyway," Kordie mumbled. "You would thank me."

"Beer, liquor, or wine?" Rory asked her, changing the subject.

Kordie sighed as she slid onto the barstool next to Keith. "Make it liquor."

"I'll take the same," Keith added. "Since you forgot to ask me."

Rory slid Keith's bourbon across the bar. "I keep hoping you'll go run with a pack and leave me alone."

He glared over his glass, taking a long drink as Kordie laughed. *Shifters* didn't have any animalistic qualities other than being able to turn into one, and Keith hated it when the girls insinuated otherwise.

"What are you smiling at?" Keith said to Dume. "You have horns, for aether's sake."

Dume shrugged. "And you have dog breath."

Rory and Kordie were both leaning over laughing as Keith flipped them off.

"I like your hair today, Kordelia," Keith said with a flirtatious grin. "The purple brings out the green in your eyes."

Kordie grabbed an olive from the bar tray and threw it at him. "For the last time, I am not having sex with you."

Keith dodged the assault and wound his arm around her shoulders. "You might change your mind."

It was the same song and dance they did every day, and Rory suspected there was something there under the playful banter.

"Do you close tonight?" Dume asked.

"Yeah," Rory replied. "But I'm off tomorrow."

Kordie perked up. "You never have Fridays off."

"I know." Rory leaned on the bar. "We need to do something that doesn't involve Whiplash."

"Like what? Go to a different bar where we have to pay full price?" Keith joked.

Rory popped him in the arm with her bar rag. "We could go dancing."

Dume groaned, Kordie clapped, and Keith pointed at her. "I like where your head's at."

"It's settled," Kordie declared. "Let's meet at Wonder at nine o'clock tomorrow night." Wonder was a popular night-club a few blocks away from the bar.

Rory slapped the bar and straightened. "Sounds like a plan." A customer waved her over. "I'll be right back."

After serving a few others, she walked back to her friends and noticed their attention focused on the essence screen behind her. "What's so interesting that even Dume is glued to the ES?" she asked, but when she turned, her words died in her throat.

"The Butcher killed someone else," Keith said grimly. "What kind of sick fuck sews someone's hands to their shoulders?" He shuddered. "Could you imagine having to poke a needle—" He stopped to gag.

Kordie wrinkled her nose. "That is what you're the most concerned about? The Butcher is murdering people and stringing them up on meat hooks."

Dume was quiet as he looked at Rory. "I'm walking you home from now on."

She waved him off, trying to look unbothered despite wanting to crawl out of her skin at her friends' disgust. "My *Fey* strength makes me stronger than most other mystics. I do not need, nor do I want, an escort."

"And if The Butcher is a *Munin* and wipes your memory clean before they attack?" he challenged, making her grimace. "You wouldn't remember any of your training."

Munins controlled memories, but surprisingly enough, they hated being around people and stuck together. A

Munin compound was located outside of the city, and they kept to themselves. Even if she were not the culprit herself, Rory doubted a *Munin* would care enough about others to commit a string of murders.

"You know as well as I do that's not the case," she replied tersely. "You're not escorting me like a child, and that's final." His knuckles turned white around his glass of water.

"After what happened to Cora, I can't risk losing you too," he said quietly.

Kordie and Keith averted their gazes, knowing Rory's sister was a sore subject for both her and Dume. "I'm not Cora. Don't forget I bested you in training last week. I can take care of myself."

"Once," Dume stressed. "We've been training together since we were sixteen, and you've only beat me *once*."

"I thought you only trained as kids," Keith said. "I want to watch next time."

"We don't train anymore," Dume said, shaking his head. "It was for fun. As teens, she begged me to teach her what they taught me in enforcer training, and once my classes stopped and I joined the force, so did our lessons." He looked at Rory suspiciously. "How did you improve so much since the last time we sparred?"

They were interrupted by a customer turning up the ES as it called The Butcher dangerous, warning the public to walk in pairs, and Rory sighed when Dume gave her an "*I told you so*" look.

She turned to the ES with a frown. They'd found this victim fast. Because of the locations she picked, it normally took days, sometimes weeks, to find the body.

She turned back around. "Maybe the victims deserved it."

Keith nodded. "You could be right. Remember last year when they said one victim was wanted for suspected murder?" The *Shifter* looked thoughtful. "If The Butcher is a vigilante, that's a different story."

Dume rubbed his forehead. "This isn't a supermystic movie."

Keith ignored him and took a drink.

There was a sinking feeling in Rory's gut. What would her friends think of her if they knew? She would lose them all.

Her thoughts were interrupted by yelling on the other side of the room, and when she looked up, fists flew. "For aether's sake," she muttered and rounded the bar. Secretly, she was thrilled at the prospect of hitting someone after that unflattering news report.

Dume stopped her. "Don't even think about it." He stood and made his way to the fighting duo as other patrons stood back, giving them ample room. He grabbed one man by the arm and pulled him back, earning him a right hook to the jaw.

Dume's head snapped back, and when the man saw who he hit, his face drained of color as he backed away with his hands raised. "I was aiming at him," the guy claimed, pointing at the man in Dume's hold.

"Fighting is not permitted. You could have hurt someone," Dume said calmly. "I won't take you two to headquarters, but if I see you in this bar again, I won't be lenient." He turned to the crowd. "Who can take them home?"

A few people raised their hands and approached each man, grabbed them, and hauled them to the exit. The first two men passed through the door without opening it, and Rory shuddered.

They were *Eidolons*, otherwise known as phantoms. They could pass through any non-living objects, except iron, and it was unsettling to witness. Most buildings had iron built into the walls and entrances, but Whiplash had iron bars that pulled down after closing.

The other man from the fight was being led out by a woman who spoke in a heated whisper, and Rory shook her head.

Dume kept a level head despite taking a punch to the jaw, but Rory would have swung and relished in the crunch of bone. She closed her eyes, disgusted with herself. After Cora died, her obsession with vengeance turned her into a monster more and more every day. Now she understood why no one other than *Aatxe* could be enforcers. Enforcers upheld the law and protected the citizens of Erdikoa.

Dume was an *Aatxe*, and they were well known for their gentle souls; they wouldn't abuse their power as enforcers and would treat offenders like mystics instead of animals, no matter their crimes.

All *Aatxe* had similar builds and tiny, bull-like horns sticking out of their hair that Rory and Cora teased Dume about when they were kids. He'd threatened to headbutt them both on more than one occasion.

Once the crowd settled down, Dume returned to his seat.

"You should have decked that guy," Keith said to him. "You're going to have a bruise."

Dume ignored him and turned his dark eyes to Rory. "Can I get another water, please?"

She reached across the bar to pat his head, but he swatted her hand away, the brief contact making his almost white soul flicker. "Sure, you can, you big ol' teddy bear." He mumbled something under his breath as she refilled his glass and gave it back.

A large, handsome man sat down at the other end of the bar and lifted his hand to get Rory's attention.

"I'll be right back," she told the trio in front of her.

She approached the man and smiled, but the moment she was in front of him, her breath caught. Something was off, and anytime she felt this way, it meant a black soul was near.

The man looked her over before his mouth pulled into a sexy smile. "It must be my lucky night."

There was something sinister behind his words, and it made Rory sick to her stomach. "What can I get you?"

The man leaned on the bar. "I'll have a RollMan beer, please."

Once she was clear of the stifling air surrounding the man, she released a long breath. It was unusual for her to encounter two black souls this close together because there weren't as many black souls as one would think.

Sure, there were plenty of shades of grey, including dark grey, but they still had a chance of redemption. Once a soul was black, there was no hope for them. Silently, she ran through her options as she grabbed a bottle from the cooler and popped the top. She would tail the man tonight, but to do that, she needed to keep him here until closing.

She set the beer down and smiled. "I just need to see your mystic card."

Annoyance flitted across his face as he pulled his wallet from a messenger bag sitting on the floor. Rory thought she heard the distinct clink of glass from the giant bag but brushed the thought aside when the man held out his card. Rory made quick work of memorizing the address before handing it back. *Jessie Hines.* "Anything else I can get for you?"

"Just the beer," Jessie said with a charming smile.

Rory noticed him eyeing the crowd, and a chill crept up her spine. He stood and walked to the bathroom, and when he returned a while later, he had a young woman with him.

Rory cursed under her breath. She didn't bring her things with her, and she needed them to *take care of business.* Usually, she kept her bag locked in her work locker until she needed it, but she hadn't brought it back yet from her last kill.

She motioned for Brax, the other bartender, to follow her to the back, and once through the door, she put on a pitiful face. "I feel like shit," she told him.

He took a cautious step back. "What's wrong?"

"I'm not sure, but I think I might puke." She made a show of holding her stomach with a grimace.

He took another step back and waved her off. "Go home. No one wants to clean up vomit. I'll pull Haxton from the lounge to take your place."

"Thank you," she said with a weak smile and returned to her friends at the bar. "I'm heading home early. I don't feel great."

Dume squinted his eyes. "You don't look sick."

Keith scooted away from her as Kordie leaned over the bar to feel her head. Her soul was the perfect mixture of pink and purple, and it throbbed until she removed her hand. "She's clammy," Kordie announced.

"I think it was something I ate," Rory lied. "I'll catch up with you guys tomorrow night. I'm sure I'll be fine by then."

She turned and left without giving them time to argue, praying she would get back in time.

She made the three-block trek to the warehouse district where her storage unit was located. It was a sketchy area where most of the essence lights were burned out and surveillance cameras were nonexistent.

After raising the garage-like door just enough to slip inside, she flipped the light on the wall. When the bulb flickered on, a faint buzzing filled the space.

The inside was set up with a dresser and a locked safe the size of a closet against the far wall. Quickly, she changed into her signature black leggings, black hoodie, and black enforcer boots. She kept extras here for nights like this.

After unlocking the safe, she stuffed an enforcer-grade backpack with a set of chains, a meat hook, a bottle of intoxicant, a large kitchen knife sheathed in leather, and her sewing kit.

Most of the things she used came from the underground market, a place crawling with grey souls of various shades and merchants selling things you couldn't legally find in Erdikoa.

She double checked her bag, made sure her long hair was secured in a tight bun, and left. On her way back to the bar, she cursed herself for not looking at what type of mystic Jessie was. She was too focused on memorizing the address.

She was an idiot.

Her black attire helped her disappear into the shadows as she slunk through the back alleys around Whiplash. The bar closed in an hour, and she hoped she wasn't too late. Earlier, she typed Jessie's address into her city guide app, saving it in the event she'd need it. If the man was already gone, she would stake out his house instead.

After what felt like forever, Jessie and the younger woman exited the bar, and Rory sent a silent thanks to the *Seraphim*. She waited for the two to get to the next crosswalk before creeping out of the alley to follow. She stayed close to the buildings with her hood up, ready to hide if either of them turned around, and even though she was a safe distance behind them, she could never be too careful.

Jessie turned down a side street in the general direction of the address on his mystic card. Rory stepped out of the shadows to skirt around a stoop when a voice stopped her.

"Is everything alright?"

Her head swiveled to see an older *Aatxe* standing at the top of the stoop with his keys stuck in the door.

"If someone is chasing you, I can call the enforcers straight away," he offered. She could tell by the way he carried himself he had been on the force in his youth.

"That won't be necessary," she assured him. "I..." She couldn't think of a single thing to say.

The *Aatxe* took a step down, concern etched on his face. If only he knew *she* was what went bump in the night.

"I watched the new supermystic movie," she blurted, making him halt. "*Fey* aren't allowed to be enforcers, and it's fun to pretend."

Her face heated with embarrassment because it was half true, though she was too old to be playing pretend. *Please buy it.*

The old man chuckled. "Carry on, then. Wouldn't want to stop you from saving the city."

He turned back to his door, cranked the key to open the knob, and disappeared. Rory released a long sigh of relief.

She swore as she hurried down the sidewalk. If she ran, it would draw attention, something she did not need more of.

When she rounded the corner, Jessie and the woman were nowhere to be seen, and panic clawed at her chest.

Forget being seen; she couldn't let anything happen to that woman. Rory took off down the sidewalk, and once at the end, she stopped to catch her breath as she wiped the sweat from her forehead. Just because she had extraordinary strength and speed did not mean she had endurance.

Righting herself, she looked at her navigation app and turned down an alley as a shortcut to Jessie's apartment building. A red high heel in the middle of the side street had her skidding to a halt.

Her vision tunneled as she stared at the shiny shoe, knowing it hadn't been there long. *No, no, no, no, no,* she chanted as she spun around and scanned her surroundings. Her eyes caught on a large dumpster not far away, and it was then she noticed drag marks from the lone shoe to the side of the black metal bin.

She dropped her bag to follow the drag line as dread collected in her chest, knowing what she would find. Using the rungs on the side of the dumpster, she hauled herself up and peeked over the side as the putrid smell of garbage assaulted her nose.

A sob escaped her when she saw the young woman's lifeless body crumpled on top of the waste. Bruises marred her neck and mascara streaked her cheeks. Rory jumped down, no longer able to stand the sight of her failure, and after sending in an anonymous tip on a dead body to the local enforcer unit, she grabbed her backpack and ran to the address on Jessie's mystic card.

That asshole would pay.

. . .

When she approached the address from the card, her stomach dropped. The apartment building was nice. *Extremely* nice. The area wasn't upscale per se, but this building was.

Normally, Rory would give her victims a potion and lead them to the warehouse district, where no one would hear them scream. The potion she frequently bought from Fiona, an *Alchemist* in the underground market, made whoever breathed it in inebriated to the point of pliancy. They did whatever they were told and presented with a drunken demeanor.

There were cameras in buildings like this, and if she tried to drag an intoxicated man twice her size through the building, it would catch someone's attention, especially since sometimes it made them loud drunkards.

She pulled her hood up and took out the bottle, held her breath as she wet a rag, and stuffed it in her pocket. Opening the door as quietly as possible, she read the list of apartments on the guide.

When she found what she was looking for, she took the stairs to the third floor. Once finding the correct door, she rang the bell and took a calming breath.

The door swung open, and Jessie stood on the other side with a look of surprise. The blackness of his soul almost knocked Rory to the ground, but she forced herself to ignore it.

She pushed her hood back and smiled widely. "I hope this isn't too forward, but I memorized your address when I checked your mystic card."

Jessie's eyes tracked down Rory's body, and his brows rose as he leaned on the door frame. "Why?"

She put on a show of shyness and bit her lip. "I wanted to ask you out, but that other woman interrupted."

Jessie stared at her, and Rory held her breath. She would mow him over if she had to, but it would be easier if he willingly let her in. "I'm Rory, by the way."

His mouth curved into a smile. "I'm Jessie. What a pleasant surprise. Come in."

"Thanks," Rory said, flashing her sexiest smile.

"Have a seat while I pour us a glass of wine," he said as he pushed through a door across the room.

Rory perched on the side of a leather wing-backed chair and inspected her surroundings. The apartment was pristine, but where she expected it to be laid back like his appearance and demeanor, it was elegant. *Strange.*

Jessie appeared with two wine glasses and held one out. When he turned to take a seat, Rory noticed there was no mark behind his ear, and alarm bells blared in her mind.

That was never a good sign. Either he had it covered with makeup, which was illegal, or he'd procured a spell to keep it hidden. Also illegal.

He looked at her hungrily. "Tell me about yourself." His eyes flitted to her wine glass, and Rory fought the instinct to dump it out. It was either poisoned or she was being paranoid.

She lifted the glass to her lips and let the liquid slosh against her mouth without allowing any to slip inside. Pretending to swallow, she lowered the glass and wiped away the remnants of the liquid with her fingers. "This is outstanding. Where did you get it?"

Jessie's smug smile as he took a sip of his own wine did nothing to temper Rory's suspicions. "A friend. If you will excuse me for a moment, I need to relieve myself." He set down his glass and stood on long legs before exiting through another door.

Rory quickly switched their glasses and sat back, trying to stop her hands from shaking. When he returned, his eyes widened in surprise at the sight of Rory. It was obvious he thought whatever was in the wine would have kicked in by now.

Jessie sat down, picked up his wine, and motioned for Rory to take another drink as he took a long swig of his own. "Drink up. We need to loosen up the tension in those shoulders."

Rory smiled and took a small sip of her untainted glass as she scrutinized the man.

Within a minute or two, Jessie slumped forward, falling out of his seat, and Rory took another drink of her wine before smacking her lips. "Damn, I'm smart."

As she stood, Jessie transformed into a small, mouse of a man, and Rory jumped back. "What the hell?"

There were no *Shifters* that changed mystic forms; they were all animals. She nudged the man with her toe. He felt like a potato.

When she rolled the man over, her blood ran cold, and she stumbled back, tripping over the chair. She hit the ground with a loud thud and her hand flew to her mouth to muffle a scream.

With shaking hands, she crawled forward, pushed the man onto his right side, and looked at the mark behind his left ear to confirm what she already knew.

Jerking to a standing position, she stepped back. "It's him." On the floor at her feet was the *Merrow* who stole Cora's soul. Rory's mouth hung open as her breaths came in quick pants, and she had to stave off the dread clawing its way into her chest.

She'd been waiting for this moment since she was fifteen years old, but to have it sprung on her completely unaware had shaken her. The creators of the realms, known as the *Seraphim*, were not something she put much stock into, but in that moment, she felt blessed. The odds of this happening were slim to none.

"Shit," she hissed as she bent back down to feel for a pulse. "Please, don't be dead."

Her shoulders sagged with relief when she felt a light *thump* against her fingers. His black soul was sickening, and she jerked her hand back. The *Merrow* would die tonight, but not until she had her sister's soul and he told her where Bane was.

Deciding to proceed as usual, she looked around the ostentatious apartment for a place to hang her hook. The ceilings were high, and fortunately, so were the doorways. She pushed the coffee table to the door between the kitchen and the sitting room, propped the door open, and stood on the table to reach the top of the frame.

She only chose warehouses with catwalks or structures she could hang her chains from, but she always kept a small drill and industrial grade screws in her bag in the event something like this were to happen. She'd had a few years to hone her craft and, by now, she was prepared for anything.

After hanging the hook, she chained the *Merrow's* feet together and slid the chain through the meat hook and pulled. The make-shift pulley lifted his body, and she thanked the *Seraphim* he was small in stature. Otherwise, she didn't know if the frame would hold.

Stepping back, she surveyed the man. This was where

she'd normally slit his throat and watch him bleed out before sewing his hands to his arms, but she needed him alive.

Digging through her bag, she grabbed a rope and tied his hands behind his back, and as she was finishing the knot, she heard a sharp intake of breath.

He struggled, and as he did, he swung back and forth, making the door frame creak. Rory moved around him so she was face to face with the monster and bent her head upside down.

"Hello, fuckface." Her smile was malicious as she righted herself, positioned a chair in front of him, and sat down.

"What is this?" he demanded, but his voice held no authority, only fear.

Her smile widened. "This is your lucky day." She reached into her backpack and grabbed the knife. "If you tell me what I want to know, that is." She removed the sheath and inspected the blade.

He balked at the cold steel in her hands and struggled again. "I don't know what you're talking about, you crazy bitch."

Rory laughed as she stood and crouched down in front of him. "Wrong answer." She slashed his cheek open, and blood splattered on the front of her hoodie. "That was a clever disguise," she admitted. "A shapeshifting potion, I assume?" It was the only explanation.

He glared at her and said nothing. She shrugged. "It doesn't matter. What *does* matter is the woman you killed tonight." She slashed his other cheek. "And where my sister's soul is."

"I didn't kill anyone," he insisted. "And I didn't know the girl from the bar was your sister."

Rage burned through Rory's body, and she kicked him

in the ribs. "Not her." She made a mental note to scour the apartment for the girl's soul. It was obvious he'd taken it. "My sister was the lamb *Shifter* Bane murdered before you put her soul in a jar ten years ago. And before you deny it, I saw you." She grabbed his cheeks and yanked his face to look at hers. Blood coated her hands from the cuts in his cheeks, but she didn't care. "If you don't return my sister's soul, I will cut every limb from your body while you are still alive." And she would enjoy it.

She could practically taste the fear on him as he trembled, and his brow furrowed before his eyes widened with understanding. "Lady, that was a long time ago. Her soul is gone."

"You absorbed my sister's soul?" She tried to hide her agony, praying it wasn't true.

"No, I didn't." He struggled harder. "I swear I didn't, but I can't tell you where it is," he stammered.

She stood with a tight-lipped smile, walked around his hanging form, and cut the tendon in the back of his right ankle. He screamed, and she clamped her bloody hand over his mouth. "Where is her soul?"

Tears fell to the ground below the man as he sobbed against her hand. Pulling her hand back, she walked around him again and stared silently until he spoke. "He took it. The man you mentioned, he took it."

"Why would he want my sister's soul?"

The *Merrow*'s body shook with cries. "He didn't say. He approached me and said he would strip my name from the Crown's archives and give me a new identity so I could skip my monthly binding elixirs. He set me up a new bank account filled with more moedas than I could spend in my lifetime. H-he gave me an elixir to reverse the effects of the suppressant." The man sobbed again. "He said all I had to do was capture her soul for him. That's all I know."

She sat in the chair, perplexed. "That doesn't make sense. My sister wouldn't hurt a chipmunk."

Instead of answering her, the man wept as he swayed back and forth. Mulling over the new information, she stood and bent down in front of him again. "I want to look into your eyes when I say this, so stop crying and listen." He sucked in a few quick breaths and looked at her. "This is for watching as my sister died and then stealing her soul."

With that, she slid her knife across his throat and watched as he bled out. She wasn't sure how long she stood there, staring at the man she had dreamt of killing a million times, but when she moved again, it was with purpose.

In her fantasies, when she found him, she drew his death out and relished in his screams, but she couldn't do that in an expensive apartment building filled with people. *Damnit.*

Wandering through the apartment, she opened every door until she found what she was looking for. Her hand flew to her mouth as she held in a cry at the sight of floor to ceiling shelves filled with jars of different colored souls. *How long had he been murdering innocents?*

Pulling herself together, she made quick work as she opened each jar and set them free.

When she was done, she methodically sewed the *Merrow*'s hands to his shoulders as her mind ran wild. She had to find Bane, whoever he was, get her sister's soul back, and send him to hell.

CHAPTER 3

VINCULA

Caius choked as he sat up, his nightmare having dragged him from sleep. He couldn't get the image of blood-soaked hands out of his head. His nightmares were becoming more vivid, and each emotion stayed long after he woke.

"*Seraphim*," he muttered as he threw back the duvet and stood. He raked a hand through his hair, crossed the room, and poured himself a bourbon from the wet bar. He eyed the wine bottles in the mini wine fridge, and his insides soured. The word *poison* echoed in his mind, and without thinking, he pulled the fridge out of its cubby and placed it in the hallway.

This happened sometimes after his nightmares. Something that never bothered him before made him uncomfortable for no reason, and he was unable to be in its presence. Releasing a frustrated breath, he padded to the bathroom and splashed water on his face.

He knew they were only dreams, but the anxiety, and

sometimes fear, he felt was real. This time it was an all-consuming rage he couldn't shake, and he wanted nothing more than to shatter everything in sight.

But the worst part of his nightmares was the feeling of suffocation; the same suffocation he experienced when in the presence of a black soul.

Flashbacks to his childhood made his hands tremble, and he gripped the sides of the sink until his knuckles turned white. As a child, he was sensitive to black souls, more so than some *Fey*. No *Royal* other than the Scales of Justice could see or sense souls, but for some reason, he could. Especially the soul of his sibling, whose secret he kept, never wanting to out them to their parents.

Royals weren't supposed to have black souls, and he used to think he was crazy. He wasn't, and not telling his mother was a weight he would carry for the rest of his long, miserable life.

Gazing at his reflection, he huffed out a laugh. If only people knew the evil Umbra King was shaken to his core by a few bad dreams.

CHAPTER 4

ERDIKOA

The next night Rory and Kordie waited for the guys outside of Wonder, and Rory tried to put the night before behind her.

Kordie's hair was long and dark and fell in a sheet down her back. "Why did you change your hair?" Rory asked her.

Kordie ran a hand through her locks. "I'm changing it back tomorrow, but I wanted something sleek tonight." She paused and added, "It's dark maroon. You would love it."

Rory nodded. "I could go for a darker color, but I don't know if I trust you not to turn my hair pink."

Kordie's lips pinched together. "I promise I won't. We could add dimension with grey highlights through the bottom of your hair," she said, inspecting Rory with eager eyes. "It would look amazing, and you could see it exactly as others do."

Rory released a heavy sigh. "Fine."

She would never admit it, but seeing herself as others

did, even if it was only her hair, was something she desperately wanted. She and Cora would lie awake and wonder what certain people looked like in color. Her heart stung at the memory.

Kordie's eyes widened as she clapped excitedly. "We're doing it this weekend before you have time to chicken out."

"*Fine*," Rory grumbled again.

Kordie looked ecstatic as the guys approached, and Rory pushed her lightly.

"Ready to get fucked up?" Keith asked as he rubbed his hands together like an evil villain. "Dumey is driving us home."

"I will leave you here if you call me that again," the *Aatxe* threatened, and opened the door for the others to walk through.

Keith smirked at the girls. "He would never."

Wonder was dark with different colored essence lights flashing and twirling around the dance floor, and Rory wished she could see them in all their glory. The music was loud, and people were already drunk as they writhed against each other to the beat of the music.

"It's busy tonight," Kordie shouted over the music. "You need to ask for every Friday off."

"It's when I make the most money," Rory yelled back. "Come on, let's get drinks."

Dume parted the crowd as they walked and ordered water for himself, along with the others' drinks.

Keith pointed to an empty corner booth in the back, and the other three followed him through the throng of people. After they sat down, Kordie stretched her tiny neck to survey the room. "There are a lot of cute guys here tonight."

She elbowed Rory in the side. "Maybe you'll find a boyfriend."

Rory made a show of gagging. "I'm never dating, especially not some asshole trying to pick up *dates* in a nightclub."

Keith winked at a man across the room before turning back to her. "Dume and I aren't assholes."

"You're an asshole, wolf," she teased, and he waved her off.

"Rory is letting me color her hair," Kordie announced, like she had the biggest news in the realm.

Dume and Keith whipped their heads in her direction. "She finally wore you down," Dume said and turned back to Kordie. "Please turn her hair yellow."

"I will murder you both," Rory warned with the most threatening glare she could muster.

Her friends exploded with laughter at her serious expression. "Will you string us up like The Butcher?" Keith asked as he took a drink.

Rory's stomach soured, and she fell quiet, grappling for something to say.

"I was kidding," Keith said, setting his glass down. "I know it's scary."

She picked up her drink and tossed the rest back. "I'm going for another. Anyone need anything?"

Keith looked apologetic, but soon recovered by holding up his glass. "I'll take one."

After waiting forever at the bar, Rory turned and bumped into Dume. "Are you okay?" He could read her like a book, and for the first time in her life, she cursed their friendship.

"I'm fine," she replied. "The Butcher is gross, right?" She fake laughed, cringing at the sound.

"I would never let anything happen to you, you know that," he told her. "I would have to be dead before someone hurt you."

A lump formed in Rory's throat. *Would he feel the same if he knew what she'd done?* "I know. I'm just tired."

He knew she was lying, but he let it go, anyway. "Let's get back to Kordie and watch Keith try to get lucky with a poor, unsuspecting person."

Rory laughed lightly. "I've heard he's great in the sack; more like *they're* getting lucky." It was true, and Rory itched to test the theory, but she could tell there was something between him and Kordie. She would never overstep.

Dume's lip curled. "Never say that to him. The last thing we need is his head getting any bigger."

Rory's laugh was genuine this time. "Lead the way."

The next morning, Rory stretched and rolled out of bed, her mood tinged with a newfound determination.

After relieving herself and brushing her teeth, she trudged to the kitchen for a cup of coffee and was surprised to see a fresh pot already brewing.

"Good morning," her mother called from the stove. Her shoulder length grey hair was brushed and fixed, and her makeup was done.

Rory's heart pinched. Today must be a good day. Lenora only had one or two good days a month, and Rory always called in to work to spend as much time with her as possible. Lenora used to only have one or two bad days every few months, then every month, then every week, and now it was reversed.

"Good morning." Rory crossed the kitchen and wrapped her hands around her mother for a hug. The comfort of Lenora's bright red soul set Rory at ease. "What are you making?"

She held up a plate of fluffy pancakes. "Your favorite. Have a seat, dear. They're almost ready."

Rory poured them both a cup of coffee, added cream and sugar, and sat at the wooden table in their kitchen. Their apartment was too small for an actual dining room and instead had a small breakfast nook.

While her mother finished at the stove, Rory sent a quick text to her boss, letting him know she wouldn't be in tonight, and another to her mother's evening nurse. Often, Rory stayed with Lenora during the day and a nurse stayed in the evenings until her mother went to sleep.

"Fill me in on everything I've missed," her mother insisted as she sat across from her. "Have any men caught your attention?" She waggled her eyebrows, and Rory snickered at her mother's antics.

As a *Sibyl*, Lenora was aware she missed time between her good days and always played catch up for the first part of the morning. It was both a blessing Rory didn't have to pretend everything was fine, and a curse her mother knew she was trapped in a cage of her mind's making.

"For the last time, I'm too busy for men." Rory stuck a piece of pancake in her mouth and sighed. Her mother was a phenomenal cook.

"Not even a friend with goodies?" her mother asked, pouring syrup over her own pancakes.

Rory choked on her food and looked up. "It's friends

with benefits, and no, for aether's sake." She preferred one-night stands.

Her mother laughed, the sound like music to Rory's ears. "Whatever you say, dear. How is work going?"

Rory's head bobbed as she ate and answered the next question she knew was coming. "Good, and Dume is doing great. He's still an enforcer, and Keith still drives him crazy."

Her mother smiled. "I love that boy. Tell him to come by today, and I'll make you two dinner."

"Great idea," Rory said, wiping her mouth. "I'll text him now." She fired off a text and sat her phone back down. "What do you want to do today?"

Her phone pinged with Dume's response, and Rory read it aloud. "*Tell Lenora I want homemade roast.*" Rory grinned. "He's coming."

Laughing, her mother took a drink of coffee and waved her hand. "I'll cook that boy whatever he wants." She pointed to Rory's phone. "Did you get a new phone?"

Rory rubbed her stomach as she sat back. "The essence sensor on my old one shattered when I dropped it."

Everything in Erdikoa was powered by the essence, the magical power that gave mystics their abilities, of the inmates in Vincula, or as some called it, the prison realm. When mystics entered Vincula, they lost their essence until their sentence was paid in full.

The technology in Erdikoa had sensors that absorbed the essence, giving them power. Rory didn't know how it actually worked, and she didn't particularly care.

"You break your phone more than you change your socks," her mother tsked.

It was true. Usually, she dropped them during her kills, but her mother didn't need to know that. "I'm a klutz."

Her mother set down her coffee mug. "You're *Fey*. It is impossible for you to be clumsy."

Rory stood and gathered their plates. "Do you want me to call Dad?"

Her mother and father, Patrick, divorced not long after her mother's abilities manifested when Rory was ten. It took years for the visions to fully take over.

Her father wanted to stay, begging Lenora not to kick him out, but her mother insisted on the divorce. It killed him to leave, but he respected his wife's wishes. When she was having a good day, he wanted to visit, but sometimes her mother didn't want to see him. She said it was too hard.

"Not today," her mother said in a strained voice.

Rory kissed the top of her head. "Okay, Mom. I love you."

Fifteen minutes later, a knock sounded through the apartment three seconds before Dume threw open the front door with a wide smile. "Lenora!"

He ambled across the room and wrapped his arms around Lenora's neck, making her laugh. "Hello, love. I've missed you," she said, patting his arm as she pulled back.

Dume was a son to her, and he deserved to spend the good days with her as much as Rory did.

"I've missed you, too," he replied, and pecked her cheek.

"I like your hair," Rory said as she set everyone's plates on the kitchen table. It was shorter than yesterday, Kordie's doing, she assumed.

Dume took his seat at the table and ran a hand between his horns. "It was getting too long."

Rory chuckled and stood to grab drinks from the fridge but froze when she saw her mother's eyes glass over. "No," she whispered as she hurried to the doorway between the living room and kitchen. She placed her hands on her mother's shoulders. "Mom?"

Dume touched Rory's shoulder lightly. He'd seen this happen before, and they both knew what it meant. The good day was over.

Lenora's eyes went clear for an instant, and she locked her hands onto Rory's upper arms. "Two were one, and one is yours."

Rory's eyes burned. "Mom, it's okay. Let's get you to bed."

"No," her mother insisted and snatched her hands away. "Listen to me Aurora, do not let him fool you; his darkness is poison. Only the golden child can save you."

A tear slipped down Rory's cheek as her mother's eyes glassed over again. Dume pulled Rory back and led Lenora to her room at the end of the hall.

When he returned, Rory looked at him with tear-stained cheeks. "She didn't even get the entire day. It's getting worse."

Dume guided Rory to a kitchen chair and laid a fork on her plate before taking his place across from her. "I know. Let's finish these pancakes and watch a movie on the couch. Your choice."

Rory was grateful for her friend, but her heart still sank. If her mother's days were getting shorter, then pretty soon, they wouldn't exist at all.

CHAPTER 5

Rory sat in a chair, watching her mother on the couch as the morning sun shone through the front windows of their apartment. Her eyes burned as memories of the day Lenora's abilities manifested swirled around her.

"Hey, Mom!" ten-year-old Rory called from the door as she ran in with her backpack bouncing against her body. "Guess what!"

Her father poked his head around the hallway, and dark eyebrows shot to his hairline. "What?"

She reached into her bag and pulled out her math test. "I got the highest score in class today," she beamed.

Her mother clapped excitedly, and Rory's smile widened. Lenora always made a big production of her children's accomplishments and encouraged them when they failed.

Patrick crossed the room and took the paper from her. "This is going on the refrigerator," he announced as he made his way to the kitchen. "We're proud of you, squirt."

Rory planted her small hands on her hips. "Don't call me that, Dad. I'm practically a teenager."

Her mother chuckled and walked into the kitchen. "What do you want for dinner? I'll make your favorite."

Dume and Cora walked in the front door, chattering back and forth. "Rory, did you tell them?" Dume asked eagerly, as if he'd made the grade himself. Cora's lips were curled into a small smile. Her twin hadn't done as well, and Rory felt a pang of guilt for celebrating her own win.

"She did," Patrick said as he ruffled Dume's hair between his horns and placed a kiss on Cora's head.

"I want pizza," Rory decided. Her mother was the best cook in the entire realm.

"Yes," Dume and Cora said, high fiving.

"Pizza it is," Lenora announced, shuffling around the kitchen to gather ingredients.

Cora smiled brightly. "She's the smart one. I'm the pretty one."

Rory shoved her sister lightly. "We look the same, dork." Cora shrugged. They weren't identical, but the similarities were uncanny.

Rory's mother dropped the jar of tomato sauce and stood still. Her gaze was on the wall in front of her as Patrick rushed over.

"Did you cut yourself?" He checked her bare feet covered in glass, but she didn't answer.

"Mom?" Cora asked, giving her a weary look.

"What's happening?" Dume whispered to Rory.

"I don't know."

Her mother turned, and the sound of crunching glass beneath her feet made Rory flinch. "She's not supposed to be

*there. He's bright because his darkness hides." Her eyes locked
on Cora. "You shouldn't be there!"*

Her words were gibberish, and Cora shrank into herself.

"Mom?" Rory asked. "You're scaring me."

*"You two take Dume to play in your room," her father said
softly.*

*Rory knew something was wrong. "What's wrong with
Mom?" she demanded. She was almost an adult now, and she
deserved to know.*

*Cora placed her hands on Rory's shoulders, urging her to
leave. "Her abilities are starting," she murmured. Cora had
always been the smart one, despite what she'd said earlier.*

*Rory sucked in a sharp breath and shook her head. She knew
what that meant. Her parents started preparing her and Cora
for this moment as soon as they were old enough to understand.
They didn't want them to be scared when they first witnessed it.*

They were scared anyway.

Rory shook her head to pull herself from the hellish
nightmare. "I miss you," she whispered to her mother.
"More than anything."

Rory called in to work again. She didn't have the emotional
capacity to deal with customers tonight, and when the night
nurse showed up, she left to look for a release.

Sex was her way of decompressing, and tonight, she
needed it more than ever. She headed downtown to Wonder
and started her perusal.

After grabbing a beer, she turned and leaned her elbows on the bar. It wasn't long before a man approached her. He was a little taller than her with perfect teeth, shaggy hair, and a sharp jawline.

"Can I buy your next drink?" he asked when he was close enough for her to hear.

She eyed him up and down and decided he would do. "Sure."

"What is a woman like you doing out by yourself?"

She took a swig of beer and shrugged. "Just looking for a little fun."

Her insinuation was clear, and the man's face lit up like a teenager seeing a girl's tits for the first time. "I'm Wyll."

"Rory," she said, wrapping her hand around his. His soul was a light shade of green. When he turned his head slightly, her eyes flitted to the mark behind his ear. A *Sylph*. *Sylphs* manipulated air, and she wondered if he was skilled enough to use it in bed. Some were.

"Would you like to take this conversation to your place?" she asked as she set her beer on the bar. "It's hard to hear with all the loud music."

He chuckled and motioned for her to follow him. "I would love that."

By the time they stumbled into his apartment, they were ripping at each other's clothes as their mouths moved in a sloppy dance. She was desperate as she shimmied out of her jeans, and his eyes were hungry as they raked down her body.

When they were both naked, he pounced. Her hands went to his already hard cock and stroked him a few times, making him moan into her mouth as he reached for her pussy.

His fingers rubbed circles over her labia, and she tried not to huff out a frustrated breath. Some men couldn't find the clit if it slapped them in the face. She reached down and moved his fingers to the right spot, but he couldn't keep them in one place.

"Grab a condom," she told him, giving up on foreplay, and he reached down to his pants, pulling a packet out of his back pocket. *Someone was confident tonight.*

He quickly sheathed himself and guided Rory to the couch. It took him a few tries to push into her entrance, and when he did, he grunted. "This feels incredible." He looked at their connected bodies. "I never expected it to feel this good."

Oh, fuck. "Is this your first time?" she asked incredulously.

"Yes," he admitted. "But I've studied what to do." *Not well enough if he couldn't find the clit.*

Rory closed her eyes and sighed. "Alright, I'll try to show you." She grabbed his hand and placed his thumb over her clit. "This is the clit. Do not move your hand lower. If you do, it does no good."

He stared at his thumb and nodded. "When you thrust, don't jackhammer. Start out at a steady pace and rub circles with your thumb at the same time." He nodded again. "If I say harder, that does *not* mean faster. You'll thrust harder than you were, and if I say faster, you'll thrust faster, not harder. If I tell you to do both, do both. Understand?"

He smiled. "Got it." He moved his hips and pushed down on her clit.

"Rub circles," she instructed. He obliged, and she sighed as she closed her eyes, letting the sensation take over. "Go a little faster."

She lifted her hips to meet his with each stroke. At least he was a fast learner. "Yes," she breathed. "Like that." Her hands massaged her breasts, and she moaned. "Faster."

His body began to convulse, and her eyes flew open. "Hold it. You have to last longer. *Do not come yet.*"

As soon as the words left her mouth, his dick began to pulse. "I can't stop," he said in a tight voice right before his cum filled the condom.

Rory stared at the ceiling miserably. "Pull out slowly and take off the condom without spilling it. Tie the end and throw it away."

He pulled out, and with shaky hands, tried to remove the condom, but fumbled it. It landed on Rory's stomach, splattering cum across her torso. She yelped and stood, throwing him to the floor. Her glare pinned him to the ground as he gaped at his cum dripping down her stomach.

"Get me a wet towel," she snapped. "And next time, be careful."

He scrambled to the bathroom and came out with a damp hand towel, and she snatched it out of his grasp. Without another word, she cleaned herself, dressed, and slammed the door on her way out.

So much for forgetting.

On Monday, Rory pulled herself together, asked the night nurse to come in early, and called Kordie's salon.

"Kordelia's Beauty Bar," her friend's voice chirped on the other end of the line.

Rory disguised her voice, making it as high pitched as possible. "Do you have a color spot open this afternoon?"

"Unfortunately, we're booked for the rest of the month for color. Would you like to make an appointment for next month?" Kordie's voice was polite and professional, and Rory held in her laugh.

She sighed dramatically into the phone and in her normal voice said, "I guess we'll have to skip the color then."

"Get your ass down here," was Kordie's immediate response. "There is no way I'm missing this opportunity."

"I don't want to put you in a tight spot," Rory countered. "Really, we can do it next month."

"I was lying. I have plenty of time this afternoon. We'll get you in and out before your shift tonight." Kordie hung up, not giving Rory a chance to argue.

When Rory walked into the salon, she plopped down in an empty chair as her friend finished her last client. When the woman walked out of the salon with hair that looked to be light grey streaked with black to Rory, Kordie crooked a finger. "Get over here."

"I'm nervous," Rory admitted as she sat.

Kordie wrapped a dark cape around her shoulders. "Don't be. I'm the best at what I do."

"Have your way with me." Rory twisted in her seat. "But do NOT put a bright, obnoxious color in my hair. I will not hesitate to burn your shop to the ground."

Kordie harrumphed. "Are you saying you think my hair is ugly?"

The *Alchemist's* hair was back to the same color it was a few days ago. *Purple*, she remembered.

"You can pull it off," Rory grumbled. "I cannot, nor do I want to."

"Trust me." With that, Kordie began mixing potions on the table next to her before saturating Rory's long strands. "I'm going to add the silver strands to the ends starting here," she said, motioning to the area around Rory's ears. "Then I will melt your root color so it blends seamlessly."

"I have no idea what that means," Rory replied. "Do what you want."

Kordie began separating and coloring, and within an hour or so, she poured another potion to dry the hair. The potions worked fast, and she was surprised her long hair didn't take longer.

"Done," Kordie announced, handing Rory a mirror to look at the back.

Rory gawked at her reflection. It looked amazing. The grey wove subtly into her hair, giving the ends dimension, and the rest was black.

She turned to look at Kordie, who had a smug smile on her face. "I told you."

"You're good," Rory admitted. "I love it."

"Let me clean up and we can head to Whiplash," Kordie said as she bustled around the room to put stuff away. "I can't wait for the guys to see."

"What happened to your hair?" Dume asked as he sat at the bar and grabbed a cherry from the bar caddy.

She touched the ends. "You don't like it?"

He shrugged. "It looks good. I didn't think you'd go through with it."

Rory smiled. "It does look good, doesn't it?"

A loud whistle sounded from behind Dume, and Keith sauntered toward them. "You look hot." He plopped onto the stool next to Dume, much to the *Aatxe*'s dismay, and grabbed the drink Rory put in front of him. "You should have let Kordie get her hands on you months ago."

"That's what I said," Kordie chimed in.

"Now that we have all established that my hair looked terrible before, can we stop talking about it?" Rory griped.

"You were hot before," Keith amended. "But you're hotter now."

"You look fine either way," Dume told her. "Stop being vain."

Rory popped his arm with her bar towel. "Stop being a jerk."

From there, their night proceeded as normal, and Rory was thankful for her friends who, over the years, became her family. Without them, she'd be lost.

CHAPTER 6

"Are you insane?" Keith demanded as he stared at the forest in front of them. "There's no way in the seven rings of hell you can beat me. I'm a *wolf*, Rory."

"And I am a *Fey*, Keith," she returned.

Dume stood between Keith and Kordie with his arms folded across his chest. "It's a fair match. I'm interested to see who wins."

Keith's mouth fell open as he looked at their friend, and Rory tried not to laugh. "You're all delusional."

Kordie, whose hair looked white, said, "I'm just happy to be excluded from today's activities. I hate running."

Months ago, they arranged their work schedules to have Wednesday afternoons free.

They did random things like going to the movies, hang out at someone's house, go out to eat, and sometimes, they'd go to the sports complex downtown and swim in the indoor pool, play paddle ball, or whatever else they felt like. It was the highlight of Rory's week. Today, they stood at the edge of the park, staring into the woods.

"I can put you on my back, and we could race with them," Dume said, smirking down at Kordie.

She glared at him, and Keith rolled his shoulders. "Let's get this over with. Loser buys everyone a round of drinks."

Rory bounced on the balls of her feet. "Deal."

Keith shifted in a flash. Rory would never get over how fast they changed, or that when *Shifters* changed back, they were fully clothed. She used to beg Cora to shift when they were little, then try to ride her. It drove her sister crazy.

Kordie moved forward and turned to face them. "To the treehouse and back. No cheating."

There was an old treehouse deep in the woods that Rory, Cora, and Dume found when they were kids. No one knows who built it or where it came from, and most of Rory's childhood memories with Dume revolved around it.

Kordie raised her arms. "On three. One. Two. THREE!"

Keith and Rory took off side by side. They stayed close together, not wanting to lose sight of the other, and Rory grinned as she pulled ahead. Not by much, but enough. She heard the wolf growl beside her, and she laughed as the wind whipped through her ponytail.

Sweat trickled down her forehead as the treehouse came into sight, and she pulled up, touched the tree trunk, and ran back. She could hear Keith on her heels and pushed faster, but before long, the dark wolf met her stride for stride. As they approached the treeline, Keith pulled ahead and crossed their imaginary finish line seconds before her.

Rory slowed and fell to the grass, breathing hard. Keith's snout appeared in her line of sight with a lupine smile, and she swatted his nose away. "No need to gloat, you mutt."

Keith shifted and held out his hand. "Don't be a spoil-sport. I told you I was faster."

She sat up and grabbed his hand. "You barely beat me."

Keith tugged Rory's hair. "You're too competitive for your own good."

"Good job," Dume said, clapping him on the shoulder.

Kordie placed her hand on her chest in mock surprise. "Did you give Keith a compliment? Is the realm ending?"

Dume frowned. "I give credit where credit is due."

"You owe me a drink," Keith said, pointing to Rory. He wasn't even out of breath.

"How about a cold beer?" she asked, poking him in the side. "But not at Whiplash. I need a break from that place."

"Birdie's?" Kordie suggested. "They have the best potato sticks."

Potato sticks were exactly as they sounded—potatoes cut into small sticks and fried. They were Kordie's biggest weakness.

Keith picked a leaf from his hair and flicked it to the ground. "I'm in."

"Me too," Dume said. "We need to hurry before it gets crowded."

They all tromped across the grassy field toward Keith's truck. He was the only one of them with a vehicle because his parents were both *Munin* and lived in the *Munin* compound outside of the city. Everyone else walked where they needed to go or took public transport.

When they were all piled in, Rory leaned her head back on the seat. "I'm beat."

Keith pushed the button on his truck, making it roar to life before reaching over to pat her knee. "Perk up, or I'll shift and lick your face."

. . .

The group sat around a tall table at Birdie's and ordered drinks from the server. Birdie's was a small sports bar near the park with good food and cheap drinks.

"Where were you the other night?" Keith asked her with his eyes glued to the arrowball game on the ES behind her. "You weren't at work."

Rory flicked her eyes to Dume, and he looked back knowingly. "I called in and went to Wonder."

"Was he any good?" Kordie smirked.

"For aether's sake," Dume mumbled, but Keith's attention was on Rory.

"He was a virgin," she muttered, and the others paused before they burst out laughing. "Shut up."

"Did he at least stick it in the right hole?" Keith asked through his laugh.

Rory lightly banged her head on the table. "I had to show him where my clit was."

A deep laugh rumbled from Dume's chest, and Rory lifted her head as she twisted her mouth to the side to hold in her own. Despite his shy nature, Dume wasn't a timid virgin, and when they were in their late teens, he'd asked Rory what he was supposed to do. She'd drawn a diagram, and he studied it like it was the most important test of his life.

"At what point did you realize it?" Kordie asked, taking her drink from the server.

"As soon as he was inside me, he looked like he'd discovered gold," she groaned. "It wasn't that bad once I told him what to do until he came in three seconds."

Keith slapped the table as he laughed. "This is the best thing I've heard all day."

"That's not all," she said, smiling at the ridiculousness of the situation. "He dropped the condom on my stomach when he took it off. There was cum everywhere."

Kordie slapped her hand over her mouth, and Dume's laughter boomed through the air. "When is the next date?"

A balled-up napkin bounced off his head. "I hate you three," she grumbled and held up her glass. "Cheers to me beating the wolf next time."

They all raised their glasses as Keith added, "And to your delusional dreams."

Rory woke with a start to a loud banging sound. She jumped out of bed and bolted to her mother's room, finding it empty, and panic seized her as she raced to the living room.

She stopped dead in her tracks as she looked around. Writing covered the walls, and her mother stood on a chair, scribbling with a marker. Rory jerked when she realized her mother was writing the same phrases over and over.

Two were one, and one is yours.

Do not let him fool you.

His darkness is poison.

Only the golden child can save you.

"Mom," Rory rasped. Her mother ignored her as she continued to write. "Mom, please stop."

She touched her mother's side, worried she would fall. "Mom, please."

Her eyes burned as she fought the urge to cry. Finally, her mother stopped and turned. "I must make you understand, Aurora."

Rory nodded her head. "I understand. Come down before you fall."

Her mother finished the phrase she was working on and held Rory's shoulder as she stepped down. "Only the golden child can save you. Trust him."

"Okay, Mom, I will. I promise."

Her mother seemed pleased and walked to her room in a daze. When her door clicked shut, Rory sank to the floor and let the tears flow freely.

After the day's events, Rory worked on muscle memory alone. She couldn't get the message from her mother out of her mind. Yes, it was true a *Sibyl's* mind was scrambled, but it was scrambled with every possible future in the realms. What her mother said was a real prophecy, but the question was whether it was *actually* meant for Rory.

Two were one, and one is yours. Do not let him fool you. His darkness is poison. Only the golden child can save you.

What in the hell did that mean? She would never know. Instead, she would agonize over it for the rest of her life.

A knock on the bar top pulled her from her spiraling thoughts, and Keith's concerned face looked down at her.

"Everything okay?" he asked. "I don't think I've ever seen you this down."

For all of his antics, Keith's soul was kind. It was a vibrant blue Rory loved to look at from time to time.

She dropped her rag on the bar top. "No." Leaning forward, she whispered, "Do you know anything about prophecies?"

His head popped back. "Prophecies? Did your mother say something?"

She chewed on the inside of her cheek. "Do you know anything about them or not?"

He sat down, watching her before finally saying, "I don't know much, but I know if a *Sibyl* can speak one clearly, it is to be heeded. What happened?"

She hung her head, not wanting the stress of worrying about her future to this capacity. "My mother spouted a prophecy when Dume was over. She was having a clear day, and everything was great, until it wasn't. She grabbed me by the shoulders and demanded I listen to her."

Keith whistled. "What did she say? Also, why wasn't I invited?"

Rory ignored his whining. "Two were one, and one is yours. Do not let him fool you. His darkness is poison. Only the golden child can save you," Rory recited for the thousandth time. "And that's not all. When I walked into the living room this morning, she had scribbled it on our walls."

Keith reached out and grabbed Rory's wrist, and when their skin connected, his soul throbbed that beautiful blue she loved so much. "You need to take this seriously," he said. "I have heard of *Sibyls* delivering coherent messages like this."

"What does it mean? Gold? Darkness? A *child*? I don't understand it," Rory groaned. She assumed the darkness was her secret pastime, and she wondered if this was a sign to stop. The only thing that didn't fit was the 'he,' but it could refer to the change Bane caused within her.

"I don't know, but pay attention to everything around you." The graveness of his tone worried her.

She patted the top of his hand that held her wrist. "I will. Thanks for listening, Wolfy."

He pulled his hand back, and the blue winked out. "You know I hate when you call me that."

She grinned. "What do you want to drink?"

Before he could answer, a group of enforcers led by Dume stepped through the door, and the look on Dume's face made Rory's body go numb as the group headed in her direction.

"Dume?" she asked, forcing herself to stay calm, but deep down, she knew what this was.

Dume shook his head and brought his fist to his mouth before speaking in a broken voice, "Aurora Raven, you are under arrest for the murder of Jasper Witlow and the suspected murders of twelve others."

Keith stood, knocking his stool to the ground. "Dume, what's going on?"

Another enforcer with a long, pale braid stepped forward when Dume was unable to speak. "We have video surveillance of Miss Raven entering Mr. Witlow's apartment around the time of the crime and leaving approximately two hours later." The *Aatxe's* blue gaze hardened as she looked at Rory. "And judging by the state of the crime scene, we suspect she is The Butcher."

Rory hated herself for not turning away when she saw how nice the building was, but in the end, she'd gotten the information she needed. What she didn't understand was how they knew it was her. She'd kept her hood up while entering the building. *Until Jessie answered the door,* she remembered, cursing herself for being stupid. There must have been cameras in the hallway.

Keith's face leached of color as he turned to her. "Tell them you didn't do this."

She grabbed her purse and stepped around the bar.

Before she allowed them to take her away, she turned to Keith. "I had my reasons, though I'm sure they aren't good enough to excuse what I've done." Her voice warbled. "I love you, and tell Kordie I love her, too."

She turned to Dume, who was staring at her with so much pain on his face, it almost brought her to her knees. "And you, please don't let my mother suffer because of me."

With that, she held out her hands and let her oldest friend cuff her before the other enforcers grabbed each of her arms and hauled her away. Their souls were bright, blinding almost, a direct contrast to hers.

She guessed her mother's prophecy was right; the dark turned out to be her destruction.

Dume insisted on being the one who rode in the back with Rory, and seeing him across from her made her wish she was alone.

"You must think I'm disgusting," she whispered.

He stared ahead, refusing to look at her.

Her chest stung. "Don't worry, you'll be rid of me soon enough. My soul is as black as theirs were, and I'll meet them in hell soon enough."

Silence followed her declaration as they continued to The Capital.

They were taking her to the Scales of Justice, a *Royal* who was said to look upon someone and know the perfect punishment for their crimes. There were only three *Royals* in the realms; Gedeon, the Lux King, who controlled light; Adila, the Scales of Justice, judge of the guilty, and Caius, the Umbra King, who controlled shadows.

Historical texts state there had once been a fourth *Royal*, Atarah, who ruled over Erdikoa as the Lux Queen, but Caius murdered her, caught standing over her body, soaked in blood with his dagger in hand.

Upon her death, Atarah's power transferred to Gedeon, and Adila locked Caius away in Vincula. Rory shivered at the immense power the *Royals* possessed.

Now, she would go before the Scales of Justice, and there was nothing anyone could do to save her, not that she wanted them to. She only wished she'd found her sister's soul first.

Rory had never seen The Capital or the palace, and when she stepped from the van, her breath caught in her throat at the sight. It was the largest building she'd ever seen and must have been the size of six city blocks in every direction. It was white with metal details the same color as gold moedas, and it shined like new, despite being thousands of years old.

"Holy aether," she breathed.

At first, she wondered why Dume never mentioned how grand the palace was, but then she remembered the *Seraphim* enchanted The Capital so that anyone who left, other than the *Royals*, lost their memory of anything inside The Capital's walls, but when they reentered, they remembered everything.

Her teachers in school said it allowed the *Royals* to move around outside The Capital undetected. It was also why there were no pictures of the *Royals* in their history books or museums until after their deaths.

Rory's trance broke when Dume stepped away and another enforcer guided her through the side entrance. They must not want the scum of the realms gallivanting through the ornate palace where anyone could see.

They led her down a dark hallway lined with empty cells, and the sight sent a chill down her spine. Supposedly, the punishment was swift; either you went to Vincula, or you went to hell. Rarely did a person have to await trial.

At the end of the hall was a set of large doors, and once opened, they revealed a small chamber. The floor was concrete and slanted toward a drain in the floor, and at the front of the room were three concrete steps leading to a small dais.

This was not what she expected. "What is the drain for?" she whispered to the enforcer on her left.

"The blood," he answered with no emotion.

Rory's body shook. All her strength disappeared as she stared at the drain that would soon be filled with her blood. She hoped her death was quick and painless.

A door to the left of the dais opened and in walked one of the most beautiful women she had ever seen. Her hair was the same shade as Keith's, and the front was pulled back with the rest hanging down her back in waves. Rory was surprised to see the woman's ears had the same slight point as hers, and she found it difficult to look away.

Were Royals a type of Fey?

An eerie quiet filled the room as the Scales of Justice took her place on the dais and turned to Rory. The woman nodded her head to the enforcer holding Rory's arm, and he pulled her forward until she was in front of the breathtaking *Royal*.

She refused to cower. She'd made her bed, and now she would lie in it. Staring down the woman in front of her, she wondered why they needed this meeting at all. Everyone knew what the verdict would be.

"I am the Scales of Justice," the *Royal* began. "Though I'd prefer you to call me Adila."

Rory jerked in surprise. *Why would she need to call her anything?* "Nice to meet you," she replied, unsure of what to do. "I'm Rory."

Adila inclined her head. "I know who you are, Aurora Raven." She continued to stare as she descended the stairs gracefully and held out her hand. "Show me your soul."

Rory looked away in shame. "We both know what you will see."

"I wouldn't be so sure," Adila countered. "Give me your hand."

Her tone was commanding, and Rory had no choice but to obey. Once their hands were touching, Adila stared at Rory's chest, and the corner of her mouth lifted slightly. *The Scales of Justice must enjoy sending dirtbags to hell*, she thought to herself.

Adila motioned for the enforcer to let go. When he dropped her arm and stepped back, Rory closed her eyes. She didn't need to see whatever they were going to do to her.

"Aurora Raven, you are sentenced to five-hundred years in Vincula, effective immediately. Your next of kin will be informed of your incarceration. When you return, you will have no memory of your life in the dark realm, but you will remember your transgressions and your life until now."

Gasps were heard around the room, including Rory's, as her eyes flew open. "Pardon me?" she said, dumbfounded.

Adila held out her hand, and an enforcer handed her a clipboard with a pen attached. She looked it over, nodded, and then scribbled something before handing it over to Rory. It was filled with typed text, and at the bottom, Adila had written the length of her sentence and signed it.

"Sign," the enforcer next to her said. She jotted her name and handed the document back.

Adila gave her a small smile. "Your soul is a beautiful shade of grey, Miss Raven. I will see you soon enough."

Without waiting for a reply, Adila reached forward and touched Rory's shoulder. A force pulled at her, and within seconds, the realm faded away as she fell into nothing.

CHAPTER 7

VINCULA

The Umbra King tapped his fingers impatiently on the obsidian arm of his throne, staring at the far side of the room. He received word to expect an arrival, and he couldn't help but ponder what the person had done.

When mystics were sent to Vincula, their crimes ranged anywhere from armed robbery to murder, though the murders were usually done by accident or justified.

Those who rape, abuse children, and murder for no reason other than their own entertainment skipped Vincula and were sent to hell, no questions asked. It's a simple decision really, seeing as their souls were blacker than the Vincula night sky.

Except for Caius. Adila couldn't leave the prison realm without a ruler, could she? Since he was a *Royal*, his little sister couldn't see the color of Caius' soul, but she felt it all the same and *graciously* spared him from an eternity with Orcus.

His anger welled within him, and he gripped the stone beneath his hands as images of Atarah lying on the ground in a pool of her own blood assaulted his mind. He'd never forget the look on Adila's face as she doled out his punishment. Five-hundred years trapped in Vincula. The longest sentence in all the realms. *"This is for your own good, brother."*

He bided his time until he could exact his revenge that would very well seal his fate, leaving his sister no choice but to send him to hell, anyway.

Five-hundred years was a long time, and resentment had festered within his soul. He knew he was beyond the point of salvation.

Opening her eyes, Rory scrambled backwards across the cold floor. Gone was the concrete of the judgment chambers, and in its place was a grey marble circle in the middle of a sea of black marble floors. Torches lined the walls, giving just enough light to see, but not enough to make out minor details across the room.

She looked around as she climbed to her feet. *Vincula.* Her awareness heightened, and she spun in a circle, searching for someone to tell her what to do. There were no chains encircling her wrists and no cell holding her captive, confusing her already muddled mind.

Rory hadn't seen him, not at first. Not until his commanding presence drew her eyes across the room and almost knocked her to the floor again. Lounging casually on his black throne was a man who exuded such raw power, she could feel it down to her core. Something was different about him, but he wasn't close enough for her to see him clearly in the dim lighting.

There was a walkway of light grey marble running from the throne to the circle on which she stood, and on either side, different people gathered with various degrees of curiosity. She didn't know who they were, but she knew the man in front of her was the Umbra King.

The crowd stayed quiet as Rory stared across the massive room at the king, and something compelled her to go to him, but she held fast. Achingly slow, he rose from his throne and descended the dais as shadows rippled in his wake, making Rory's eyes widen. He was the king of monsters among men and the villain of everyone's nightmares.

His measured steps against the marble floor were the only sounds as they echoed through the air. She was sure no one was breathing; herself included.

He walked with a dangerous grace that would send the fiercest mystics skittering, and the shadows permeating the air around him were vicious in their own right.

He was tall and muscular, wearing a fitted black button-down shirt opened at the top, perfectly tailored black slacks, and silver rings adorning both hands. His bright golden eyes stared her down, and when he was close enough for her to see his terrifyingly beautiful face, she stepped back in horror. *It couldn't be.*

As her eyes traveled the length of him, she nearly fainted from shock.

He stood out against the rest of the room, not because he was the king, but because he was in vivid color. His skin was a hue she'd never seen before. *Sun-tanned beige*, her soul whispered in the back of her mind, and his hair was *blonde*.

While seeing him in color was a shock, it wasn't what left her speechless. She didn't know much about the notorious Umbra King, but what she *did* know was ten years ago she watched him murder her sister.

The king stared at Rory, and she dug her nails into her palms as anger and disgust rippled through her. He cocked his head to the side, and she forced herself not to squirm under his scrutiny.

Without taking his eyes from hers, he held out his arm and snapped his fingers. Within seconds, an enforcer she recognized from her sentencing hurried to his side and placed a sheet of paper into his waiting hand. After the man retreated, the king scanned the document.

As he read, his face morphed from one of curiosity to one of disgust and anger. "Aurora Raven." His voice was deep and filled with an icy calm that raised the hairs on her arms.

"Umbra King," she spat back. Her voice lowered so only he could hear as she said, "Or should I call you Bane?"

An amused look crossed his face as he took a step forward, and shadows curled around them both. Before she knew what was happening, a shadow grabbed her chin and forced her to look at him. "You will address me as 'Your Grace,' or I will carve your tongue from that pretty mouth of yours."

Blind rage filled her, and if it were not for the fact he held her sister's soul, she would have tried to rip his head from his neck with her bare hands and bathe in his blood.

Her traitorous body reacted to the masculine sex appeal radiating from him, but no amount of attraction would dull the hatred she had for the man before her.

His face was cold and impassive. "How did you convince

my sister to spare your life?" Again, she stayed silent, and the shadow released her chin as he turned his attention to the paper in his hand. "Your contract is for five-hundred years." He circled her slowly, and she could feel his eyes raking over her in cold assessment. "Congratulations. You have been given the longest sentence of any mystic in the history of the realms."

"I suppose she thought five-hundred years with you was worse than hell," Rory deadpanned.

As he walked into her line of sight, he stepped close enough that she could see the different shades of gold in his eyes. "I promise, little butcher, after your time with me, you will wish she sent you to hell. My only regret is when you return to Erdikoa, you will not remember your time here." His breath fanned over her skin, and goosebumps cascaded to her toes.

The king turned to address the crowd as he walked away from her. "It seems the worst of you has graced us with her presence." He paused as a hush fell over the crowd. "Miss Raven has not only taken a life; she has taken *thirteen*."

Gasps and murmurs moved through the crowd, and Rory straightened her spine. She knew her crimes were horrendous, but she would not allow herself to regret them.

"Some of you who have been here only a year or two may have heard of her." The king stepped back and swept his arm toward her with fanfare. "She is otherwise known as The Butcher."

A man standing at the edge of the crowd recoiled and turned to the woman next to him, whispering in her ear. From there, the information of who she was spread through the crowd, and the looks of curiosity soon turned to those of fear.

The smile the king directed at her was one of pure malice, and her own face twisted in disdain. He turned back to the crowd. "As you know, inmates convicted of murder are sentenced to work in the palace so the legion and I can monitor their behavior." Shadows pushed her from behind until she was stumbling closer to him. "Miss Raven is no different."

The announcement elicited more murmurs from the crowd, and he held up a hand to silence them. "I trust you will give her the welcome she deserves."

He strolled down the marble walkway and exited through a door at the back of the dais without looking back. The crowd dispersed quickly, presumably returning to work, and Rory fought to hide her smile.

The king unknowingly gave her the opportunity of a lifetime. She would scour the palace until she found her sister's soul, and then she would send the king to wait for her in hell.

A rough hand grabbed her by the arm and dragged her across the large room. She turned to shoot her best glare at whomever was handling her, but her throat dried at the powerful mystic pulling her along.

"Samyaza," she whispered, more to herself than to him.

She thought he was a myth, a bedtime story told to children to keep them in line. He was said to be the commander of the Vincula legion, brutal beyond comprehension, and sent directly from the aether by the *Seraphim* themselves. The books never said what type of mystic he was, and for the first time since arriving, fear gripped her like a vise.

Her eyes tracked over him from top to bottom. His light hair hung past his shoulders, obstructing her view of his face, and the white wings protruding from his back were large, even when tucked tightly against his back.

He wore armor she'd seen in supermystic movies and old story books. Taller than the king, he was imposing, and when he finally turned his face to hers, she bit her tongue to keep from screaming.

His features were severe, and the way his eyes burned into hers, she wondered if he possessed the ability to create fire.

"Yes," he said in the deepest voice she had ever heard. "I prefer Sam."

Did he expect her to call him by such a casual name? She would be too busy shitting her pants in his presence to call him anything at all.

She nodded in acknowledgement and turned her eyes forward. If she stared at him too long, would she die? Probably.

"Tell me why you called the king Bane," he said, leaving no room for argument.

Her head snapped back to him. "That is what he said it was, but I know now it was a lie."

The commander's eyes narrowed. "Are you drunk?"

Jackass. "Of course not. That is what he told my sister his name was, but as I said, it was a lie."

He removed his hand from her arm but kept walking. There was no way she would stop until he told her to, and he knew it. "Is your sister here, too?"

"She had one of the brightest souls I have ever seen," Rory said, clearing the emotion from her throat. "She would no sooner be here than the Scales of Justice herself."

Sam was silent as they walked, and she assumed their conversation was over, but then he said, "Then it was not

Caius who spoke with her. He has been locked in Vincula for almost five-hundred years. There are only a few months left in his contract."

The king had a contract? Her mind cataloged the information for later. She'd heard he was locked in Vincula indefinitely for killing his own sister. A myth.

"I saw him with my own eyes," she insisted. "I'm not blind."

His cold features remained impassive. "Think what you wish." Something nagged at her to believe him, but she knew what she saw. It *was* weird the king wasn't in color all those years ago.

"Why did he say I have the longest sentence in history if his is just as long?" *They were all jackasses.*

Ignoring her, Sam led them down several flights of stairs before arriving in a dank hallway lined with doors. The air was thick with moisture, and the torches provided just enough light to avoid running into the walls. She would kill for a flashlight.

The behemoth stopped in front of a door labeled 21030 and swung it open. He gently pushed her inside and closed the door behind them. As she looked around, she saw they stood in a small, tidy room with a lantern, a bed, a nightstand, and a dresser. There was a door on the left wall she guessed was a bathroom.

"Welcome home," he said, ushering her across the room, which was a total of five steps.

She turned to him. "No dungeon?"

His hard eyes stared at her, void of emotion. "There is no need for a dungeon. If anyone steps out of line, they are put to death."

Rory recoiled. "I understand that for me, but for *everyone?*" She was horrified.

Again, Sam's face remained stone-like. "You forget, everyone here has committed some type of serious crime. They are not here for petty theft." He pushed open the door to the left and gestured inside. "Washroom."

The commander sounded a million years old when he spoke. She paused. Maybe he was. Inside the door was a small room with a shower, sink, and toilet. *Thank the Seraphim.*

"You will be measured by a seamstress. Once your uniform and night clothes are finished, they will be delivered to your room. Place your soiled clothes in the basket," he said, pointing to a small basket by the door. "Laundry is collected twice a week."

"Do I set the basket in the hall on those days?"

He shook his head slowly. "Why would you do that?"

"How else will they collect them?" she asked, wondering how he led an entire legion with a brain full of rocks.

His brows rose. "They open your door, pick up your basket, close your door, and leave," he said, as if speaking to a child.

She stared at him incredulously. "What if I'm naked?"

Sam threw his head back with a booming laugh, and the sound startled her. "You no longer have privacy. Welcome to Vincula." He turned to leave but paused. "Someone will be by to collect you once Caius assigns you a position among the palace staff."

Without another word, he left, leaving Rory alone in her new home for the next five-hundred years.

~

Rory stood in the bathroom and splashed water on her face as her brain tried to grasp the concept of being alive for multiple lifetimes. Mystics lived to be anywhere between one-hundred and two-hundred years old. But five-hundred plus another one-hundred and fifty when she was free? It was unfathomable.

The door to her room burst open, and a blur of fabric bustled in like a whirlwind. Rory straightened, prepared for a fight. It was only a matter of time before the other staff began making her life a living hell, if their reaction in the throne room was any indication. Well, more than it already was.

A short woman with dark hair cut into a long bob stood by Rory's bed, dropping the bundle of clothes she held. She turned her wide eyes to Rory and tilted her head.

"Why does your face look like that?" she asked.

Rory's eyes narrowed. "What is that supposed to mean?"

A laugh burst from the woman's chest. She looked to be in her thirties with the slightest lines by her eyes, presumably from laughing. *Or squinting.* "I mean, you look like you ate a lemon for the first time."

Rory crossed her arms but said nothing as the woman picked up a dress and beckoned her closer. "I'm here to measure you, not beat you."

Dropping her arms, Rory crossed the tiny room reluctantly. "What do you need me to do?"

"Put this on," the woman said, picking up another dress.

Rory tugged her shirt over her head and tossed it onto the bed before grabbing the dress and wiggling it on. It was short-sleeved, black, and had three buttons at the top. It fell just below the knee, and her face slackened. "You have got to be kidding me."

The woman shrugged and gestured to her own uniform. "We all have to wear it." Rory glanced at the woman's dress, noting she also wore a greyish apron with large pockets.

"I'm Bellina, by the way," she said.

"Rory. Are you scoping me out to find the best way to torture me?" She had no time for games.

Bellina shook her head with a light laugh. "You wouldn't be here if you were as evil as they say." She looked at her with curiosity. "Though it is unsettling that you hung your victims on hooks."

Rory hiked a shoulder, no longer needing to pretend she wasn't a monster. It was freeing. "Their souls were black, and in my opinion, they were nothing but meat suits for pure evil."

"You're a *Fey*," Bellina discerned. "I'm a *Visitant*." She moved her hair aside to show the tiny mark behind her left ear.

Rory's brows rose. *Visitants* were usually peacemakers. They had the ability to control the moods of those around them. "How did you end up here?"

"I am no different from you," she said with a tight smile.

Rory held up her arms while Bellina pinned the fabric at her sides. "You killed thirteen people and hung them on meat hooks, too?"

Bellina shook her head with a smile. "No." Her expression turned serious. "I killed my father-in-law." Rory tried not to show her surprise. "I discovered he beat my wife repeatedly when she was a child. Her mother died during childbirth, and he blamed her." Her fists tightened around the fabric. "She was just a child." Her voice was barely a whisper, and her eyes were distant. "My wife told me upfront she had issues dealing with trauma from her childhood. I thought she meant from growing up without a mother, and I never pushed the issue. I knew she would tell me when she was ready."

"She has nightmares," she continued. "I would find her in our room crying, and it broke my heart that I couldn't help her, until one day, she opened up to me. She admitted she was terrified he would try to hurt her again." Bellina lifted her gaze to Rory's. "I would sooner die than let him touch her, and I couldn't stand to see her living in fear. I would put a knife in his gut ten times over."

Rory nodded. "Too bad we weren't friends in Erdikoa. I would have done your dirty work."

Bellina fumbled the garment she was holding before she burst out laughing. "I knew I was going to like you. Take that dress off so we can measure your pajamas. You can either wear a two-piece flannel set or a shift."

Rory stared at the offending fabric in the seamstress' hand. "A shift? I'm not two-thousand years old." She tended to run hot in her sleep and knew she would sooner sleep naked than in the flannel. Sighing, she pointed at the white fabric. "The shift."

Bellina smirked. "You get credits for ten items of clothes, five sets of undergarments, and two pairs of shoes a month to spend in town. The clothes there are normal."

"We're allowed to leave?" Rory asked, surprised. "And we get credits?"

Bellina nodded. "You also get credits to spend on extra non-necessity items like beer, pastries, and games. This realm is nothing like the nightmare we were told. In some ways, it's better than Erdikoa." She paused. "Except for the no sunlight thing."

According to Rory's history classes in school, Vincula's days were the equivalent of dusk in Erdikoa, and the nights were pitch black with no stars or moon except once a month when the moon was full in Erdikoa. When this happened, in Vincula, the moon and stars made an appearance for the inmates to enjoy. It was called the Plenilune. She tried not to slump at the knowledge that she wouldn't feel sunshine on her face for a very long time.

On her mother's good days, they would sometimes meet her father at the park for a walk or picnic, something she would never do again.

Tears pricked her eyes, and she turned away. She could only hope Dume and her father would make sure her mother was taken care of.

The enforcers would have notified her father of her incarceration. At least she hoped they did. She knew he would never leave her mother alone, but sometimes it hurt Lenora to see her ex-husband on her good days. It would be better if Dume lived with her instead.

Pain squeezed her chest at the thought of never seeing her again. By the time her contract was over, her mother would be long dead, as would her father and her friends.

A finger tapped her forehead. "I know that look," Bellina said softly. "Get out of your head. If I had my abilities down here, I would help, but you'll have to calm down on your own."

The shift fell over her shoulders, and Rory looked down. The straps were small, the front met in a V just above her bust, and the bottom hit about mid-thigh. It was made of a soft, white silk and was basically a nightie instead of the dreadful smock she was expecting.

"How long are you here for?" Rory asked.

Bellina motioned for her to turn and began adding more pins. "One-hundred years. I've been here for two."

"That isn't so bad. There's still a chance you can see your wife again." Rory peeked at Bellina over her shoulder, and the *Visitant's* eyes met hers.

"That is what keeps me going. Lexa was only twenty-nine and a *Fey.*"

Rory nodded in understanding. *Fey's* lives were on the longer end of the spectrum.

"We're done," Bellina announced and motioned for Rory to remove the garment. "What is your shoe size?"

"Twenty-four and a half," Rory responded, wondering what type of shoes she had to wear while working.

Bellina packed away her supplies as she spoke. "Your new clothes will be here by this evening."

"That fast?" Rory thought sewing took longer, but then again, she'd never sewn a day in her life.

The woman nodded as she gathered the dresses. "There should already be uniforms and shifts in your size. If not, it doesn't take long to resize them."

"How many seamstresses are there?" Rory inquired as she wondered if the Vincula palace was as large as the Erdikoa one.

Bellina opened the door and as she left, called over her shoulder, "A lot. Welcome to Vincula."

CHAPTER 8

Later that night, Rory stepped out of the shower and slipped her shift over her head. When they delivered her new clothes, they took her old ones to wash. She'd have to wait until they brought them back before she ventured into town.

She found a comb and other toiletry items under the sink and began working the knots from her hair when someone knocked on her door. Before she could cross the room, the door opened, and Samyaza stood on the other side, looking imposing as ever.

"Caius has summoned you," he said robotically.

Rory glanced from her shift to the mountain in front of her. "Now?"

He said nothing and stepped aside for her to exit into the hallway.

She waved her hands over her body. "I need to change first." There was no way she was seeing the king like this.

Sam glared at her. "You will come now of your own accord, or I will drag you. The choice is yours."

She huffed, jabbed her feet into a pair of slippers they'd

given her, and followed the commander down the dark hall. By the time they reached the top floor of the palace, her calves were locking up, and she was sweating. "Is this part of the torture?" she asked between pants, never realizing how much her *Fey* strength helped her until now.

"Come," was his only reply. She lifted her middle finger to his back and before she could lower her hand, he spun around and grabbed her wrist. "If you do that to the king, you will no longer have a finger to raise."

She snapped her jaw shut from its unhinged position and nodded dumbly. "Sorry," she whispered.

Sam's eyes bounced between hers, and she thought the corner of his mouth lifted a fraction. "No, you are not."

He stopped in front of an enormous set of wooden doors and knocked, and Rory couldn't quell her nerves. Someone who had the infamous Samyaza knocking was someone to be feared.

The doors opened, and shadows retreated across the room. Rory recalled the smooth feel of them against her skin and shivered.

Sitting behind a large, cherry wood desk was the Umbra King. She wasn't used to seeing people in color, and looking at him was a shock all over again.

His blonde hair was slightly mussed, the top few buttons of his shirt were undone, revealing a strong, tanned chest, and one of his elbows rested on the arm of his chair. Despite his light hair, he was the living embodiment of enchanting darkness.

He watched her step into the room, and his eyes traced clinically down the length of her shift before settling on her exposed thighs. Instead of fidgeting under his inspection, she set her jaw and stared him down.

"Miss Raven," he drawled. His voice was rich and smooth, and she felt his shadows on her back, forcing her to walk. She was tired of that. When she stood in front of him, he leaned forward. "You have been assigned to kitchen duty, and you will help the maids when needed."

Surprise ricocheted through her. She was certain she would have been tasked with mucking the stables or something equally horrible. *There are no horses in Vincula,* she remembered. Because of the lack of sunlight, the only animals and plants in the realm were nocturnal.

"You will be on the third shift," he continued. "You are to report at three a.m. sharp."

Rory's eyes bulged. She wasn't certain of the time, but she assumed it was ridiculously late. "I haven't slept in thirty-six hours."

His eyes lifted. "That is not my concern."

He stood, walked to a door on the far side of the room, and disappeared. She stared after him in disbelief. Had he really dragged her halfway across the palace to tell her something that could have been relayed through Sam in one sentence?

She looked around the room for the first time since entering and realized it was his office. Bookcases lined most of the walls, and it was much brighter than the hallways.

Noticing a set of filing cabinets at the back of the room, she pointed at them and turned to Sam. "What are those for?"

His eyes flicked to the cabinets. "Contracts."

She didn't understand why they needed paper contracts; their sentencing was bound by magic. "Why do they have paper contracts?" she mused as Sam led her from the room.

He lifted a light brow. "What an odd thing to ask."

She shrugged. "It's an odd thing for a *Royal* to do."

"The contract has information on each inmate, their crimes, and their sentencing," he explained. "The king cannot memorize every inmate, and they are used for reference if needed."

"Oh," was all she could think to say.

When they arrived at her room, she wiped sweat from her forehead and prayed the kitchens were on the same floor. She knew an inmate's appearance stayed the same during their time in Vincula, but she hoped her muscles would learn to take the stairs without killing her every time.

They weren't bad when she went down the first time, but after going up and then back down again, she was dying.

Sam opened her door and said, "Change. Work starts in an hour. I will show you the way." It was worse than she thought.

Grumbling under her breath, she grabbed one of the hideous uniforms from her dresser and stomped to her washroom. When she emerged, Sam tipped his head to the hallway. "I would prefer to get to sleep at some point tonight," he informed her.

She glared at him, but quickly schooled her face into one of indifference. He didn't seem the type to tolerate back talk. Her work boots were by the door, and she pulled them on as quickly as possible before following him down the hallway and into the kitchens.

"Nina," he called out. "Fresh meat!"

This time she did glare, and to her surprise, he smirked. A girl who looked to be a couple of years older than Rory stepped out of a closet and frowned. "Good. Staying up late for her was not on my agenda."

She was beautiful, with curves that would make Rory

jealous if she weren't in prison, and smooth skin the color of Lenora's porcelain cats she displayed in her room. Nina eyed Rory in cold assessment, and her scowl deepened.

"If it isn't the famous Butcher." The repulsion was clear in her voice, and Rory steeled her spine. Nina stepped back into the closet and grabbed a bucket full of cleaning supplies.

Sam turned to Rory. "Remember what I said about transgressions," he warned before turning on his heel and leaving her alone with the sour woman.

"What color is your hair?" Rory asked, without thinking. It was a shade she did not see often.

Nina's face screwed up. "It's red. Did they not teach you colors in school?" Rory itched to slap her, but before she could snap back, the bucket of supplies was thrust into her hands. "I hope you like scrubbing grease." She tilted her head. "You do know what an oven is, don't you?"

Ignoring Nina's jab, Rory laughed under her breath at the cliché of being assigned the grunt work after all. "Where will I be starting?"

A cruel smile spread across Nina's face. "Follow me."

The woman led her through a series of kitchens, pointing out various ovens and stoves. *Why did they need so many kitchens?* Rory thought to herself. Seemed like overkill.

"Do not stop until they are spotless," Nina sang before leaving.

Rory bent in front of the first oven, exhaustion making her body groan. Her eyes crossed at the sheer amount of grime coating the metal. It was obvious they had not been cleaned in some time.

Her mother kept their kitchen appliances immaculate, passing the habit down to Rory, and because of this, they were easy to clean. The thought made her sit back on her bottom, and the cool stone soaked through her dress.

For the first time since being arrested, she cried.

Her hands covered her face as pictures of her mother assaulted her. Her bright smile on good days, her dwindling state of mind, and her barrage of questions over breakfast. Rory would never get to laugh at her mother's silly questions again.

As a sob ripped from her chest, a warm, weathered voice filled the room. "You don't seem the type to cry over a little grease."

She lifted her head, and a man who looked to be roughly one-hundred and twenty years old stood across the room with his hands in his pockets. She searched his face for the usual taint of disdain but found none.

A sharp retort was on the tip of her tongue, but something made her swallow it. "My mother is a *Sibyl*, and I was her only caregiver." She didn't know why she told him.

Understanding filled his eyes, followed by pity. "Do you have any other family to care for her?"

"No," she replied, anger filling her voice. "My sister was murdered, and my parents divorced when my mother's powers manifested. My father will step up, but she wouldn't want him to." Her answer brought on a fresh wave of tears.

"I heard you're sentenced to half a millennium." He whistled. "But not hell."

She hardened her gaze and waited for the blow. "Go on, then. Call me whatever you'd like."

The man shook his head. "The Scales of Justice is never wrong. If she sent you here, I suspect there's a reason."

Rory looked down, not wanting to meet his eyes as

shame heated her skin. "I am a monster," she rasped. "I did everything they said."

He nodded. "I'm sure you had your reasons." Before he turned to leave, he said one last thing, "Dry your tears or they will eat you alive. Kitchen staff will be here in an hour."

Dragging her hands across her face, she nodded, but before she could thank him, he disappeared. Sighing, she climbed to her knees and started to scrub, realizing she hadn't asked the man his name.

Caius lingered outside the doorway to the kitchens, cloaked in shadows. He told himself he came for his usual late night sweets, but he knew it was a lie. His curiosity about Aurora Raven led him here against his own protests.

After overhearing her conversation with Max, a man convicted of breaking his neighbor's legs with a shovel for disrespecting his wife, Caius stopped himself from entering the room.

The woman wept over her mother, concern and regret lacing her every word, but those were traits black souls did not possess. *Unless she's acting.* Admitting to her crimes so freely suggested she was exactly what he thought her to be. Black inside, no matter how beautiful on the outside.

It was obvious his sister knew this woman would tempt him because physically, Aurora was everything he sought in a partner when he could still move freely between the two realms.

Adila also knew he hated black souls more than anyone. As a child, he would cower when one was near because the feeling of them covered him like poisoned vines.

Being locked in Vincula weakened his power, and although he was still strong, it was possible his ability to sense black souls was gone. Until now, he had not been around one.

After Max left, Caius stepped from the shadows through the doorway toward Aurora. "Your face looks a bit swollen, Miss Raven."

The woman looked up, hatred transforming her face, and Caius chuckled lightly. She'd called him Bane with the same look, and the memory made him study her more closely. "Who are you?"

A black soul in Vincula, calling him by anything other than his given name or title, was not an ordinary inmate.

She threw the brush she held into the bucket of soapy water and glared. "I am The Butcher, *Your Grace*, and I will not hesitate to string you up with a dagger in your heart." He had no doubt she meant every word. There were two ways to kill a *Royal*: a dagger to the heart or decapitation, and she clearly had a thirst for blood.

His anger rose fast, and shadows struck like vipers, knocking her on her back as they gripped her throat. "You are a vile creature, and if you threaten me again, I will send you to hell myself."

Her chest heaved as her face reddened. Despite his aversion, he couldn't help but drink in her body.

Her grey eyes sparked with fire, standing out against her dark hair, streaked lightly around the ends. She was fit, with lean muscles, small tits, and long legs. Her face was one of the most beautiful he'd ever seen, and he ground his teeth. *Fucking Adila.*

Aurora Raven would be his greatest temptation. The thought made him release her and take a step back. "Finish scrubbing my kitchens, and mind your tongue, or you will lose it."

He left, his late-night snack forgotten as he decided to have Sam travel to Erdikoa and find out everything there was to know about the notorious killer.

Caius needed sleep, and tomorrow, he would find a way to relieve the tension brought on by the woman he left behind.

Rory thought her arm was going to fall off. Who knew cleaning ovens was such a workout? She'd been cleaning for so long the breakfast crew had come and gone, and now it was quiet again, save for a few staff members preparing breads.

She couldn't shake her encounter with the Umbra King, and not for the first time, she hated herself for being stupid. Playing it smart was how she would find her sister's soul, not pissing off the man who held it.

Her knees cracked as she stood, and she was glad she finished before the lunch crew came in. If she never had to scrub another oven for the rest of her life, it would be too soon. She hauled her bucket to a nearby sink to rinse the grease and grime from her supplies before heading out.

After putting everything away, she asked a passing maid where Nina was. She didn't know if she was supposed to check out for the day or not and decided she'd rather be safe than sorry. The last thing she needed was an extra shift.

Finding her way to the room number given to her, she knocked on the door, and it swung open as soon as she touched the wood. Her mouth dried at the sight before her.

"I'm ready for you," Nina purred over her shoulder to Caius, who stood naked behind her. The head maid was on all fours, wearing only a bra as she presented her bare ass like a bitch in heat.

The king met Rory's stare and pinned her in place.

"Are you here to watch, Miss Raven?" he asked in a rough voice as his hand found his hardening cock.

She stared at the king's muscular body; he was a magnificent suit harboring a murderous beast.

Nina twisted her head toward the door. "Shut the door, you fucking pervert." The woman's voice grated on Rory's nerves, and she clenched her fist while glaring daggers at the king's shadows billowing on the ground around him. If they grabbed her, she would make it her life's mission to light the palace up like an *Aatxe* soul.

"Or is this your thing?" Nina continued as she sat back on her heels. "Did you watch your victims fuck before acting out your own sick fantasies?"

Rory's body vibrated with anger. The *fuck you* sat on the tip of her tongue, but she swallowed it. Caius watched her darkly as she grabbed the handle of the door and slammed it shut as she left.

Her anger at the words from that horrible woman's mouth grew as she stomped through the hallway. She knew the staff would hate her, but to see her sister's murderer look at her like she was filth was too much.

At least her victims deserved it. Cora had the sweetest soul in all the realms, and he stole it. She knew her methods were cruel and disturbing, but she couldn't find it within her to care.

∾

Caius stared at the door as it slammed with Aurora's anger, and the second she was gone, his cock deflated. He pumped his hand and closed his eyes, but the traitorous appendage wouldn't cooperate. He frowned at Nina's back.

When he was free to pass between realms, Caius only fucked women in Erdikoa, but since being locked in Vincula, he took mistresses who weren't sentenced very long, allowing him to switch often. Nina was his current mistress, and at the moment, he cursed the day he first took her to bed.

They wouldn't remember him when their time was up anyway.

Running a frustrated hand through his hair, he bent over and grabbed his clothes.

"What are you doing?" Nina asked. "Don't let her ruin our fun." Her smile was coy as she ran a hand up his chest.

He pushed her arm away. "We're done here."

Nina's sharp intake of breath made him dress faster. He needed to leave.

"Caius," she said before he held up a hand.

"I'm leaving, and you will not follow, nor will you question my decisions again."

Her mouth snapped shut, and anger took over her sharp features. As he left, she stomped to her bathroom and slammed the door as Aurora had.

The difference was he didn't care if Nina opened hers again.

CHAPTER 9

ERDIKOA

Dume walked into Whiplash and sidled up next to Keith, who was staring glumly at the man tending the bar. Just because they learned their best friend was a mass murderer didn't mean they would stop meeting after work as usual, especially when they needed each other the most. When he left The Capital, he called Kordie to confirm they were still meeting.

He didn't remember what happened, but he read the transcripts. When there was a trial, one copy of the transcripts was kept at the palace and another in the sector where the offender was captured.

The three friends could have picked a different meeting place, but Whiplash was centrally located to their jobs, and deep down, Dume knew they were holding on to a small piece of Rory, despite what she did.

The *Shifter's* eyes moved to Dume. "You're back earlier than I thought you would be."

Dume grunted and signaled the bartender to order a beer. He didn't drink, but today he would make an exception. "The trials are never long."

A heavy cloud settled over the conversation. *Rory was The Butcher.* Dume still couldn't believe it. How she had fooled them all was beyond him.

"Was she scared?" Keith asked quietly.

Dume grabbed his beer from the bartender and chugged it. "I don't remember, but you know as well as I do nothing scares Rory."

Keith swallowed hard. "I figured going to hell might be an exception."

Dume held up his mug for another. "She wasn't sentenced to hell."

Keith's head swiveled toward Dume so fast, he thought it might twist off. "What do you mean? She murdered thirteen people." His forehead wrinkled, the confusion Dume felt blanketing Keith's face.

"The Scales of Justice sentenced her to five-hundred years in Vincula." Dume chugged his new beer. "It doesn't make sense."

"Are you talking about The Butcher?" a high-pitched voice asked from behind them. "She worked here, didn't she?"

They both spun to look at her, and Keith nodded. News of The Butcher's identity spread through Erdikoa within hours of her arrest.

A small woman who looked to be a few years younger than Dume stood at their backs. She had strawberry blonde hair, and light freckles covered every inch of exposed skin. Her green eyes widened with excitement. "The Scales of Justice spared her?"

The hope in her voice had Dume and Keith looking at each other stupidly. *Who was this woman?* Dume thought he knew all Rory's friends.

"You knew Rory?" Keith asked cautiously.

The woman shook her head. "Her name is Rory? The news said Aurora."

"It's a nickname. Who are you, and why do you care?" Dume said curtly.

The woman set her jaw and pulled herself to her full five-foot nothing height. "My name is Sera, and I care because she saved my life."

"Who saved your life?" Kordie's voice said from behind Sera, causing the woman to spin around.

"Rory," Keith and Dume said at the same time.

Kordie's face was thoughtful as she regarded Sera. "Rory is dead."

"They said she's in Vincula," Sera informed her, pointing at Dume and Keith.

Kordie rounded on Dume. "What is she talking about?"

"Adila sentenced Rory to five-hundred years in Vincula." The lump in his throat grew.

Keith pushed past Dume to stand in front of Sera. "What do you mean, 'she saved your life?'"

Sera looked between the three. "I didn't know her name, but I'll never forget her face." She pointed at the ES above the bar where Rory's picture covered half the screen with scrolling text. "One of the men she killed attacked me. She ripped him off me and told me to run. I later saw him on the news as a *victim*," she sneered. The woman's chin lifted defiantly. "Say what you want about her, but I think she's a hero."

The group stared at Sera, at a loss for words. Dume's

mind raced as Adila's words from the transcript ran through his mind. *"Your soul is a beautiful shade of grey, Miss Raven."*

"In the van on the way to The Capital, Rory said, 'my soul is as black as theirs were.'" Dume recalled.

"Her soul isn't black," Sera snapped.

"Maybe they deserved it," Keith recited. "Remember? That day in the bar when we were talking about the murders, Rory said, *'maybe they deserved it.'*"

"And you said life wasn't a supermystic movie," Kordie added, looking at Dume.

"Well, you were wrong," Sera said, glaring at the *Aatxe*. "If she were murdering for fun, why didn't she kill me too?"

Dume scrubbed a hand down his face. "She was obsessed with being on the force."

Keith blinked. "What does that have to do with anything?"

"After Cora was murdered," Dume explained. "She became obsessed with enforcers. She even wrote a letter to the Scales of Justice asking to make an exception and let her on the force." He snorted at the memory. "Lenora never sent it. The older we got, the less she talked about it, and I thought her fixation had petered out."

"She became her own version of the Scales of Justice," Kordie concluded as she plunked onto a stool. "Why didn't she report the crime after she saved her," she asked, jerking a thumb at Sera. "Why kill them in such a terrifying manner?"

"And if her other victims were the same, why not report them, too?" Keith mused.

Dume pinched the bridge of his nose. "Cora." He looked at his friends. "She harbored a lot of guilt and anger after Cora died. She watched as her sister was murdered, and it really fucked her up."

"She wasn't fucked up," Sera growled. "Stop speaking about her as if she were a cold-blooded killer. Her ways were... horrible at best, but she is still a hero."

"She was a crazy bitch," a man to their right slurred.

Sera spun around, cocked her arm back, and slapped him across the face. He stumbled to his feet, pissed. Dume stepped between them and looked over his shoulder at the pint-sized fireball. "You should go."

She harrumphed and stomped away with her head held high, but before she stepped through the door, she held her middle finger in the air. Dume's lips twisted to hide a smile.

"Go home," Dume told the drunkard and looked at the bartender. "Don't serve him again." The drunk man grumbled under his breath as he left.

"What if she *is* a supermystic," Keith blurted, and Kordie popped him in the back of the head.

"Supermystics aren't real, idiot, but she was something else, and I don't mean the villain the news is making her out to be."

Dume nodded. "I have to go." He threw moedas on the bar. "If one of her victims was a suspected murderer, and another was a rapist, there may be more people she saved willing to come forward."

If there was more evidence Rory wasn't the heartless killer the news made her out to be, he would find it. He *had* to find it.

For his own sanity.

CHAPTER 10

VINCULA

Rory dragged herself out of bed, wishing she could take a longer nap. Exhaustion pulled at her, but sleeping all day wouldn't help her adjust to the third shift schedule.

The other kitchen staff told her dinner was served at six o'clock, and her stomach demanded she join.

Her uniform was crumpled from sleep, and she made a mental note to venture into town tomorrow for casual clothes. The clothes she arrived in magically disappeared while being laundered.

Winding through the dark hallways soothed her, and when she stepped into the brightly lit dining hall reserved for the staff, she relaxed. The room was large and had several rows of picnic-style tables where people were sprinkled about, talking and laughing amongst themselves.

When the closest table noticed her arrival, they fell quiet. The rest of the staff followed suit, and before long, the entire room stared at her in a deafening silence.

Keeping her shoulders back, she walked to the serving line, but the stack of plates was snatched from the table by a woman standing nearby. Rory heard a few snickers around the room and fought the urge to grab the plates from the woman and throw them on the ground.

If they wanted a villain, she would give them one.

Instead, she proceeded to the line and looked for anything she could eat with her hands, but as she passed each tray of food, someone pulled it back. She whirled on the other staff and stared them down, table by table.

A movement at the back of the dining hall caught her attention, and when she looked up, Samyaza stalked through the room toward her. She had half a mind to give him a reason to send her to Orcus now, and if it wasn't for Cora, she would have.

He stepped around her and grabbed a plate that miraculously appeared where the stack had been. Food filled the buffet, too, and he piled his plate high before turning and leaving without a word.

Rory's shoulders fell as she turned on her heel and walked toward the exit, but she only made it a few steps before mashed potatoes splattered against her chest. She stopped cold and searched for the one responsible.

"Evil bitch!" someone yelled as they hurled a spoonful of green beans her way.

That was all it took to set the others off. Rory was pelted with food from all angles, accompanied by insults she deserved. She would not cry, and she would not run. She retreated down the aisle, taking the punishment with poise.

As she stepped into her room and surveyed her clothes, she smiled. Ironic how they refused to feed her dinner, yet they gave her food, anyway.

She looked around the room for something to scrape the edible weapons onto. It was gross, but she was starving and didn't eat during her shift.

A knock on her door almost made her jump out of her skin, and before she could ask who it was, the door opened, and two large wings cast a shadow across her face.

Sam entered quietly. "Eat," he commanded and shoved the plate he'd made into her hands. She watched his large wings tuck in tight as he ducked through her doorway and disappeared.

Rory's alarm clock blared at two-thirty a.m. the next morning, and she reached blindly to hit the snooze button. She was met by cold, rattling metal, and reality crashed into her, jolting her awake.

There were no electronics here, and the clock on her bedside table had literal bells that made her want to stomp it to bits. Turning it off, she stood and stretched before using the bathroom and getting ready for her shift. Briefly, she wondered if women had periods here since their bodies essentially froze in time.

She seemed to be the only person on three a.m. kitchen duty, but she'd passed other staff in the palace yesterday on her way to the kitchens.

The head cook at the end of Rory's shift the day before told her to peel potatoes today. While it sounded terrible, it had to be better than scrubbing ovens.

She passed through the first kitchen into the next and screamed at the top of her lungs when she came face to face with the Umbra King.

His blonde hair was messy, and his silk sleep pants hung low on his hips. He wasn't wearing a shirt, and the deep V at his waist drew her eyes downward.

"My eyes are up here, Miss Raven," he drawled. *Damn him.*

"What are you doing here?" she asked, fighting down the heat creeping into her cheeks.

"This is my palace," he said, waving around a spoon. "What are you doing here? Ah, that's right. You murdered thirteen innocent people."

Dipping his spoon into what looked like custard, he brought it to his mouth, never breaking eye contact. She crossed her fingers and hoped that he choked.

Ignoring him, she walked around the middle island toward the back kitchen supply closet and mumbled, "None of them were innocent."

"What was that?" he called after her. She kept walking, but shadows snaked around her like ropes and held her in place. Wiggling did no good, and she closed her eyes, wishing she were anywhere but here. "I said..." Caius walked closer. "What was that?" His breath tickled the back of her neck, and she wondered if head-butting the king was a punishable offense.

"I said, I wish you had been one of them," she replied. The shadows tightened, and one wrapped around her ponytail, twisting her head to look at him behind her.

"Tell me," he murmured. "Did you lure them to their deaths with the promise of a good fuck?"

Rory tried to burn a hole through his face with her eyes. "Why? Interested?"

His shadows moved, still restraining her arms and legs, but freeing her body and hair. Caius walked in front of her, tracing his eyes from her face to her chest to her stomach.

His eyes found hers again, and they were filled with such heat, she thought she would burn alive. "Are you offering?" Her entire body throbbed, which pissed her off.

Her mind flashed back to the image of him standing behind a naked Nina. "I prefer not to lower myself to Nina's sloppy seconds," she crooned with a snarky smile.

He stepped into her space and lowered his towering frame. "Do you prefer to be strung up, like your victims?"

The way Caius looked at her curdled her insides, and she strained against the shadows binding her limbs. "Do not pretend to be better than me, *Bane*, or Caius, or whatever the fuck you're going by today. I know what you did." She spit in his face for good measure, but a shadow blocked it from hitting him.

He remained unmoving as he studied her. Finally, he stepped back before rescinding his shadows. "And what is it you know?"

She shook her arms as the blood returned. "I watched you murder my sister and steal her soul." Her words held such venom that she barely recognized her own voice.

He seemed to contemplate her words before saying, "I killed my own sister, Miss Raven. Why are you surprised?"

She forced her feet to stay rooted to the floor instead of lunging for him. He simply walked back to the counter, grabbed his bowl, and left.

Later that night, Rory sat under the shower's hot stream and leaned her head back. Her hands had blisters the size of

Erdikoa because, as it turns out, peeling potatoes all day is *not* easier than cleaning ovens.

She'd shoved a few rolls into her apron and snuck a piece of breakfast steak before the lunch crew came in, and it was all she'd eaten today. Her stomach rumbled, but there was no use in trying the dining hall again.

Once she was out of the shower, Rory climbed into bed, not bothering with pajamas. She was exhausted, and it wasn't long before sleep pulled her under.

Rory was lying in a field of wildflowers, staring at a ceiling fit for a king. A grey and black chandelier hung above her, and when she turned her head from side to side, the Umbra King's throne room surrounded her. Her dark surroundings were in deep contrast with the soft grass beneath her. "Even in my dreams I'm stuck in Vincula."

"Miss Raven?"

Rory looked up and saw Caius wading through the thick field and groaned. "Figures my first full night's sleep would be haunted by the likes of you."

His head appeared in her line of sight. "Your soul is black, Miss Raven. You are a walking nightmare in and of yourself."

She sat up and twisted herself to glower at him. "You murdered your own sister, but you speak to me like I disgust you for similar transgressions."

He positioned himself in front of her and sat on the grass. "Thirteen," *he corrected her.* "You murdered thirteen people. Not just one."

"You killed two." *She ripped a handful of grass from the floor and threw it in his face. He had no shadows here, and his hand wasn't big enough to deflect the entire assault. He tried blowing blades of grass from his mouth but ultimately had to pick them from his tongue with his fingers.*

Rory leaned forward, laughing with satisfaction. "You deserved it."

"That wasn't very polite," he said in a low voice. "You need to grow up."

She threw another blade of grass half-heartedly. "Not everyone is five-hundred years old." She eyed him skeptically, recalling his naked body positioned behind Nina for the hundredth time. "Which is really fucking weird. Why do you fuck women hundreds of years younger than you?"

He studiously ignored her as he picked the grass off his shirt. "Who else am I supposed to fuck? My siblings and I are the only immortals in the realms."

Rory scrunched her nose. "It's still weird."

"It is not something you need to concern yourself with," he replied. "I do not consort with people like you." At his condescending words, she lost her composure.

"Will you shut up?" she snapped. "They deserved it. I saved people, you know. Me, not you. All you did was kill for your own gain. Do not judge me when your hands are bathed in blood."

There was a breath of quiet before he asked, "What do you mean, 'they deserved it?'"

She still ripped at the grass. "They were black souls so suffocating it was hard to be around them." She could feel his attention focused solely on her. "I followed them, and—"

"Why?" he asked, cutting her off. "If they were difficult to be around, why would you follow them?"

She looked at him and wondered how he could be so old,

yet so dense. "Because a black soul will commit a crime, eventually. They can't help themselves."

"You do not know that," he argued. "You killed them because you assumed they would commit a crime?"

"I followed them for days, sometimes weeks, to keep an eye on them," she explained. "Some committed small crimes that were none of my business, and after a while, I left them alone." It still bothered her, letting them go. What if the next day they hurt someone? "But some tried to hurt people in the worst ways, and I stopped them." She quit messing with the grass and lifted her gaze. "Forever."

He didn't respond, and she wished something would make noise to fill the silence. Suddenly, music blasted through the room, and she startled like Keith in a phantom house. They were fun houses at carnivals where Eidolons popped through walls and scared the shit out of you.

She remembered she was dreaming and laughed quietly to herself.

Caius lifted a brow. "Discussing murder is funny to you?"

She motioned her hand around the room. "I wished for noise and conjured music."

He stared at her. "There is no music."

The music stopped, and she wished the chandelier would fall on his head, frowning when it didn't. "How is it you have finagled your way into my dream? Leave."

"Perhaps it is you who has intruded on mine," he countered.

"I didn't know the evil king slept." His presence irritated her, but despite the hostility in the air, they had a sort of familiarity, and it unsettled her more than anything.

He bit his lip, and she could tell he was trying not to smile, *which pissed her off more. "Is that what they're calling me now?" he asked wryly.*

"Is that not what they have always called you?" She hoped her taunting pissed him off, even if it was only a dream.

A humorless laugh escaped him. "They called me much worse."

"Because you killed your sister?" Rory asked crossly.

His eyes were focused on a flower as he plucked it from the floor. "Things are not always as they seem."

"I suppose you didn't kill my sister, either, and my own eyes deceived me?" she asked through clenched teeth. They were headed toward dangerous territory.

His fist closed around the delicate petals in his hand, crushing them, and they fluttered to the ground. "If I said no, you wouldn't believe me."

Bells echoed through the enormous room, and Rory jumped to her feet, prepared for a fight. Instead of the danger she expected, Caius moved next to her and looked around. "Time to wake up."

Rory reached blindly for her alarm clock, and when she couldn't find the button to stop the bells, she knocked it to the floor. She vaguely remembered dreaming, but as dreams do, the memory of her wonderland faded away until it was nothing but a feeling in the back of her mind.

The palace was vast, and Rory's feet ached as she explored every inch she could. She was still trying to adjust her sleep schedule and needed something to keep her awake until an appropriate hour. It would also help when she began her search of the palace.

There was a smaller staircase by the kitchens no one ever used that she never noticed before; the steps were dusty, and the torches were out. Intrigued, Rory grabbed a torch from the nearby wall and looked around before slinking up the abandoned stairwell. The last thing she needed was someone reporting her to the king.

The stairs ended on a small landing with a single door at the top. "Interesting," she murmured and tried the handle. Locked. *Shit.*

Her curiosity was going to eat her alive if she didn't find out what was behind that door. Running back downstairs, she hurried to her room, grabbed a few hairpins, and bolted back up the stairway, thankful no one was around.

Once in front of the door, she bent over as she gasped for breath. Her legs ached, and her lungs burned. Running laps around the palace courtyard for conditioning shot to the top of her to-do list.

Pulling the two pins out, she stuck them into the deadbolt. Lock picking was something she mastered years back after her first kill.

The news said she killed thirteen people, but she killed fourteen. After her first kill, she puked and cried, and abandoned the body in the alley where she killed him.

The enforcers found the body the same night but ruled it an illegal trade gone badly. Rory knew she needed better places to execute her *victims* and researched until she was blue in the face. One *netsite* led her to a warehouse that used to house a butcher shop and meat packing plant.

She went to check it out, and when she found the door locked, she taught herself to pick locks with the help of different videos on the *esse-net*. Once inside, she was fascinated with the meat hooks hanging in broken freezers and the pulley system over a huge drain in the floor.

It was the day The Butcher was born.

Now, she was thankful for her self-taught skill as she moved the pins around until the latch clicked. When she pushed the door open and entered the room, she couldn't believe her eyes.

The entire ceiling showed a blue sky with a few clouds and bright sunlight. With her head craned back, she studied the ceiling to figure out how it was possible.

"Essence screen," she murmured. The entire ceiling was one giant screen. She closed the door and looked around the room. It was a large bedroom decorated beautifully with a feminine touch.

An enormous sleigh bed sat against the far wall, and upon further inspection, Rory realized the entire frame was made of a metal the same color as gold moedas. "Aether," she breathed.

The rest of the room was more of the same; the beautiful metal detailing covered everything, and Rory couldn't help but run her fingers along every surface she could reach.

The entire room was bathed in faux sunlight, and Rory almost cried from the sensation. She didn't think she would feel the light on her face again for a very long time, but it seemed she found sunshine in a bottle.

It was then she really inspected the room and noted there was no dust collected anywhere. The stairs were untouched, but this room was immaculate. There were two doors on the back wall of the room, leading to a bathroom and a closet.

"Whose room is this?" she asked aloud. It was obvious

by the stairs no one had been here in a long time, so how was it clean? A spell, maybe? The room *was* fueled by essence, after all. Another mystery.

She pulled open drawers to hunt for clues as to who stayed here, but all she found were basic toiletries and cosmetics. Gorgeous gowns hung in the closet, as well as tailored women's pantsuits.

Had the previous Umbra King's wife stayed here? When Rory pulled open the slender drawer at the top of the vanity, she stared in awe. It was a built-in jewelry box, filled with exquisite jewelry of every kind. There was a small box next to the earrings, and when she flipped the lid open, she nearly squealed with joy. "Jackpot." A golden key sat inside, and while it could be to something else, it matched the room and was the size of the lock on the main door.

She wasn't a thief, but for this room, she would make an exception. Looking around one last time, she tucked the key in her pocket and slipped through the door onto the small landing at the top of the stairs.

"Please work," she prayed. The key slipped into the deadbolt and turned, locking the door. She opened the door again, ran to the bathroom, and grabbed a towel.

She did a silent victory dance when she locked the door again and scrambled back down the stairs to continue her exploration of the palace. On her way down, she used the towel to dust the stairs. If people noticed footprints, it would draw unwanted attention to the room.

Afterward, she took the main staircase to the next floor, which were the legion's quarters. It made sense, she guessed, but wouldn't they want their own homes?

"Their rooms are likely bigger than yours, dumbass," she mumbled to herself.

"They are," a familiar voice said from behind her.

She spun around to find the Umbra King standing a few feet away, watching her intently. "Oh," she replied as the stolen key burned a hole in her pocket.

"Are you lost, Miss Raven?" He had one hand in his pocket while he raised the other to his mouth and ran a thumb across his bottom lip as his eyes roved over her. The rings on his hand glinted in the torchlight, and while she'd never thought rings on men were attractive, they worked on him.

She jolted at her own thoughts. Why did she keep thinking like that? *This man murdered your sister,* she reminded herself. At least she thought so. It had been ten years since she'd seen him, but his face wasn't one she could forget.

Then why did doubt cloud her mind when he was near? And why did his face anger her less and less after such a short amount of time?

No. It was him. Her shoulders straightened as she met his stare straight on. "I was getting to know the layout of the palace. Am I not allowed to do that?"

His hand dropped. "If you are looking for an escape from Vincula, there isn't one."

Her eyes turned to slits. "I'm not an idiot. If you'll excuse me." She turned to leave, but a wall of shadows stopped her. She glared at them and swore a silent oath to find a way to kill the stupid things.

"I will show you around. I wouldn't want you snooping where you don't belong," he said, and approached her side. "I don't trust you."

Her glare could have sliced through steel. "I don't trust you either."

"Good," he replied as his eyes roamed her face. The wall of shadows dissolved, and he motioned for her to follow. "As you pointed out, this is where the legion lives."

"Why don't they live in town?"

His eyes cut to her briefly. "They can if they wish. Most prefer to stay here where someone else does their laundry and cooks for them."

"Typical men," Rory muttered.

The king's mouth pulled up slightly. "You can do your own laundry and cooking, if you'd like to prove your independence."

"I already do," she said under her breath. After the incident in the dining hall, she cooked herself food in the kitchens before her shift ended and ate half when no one was around and the other half in her room at night.

His eyes shifted to her again. "Excuse me?"

She refused to look at him as they walked. "I cook my own food, *Your Grace*."

He stopped abruptly and folded his arms across his chest. "Are you above eating with the others, or is the food not to your liking?"

She kept walking, but another shadow wall blocked her passage. "Fucking hell." She turned to him. "You will be delighted to hear I am not allowed to eat with the others. The first and last time I tried, I was refused food. Until they covered me in it, that is. I'm sure you will relish in my humiliation for the rest of the evening." She was embarrassed, as much as she hated to admit it.

He regarded her thoughtfully. "Are you surprised?"

"No," she answered honestly. "If you won't show me around, I would like to go to my room, please."

The politeness she afforded him seared a hole through

her tongue, but pissing off her warden would do her no favors.

He tipped his head toward a set of stairs at the end of the hall, and Rory groaned. "You couldn't at least bring elevators to this cursed palace?"

He chuckled, and the sound surprised her because it wasn't full of mockery as usual. "The only place in all of Vincula with power is the *Royal* quarters, powered by my essence." After seeing the sky room, she knew that was a lie.

"Wait. You're an inmate as much as I am, yet you get power? That is bullshit."

The mirth on his face slipped away, and his jaw tensed. "I may be locked away, but I am no inmate. I am your king, and it would do you well to remember that."

His tone made her eyes bulge slightly. He looked to be three seconds away from strangling her. "Where are your quarters?"

He continued toward the stairs, leading them up. "Are you planning a visit, Miss Raven?"

She smiled sweetly when they reached the next floor, ignoring the ache in her calves. "How else will I ravish you, Your Grace?"

She yelped when he backed her into a wall, and a shadow squeezed her throat lightly. "You couldn't handle the way I fuck, Miss Raven." Her chest was heaving when he stepped back and turned.

"Seemed pretty basic to me," she mumbled, rubbing her throat.

He didn't turn around as he continued down the hall. "I do not waste effort on unimportant things." Rory smiled to herself at his dismissal of Nina.

"Smug is not a good look on you, Miss Raven."

Her jaw dropped. Did everyone have eyes in the back of their heads? She hurried after him. "Where are we?"

"The guest floor," he replied.

Her brow furrowed. "Who in the hell would visit Vincula?"

She was beside him now, and his eyes cut to her. "Vincula is a beautiful place." His eyes grew distant. "My friends and siblings from Erdikoa would often visit."

"Would?" she echoed and immediately wished she could snatch the question back at the look on his face.

Why did she care about his pain? She didn't.

"The two rooms at the end of the hall are for the *Angels*," he said, ignoring her question.

"*Angels?*" Like the feathered mystics from fairytales? "Sam," she realized aloud.

Caius' mouth thinned slightly. "You speak informally as though you know him well."

"He told me to call him Sam," she said defensively. "And he is nice to me." Kind of. She wasn't sure he liked her much.

"Interesting," Caius murmured. "I think we're done for today."

A slight twinge of disappointment pinched her chest. She needed to see more of the palace, and while it was better to search without the king watching her every move, having someone explain the layout was helpful. She would ask Bellina.

Silently, he led her back to the staff quarters and left as she stared after him.

CHAPTER 11

Nina flounced into the kitchens not long before Rory's shift was over and gave her a cruel smile. "I heard you've been making food and sneaking it to your room."

Rory stiffened. "And?"

"And you will eat with the others in the dining hall, or you will not eat at all." Nina looked positively delighted, and Rory dug her nails into her palms to keep from punching her. "It opens for lunch soon. I suggest you hurry." Nina turned to the other staff still in the kitchen. "If any of you allow her to leave with food and I find out about it, you will not be pleased with the work you are assigned."

Anger roared in Rory's ears. She threw her rag in the laundry bin by the door and stepped through it, needing to be alone before she did something she'd regret. Nina knew as well as she did the dining hall wasn't an option.

Unable to look at Nina a minute longer, she marched out the back door of the kitchens and across the stone courtyard surrounding the palace. When she reached the edge of the massive space, she slipped through a small man-sized gate at the back.

It surprised her to see a garden filled with various lush plants and beautiful flowers. The stone walkway twisted in a spiral toward a large flower in the middle. The plant was huge, with a bell at the top.

"Fitting you should find the reaper flower," a voice said from behind her. "It blooms once a year and smells of death."

A small, growl-like sound emitted from her chest. "Fitting you should find me to gloat."

In her peripheral, he stepped next to her, but she refused to look at him. "You will need to refresh my memory. I'm right about many things."

The pebbles beneath her feet crunched when she turned on her heel to flee, but shadows stopped her retreat. "I am fucking sick of these things," she half-yelled as she swiped her hand through them. To her surprise, they scattered despite being solid seconds before.

"Refresh my memory," he repeated. "What has the little butcher wound up today?"

She spun on her heel again to face him, red hot fury seeping from her pores. "Nina made sure to tell the kitchen staff to stop me if I tried to take food to my room. Seeing as you were the only person who knew, I have you to thank, no?"

"You made quite the impression on the staff." He smirked. "They are giving you the welcome they think you deserve."

"And you?" she challenged. "Do they give the infamous sister killer the treatment he deserves?"

She was shoved to the ground, but shadows cushioned her fall, preventing the gravel from cutting her knees.

He strolled toward her, his expression lazy. "I must admit, Miss Raven, I enjoy seeing you on your knees." His pupils flared.

She recognized the lust in his eyes, and she fought to keep her expression neutral.

The shadows kept her pinned in place as she struggled, and the king smiled. "You despise me for two deaths, yet you have taken thirteen lives. Does that seem rational to you, or are you as deranged as they say?"

He would swing headless for all his people to see, she vowed silently to herself.

"You are nothing but a hypocrite." His words should have held venom, but they held nothing but amusement. Giving her his back, he walked away, but not before calling over his shoulder, "I hope you have the day you deserve, Miss Raven. I know I will."

Once he was out of sight, his shadows released her, and she glowered as they retreated. "You are assholes too," she hissed after them.

A plan formed in her mind, and she wanted to scrub her skin clean at the prospect. She saw his desire, and she would use it to her advantage. The king may hate her, but he was attracted to her, too.

Nothing brought down a man's defenses like sex.

Rory was lost in her own thoughts as she wound through the palace garden for an hour. If she was going to do this, she would do it right. Seduction was nothing new to her. When she wanted a good fuck, she found one.

The first thing she needed to do was use her credits for new clothes. She would buy comfortable items, including jeans that showcased what little butt she had and whatever else she could find to make the king drool like the dog he was.

She *would* do this. Her sister's soul depended on it. An hour passed before she marched back inside like a soldier heading into battle.

Throwing the door to her room open with newfound determination, she began ripping off her wretched uniform but stopped short. On her bed sat a tray of food. There was a burger, potato sticks, and what looked like a glass of lemonade.

She approached her bed slowly and poked at the food. Her first thought was, *they had burgers here?* It dawned on her they must have shipments brought in from Erdikoa, which would explain the modern clothes and whatever else was in town Bellina told her about. There was nothing like this in the kitchens, and she surmised it came from town.

It could be poisoned, but she was starving enough to risk it. Grabbing the burger like a wild animal, she bit into it and moaned. It was delicious. She lifted the bun to see what was on it. There were no condiments, only lettuce, tomatoes, pickles, and onions.

Setting her burger down, she picked up the tray and placed it on her nightstand before taking a seat on the bed to eat the rest. News in the palace travels fast, and Bellina must have heard what Nina said to her in the kitchens and grabbed it for her. She was a lifesaver.

After scarfing down the rest of her meal, she took a shower, relishing in the warm water as it pelted against her skin. Showers were her only reprieve as of late.

She needed to get the king alone, but how? She might not have to. Somehow, he kept finding her. Her lips curled into a smile as she rinsed her hair. This might be easier than she thought.

Rory meandered her way through the halls to the seamstress's quarters in search of Bellina. No one else would speak to her aside from hurling insults, and she needed a guide around the town. A dark bob caught her eye, and she made a beeline to the back of the room.

Glares were thrown her way as she passed the other workers, but she ignored them when Bellina spotted her and waved. "What are you doing here?"

Rory leaned on Bellina's workstation with puppy dog eyes. "I was hoping you could show me around town today and help me order clothes."

Bellina clapped excitedly with a wide grin. "I love shopping! Let me clean up, and we can go."

Rory stepped outside the front of the courtyard for the first time since arriving in Vincula and was taken aback. Her eyes widened as she took in the bustling town. The brick buildings lined the modern streets, oil lamp posts dotted the sidewalks, and people were everywhere, as well as legion officers on patrol.

It wasn't a city like Erdikoa, but it was more civilized than she'd imagined. What took her breath away was the beauty of the town silhouetted against the twilight sky. She knew she'd miss the sunshine, but the dusky sky was just as beautiful. The sunset wafted over the town like a blanket, and various plants decorated the buildings.

"This..." she began, but her voice trailed off.

"Is gorgeous," Bellina finished for her. "I couldn't believe it the first time I saw it. I expected a muddy, dreary mess, but in some ways, I like Vincula more than Erdikoa."

Rory could only nod, still in shock. Keeping up with Bellina was harder than she thought. The woman's tiny legs moved fast, and Rory took long strides so as not to be left behind.

"Where are you taking me?" she asked.

Bellina pointed to a shop across the street. "We'll order clothes first, and then I'll show you around. Have you received your card yet?"

Rory furrowed her brow. "Card? I've heard nothing about it."

"Those assholes," Bellina huffed. "You're supposed to be given one on your first day. You show it to the vendors to keep track of your credits. There is no money system here. Every inmate gets credits for each shop per month to get whatever they'd like."

"How do they scan cards with no essence?" Nothing about this realm made sense.

Bellina pulled out her own card to show Rory. "It has your name and number on it. They look you up by your number and mark how many credits you spend."

Rory grabbed Bellina's arm, forcing her to stop. "How is this a prison if we are given things for free, no matter where we work? I don't understand."

Bellina shrugged. "I told you it isn't the hell they've painted it to be. We're treated well, as long as we follow the rules. I know you hate the king for whatever reason, but he is good to us and makes sure we are taken care of. Rumor has it the *Seraphim* thought being in Vincula would help change souls for the better, and even though we don't remember our time here, our soul is changed all the same."

Briefly, Rory wondered if there was a chance for her soul but shook off the notion. She didn't want redemption. She wanted retribution.

"That is brilliant," she said finally. "Rehabilitation for the soul."

Bellina nodded. "If everyone wasn't a dick to you, I think you'd like it." She stopped in front of the shop. "Do you at least know your number?"

"Like my phone number?" Rory asked. "Or my mystic number I was given by the Crown?"

Bellina puffed out a burst of air. "They told you nothing. It's your inmate number for Vincula. It will be printed on your card and above your room."

Rory perked up. "I know my room number."

"Perfect." Bellina grinned as she opened the door. "You can give it to them this time since you're new, but you'll need your card next time."

The shop was like any other clothing store in Erdikoa but without technology. There were jeans, jackets, shirts, dresses, and anything else you could think of from the other realm.

Rory reached out to touch a shirt. "Do they have these imported?"

"Ding, ding, ding," a deep voice said.

She spun around, facing a man who looked to be her age or a few years younger. He had a mischievous smirk, and his hair was like Nina's, only darker. "What color is your hair?" She grimaced at her lack of manners.

"You're weird," he replied with an amused smile. "It's auburn. You've never seen it?"

"I can only see the color of souls," she admitted. "I have grey-scale sight."

"What is that?" Bellina was eyeing the man's hair.

Rory played with the end of her hair to give her hands something to do. "I can only see in shades of grey, black, and white."

The guy whistled. "Damn."

"My hair is dark brown," Bellina offered. "Almost black."

"And my gorgeous eyes are hazel," the man added, making Bellina roll her eyes.

"You're The Butcher," he said, sticking out his hand. "I'm Asher."

"Leave her alone, Ash," Bellina chided.

Rory shot Bellina a withering look. "I'm in no position to pass up someone being nice to me." She turned back to Asher to shake his hand. "I go by Rory."

"Rory. I like it." He tossed his arm over Bellina's shoulder and bent down to smack a kiss on her cheek. "I told Bell to bring you out with us, but she keeps refusing."

Rory understood. "You'll get a bad rep if you're seen with me."

Bellina pushed Asher away. "Don't call me that. I told

him we needed to give you time to adjust first, but you are welcome out with us anytime. Everyone here is a criminal, so they can fuck off with their judgment."

A laugh burst from Rory. "I knew I liked you." She turned to Asher. "You know of my atrocities. What are yours?"

He seemed embarrassed, which struck her as odd, seeing as how she was a serial killer.

"Armed robbery of a bank when I was twenty-two," he said, regret lacing his voice.

Rory wondered how long he'd been here. His phrasing suggested a while. "How old are you now?"

He ran a hand through his hair, and Rory couldn't help but notice how his biceps bulged. "Fifty-one." He chuckled. "In a twenty-two-year-old's body. How fucked up is that?"

She lifted a shoulder. "At least you're a hot fifty-one-year-old. Gives a whole new meaning to the age-gap kink."

He threw his head back with a loud laugh. "This is my last year, thank the *Seraphim*."

"Lucky," Bellina muttered as she plucked a shirt off the rack.

Asher reached over and tweaked her nose. "I'll miss you."

Bellina's expression grew somber. "No, you won't. You won't remember us."

Silence fell over the group. "I'll remember you both enough for all of us," Rory tried to joke. "I was sentenced as long as the king."

Asher clucked his tongue. "I heard. Tough break. Next time, maybe only kill seven."

They laughed, but then he asked her, "Why'd you do it? I have to know."

Bellina slapped his chest. "You can't just ask people why they killed someone."

Rory smirked at Bellina. "You did."

The seamstress shrugged. "I knew we'd be friends, but there's no guarantee you won't get sick of this one," she said, motioning to Asher.

He looked at Rory expectantly. She knew it was natural for others to be curious, but the thought of having to tell the same story over and over irked her. "I need to hand out flyers and put this to rest." She looked up, mental exhaustion taking over. "They were all black souls I caught in the middle of trying to hurt someone."

Asher stared for what felt like hours. "Good for you." He slapped her on the shoulder. "We're going out tomorrow night. Come with us."

Rory glanced at Bellina. "Who is 'us?'"

"Asher, Max, and me. Max is older, but he's fun. Drinks like a fish. Tallent, Kit, and Cat might be there too." She looked at the apprehension on Rory's face. "They couldn't care less what you did. We're all here for a reason."

Rory swallowed hard. "Screw it. I'm in."

Asher lifted his arm for a high five, and she laughed, slapping his hand in the air. It was nice to have friends again.

Asher tagged along as Bellina showed Rory the rest of Vincula. It was amazing, and she couldn't get over how many shops there were. There was an extensive park with gravel in place of grass, cobblestone walkways, random lawn games, picnic tables, and even a large lake nestled in the back.

Plants similar to the ones in the palace garden were everywhere, giving it appeal.

"There are fish in there, too," Asher said, pointing at the water where people sat on piers, holding fishing poles and talking quietly.

"This place is incredible," she breathed. "Maybe five-hundred years won't be so bad."

From the foliage to Rory's left, a black panther emerged, and Rory screeched, backing up and bumping into Bellina.

Bellina steadied her and giggled. "That's Lo. She's like the Vincula mascot."

"Why are you talking about a killing machine like she's a *Seraphim*-damned house cat?" Rory demanded. "Are you crazy?"

Asher walked forward and stroked a hand down Lo's silky coat. "She basically is a house cat. Just bigger."

A deep rumble sounded from the panther's chest, and she nipped at Asher's arm. He jumped back and frowned, and Rory pointed at the enormous cat. "I'm not going near her." Like an idiot, she addressed the panther like a person, "Sorry, kitty. I would rather not chance you taking a chunk out of my leg. I need them to run away."

The panther's head tilted to the side as her tail twitched. She turned and disappeared back into the lavish brush, and Rory looked at the other two. "Did you lure me out here to feed me to her?"

The two busted up laughing while Rory stood with her hands on her hips. "It wasn't that funny."

Bellina nodded as she laughed so hard she sounded like a teapot. "It really was. You should have seen your face when Lo stepped out." She swiped at her eyes as her laughter died down. "She's harmless. The shop owners let her inside, and I've seen her in the palace a time or two."

Rory stared. "You're all insane. What happens when she turns on you?"

Asher shook his head. "You run." She blinked at him, and he laughed. "I'm kidding. She wouldn't hurt a fly."

"Are there more?" Rory asked and slid her gaze to the bushes where the panther disappeared.

"Not that we've seen," Bellina said. "There are other animals, but they keep to themselves."

Rory shuttered. *Great.*

CHAPTER 12

Rory walked back into the palace, wanting nothing more than to fall into bed. She was loaded down with her shopping bags from their trip and needed to sort everything out. Specifically, she needed to plot out how she would run into Caius while wearing her new dress. She also needed a reason to wear the scandalous garment.

Bellina stayed in town longer, and since Rory was not entirely familiar with the palace layout, she took a wrong turn and ended up in the throne room. The doors were open, which seemed strange, and she took the opportunity to look around without prying eyes.

Her eyes kept finding their way to the door behind the throne, and before she could stop herself, she was in front of it, grabbing the handle. This was either incredibly stupid, or it would pay off for later. She crossed her fingers and hoped it was the latter.

The door opened to a hallway with a long ornate rug covering the marble floor. After closing the door quietly behind her, she tip-toed her way to the first door. She missed her ability to move undetected, but the rug helped absorb any sounds her boots made.

She could see there were only two doors in the entire hallway: the one she stood in front of, and another at the very end. Which should she try?

Shrugging, she pushed open the first door and poked her head inside. It was dark other than a sconce by the door and another behind a large desk.

"The king's office," she whispered with wicked delight. This must be a second entrance.

"Yes," Caius said, his voice floating through the dark. "My office."

Rory yelped, letting the door close in her face. She turned to run, but the door flew open, and shadows wrapped around her arm, stopping her retreat.

That was it. She was carrying a torch to keep the damned things away from her.

"Where are you going, Miss Raven?" His voice was rich and enchanting, like a song.

She counted to three and stepped into his office, swiveling her head slowly to find him. It was dark, and she had a feeling he'd cloaked himself in shadows to hide. He revealed himself as he sat in a high-back chair in what looked to be a reading nook across the room.

One ankle rested on his opposite knee, and a book sat open in his lap. His head was bent as he read, and in his other hand, he held what looked to be a glass of liquor.

"Didn't anyone tell you it's impolite to sneak around?" he asked without looking up.

A lantern burned bright on the table beside his chair, and when he raised his head, her breath stalled. She hated how handsome he was. So handsome, it was hard to tear her gaze away.

"I was lost," she fibbed. Not a *complete* lie.

He closed his book and set it on the side table. "I don't appreciate being lied to." He stood and prowled across the room. Everything about him was sleek and effortless, and she wanted to throw something at him.

"What makes you think I'm lying?" She tilted her head slightly. "Do you possess the ability to detect lies?" Cuffing her arms, she feigned boredom. "They left that ability out of the history books."

A smirk pulled at the side of his mouth, and once in front of her, his eyes explored her face. "Why are you here?"

"I was looking for you," she said sweetly.

His expression didn't change. "Most women are."

"Do they want to cut out your heart, too?" She fluttered her eyelashes dramatically.

A laugh rumbled from his chest, taking her by surprise once again. "I like when you're honest." His face shifted from amusement to a cold calmness as he took another step forward. "But I would like you even better on a spike, which is where you will be in hell if you threaten me again."

Her eyes flared slightly as she took a step back, trying not to show fear, but his face broke into an amused smile again. "Ah, so you meant it."

She stopped and pinched her brows together. "Excuse me?"

He strolled back to his reading chair, sat down, and lounged like the king he was. "You would have immediately told me you were kidding." His eyes roamed the length of her. "It's too bad. You might have even gotten on your knees, and you know how much I like you on your knees, Miss Raven."

Her body heated against her will, and she ran through every unsavory image she could think of to dampen the flames inside her. *Being horny would make seducing him easier*, she reminded herself.

The organ beating in her chest had long been dead, and separating sex and feelings was something she did well.

The feeling unsettled her. Not the act of having sex with him, but the fact her body *wanted* to. She closed her eyes and willed herself to remember the night of Cora's death.

"Miss Raven," Caius' voice said, cutting through her thoughts. He picked up the book on his side table. "While I am sure you were dreaming of taking my cock into that smart little mouth of yours, I would prefer it if you acted it out for the class."

It felt like a test. She had no doubt he was telling the truth about women throwing themselves at him. *Like Nina.* But he seemed like a man who liked the chase, and if the look in his eye was any indication, he hadn't had one in some time.

Still lugging her shopping bags, she shrugged and walked to the door. "What made you think the cock was yours?"

She practically ran through the door, moving faster than she ever had before.

When she burst through the exit leading to the dais, she spotted Nina climbing the steps. The woman stopped, and a sneer transformed her pouty mouth. "What were you doing in there? Everything beyond that door is off limits."

"Not for me," Rory replied coyly, taunting the woman who was making her life miserable, and as soon as the words left her mouth, she regretted them. Nina looked like someone with a vicious streak, and the last thing Rory needed was more shit from her.

"Not likely, gutter trash," Nina fumed. "Get back to your room and stay out of sight. It would be a shame if you were caught by the wrong person, wouldn't it?"

Rory didn't dignify the maid with a response as she left. Nina opened the dais door, and for some reason, it pissed Rory off. It would be difficult to seduce the king with Nina occupying his dick.

A sigh left her lips. She would figure it out. She always did.

~

Caius stared at his office door. *What made you think the cock was yours?* He couldn't decide if he wanted to cut her tongue out or suck it into his mouth.

"Fuck you, Adila," he said into the empty room and leaned forward to rest his elbows on his knees.

If he couldn't feel the suffocation of Aurora's black soul, then why couldn't he have her warm his bed? This was assuming she wanted him, of course. While he wanted nothing more than to fuck her mouth into submission, he would never force her.

He stood, frustrated. What was he thinking? It didn't matter if he could feel her soul or not; he knew what resided within her, and he hated it.

There was a knock on his door, and he foolishly opened it, thinking it was Aurora. Nina smiled and walked into the room, swaying her hips, and he fought a frustrated sigh.

"I've missed you." She pouted, and he forced himself not to grimace.

"What do you want, Nina?"

Her nostrils flared slightly. "Did Aurora bother you? I saw her sneaking through the door."

"That is none of your concern. Leave." He gave her his back as he crossed the room. Nina made a noise but wisely kept her thoughts to herself and left, slamming the door.

The door to his office opened again, and in walked Samyaza, his eyes watching Nina. Once she was out of earshot, he turned back to Caius.

"Why do you look like that?" he asked as he took a seat on the large, cushioned bench Caius had brought in to accommodate his friend's wings.

Sam could shift into a wingless form, but the *Angel* hated to, unless necessary. Caius eyed Sam's wings and was thankful he wasn't born with any.

Sam threw a dinner roll and hit him on the side. "Stop staring at my wings and answer me."

Caius popped a brow. "Did you pull a dinner roll out of your pocket?" He toed the bread.

Sam brought another roll to his mouth, ripped off a bite, and smiled as he chewed. "It was in my hand, but you were too busy stewing to notice."

"I was reading," Caius argued. It wasn't a lie. He was reading earlier.

"You were standing with no book when I walked in." Sam shoved the rest of the roll in his mouth and, after swallowing, said, "Tell me."

"Nothing is wrong." Caius picked up the roll and tossed it in the trash bin next to his desk. Aurora's contract peeked out from under a few papers, and he reached for it. Normally, he would file it away the same day the inmate arrived, but he couldn't stop himself from rereading her charges.

Thirteen murders, most of them men. It was unbelievable. When Max, the palace gardener, was speaking with her in the kitchens, she'd said, "*I am a monster.*"

"What is your obsession with Aurora Raven?" Sam asked from directly behind him.

Caius didn't scare easily, but when an oversized pigeon snuck up behind someone, even the bravest of men would yelp the way he did. "You need to wear a bell," he griped. "And I do not have an obsession, but I am curious as to why Adila sent her here."

Sam took the contract from Caius' hand and walked to the cabinet to file it away. "It is not your place to question the Scales of Justice. She would not have sent Aurora here without reason."

"I don't trust it," Caius said, taking a seat at his desk. "I want you to go to Erdikoa and gather whatever intel you can on the woman. Her mother is a *Sibyl*, and her sister is dead." He rubbed his jaw. "I want to know everything."

Sam looked skeptical but said nothing. They may have been best friends, but at the end of the day Caius was in charge.

"When do you want me to leave?" Sam asked quietly.

"After the Plenilune ball."

When Rory returned to her room, she stopped short at the tray on her bed. Her smile widened. She'd forgotten to thank Bellina for saving her from starvation. Her friend must have realized Rory didn't stop for food after shopping.

After setting her shopping bags down, she crossed the tiny room to her bed and inspected her dinner. She would have been happy with bread and water, but Bellina pulled out all the stops. A steak sat next to a baked potato topped with butter and cheese.

Guilt made her shoulders sag. She hoped her friend wasn't spending all her food credits on Rory. Tomorrow, she would seek her out and demand she use Rory's credits instead.

Her heart swelled at the thoughtfulness of her friend, and she sat down to dig in. The steak was juicy, and the baked potato was still warm enough to melt the butter.

Rory stopped chewing and looked at her plate. If it was another member of the staff leaving the food, there was probably spit in it. With a shrug, she continued to eat, savoring the taste. It never occurred to her to use her credits in town for food.

Her shift usually ended between breakfast and lunch, but after she showered and put herself together, it was midafternoon. She remedied starvation by stuffing as much food from the kitchens in her mouth as possible when she arrived at work. The other staff didn't arrive until five a.m., and there was no one around to report her to the queen bee.

Delaying her shower to grab food would be worth it, and she hoped they had a grocery store where she could get items that didn't require a refrigerator.

She blew out a long breath at the memory of her encounter with Nina. There was no doubt in her mind she would pay for it, but seeing the look on that wench's face was priceless.

Her mind drifted back to Caius. He made it clear Nina meant nothing more than a quick fuck to him, which was lucky for Rory. She wasn't the type to steal another woman's man, but not only was Caius not Nina's, Nina was a cunt, making the task more enticing.

Rory shook herself. How could she look into the face of her sister's murderer and still feel attraction? Maybe she was more messed up in the head than she thought.

Placing her tray on the nightstand, she threw herself back on her bed with a sigh. Could she really go through with this? *She had to.* Figuring out the layout of the palace was crucial, specifically where Caius' room was located. That was where she was likely to find Cora's soul. Or maybe in his office.

The other door in the hallway must lead somewhere, but she couldn't get caught by Caius again. What did he do all day? That was her second order of business. Could she follow him undetected?

Not for the first time, she cursed the realm for taking her abilities. Knowing his schedule would help with her plan to seduce him, though if she could find Cora's soul on her own, she wouldn't need to.

Sitting up, she stood and picked up her shopping bags to put her things away. She needed to get to sleep and prepare for the days ahead.

CHAPTER 13

After work the next day, Rory took the fastest shower she could, changed into a pair of leggings and a hoodie, and set out to find the king. Surely he didn't sit in his office all day. Knowing where to start proved to be difficult, and her plan didn't seem as clever as she stood in her room with no direction.

The best places to start were where she'd seen him before, and she made her way back to the throne room. She pulled up short at the crowd of people gathered in the enormous room, all staring at Caius lounging lazily on his throne.

Rory stuck to the shadows, knowing if the others saw her, they would kick her out, or worse. *What were they doing?* A grunt filled the air, and her head whipped to the circle at the other end of the room. A man was on the ground at the end of the marble walkway, looking around.

They're either receiving a new inmate or punishing one. Unable to help herself, she inched closer for a better look.

Her eyes flicked to Caius, who was watching her instead of the new arrival.

Shadows cloaked her, and while they weren't dark enough to prevent her from seeing, they were dark enough the others wouldn't notice her. *He helped her.* She looked back to him, but his gaze was on the man, and as Caius stood, she was reminded of how tall he was. He had to be a good seven or eight inches taller than she was.

His body was powerful as he walked across the floor, and she thought back to her own arrival. It was déjà vu as his footsteps filled the quiet air, and the newcomer trembled on the ground.

When Caius stopped, he held out his hand for the contract, looked it over, and raised his eyes to the man. "Bruce Stewart. Sentenced to one month." Caius motioned to the paper. "I believe you have the shortest sentence in the history of Vincula." His eyes returned to the contract, and he chuckled. "For approaching an *Aatxe*, pointing an unloaded gun at their chest, and demanding they arrest you."

Bruce wasn't paying attention to the king. His eyes were darting around the room.

"Mr. Stewart, someone will take you to your apartment, where you will be briefed on the rules of Vincula. You will report to me in the morning for your assigned work. Understood?" Caius' voice was amused but kind, and Rory clenched her jaw.

He'd shown her no such kindness upon her arrival. Humiliation had been his weapon of choice that day, and because of it, her life in the palace was miserable.

Bruce nodded as he stood. "Thank you, Your Grace."

An *Aatxe* in the legion stepped forward and motioned

for the new inmate to follow her, and Rory glanced around the room for Samyaza. Did he only escort the worst of the worst, or was he gone? She knew the employees in Vincula could move freely between realms if they wished.

Her eyes went back to the *Aatxe*. She missed Dume. This was the longest she'd gone without seeing him since meeting him. She missed Kordie and Keith, too.

Those thoughts turned into thoughts of her mother, and hot tears pricked the corners of her eyes. She stood lost in thought, fighting the urge to cry at what her life had become.

"Miss Raven." Caius' deep voice brought her back. The room had cleared out, and the shadows protecting her vanished. "Did you need something?"

As he closed the distance between them, she turned her head to discreetly wipe her cheeks before turning back to him. "Just waiting for everyone to scatter, so I'm not executed as I leave."

His movements ceased for the briefest moment before his arrogant demeanor returned. She may have imagined it. "Why are you crying?"

She stood taller. "I'm not crying."

"Don't lie to me," he said in a low voice.

"I'm worried about my mother," she snapped. "My apologies if my emotions have offended you, *Your Grace*."

His eyes were not amused or cruel as he regarded her. "She is a *Sibyl*, yes?"

She nodded. "Yes, but it doesn't matter now."

"It does to you." He motioned to her tear-streaked face. "Is there someone to take care of her in your absence?"

Rory couldn't stand the pity and answered by walking

away. She expected shadows to stop her, but they didn't. His voice did.

"I will send Samyaza to check on your mother."

Her eyes watered as she turned to face him. "What?"

He stuck both hands in his pockets and lifted his gaze. "I'll send my commander to check on her. If she doesn't have care, we'll arrange it."

Rory's mouth moved wordlessly, and her skin felt clammy. "Why would you do that? Is this a trick?"

Caius' face darkened. "I am not the heartless man you believe me to be. Your mother should not suffer for your transgressions."

Involuntarily, her body moved forward, but she stopped herself. The instinct to hug him was strong. "Thank you." It was all she could manage without making a fool of herself.

She thought everyone except *Royals* lost their memories after leaving Vincula. Maybe *Angels* were an exception, or perhaps the king was lying. If it was a ploy to make her suffering worse, she would kill him on the spot and hope someone would put her soul in a jar next to Cora's.

Rory's arm threaded through Bellina's that evening as they made their way across the palace courtyard. It was Rory's first time "going out" with her new friends, and she hated to admit she was nervous.

Her outfit was simple, consisting of jeans, a black top, and black heeled boots. Despite being able to see the king in color, everything else was still in grey-scale, meaning her wardrobe stayed basic. She braided her hair back in two simple braids in the event someone tried to attack her because loose hair was a weakness when fighting.

Bellina bumped her body into Rory's as they walked. "There is nothing to be worried about. No one will mess with you."

Rory side-eyed her. "You don't know that."

"No one *in our group* will mess with you," Bellina amended. "If anyone says anything, we'll leave." Bellina nodded to the guard at the gate as they left the palace grounds.

One of Rory's braids fell over her shoulder as she shook her head. "Absolutely not. If I need to leave, I will, but under no circumstances will I allow you to ruin your night."

Bellina patted Rory's arm. "You are not my boss, my mother, or my wife. Therefore, you can't tell me what to do."

Rory smiled to herself. "Thanks, B."

Bellina pointed to a large building down the street. "There's the bar. Let's get drunk."

Stepping into the bar was like stepping into another realm. A band played loud music in the back, people were everywhere, and what must have been hundreds of lanterns hung from the ceiling.

"Could you imagine having to refill the oil and light all of those?" Rory said to Bellina. "I would rather scrub the ovens again."

"Be careful what you wish for, butcher bitch," Nina's voice said from a few feet away. "Or maybe you want to watch again?"

Rory bit the inside of her cheek and rotated her head to look at Nina. "You already give me the shittiest work available. Save your threats for someone else." She turned to Nina fully and gave her a sardonic grin. "And I'll have to pass on the free show. I prefer real entertainment instead of watching a bitch beg for cock like a mangy mutt."

Nina's face screwed up, and she lunged, but Rory was faster. Her hand was around Nina's neck in an instant, and she squeezed, reveling at the fear in the maid's eyes. Her hands clawed at Rory's face, but Rory held her at arm's length.

Her voice was low when she looked into Nina's panicked eyes and said, "Be careful who you attack. You like to remind me I am The Butcher, but maybe you should remind yourself."

She released Nina with a shove, and the woman sucked down breaths as she wobbled away.

Asher turned to Rory with bug eyes. "Damn, you're scary. What was that about?"

"Why?" Rory shot back. "Are you fucking her, too? Please don't ask me to watch."

Asher looked from Bellina to Rory. "What did I miss?"

Bellina whirled on Rory. "Explain."

Rory blew out a long breath. "I'm going to need a drink if I have to relive the image of Nina naked with her ass in the air."

A loud grunt sounded behind them, and Rory turned to see a man with salt and pepper hair and dark eyes who looked to be her father's age. "You must be Rory," he said. "I'm Tallent."

She shook his hand. "Nice to meet you."

He was standing with two women, one who was at least

six feet tall with a medium shade of hair, and another who was short with a mop of dark, curly hair.

"I'm Kit," the tall one said.

"Cat," the other woman squeaked. She was adorable, and Rory had to resist ruffling her hair.

"Nina's still sleeping with the king?" Kit asked as she sidled up next to Rory at the bar.

Rory grabbed her drink and nodded. "I was unfortunate enough to walk in on them." She took a long drink. Hopefully, it would erase the image from her mind.

"Tell me everything," Cat said as she grabbed her own drink and motioned for them to follow her. When they found an empty table and sat down, Cat pointed at Rory. "Spill it, butcher girl."

Rory choked on her drink, and whiskey splashed onto the table.

"Cat!" someone hissed.

The woman looked around. "What? She's The Butcher, isn't she?"

"Excuse Cat," Tallent said, shooting the woman a warning glare. "She speaks before she thinks."

She threw her hands up. "She *is* The Butcher!" She turned to Rory. "Did I hurt your feelings?"

Rory was frazzled from the back and forth, and all she could do was shake her head. "We aren't twelve," she managed after a beat. "Call me whatever you'd like."

Cat shot Tallent a triumphant smile and turned back to her. "Okay, now tell us how you ended up in a threesome with the king and Nina."

"Wait, what?" Asher butted in. "I thought you walked in on them?"

"She did," Bellina confirmed. The seamstress turned to her and whispered, "Is that all?"

"We did *not* have a threesome," Rory insisted. "I finished my first shift and went in search of Nina. One of the palace staff gave me her room number, and when I knocked, the door flew open." She shuddered.

They all howled with laughter. "I hate you all," she grumbled.

Asher sat beside Rory and leaned in. "If you ever decide to have a threesome, I volunteer."

A piece of ice sailed across the table at him, and when he looked up, Bellina hurled another. "You're a pig." He shrugged and looked at Rory with a sly grin.

"You couldn't handle me," Rory told him and took a drink of her whiskey. "Good try, though."

The table erupted with more laughter, and Asher feigned offense. Rory's shoulders eased a fraction as she fell into easy conversation with the people she hoped would become her new friends.

"What does everyone do?" Rory asked the table.

"I work at the bakery downtown," Cat said with pride. "I'm damn good at what I do."

"Do you make donuts with cream cheese in them?" she asked. "I would kill for one. Not literally. Well, maybe."

Asher's drink shot through his nose as he laughed.

"Of course I do," Cat replied. "I'm no amateur."

"I work at the library," Kit added. "If you like to read, I can suggest any type of book."

"I didn't know there was a library here," Rory replied thoughtfully. She didn't like to read, but if there were history books to give her more insight into Caius, that would be helpful.

Kit nodded. "There's a lot of neat stuff in Vincula. I'm sad I'll have to leave."

"What did you do?" Rory asked.

Kit smiled deviously. "I broke into one of the administration buildings for the local grade school and burned it to the ground." Rory gaped, and the woman shrugged. "They were trying to ban books they deemed unfit. It was bullshit."

"How did you get in? Aren't the schools locked down tighter than The Capital?"

Kit turned her head and pointed at her mark. "I'm an *Eidolon*. The roof of the building didn't have iron in it."

Rory almost dropped her glass. What kind of supermystic shit was that?

She turned to Tallent. "And you?"

The man took a long drink. He was quieter than the rest. "I work at the hobby store, and I sold stolen art in the underground market." He shrugged. "I'm a hawk *Shifter*."

"I'm a *Sylph*, and I shot my brother in the leg," Cat added casually.

"What did he do?" Rory asked her.

Cat took a drink and smacked her lips. "He cut off my hair in my sleep." She motioned to her short, curly hair. "I look like a paintbrush." The table burst out laughing, but Rory was a little scared of the pint-sized woman. Her short hair was cute, but clearly she hated it. Who shot their brother over a haircut?

After some time, Rory excused herself to the bathroom, and on her way back to their table, someone knocked into her shoulder, hard. She almost lost her balance, and a burly man with a long, black beard sneered at her.

Unease skittered across her skin when he took a step

toward her, invading her space. "Excuse you," she said as she stepped back.

His hand tightened around his beer bottle, and she wondered if it would break from the pressure. The look of pure hatred on his face was one she'd not encountered yet, and it unsettled her.

"You don't get to speak to me as an equal, little butcher bitch," he snarled and took another step forward. Was butcher bitch her nickname now? *Original.* "If I see you disrespect Nina again, I will return the favor tenfold."

"Is everyone here fucking her?" she said, poking the already enraged bear.

His sheer size had her heart racing, and she cursed her smartass mouth, but before she could figure out an exit plan, the old man from the kitchen grabbed the man's shirt and pulled him back. "Get out of here, Ronny."

Ronny spit on Rory's shirt, and she stared down in shock. The older man had surprising strength as he hauled Ronny toward the door and said, "Go home."

Ronny shrugged the old man's hand off his shoulder and stalked out of the bar. Asher and Bellina pushed their way through the crowd, calling Rory's name, and it was then she realized the bar had gone quiet.

"What happened?" Asher demanded, all jest from earlier gone.

"Ronny," was all the old man said.

Bellina grabbed napkins from the bar and handed them to Rory. "That asshole. He's been in love with Nina since she arrived."

Rory glanced toward the exit and decided to avoid him at all costs.

"What kind of mystic is Nina?" Rory didn't know, and the maid's hair always hid her mark.

"*Alchemist,*" Asher answered. "Rumor is she would manipulate men and then steal their money."

"Of course she did," Rory muttered under her breath.

The old man held his hand out. "We haven't been formally introduced. I'm Max."

Rory put her shaky hand in his. "Rory. Thank you for that."

He tipped his head in acknowledgement and stepped around her to order a drink. "What are you drinking? It's on me."

Rory waved him off. "I appreciate it, but I think I'm going back to the palace."

Bellina motioned for Kit to bring her purse from the table. "I'm going with you."

"No," Rory said, motioning for Kit to stay put. "I'm fine." Kit stood with Bellina's purse half suspended in the air before plunking back down in her chair.

Bellina's hand motioned to Kit again, but the woman merely raised her middle finger in return.

"Please let me walk you back," Bellina tried again.

Rory shook her head. "I murdered thirteen people all by myself. I think I can manage to walk back to the palace alone."

A silence fell on those around them, and Rory guessed her dark humor wasn't well received, but before she could apologize, Max's booming laugh filled the space. "Yeah, you'll be alright. Come on, Bellina. Leave the girl be."

Rory shot Max a grateful smile and left.

CHAPTER 14

Caius woke with a start, a sheen of sticky sweat coating his body. He scrubbed a hand down his face and threw his comforter back. "Fuck."

Another nightmare. They'd become more frequent over the last few years, and sometimes, he had them while awake. Sam said he dozed off from lack of sleep and didn't realize it, but Caius knew that wasn't the case.

Tonight's wasn't as bad as some, but his heart still beat against his ribs. Throwing his legs over the edge of the bed and standing, he walked to the closet to dress.

He crossed the room to a bookshelf and pulled out a book to hit the button hidden beneath. The shelf slid sideways, revealing a dark stairwell leading to an underground tunnel.

Tunnel wasn't the correct word; it was more of an ornate hallway leading to the palace gardens. He flipped the switch to the essence lights, stepped inside, and pushed the button on the stone wall to close the hidden door.

Once at the end, he pushed open the door and stepped

into the palace gardens. They were located outside of the palace walls to help conceal the entrance to his tower, and he thanked the *Seraphim* for their ingenious design. It was created as an escape in the event of an emergency, but he used it to come here undetected.

It was strange really, how they created the realms, designing things they deemed important, like The Capital in Erdikoa, the Lux Palace, the Umbra Palace, and the essence system. Then they left, making the *Royals* and other mystics figure everything else out on their own. They never returned, nor did they speak with anyone, not even the *Angels*. What was the point?

Caius stopped trying to figure out the universe when he was imprisoned by his own sister. He meandered through the winding paths and eventually found his way to the small pond hidden behind the lush greenery.

It was much smaller than the lake in the park, and there were no piers or fish. It had posts with lanterns placed sporadically along the walkway, giving off the faintest glow. Only a handful of people knew the pond existed, and he wanted to keep it that way.

Someone sat on the shore, and he stopped short as he closed in on the water. He debated turning around, but before he could, Aurora's red, splotchy face turned to him. He waited for a quick remark or murderous glare, but all he got was her back as she turned away.

Caius had never been unsure of himself a day in his life, but he didn't know what to do as he stood with his hands at his sides, staring at a woman he should despise. His instinct told him to go to her, but his brain screamed at him to go back inside.

"How did you find this place?" was what he settled on.

He saw her chest rise as she sniffled and dutifully ignored him. His gut tugged him toward her, and his feet moved without permission.

"Is it not part of the gardens?" she asked, still refusing to look at him.

Her voice held none of her usual bite, and he hated it.

"Technically, yes," he replied. "But no one spends enough time in the gardens to find it."

"What do you want, Your Grace?" she asked, her snark working its way back into her voice, bringing a whisper of a smile to his lips.

He huffed out a laugh and asked, "Crying over your mother again?"

Her head turned eerily slow to look at him, and by the time their eyes made contact, hers were filled with hate. "Never speak about my family again."

His brows rose. "I will speak of whomever I wish." She turned away from him again. "Why were you crying?" *Fuck subtlety.*

"I wasn't. My allergies are terrible here with these night-time plants."

"As bad as you are at lying, I'm surprised you were not arrested sooner."

Aurora rose and stomped off, but she didn't get far. "Call off your dogs," she demanded through clenched teeth as she struggled against the shadows he used to stop her.

"They're not mine." He turned to look at her. "Why were you crying, Aurora?"

"Why do you care?" she shot back. "I'm getting the treatment I deserve. Isn't that what you wanted?"

"Walk with me," he said, releasing the shadows surrounding her.

He saw her hesitation, but eventually, she conceded and followed him as he walked around the pond. "What do you think you deserve, Miss Raven?"

Her brows came together. "What?"

"What treatment do you think you deserve?" he clarified.

The silence seemed to stretch forever, but then her mask of cool indifference blanketed her face when she answered, "It doesn't matter what I think. There will always be someone who thinks of me as their villain. The least I can do is be a damn good one." She looked at him. "Everyone loves to hate the villain, including you."

"Am I your villain, Miss Raven?" He didn't know why he asked, but he was interested in her reply.

He wished he hadn't because her response was immediate. "Yes."

Their gazes collided in a battle of wills, and he leaned down so his lips grazed her ear. "Then I'll be a damn good one."

With that, he left her standing in the glow of the lanterns, putting much needed space between them.

That fucker, Rory thought as she watched Caius leave. She'd been too shaken by her encounter with Ronny to take advantage of her time alone with the king, but even if she'd been in her right mind, she was ill prepared.

Dealing with Caius wasn't like dealing with men she picked up from the bars. Not only was he a king, but he was also a master manipulator.

The way he'd spoken to her tonight bordered on caring,

and she knew that wasn't something he was capable of. It was time to throw everything she had into her plan and find Cora's soul so she could kill the king and be done with it.

He always knew when she was lying, and she needed to get better at it. She would practice in her bathroom mirror like an idiot if that was what it took.

She hurried back into the palace, but when she entered the back door to the kitchens, a woman with dark hair lined with white streaks cut her off. Rory paused, unsure of what to do.

Did she need to prepare for a fight, mumble an awkward excuse, or ask her about the weather?

"You were scared," the woman said.

Rory stared dumbly. "No, I'm not." *What is with the people in this realm?*

"Not now," the woman clarified. "When you were walking back to the palace. You were scared."

Is she being monitored now? "I'm scared of the dark," Rory lied as she tried to walk around her.

"Liar," the woman called after her. *Did everyone here have built-in lie detectors?*

Rory spun around and threw her arms up. "What do you want me to say? Who are you, anyway?"

"I want you to tell me why you were afraid. A serial killer running through the streets looking as though she'd seen a ghost isn't normal." The woman leaned a hip on the counter and grabbed a knife from the block to pick at her nails. "I'm Lauren."

Rory gave up. "A guy at the bar threatened me, but to be fair, I threatened Nina first."

"Ah, Ronny," Lauren concluded. "He's an asshole." She looked at Rory with a serious expression. "He's also dangerous. His soul was a dark grey, and sending him here was a risk. Do not find yourself around him alone."

With that final warning, Lauren turned and pushed her way through the back entrance, disappearing into the night.

Rory shook her head in disbelief. If Lauren meant to make her feel better, she did a terrible job.

As she approached her room, Rory wished she'd slept in the garden when she saw Nina and two men standing in the hallway of the staff quarters. They abruptly stopped talking and stared at her with various looks of malice.

A warning crept down her spine, and she took measured steps toward them. If they wanted a fight, she would give them one, but without her *Fey* strength, she wouldn't win.

It pissed her off how the staff acted like she personally wronged them. They were criminals as well, and yes, her crimes seemed much worse, but their judgment was harsh. Almost too harsh, and she wondered if she had Nina to thank for that.

They didn't speak to her or touch her when she stepped around them and into her room. She sagged against her door. Despite the serenity of Vincula, she feared she would die, whether it be at the hand of a fellow inmate, or after she exacted her revenge.

One thing was certain, she wouldn't leave Vincula alive.

CHAPTER 15

The next afternoon, Bellina and Rory sat in the bakery where Cat worked. Rory was grateful Bellina hadn't brought up the night before. A small mercy, though Cat was a different story.

"Don't sweat it, butcher girl," she called from behind the counter. "No one takes Nina seriously, and Ronny is nothing but a love-sick dick."

"Thanks," Rory mumbled around a mouthful of donut.

"Are you wearing that saucy dress you bought to the Plenilune ball?" Bellina asked, shimmying her shoulders.

Rory took another bite of her donut and looked at Bellina as she chewed. "What is the Plenilune ball?"

"The staff really goes out of their way to keep things from you," her friend said, shaking her head. "The Plenilune is in three days, and every month the king throws a ball. It's not as pretentious as it sounds. There are no poofy dresses or ballroom dancing."

"The entire town is invited," Cat chimed in. "Every shop in town pitches in, so there's a variety of food."

Rory set her donut down. "Of course, it's in three days," she muttered. "I *have* to wear that dress because I'm out of credits." The dress left nothing to the imagination, and she could only imagine what the staff would think of her once they saw her. Her plan had been to catch Caius *alone* in it.

She could hear the insults now. *Whore. Butcher slut.* She sighed.

Bellina shimmied her shoulders. "You're definitely getting laid."

"As great as that sounds, everyone in this realm hates me," Rory reminded her.

"No, they don't. Most of them, maybe, but not all. Everyone liked you last night." Bellina shoved a forkful of cheesecake into her mouth. "Besides, even your worst enemy will want to fuck you in that thing."

"I don't know what your dress looks like, but I already want to fuck you in it," Cat offered.

Rory laughed as she stood. "I have to get back so I can go to sleep. Three a.m. comes early."

Bellina set her fork down and leaned back in her chair. "I can't believe they put you on the early morning shift. At least you get two days off each week."

"It doesn't surprise me." Rory replied. "The upside is if the ball is in three days, I'm off the next morning."

Rory turned to leave and almost ran headfirst into Nina. She seemed to pop up everywhere. "Get out of my way," the maid snapped as she shouldered past.

Rory ignored her and left with a wave in Bellina's direction.

As she trekked back to the palace, she thought about how she would wear her hair and if she'd get to spend time with the king or not. If she was going to wear the dress in front of the masses, she would put it to good use.

The morning of the ball, Rory rushed around the kitchens, trying to finish her duties as fast as possible. She needed plenty of time to get dressed and convince herself to go.

The ball started at five, and she agreed to meet Bellina, Asher, Kit, Tallent, and Cat at five-thirty. Max said he would rather eat nails than go, and Rory was inclined to agree.

She was almost done when Nina strolled in with a sardonic smile on her face. "I'm glad I caught you," she said in a sickly-sweet voice. "There has been a change in the schedule for tonight."

Rory stiffened. "I'm sorry to hear that. Now, if you will excuse me, my shift ended."

She put her rag in the bin and began to untie her apron, but Nina's voice stopped her. "I am afraid you'll be working the ball tonight." She walked into Rory's line of sight. "You will take empty plates and glasses from the guests, make sure the food and drink tables are full, and stay to clean up the throne room once the night is over."

Rory stared at Nina with wide eyes. "This is low, even for you," she hissed. She should have expected this.

"It's already been cleared by the king." Nina's smile was wide and cruel. "Report at four-thirty sharp."

When Nina left, Rory lost her temper, grabbed a butcher knife from the counter, and hurled it against the wall.

The blade felt good in her hand.

～

Rory waltzed into the ballroom at four-thirty wearing a
long, black, silk dress with slits to the top of each thigh. The
top was rigid and held up by two thin straps and the neckline plunged to her navel, showcasing the little bit of breasts
she had.

Nina hadn't specified what Rory had to wear, and if she
was going to suffer, she was going to do it in style. Her hair
fell in a sheet down her back, and the left side was pinned
back with a black metal pin. Her makeup was done, and her
lips were blood red, according to the label on the tube. She
looked damn good, and she knew it.

The hair, skin, and body products in Vincula were
modern, otherwise she wouldn't know what to buy. It really
wasn't bad in the prison realm, and if her friends and family
were here, she would enjoy it.

One maid working the ball saw her walk in and shook
her head. "Where is your uniform, girl?" The woman was
older, with a tight grey bun and a frown on her weathered
face.

"Nina didn't say I needed to wear my uniform." She
shrugged. "Sorry."

The woman huffed and waved her toward one table.
"I'm Gracie." She pointed to things and explained when to
fill and when to clear off the other tables used for
dining. Gracie was an odd name for an old woman, but
Rory simply nodded as she rattled on.

Once the maid finished, Rory took her post behind the
beverage table and periodically scanned the growing crowd
for her friends. There were no phones in Vincula, and she

hadn't been able to let them know she wouldn't be joining them tonight.

Spotting Asher as he entered the room, she slipped out from behind the table and made her way to him. When his eyes landed on her, he scanned her from head to toe and whistled.

"Damn, are you sure you don't want to fuck me? Because I would leave with you right now," he said with a playful wink.

She shoved him lightly. "Nina is making me work tonight."

"What?" he asked incredulously.

"She does what she can to make my time here a living hell," she sighed as frustration boiled her blood. "I have to get back or old lady Gracie will hunt me down and kill me herself."

Asher nodded. "I'll tell the others, and if you get the chance to poison Nina's drink, take it."

Rory laughed and waved as she slipped back behind the beverage table right as Nina approached with hate in her eyes. "What are you wearing?" she demanded.

Rory popped a hip. "Is there a problem?"

"Why aren't you in uniform?" Nina's face seemed to darken in color, matching her hair.

"Because I don't have to be." Rory held out a glass of wine. "You look like you could use this."

Nina snatched the glass and threw the wine all over the front of Rory's dress. Rory jumped back and held her hands out as wine trickled down her chest, and when she looked up, Nina smirked. "Oops." She stomped away, and Rory seethed as her skin turned sticky.

A few people were looking at her, some with grins, some

with pity. Grabbing a few napkins from the nearby dessert table, she dabbed at her dress, but her attempts were futile.

She returned to her station, all hope of a decent night gone.

She felt the moment he entered the room. Everyone must have because the talking died down to a murmur as Caius approached his throne. He turned to the crowd with a lazy smile.

He looked exquisite in a finely tailored suit that hugged his muscular arms and thighs perfectly. *For aether's sake, looking like that should be a crime.*

"Happy Plenilune. Enjoy the night; you have earned it with your hard work this month." A maid placed a highball glass in his hand, and he raised it in toast. The crowd responded in turn, and it was obvious the subjects of Vincula adored their king.

She was constantly having to separate what she'd been taught about Vincula from reality, as it all seemed to be a lie. The king's eyes collided with hers, and she held her breath.

His eyes drifted down her body, and when they made their way back to her face, he wore an indiscernible expression. Without breaking eye contact, he reached out his hand and snapped, summoning a nearby maid.

His eyes never left hers as he spoke with the girl before sending her away. Not a minute later, the same maid tapped Rory on the shoulder. "The king needs to speak with you."

Rory snapped her head back toward Caius, and the side of his mouth lifted a fraction. When she approached the bottom of the dais, he motioned for her to come closer, and once in front of him, he snapped his fingers again.

The same maid appeared with a rag and a jar of something Rory didn't recognize. The maid handed the items to her and scurried away.

"On your knees, Miss Raven," the king purred.

Rory looked at the things in her hands. "What is this?"

Caius leaned back with his arms draped on each side of his throne. "My shoes are looking a little dull. Shine them."

Her jaw almost hit the ground as she stared at him. "You have got to be kidding."

His brow rose slightly. "Do I look amused?"

"Yes," she muttered as she bent to her knees.

The same maid brought a stool for Caius to prop his feet on, and he motioned for Rory to begin. The room quieted down and watched as Caius seized a chance to humiliate her in front of the entire town. Again.

As she sat on her knees, the slits in her skirt rode up, exposing her bare hips. The king's eyes caressed her skin, and she could have sworn the gold in his eyes darkened as his pupils expanded. She suppressed a triumphant grin.

Looking up, she smiled innocently. "You did say you liked me on my knees."

He brought his thumb to his lip and trailed it over the pillowy flesh, something she noticed he did often. "Yes," he said in a rough voice. "I do."

She returned to her task, and when her hand grabbed the back of his shoe, she ran it slowly over his pant leg until she was gripping his calf. His muscles tensed beneath her hold, and she fought another smile.

She ran the rag methodically over his shoes, shining the leather to perfection, and periodically, she would lean back and dab non-existent sweat on her chest with her free hand. Caius tracked her movements, his eyes growing darker by the minute and when his shoes were finished, she used his leg to help her stand.

Her hand crested the top of his thigh before she straightened with a sly smile. "Is there anything else you need, Your Grace?"

Shadows discreetly trailed under her dress and up her legs in a way that instantly made her wet, and she bit her lip to stop a moan. "This is a dangerous game you are playing, Miss Raven." He leaned forward, and his shadows retreated. "One that will leave you broken if you are not careful."

She leaned down to position herself in front of him. "I'm counting on it."

Straightening, she walked away, swishing her hips for him, full of satisfaction.

CHAPTER 16

Caius prowled the castle looking for *her*. She'd teased him enough, and it was time to teach her a lesson. He rounded the corner to the kitchens, hoping she was cleaning up after the ball, but she wasn't there.

Where could she be?

His instinct told him the gardens.

He pushed his way through the back entrance and wound through the path leading to the middle of the maze. Black heels discarded on the ground caught his attention, and he grinned. "Hello, Miss Raven."

"Your Grace," came her reply, and his pants tightened at her sultry tone.

"I don't like to be teased," he said as he strolled toward her voice.

The plants nearby rustled. "How is that my problem, Your Grace?" Her voice held a challenge he was happy to accept.

"I suggest you run, Miss Raven."

A loud gasp made him feral, and when he heard the slapping of her bare feet against the concrete, he began to count. "One." Her footsteps moved farther away. "Two." His heart thundered in his chest. "Three."

Rory was thankful for the slits in her dress that allowed her to run. The sound of Caius' footsteps pounding the pavement behind her sent a thrill through her.

Her lungs were burning as her legs pumped faster toward the opening to the pond. There were trees and plants to hide behind, and she pushed harder, refusing to glance over her shoulder.

The full moon and starry sky aided the lanterns, helping her see, and she almost cried out with relief when she crossed the archway out of the garden. Stopping at the shoreline, she turned around, searching for cover, but shadows enveloped her.

She screamed, and a shadow wrapped around her mouth to muffle her cries. The lights from the lanterns surrounding the pond disappeared with the shroud of shadows, taking away her sight completely.

When the darkness receded, Caius stepped from the shadows like a beast of the night, and his golden eyes flashed as they raked down her body. His approach was slow, and a cocky smirk transformed his face into one of arrogant beauty.

"What were you doing tonight, Aurora?" he drawled.

The shadows disappeared from around her, and she forced herself not to shake in his overwhelming presence.

"What do you mean?" she asked, biting her lip for effect.

He stepped closer. "You know exactly what I mean." His

hand reached for her neck but stopped. "What game are you playing? You have made your loathing for me clear, but your actions suggest otherwise."

"Does it look like I hate you?" Her eyes dipped to her breasts, where her nipples were visibly hard against the fabric of her dress.

The king went utterly still, his eyes glued to her chest. "Do you want me to touch you, Miss Raven?"

She tried to take a step forward, but his shadows wrapped around her legs to stop her. "Do you want to touch me, Your Grace?"

He stepped back, and her hope dissolved, but then she felt a hand wrap itself gently around her ankle.

No. Not a hand, a shadow. She didn't dare move as it trailed up her leg, and the king watched her with rapt attention.

"Is this what you want?" he asked in a gravelly voice.

As the shadow traveled higher, her breathing picked up, and as much as she hated to admit it, she was shaking with anticipation and want. She disgusted herself, but tonight, it served her well. Closing her eyes, she let herself succumb to the pleasure.

She could feel the cool shadow swirling sensually around her leg, but when it stopped at the apex of her thighs, she groaned. Her eyes opened, and her mouth parted slightly at the look on Caius' face. It was raw and primal, and if she had been wearing panties, they would have been soaked.

His eyes were glued to her leg, exposed by the slit of her dress, and when his eyes met hers, the cool night air hit her pussy as her dress was ripped even higher.

"You're bare," he all but growled.

She refused to look away. "It seems I am."

He stepped closer, but his hands stayed in his pockets. Her body was burning up, and if he didn't touch her soon, she would have to touch herself. Just as she trailed her hand south, something strummed her clit, and she lurched forward.

Her mouth formed an O, and she reached for Caius, but he stepped back again as he watched her with satisfaction. The shadow was vibrating against her clit, and everything within her started to tingle.

Her nipples were diamonds, and her legs useless as her muscles spasmed from the intense pleasure. She had no other option but to sink to her knees, no longer able to stand. The shadows holding her limbs dispersed long ago, and she leaned on her hands and knees, twitching from torturous pleasure.

"Caius," she begged. Her body pulsed, and her vision blurred. "Caius, please." Her moan cut through the night as an orgasm crashed through her. The muscles in her legs seized completely, and she was forced to roll onto her back, lifting her hips.

Her pussy clenched over and over, but the shadows didn't stop. "Please," she begged again. It was too much.

Another climax was building, and her stomach tightened, preventing her from catching her breath. She cried out through another orgasm, and her clit felt raw from the continuous vibration because it never stopped.

She never knew pleasure could be torture, and when she tried to press her legs together, more shadows pried them apart.

"Please, stop," she breathed, and as soon as the words were out of her mouth, the shadows disappeared.

She squeezed her eyes closed as shame coated her cheeks,

and the urge to ask him for more sat on her tongue. It was excruciating, but in the best way, and when he stopped, she regretted asking him to.

Her body went limp except for her heaving chest. Caius sauntered to where she lay sprawled on the ground and crouched down. "Do not challenge me unless you are prepared to lose, Aurora."

He stood and disappeared through the arch as she lay panting on the ground, staring at the starry sky.

An hour later, Samyaza stepped into Caius' office, and Caius said without greeting, "I need you to check on Aurora's mother while you're in Erdikoa."

Sam adjusted the neck of his tunic. "What am I checking on, exactly?"

"She is a *Sibyl*." They both fell silent.

"And she doesn't have a caregiver," Sam guessed.

"Not to Aurora's knowledge."

"I will see it is taken care of," Sam assured him as he clapped Caius on the back. "I will return when I have the information you've requested."

Caius tipped his head as his friend opened the door. "Thank you."

Shadows exploded around Caius the moment the door to his office closed as his restraint snapped, and he stabbed a hand through his hair. *Why was he concerned with Aurora's life before Vincula?*

He was losing control where she was concerned. The want to touch her more than anything consumed him, but he knew the moment he had her, he would never give her up.

This all-consuming feeling after only a few weeks was egregious.

The way she fell to her knees was a sight to behold, and her mouth parting as she whispered his name almost broke his resolve. She was a fool if she thought he didn't know she was seducing him on purpose, and he assumed it involved her sister's death.

He rubbed the tension from his forehead as he looked around his office at the mess he'd made. A bone deep exhaustion settled over him, and he decided the mess could wait until morning.

CHAPTER 17

ERDIKOA

Sam appeared in his arrival bunker at the palace in Erdikoa and quickly shifted into his discreet, wingless form. As an *Angel*, he could shift between several forms at will. He liked his true form best, but his many wings would reveal his identity to the citizens of Erdikoa, something he couldn't allow.

Grabbing his street clothes from his closet, he padded to the bathroom, changed, tied his long hair into a low bun, and examined himself in the mirror. The citizens in the city would stare at him, knowing he was different, but they wouldn't be able to put their finger on why.

There was more to Aurora Raven, and he was determined to prove she was not the black soul everyone believed her to be. Sam could tell Caius wanted her, but the king was holding himself back.

Caius was his best friend, and what happened to him all those years ago was unfair. Adila refused to hear him out and sentenced him immediately. Sam always liked Adila, but something about her treatment of Caius at his trial rubbed him the wrong way.

Sam left his bunker and found Lauren in the hall. She was one of the few *Angels* stationed in the realms, and she was stunning. The two of them weren't dating, but they often kept each other company.

His hand twitched, wanting to run it across the smooth light brown skin of her exposed shoulders. Her dark hair had streaks of white framing her face, and the soft curves she sported made him want to yank her back into his bunker.

She was one of the best fighters he knew and was fiercely protective of those she deemed worthy. She had his respect and his bed. "Are you on your way back?" he asked.

She lifted on her toes and patted his cheek. "Why? Miss me?"

He nipped at her hand. "Always." She helped monitor the inmates in Vincula, but instead of being in her winged form, she preferred to stay shifted to blend in. "What errand does Caius have you on now?"

"Researching Aurora Raven," he replied. "Have you met her yet?"

"Ahh," Lauren said knowingly. "Briefly. He has never been interested in an inmate's life before Vincula. Why now?"

Sam nodded. "She is The Butcher. Caius despises what she represents, but he's drawn to her. I believe his desire will border on obsession before long."

Lauren sighed. "I can tell she is not what she seems. Let me know what you discover."

She turned and opened the door to her own bunker and blew a kiss over her shoulder. Sam scrubbed a hand down his face and headed to the only place he knew where to start: Aurora's place of employment.

"I have tracked down four more people who say she saved them," Dume told Keith and Kordie. They sat at the back of Whiplash in a dark booth, drinking.

"I knew it," Kordie whispered. Her voice wobbled. "I knew she wouldn't kill innocent people."

"That's why the Scales of Justice didn't send her to hell," Keith said excitedly. "She *is* like a supermystic, only more gruesome."

Dume saw Keith shiver. The way Rory displayed her victims was disturbing, and that was something they would unpack later. But with every *real* victim he spoke with, a little more weight lifted from his shoulders.

Rory was his oldest friend, and he refused to believe she would murder someone without cause. "Her last victim was an undocumented *Merrow*, and they found an entire room full of empty jars in his apartment."

Keith whistled. "Damn. If they were empty, I bet Rory set the souls free." Dume thought the same thing. "There's no telling how many people he would have killed."

"Or how many he already did," Kordie added.

"What do you know about Aurora Raven?" a deep voice rumbled across the room.

All three turned their heads to see a large man with a blonde bun, glaring at the bartender. Dume rose from his seat and approached the man. "Why are you asking about Rory?"

The man turned his threatening gaze to Dume. "Rory?"

"You asked about Aurora Raven." Dume folded his enormous arms across his chest. As an *Aatxe*, he was big, but this guy was huge. "She goes by Rory."

The man looked Dume up and down. "You know her." It wasn't a question.

"What do you want with her?" Dume asked again.

"I would like to speak with you," the man replied instead of answering the question.

Dume's jaw ticked, but it wasn't in his nature to be hostile. "Come with me."

He led him to their booth in the back and introduced him to Keith and Kordie. "We are—were her best friends."

"Are," Keith corrected, narrowing his eyes at Dume.

"My name is Sam," the man said. "I need to know everything you know about her, including why she murdered thirteen people."

"Why?" Keith asked. "She's gone, and she isn't coming back until we're long dead."

Sam motioned for Kordie to let him sit, and she scooted as far away from him as possible. "It is to help her."

The three went still. "What do you mean '*help her?*'" Kordie asked. "There is no way out of a prison sentence. She'll be in Vincula for five-hundred years."

"I am aware of how long her sentence is," Sam said flatly. "What do you know?"

They all looked at each other, silently agreeing to let this man in. "I have been investigating the murders," Dume began. "So far, five people have said Rory saved their lives from her so-called victims. The first one found us here, defending Rory tooth and nail. I tracked down the other four. Her last victim was an undocumented *Merrow*, and there were dozens of empty jars in his apartment. We think Rory set the stolen souls free."

Sam's face had the emotional range of a dial tone. "Is that so?" Dume gave a curt nod. "And what of the others?"

Dume frowned. "I can't announce to the realm I am investigating a closed case. I must be discreet, and that's not easy."

"Her soul is grey," Keith added. He jerked his thumb at Dume. "He said when the Scales of Justice sentenced her, she said, '*Your soul is a beautiful shade of grey*' or something like that. It's in the transcript."

"It's odd," Dume added. "She has never commented on a person's soul. Not that I've heard of."

Sam was quiet as he absorbed the information. "How do I contact you three? I will check in to see how your investigation is going. Is there anything you need to help?"

Three sets of wide eyes looked back at him. "Who are you?" Dume asked with a mixture of awe and bewilderment. "Why are you helping us?"

Sam pulled out a cellphone and slid it to Dume. "Put in your information. I must leave." The gargantuan man paused. "What do you know of Rory's mother, the *Sibyl*?"

Dume's fist clenched around the phone, but instead of arguing, he programmed his, Keith's, and Kordie's numbers into the phone and handed it back. "Lenora? What do you mean '*what do we know?*'"

Sam pocketed the device. "Rory was her caregiver, was she not? Who cares for her now?"

Dume's eyes slid to Kordie and back to Sam. "We do."

The man nodded and stood. "I'll be in touch."

The three watched him walk away. Keith turned to Dume and muttered, "What the fuck just happened?"

CHAPTER 18

VINCULA

The vendor leaned over the counter of his food cart to hand Caius his pizza and cautioned the king not to touch the bottom of the hot box.

Caius tipped his head in thanks and left, the people in the streets making a path as they greeted him politely. He enjoyed venturing into town periodically to see that his people were taken care of.

They were criminals, but they weren't evil, though some teetered on the edge, almost past the point of redemption. A familiar voice had his steps faltering, and he turned, knowing whom he would find.

Aurora stood with a seamstress from the palace and another man who was looking at her with a mischievous grin. As she laughed, she slapped his shoulder, and he pulled her in to wrap an arm around her.

Caius' grip on the pizza box tightened and dented the cardboard. He knew the moment she sensed him because her body stiffened, and she glanced over her shoulder. Her eyes flared slightly and flicked to the pizza box in his hands.

The man with his arm around her pulled her attention away, making her laugh again. Caius both relished and resented the sound, and he hated the man pulling it out of her.

They were probably fucking, and he hated that knowledge even more.

By the time Caius arrived back at the palace and sought out Gracie to run an errand, his mood was sour, and it worsened when Nina approached him in the courtyard. Her shirt was tight and low cut to showcase her huge tits, and her skirt was short.

Her tongue ran along her bottom lip before she bit it, and he wanted nothing more than for her to disappear. "I was looking for you," she purred. "Can we meet tonight?" Her voice lowered so only he could hear. "I want to taste you."

Aurora with the man in town flashed through his mind, and something red hot burned his chest. *Would she be jealous if she saw him with Nina?* It was a theory he wanted to test, but he wouldn't fuck Nina again. She no longer appealed to him.

"Would you like to have dinner with me instead?" he asked with a forced smile.

Her eyes lit up. "Yes!" Had she been any other woman, he would have felt guilty for getting her hopes up, but Nina only wanted what she thought would elevate her status. If Caius lost his place of power tomorrow, Nina wouldn't give him a second glance. *No loss there.*

He nodded and motioned for her to follow. Spending time with Nina where they had to converse would be its own kind of torture, but he would do it until they crossed paths with Aurora.

If she was jealous, then despite her trying to seduce him on purpose, she wanted him, and if she wanted him, he would take her.

Nina's arm wrapped around his, and she wore a smug smile on her face every time they passed the other staff. Normally when he consorted with her, he took the less used halls, but that would defeat the purpose tonight.

"Where are we eating?" Nina asked excitedly. "We could try the pasta restaurant. They have a chicken parmesan plate that is to die for."

Caius' arm tightened slightly. "If that's where you'd like to go."

They walked through the streets with Nina hanging on his arm like a leech, and the stares they received made his stomach turn. *Why was he subjecting himself to this over a woman he didn't even like?*

But then it happened. Aurora was walking toward the palace with one of her friends, and when she saw Caius and Nina approaching, she stopped talking and stared. Her eyes bounced between Caius, Nina, and their linked arms, and her eyes tightened.

Caius let his smugness show, and when he smiled at her, she turned away, grabbed the other woman's arm, and practically dragged her away. His smile was stretched from ear to ear.

She was jealous.

"Are you listening?" Nina asked impatiently.

He cleared his throat. "Yes, of course."

Nina glanced over her shoulder at Aurora, and when she turned back around, her eyes were cold. Her face transformed into a bright smile, and he knew she was putting on a show. She was jealous of Aurora, and with good reason.

Nina was nothing to him, but Aurora was something, he just didn't know what.

"Come, Your Grace. Let's eat, and then maybe you can *come* later, too." Her other hand caressed the top of his forearm, and he itched to yank it back.

"After we eat, I must retire," he replied. "What was that dish you were raving about?"

Rory threw open the door to her room as rage consumed her. Today had been fun with Bellina and Asher, but all she could think about was Nina's wretched claws hanging on to Caius.

How could he return to Nina after their night in the garden? It hadn't been intimate, purely sexual, but she thought it was the start of their little game.

Nina would ruin everything, just as she ruined everything else in Rory's life.

Rory stomped to her bed and grabbed a pillow to hurl across the room, but as she reached across her bed, something caught her eye that made her freeze.

Sitting on her bed was a pizza box dented on the sides. Her hands shook as she opened it and found a thick crust cheese pizza. Picking up the box, she sat on the bed in a daze with the pizza on her lap.

It was never Bellina leaving her food—it was Caius.

Setting the pizza down, she stalked to the hallway toward the king's office. She climbed the bane of her existence, and when she reached the top, she turned around and gave the stairs the finger.

The throne room was another ten-minute walk across the massive palace, and when she finally arrived, she had to stop and take a breath. She practically ran, despite her legs yelling at her not to.

The good thing was the stairs were getting easier, and eventually they wouldn't bother her. *She hoped.*

Crossing the room, she climbed quietly up the dais and slipped through the door behind the throne. She assumed he was still strolling through town on his date with Nina. Her plan was to scribble a thank you note and leave it on his desk, but when she stood in front of the door, another idea struck her.

It was the perfect time to search for Cora's soul. *If he was truly her killer,* her soul whispered. The more she thought back to the day of her sister's murder, the more she noticed subtle differences between Caius and Bane. Their faces were the same, but their walk was different. Bane didn't wear rings, and his suit was light, not black. Then there was the problem of her seeing Caius in color, but not Bane.

She didn't know if she was fishing for differences because she wanted the king, or if it was because they *were* different.

She tried the knob, but it was locked, and she reached into the back pocket of her jeans. After discovering the sky room, she started carrying a few pins with her for spontaneous situations like this.

Working the lock until she heard a click, she silently slipped into the dimly lit room and looked around to ensure it was empty. She took a second to admire the room, and as she closed in on his reading nook, his smell filled the air.

Every person has their own smell, but they can't smell it

themselves. Rory always wondered if hers stank or some-thing. No one would tell her if it did, but no one ever told her she smelled good unless she was wearing perfume.

His was a comforting smell, but she couldn't link it to any certain thing. Her hand reached to touch the chair, but she pulled it back and shook her head. "Get it together," she scolded herself.

She made quick work of looking for any sign of jars or hiding places. When she got to his desk, she opened various drawers and found nothing but office supplies. It was disap-pointingly boring.

The long drawer across the middle was locked, and her brows rose. Why would he lock this drawer but not the others? She felt along the underside of the desk for a key, and when she found none, she looked through the drawers again, coming up empty. He must keep it on him.

Grabbing the pins from her back pocket, she unlocked the drawer and slid it open. Rory's blood ran cold. A folder with her sister's name on it stared at her, and with shaky hands, she pulled it out and dumped the contents onto his desk.

Inside was the emergency report from Cora's murder and pictures of her dead body. A sob ripped from Rory's throat as she stumbled back and covered her mouth. A flood of tears streamed down her face, and she squeezed her eyes shut to banish the pictures from her mind.

How foolish she'd been to think he was innocent. How disgusting that she'd let her hormones take over. He killed his own sister, for aether's sake. Quickly, she shoved the papers and pictures back into the file and slammed the drawer shut before locking it back.

She looked around the office with newfound determination. Running to the bookshelves, she pulled books to look behind them. When she pulled out a book on a smaller shelf, a button sat against the back of the wood.

She couldn't move. Whatever this button went to could lead her to her sister's soul, and as much as she wanted to find the jar to free Cora, the bright pink trapped within the glass would be another reminder that her sister was gone.

She jabbed the button with her finger and yelped as the bookcase slid sideways to reveal a long hallway. Her tentative steps carried her through the door, and when she found another button on the wall, she pushed it and watched the bookshelf slide back in place.

She jogged through the corridor, looking for another door, and when she arrived at a set of stairs, she groaned.

Once she reached the top, she was pouring sweat, and when she pushed open the door, she stepped into the sky room. Her jaw dropped, and she spun around to look at the door. It was another bookshelf.

Pulling out books, she looked for the button to close the door, and when she found it, she watched it close. "I'll be damned," she whispered. Her head tilted back to look at the illusion of a setting sun above her.

"Why would this room lead to his office?" she mused. It must be the queen's chambers, she realized, frowning. "Why wouldn't his queen share his room?"

Sighing, she crossed the room and slipped through the main door. At least tonight wasn't a complete bust. She knew, without a doubt, Caius killed her sister.

CHAPTER 19

Caius pulled out his keys to unlock his office after his *date* with Nina. The thought made his skin crawl.

His office was already unlocked, and his hackles rose. Throwing open the door, he stepped inside to survey the room. No one was there, and nothing was out of place. In his haste, he might have forgotten to lock it on his way out.

He ran a hand through his hair and sat in his reading chair as he replayed the night at the pond. It had only been a week, but the image of Aurora as she lost control consumed him, and it was all he thought about.

He was adjusting his pants when his door opened, and Samyaza stomped in. The *Angel* was large and stomped everywhere, and sometimes Caius thought he felt the entire realm shake.

Sam eyed the king. "You look annoyed."

Caius sat at his desk and huffed out a breath. "I am annoyed. You're back from Erdikoa sooner than expected."

The *Angel* nodded and took a seat. "I was lucky. Rory's

friends were at her place of employment. It took little effort to get information."

"Rory?" Caius asked. "Who is Rory?"

Sam's mouth pulled into a wide smile. "It is what Aurora goes by. It is much more fitting, is it not?"

"And what did these friends tell you about *Rory*?" Caius rolled the name around on his tongue, savoring the taste.

Sam sat forward, leaning his elbows on his knees. "They were already looking into her victims."

"Why would anyone in Erdikoa be looking into the murders?" Caius mused. The cases were solved.

When Sam raised his head, satisfaction blanketed his face. "Because, according to them, she was a good person."

Caius gave a humorless laugh. "She murdered thirteen people and sewed their hands to their arms."

Sam nodded. "So far, five people have come forward claiming Rory saved them from one of her victims, and her last victim was an undocumented *Merrow* with a room full of empty jars in his apartment. They think Rory released the trapped souls."

Caius sat back. "Come again?"

"You heard what I said," the *Angel* said smugly. "Her *Aatxe* friend will keep looking into the other murders, and I suspect he will find more of the same."

"Was the *Aatxe* her lover?" Caius asked tightly. "He could have been trying to free her." The thought made him want to destroy his office again.

Sam smirked, and Caius considered strangling him. "They did not say, but you and I both know Adila's word is final." He rubbed a large hand down his face. "I think they need to know she was not a monster, for their own sakes."

Caius nodded, mulling over the new information. If she was saving people, why the disturbing display? He couldn't make sense of it.

"And her mother?" Caius asked.

"Taken care of by the *Aatxe*."

Caius' frown deepened. How close was Rory to this *Aatxe* friend? "The reasons she killed don't matter," he said after a beat.

Sam stood, unfolding his long legs. "Yes, it does."

He left, and his cryptic comment hung over Caius like a guillotine.

This woman would be the end of him.

Later, Caius fisted his cock as the warm water of his shower trickled down his chest. Visions of Rory on her knees were at the forefront of his mind, and he imagined kneeling behind her in that silk dress while she convulsed with pleasure. The slits of her barely-there dress would give him easy access, made even easier by her lack of panties.

He hated himself for wanting her, and he hated Sam for giving him hope she wasn't as heartless as her crimes would suggest.

Up and down his hand went, imagining her riding him with slow, sensual movements. His name on her lips as her head fell back, and her long, dark hair brushed her breasts.

His fist moved faster as her lust filled eyes met his, and he groaned, slapping his hand against the cool tile as his balls tightened, and waves of pleasure spread through his body.

Hot strings of cum splattered against the wall and floor,

and he stood beneath the stream of water, panting. He wished he'd never seen her face.

As he wrapped a towel around his waist, the venom she spewed at him came rushing back. She hated him, blaming him for her sister's death, but she wanted him, too. He understood the sentiment.

A knock sounded at his door, and with a single thought, the shadows opened it. Everyone called them *his* shadows, but they didn't belong to him. They were the shadows in the surrounding spaces that bent to his will. The very shadows used by the *Seraphim* to create the realms.

Nina waltzed in with a smile. "I enjoyed our date tonight, Your Grace." He stared at her with a blank expression, feeling nothing for the woman in front of him.

Earlier, the thought of touching Nina disgusted him, but maybe he could force himself to forget the grey-eyed woman occupying his every thought. His feelings for Rory were hot and cold. He moved between wanting to fuck her and make her jealous and wanting to rid himself of her.

Nina sashayed toward him as she unbuttoned her dress, and he met her halfway, sliding his hand across the back of her neck to thread his fingers through her thick locks. "I'm always ready to fuck that dirty cunt of yours." The words were a bitter lie.

She dropped her dress to the floor and removed her bra and panties as he watched and dropped his towel. The faster they started, the better. He grabbed her by the throat and walked her to his bed. "On all fours."

She bit her bottom lip with an excited smile and turned her back to him before falling to her hands and knees. He rarely took her from the front because the faces she made annoyed him.

His palm met her skin with a resounding slap, and she giggled. Her arousal was visible from this angle, but he couldn't bring himself to run his fingers through it.

Rory's face flashed in front of him, and his body tightened. Once again, she robbed him of the pleasure he needed to clear his mind. "Fuck," he muttered as he stepped back. "Get dressed and leave."

Nina's head turned slowly, and anger filled her voice. "What did you say?"

"Watch the way you speak to me," he warned as he grabbed a pair of sleep pants from his dresser. "Leave."

Her expression was unhinged as she stood. "It's Aurora, isn't it? You want to sleep with that vile woman? I saw you watching her tonight."

The words she spat at him made his insides boil, and he fought to stay calm.

"I do not answer to you." He took a menacing step forward and lowered himself, so they were eye to eye. "Speak to me that way again, and I will reassign you. You're lucky I allowed you to live in the palace. Your transgressions were hardly serious enough to warrant extra supervision, yet you requested to stay here, anyway. I will not bat an eye at moving you. Are we clear?"

Her lower lip trembled. "Yes, Your Grace."

She donned her dress and was out the door before she finished buttoning it. He hung his head, and realized he needed to fuck Rory out of his system, but he knew if he had a taste, she would be his until death.

Rory looked around before bolting up the small staircase leading to her secret room. She was eager to see the sunshine, even though it was night. Her alarm clock and a clean uniform were tucked under her arm as she turned the lock and snuck inside.

Tonight, she would sleep in a soft bed under the sun. When the door was closed, the light left the room, and Rory looked for a light switch to turn on the screens. After finding none, she looked up and covered her mouth in awe.

A beautiful starry sky with a crescent moon replaced the sunshine, and she walked to the bed for a better look. "It must be on a timer," she surmised, remembering the setting sun from the night before.

Her eyes slid to the bookcase nestled on the opposite wall. Toeing off her shoes, she slipped into bed and relished in the feel of the soft sheets against her freshly shaved legs. Her eyes drifted closed with a contented sigh.

Rory's eyes opened and stared at the sunshine above her as she burrowed deeper under the covers. "Aether, this is comfortable."

"It is," Caius' smooth voice said from beside her.

Somehow, she wasn't surprised he was there, but she didn't know why. She also knew she was dreaming because a quick glance around showed the floor was covered with a field of wildflowers.

"What is this place?" she asked, looking at him.

He turned his head toward her. "This was my sister's room when she visited."

"Adila?"

His head shook slightly. "Atarah. She loved Vincula, but

she missed the Erdikoa skies. I made her this room and powered it with my essence."

"Atarah has been dead for almost five-hundred years," Rory replied. *"The room is always clean."*

"I have a trusted maid clean it. You remember Gracie from the ball," he said. *"I don't allow any other staff in here. I can't bear to let it rot."*

"The stairs," Rory said. *"They have not seen feet in quite some time."* She was prodding to see if he would admit to the entrance from his office.

"She cleans my room as well," he began. *"And there is a back entrance from my quarters."*

Rory suppressed her surprise and made a mental note to look for the other entrance.

She flipped over to stare at the sky. *"I miss the Erdikoa skies, too."*

She hated that her brain conjured a nice Caius, one who didn't kill her sister. At least that was how she felt despite her findings in his office. His face no longer elicited anger. She frowned. Her mind was a scary place.

"What are you thinking?" he murmured.

"I'm wondering why I don't hate you here. In my dream, I mean." She turned to him again.

His eyes bounced between hers. *"Why do you assume this is your dream and not mine?"*

The look on his face and the sound of his voice made her body sing. *"Why would it be yours?"*

The air was charged with sexual tension, and when he spoke again, she fought for air. *"Because here, you are mine."*

His words surprised her, but at the same time, they didn't. Since arriving in Vincula, conflict had warred within her where the king was concerned.

"You cannot claim me," she argued half-heartedly. *"It's barbaric."*

He reached over and caressed her face. *"Let me show you."*

She would let him show her anything.

Her breath hitched when he leaned over and kissed her, running his tongue over her bottom lip until she granted him entry, and from there, their want for each other ran wild. He rolled on top of her and hovered over her naked body, and Rory's eyes widened as his pants disappeared, showcasing the biggest dick she'd ever seen.

"Seraphim," *she whispered.*

"They cannot save you now," he said in a rough voice. *"Here, you are mine, and no one can keep me from you, other than yourself."* His voice was pleading, and it filled her stomach with butterflies. *"Let me have you, Aurora."*

His eyes bore into hers, amplifying her need for him. *"I am yours,"* she murmured. *"Take me."*

"Thank fuck." A warm hand ran from her neck to the swell of her breast, but his eyes never left hers.

Soon, his fingers were trailing across the sensitive skin of her stomach, making it quiver under his touch. Her hands ran up his chest until they reached his neck, and when she tried to pull him in for a kiss, he resisted.

"I want to see your face as I destroy you," he rasped, and his words both excited and frightened her.

A warm touch passed over her clit and moved to her entrance, swiping through her arousal before returning to circle with the slightest pressure.

She hummed at the sensation, and the corner of his mouth lifted a fraction. He alternated between pressured circles and lightly running his fingers south to tease her entrance before *returning to her clit, and the back and forth was making her lose her mind.*

She whimpered as she lifted her hips, seeking his constant touch. Still, he continued his languid movements, and she moved her hand down to touch herself.

His hand moved from her core to grab her wrist. "Do not touch what is mine."

The possessiveness in his voice almost made her come. "You're torturing me."

He bent forward and took her nipple into his mouth as his fingers continued to move, and she moaned, thrusting her breasts into his face as he moved to the other.

"This is too much," *she gasped.* "I need to come. Please."

The quickness with which she was closing in on her climax proved this was a dream.

She felt him smile against her skin, and without warning, he thrust two fingers inside her and hooked them toward her belly as he slowly rubbed them against her insides. Her back arched from the bed as she cried out from the sensation, and he sat up to push on her lower stomach with his other hand.

The second his hooked fingers entered her again and brushed against the spot most men couldn't find, she exploded. Her body convulsed as her mouth released sounds she'd never heard before. "Caius," *she whimpered as he continued to stroke her.*

He slid his fingers out of her, allowing her to come down from the best high she'd ever experienced. He bent forward and kissed her neck. "Beautiful."

"I need you inside of me," *she told him.* "Now."

He sat back and smirked. "I need to eat first."

She released a whine. He flipped them over with incredible strength, and she straddled his chest.

"Take a seat, Miss Raven," he drawled as he licked his lips.

She lifted herself, moved forward to hover above his face, and hesitated. "I'll crush you."

"I want you to break me," he said and grabbed her hips to pull her down.

His tongue touched every bit of her he could reach, and her already sensitive area lit up like the Erdikoa sunrise. "Fuck," she swore as she moved her hips against his mouth.

A sound vibrated against her pussy lips, and his movements came faster. The sensual feel of his tongue moving through every bit of her folds, pressing into her entrance, and then sucking her clit was something she'd never experienced.

The men she'd been with before seemed like boys compared to the king. His warm breaths against her pussy as he moved her hips where he wanted made her moan as she grabbed her breasts.

Caius pulled her down harder, and between her rocking hips and his frenzied mouth sucking and licking, it wasn't long before she burst from it all.

She felt herself clenching as an orgasm ripped through her and cum dripped between her legs. Caius continued to lick until there was nothing left. His hands released her hips, and she rose to scoot backward.

His mouth shone from her as he looked up with a wicked grin. Sitting up, he grabbed the back of her head and pulled it to his as he claimed her mouth. Unable to help herself, she lifted slightly and reached between them to grab his cock.

When she sank down, they groaned into each other's mouths as his wide length stretched her. He moved them to the edge of the bed, so his legs were planted firmly on the floor, and she rocked her hips.

Their movements were untamed, and they clawed at each other with unchecked desire. Her sensitive breasts brushed his chest with every stroke, and the feel of him moving in and out of her was addicting. He was big, but here in her dream, he fit perfectly.

Here, her body was made for his, and his for hers. She pulled back, and they both looked down at where their bodies met. He stood, and she wrapped her legs around his waist as he kissed her with slow, sensual strokes.

"Can I keep you?" he murmured against her lips.

She pulled back to look into his eyes. "Forever."

He pressed her against a wall and thrust with slow, deep strokes. It was dragging out their releases, and while she would miss their bodies joined as one, she needed to come.

As if reading her mind, his hips sped up, and he ground his pelvis against her clit. Soon, she felt him pulse and grow. She moved her hips faster to match his, and they were both breathing so hard, there was no kissing, only traded breaths.

"Rory," he said against her lips. He grunted and buried his head in the crook of her neck as he thrust one last time, sending her tumbling over the edge with him.

As they stood, connected, and catching their breaths, bells rang around them.

He sighed and gave her one last kiss. "Time to wake up."

Rory shot up in bed and looked around. She was in the sky room, and her alarm was loud enough to wake the dead. Her hand swatted the stupid thing onto the floor, and she threw herself back on the pillow with a huff.

Her pussy was wet and aching, and she groaned as she rolled over. Of course, she had a wet dream she couldn't remember. It was bad enough she wasn't getting any, she didn't need her own mind teasing her.

With a sigh, she threw back the comforter and stood to stretch. She needed to pee and sneak downstairs to her room undetected, and for once, she was thankful she had third shift.

CHAPTER 20

A few days later, Rory carried a lantern with her as she made her way through the park toward the lake. As she suspected, it was deserted at this time of night, and she released a sigh of relief.

Her small room was suffocating, and she needed to be away from other people where she could breathe in the fresh air, even if it meant staying up past her bedtime. There was too great a chance she would run into Caius in the gardens.

She walked onto the closest pier, removed her socks and shoes, rolled up her pant legs, and sat at the end to dangle her feet over the edge. The water lapped against her ankles, and she wondered if it ever rained here.

She thought of her mother, her friends, and her sister. Her heart burned, and a chasm formed in her chest. She missed them terribly, and she would never see them again, unless by some chance, the *Seraphim* let her into the aether. She doubted it, even if the Scales of Justice said her soul wasn't black.

The knowledge made her happier than she thought it

would. Killing the Umbra King would be a ticket to hell, but since he killed innocents, she hoped they would make an exception for her. Hope was a dangerous thing. It made people destroy in the name of good intentions.

"Please save a place for me," she whispered into the dark.

It was eerie how dark it was at night. In town there were streetlights, but out here, it was almost impossible to see her own hand in front of her face. The lights from the town gave the park a slight glow, but not enough. She mentally patted herself on the back for remembering to bring a lantern.

"Well, if it isn't the little butcher bitch," a voice snarled behind her.

Her heart stopped beating as she climbed to her feet and whipped around in time to see a burly man with a black beard stalking across the pier, making the wood groan beneath him. *Ronny.*

The water below was the only escape, but she wasn't sure what sort of creatures inhabited it.

She'd seen no one swim in it before, and that couldn't be a good sign. Her feet were at the edge, and she needed to decide. Fighting him off wasn't an option. He was big. *Really big.*

He was fast too, because before she could decide, he had her around the throat, and her lungs no longer filled with air. "You think you can treat one of our own like you're better than her?" he sneered and grabbed her hair with his other hand.

Nina. This was because Rory showed up Nina at the bar?

She clawed at his hand, and he shoved her into the water as he released her neck, keeping one hand in her hair. Her scalp burned, and before he pushed her under, he said, "You don't deserve to kiss the dirt beneath her feet, you dirty whore." Her head plunged under the water.

Floundering, she grappled for the edge of the pier, but he pushed her head down farther. He was going to drown her, and there was nothing she could do about it. She fought as hard as she could, refusing to let him win, but all she did was exhaust herself.

He released her, and she broke the surface, choking and trying to gulp down air. Ronny's cries for help filled the quiet night, and when Rory wiped the water from her eyes, she screamed at what she saw.

Lo, the supposedly gentle cat, was dragging him to the bank, and once on land, she pounced and ripped out his throat. It was fast, and Rory blinked to assure herself it was real.

When the panther was satisfied the attacker was dead, she walked down the pier toward Rory.

Lo sat down a few feet from where Rory hung on for dear life and looked at her.

"Please don't eat me," Rory begged, and then kicked herself for talking to an animal.

Lo cocked her head to the side, and Rory glanced at the shore and let go of the pier to swim away from the murder machine. Maybe she could climb onto the bank and run before the panther realized what she was doing.

When she waded out of the water, Lo met her at the bank, and Rory froze. "You can't still be hungry after eating that mountain of meat," Rory said, pointing at Ronny.

The panther chuffed and approached her. This was it. She was going to survive the Scales of Justice, only to be mauled by an overgrown cat.

To her utter amazement, Lo put her head in Rory's hand and nudged her. "You want me to pet you?"

The panther nudged her again, and Rory rubbed Lo's soft fur in a daze. This was the weirdest night of her life, and that was saying a lot.

Relaxing a little, Rory scratched the cat's head. "You saved my life." Lo purred. "You really are a house cat. A scary one."

She could have sworn the panther glowered at her. "Sorry," she said with a laugh. "I promise I know how vicious you really are." She looked pointedly at the dead body twenty feet away. "I won't tell anyone."

Rory shivered, the adrenaline finally wearing off and reminding her she was soaked to the bone. Her black leggings were still scrunched to her knees, and her white t-shirt was stuck to her skin.

"I'll bring you a nice, juicy steak tomorrow night," Rory promised. "But I have to get back to the palace before I die of hypothermia." She paused. "Can we die of sickness down here?"

The cat looked back at her silently, and Rory shook her head. "I'm losing it." She gave Lo a final scratch. "Thank you again." She thought about hugging the cat but didn't want her affection to be mistaken for a chokehold.

She turned to leave, but Lo trotted alongside her. "What are you doing?" *Stop asking the damn cat questions like it's going to answer you,* she scolded herself.

Lo ignored her and continued to follow her through town. A few stragglers were on the streets leaving the taverns or out for night strolls, and Rory walked faster. She looked like a drowned sewer rat. One man gave her a strange look that turned to surprise when he spotted the giant panther beside her.

Rory smirked down at Lo. "You're like an asshole repellent." The cat shook her head.

When they arrived at the palace steps, Lo licked Rory's leg and stalked away into the night.

Caius stumbled, almost hitting the ground in the middle of his office as a hellish scene engulfed him. His heart hammered in his chest as he struggled in the water.

Ice encompassed his body as he fought to breathe. A scream tore from his throat as he beat his fists against whatever held him down, but it was no use.

He was dying.

Until he wasn't.

The scene evaporated, and he slumped to the rug beneath him. His hand was clutched around his throat as he coughed, trying to expel the phantom water from his lungs.

As he stared at the ceiling, trying to catch his breath, he cursed, not understanding what happened. It was by far the worst nightmare to date, and he knew he wouldn't sleep tonight.

After gathering his bearings, he stood and left for the kitchens. If he wasn't going to sleep, then he would need as much sugar as he could get to keep him awake until tomorrow.

Rory tried to sneak through the palace unnoticed, but luck was never on her side. When she descended the second set of stairs, she was met by the Umbra King himself.

His cold gaze raked over her wet hair down to her white shirt, and she was painfully aware her t-shirt was now transparent, but his eyes didn't linger. "Why are you wet?" There was something strained in his voice, and it piqued her interest.

"I went swimming," she replied coolly, hoping he couldn't *actually* detect lies.

He met her stare, and his eyes looked wild. "They do have swimsuits available in town." He was playing at indifference, but something was wrong, she could feel it.

"I'll keep that in mind for next time."

Not wanting to think too much about his demeanor, she stepped around him and continued down the stairs.

"Wait," he called, and she turned at the gentleness in his tone. "Your *Aatxe* friend is taking care of your mother."

Rory's hand flew to her chest as she swallowed whatever sound tried to claw its way out. "You're not lying?" Hope seeped into her words, showcasing her weakness.

His eyes seemed to glow in the torchlight. "No, Rory, I'm not lying."

Her jaw hung open as she watched him leave, and she knew what he said was true.

Because he called her Rory.

CHAPTER 21

The next afternoon, Rory hid in her room. Her body hurt from her altercation with Ronny, and her pride was bruised at the fact she had failed to fight him off on her own.

Her door opened, and she lurched forward from her spot on the bed. Lauren waltzed in and looked around. Rory's bathroom door was open and her wet clothes from the night before still hung over the shower door.

The woman's eyes met hers. "I am here to speak with you regarding a death that took place last night."

Rory kept her expression neutral. If they blamed her for Ronny's death, it was a one-way ticket to hell.

"Who died?" she asked as she threw back her covers and stood.

"Where were you last night?" Lauren demanded, ignoring the query.

Rory eyed the woman. "Are you an enforcer?" Only *Aatxe* could be enforcers unless the rules in Vincula were different.

Lauren stepped back into the hall and wings exploded from her back. Rory stared slack-jawed at her. "Holy aether."

As quickly as they appeared, they vanished. "I prefer to stay shifted," Lauren told her. "But I work with Sam and the legion."

Rory nodded dumbly. "I was here last night."

Lauren turned back to the wet clothes in the bathroom. "Why are your clothes wet?"

Rory kept her face impassive. "I wanted to wear them tomorrow, and the launderers won't have them back in time. I washed them myself." *Please don't be a lie detector like Caius.*

"The man who scared you the other night, Ronny, was found dead this morning by the lake in town."

"That's terrible," Rory lied through her teeth. "How did he die?"

Lauren walked around Rory's room, touching her things. "His throat was ripped out. It looks like an animal attack; the panther maybe, but she is usually gentle." The *Angel* paused. "But there are rumors it was you. After all, you have a flair for the dramatic."

"How would I rip a man's throat out?" Rory demanded. "He was twice my size." She paused. "And Lo didn't do it."

She couldn't let the panther go down for this.

Lauren's perfectly arched brows rose. "How could you possibly know that?"

Damnit, Rory. You idiot. "Because," she started, grasping for something to say. "Because she was with me." *Idiot.*

Lauren crossed her arms. "I thought you were here all night?"

"I was," she replied. "But Lo was with me. She roams the palace sometimes. You can ask anyone."

"And she just so happened to come to your room?"

Rory nodded, confident in her lie. "Yes. She prowled into the kitchen when I was cleaning up before my shift and followed me. Some of the townspeople saw her follow me through town once." Rory cringed. That was last night, but she would leave out that detail. "She likes me, I guess."

Lauren nodded, and Rory could have sworn she was fighting a smile. "Alright. If you hear anything, let someone in the legion know."

Rory's shoulders relaxed when Lauren turned her back. "Absolutely."

She closed the door behind the woman and rested her forehead against the wood. That was close.

Rory groaned at her reflection in the mirror. Huge bruises marred the skin of her neck, as well as her arms and legs, where she hit the dock as she struggled on her way down. Her adrenaline had kept the pain away until now.

She had yesterday off, but now, two days later, the bruises seemed to be more prominent than before. Not even makeup helped.

With one last look, she huffed and left before she tried to do something stupid like tie a scarf around her neck to wear in the sweltering kitchens.

Trudging down the empty halls, she thanked the *Seraphim* no one would be in for another hour and a half, and when she stepped through the door, she screamed like a banshee. There stood Caius in his low-slung pajama bottoms, fifty-seven abs, and a pastry in his mouth.

Her hand was covering her racing heart. "Do you wait in here to scare me on purpose?"

He finished chewing and smiled, and Rory almost stumbled at the magnificence of it. It wasn't sardonic like she was used to, but a brilliant smile that lit up his handsome face. "Would you like that, Miss Raven?"

Before she could answer, his eyes stared at the arm still covering her heart, specifically the side of her forearm that hit the dock. Soon, his eyes scanned her, stopping briefly on her bruised shin. Without thinking, she hid both arms behind her back and the jerky movement displaced her hair.

It was a stupid move that left her neck exposed, and when his eyes found the deep purple bruises surrounding her throat, the realm around them seemed to stand still, as if reacting to his energy.

His look of curiosity turned frigid as he set his pastry down and closed the space between them. Each step was careful and controlled, and her legs threatened to give out. She didn't know why, but the look on his face terrified her.

"What is that?" he asked so low she almost didn't hear him.

She feigned nonchalance. "What is what?"

His eyes were virulent. "What is on your neck, Rory?"

She took a step back and hit a wall. "It's a fashion statement," she joked.

When he stood a foot away, he stared at the bruises coloring her skin, and his entire body went unnaturally still. She stood like a statue, afraid to make any sudden movements lest it make the predator in him attack.

His anger was barely leashed when he said, "Who did this to you?" He visually inspected the bruises on her limbs, touching each one with his golden gaze.

His eyes met hers, and the danger she saw there made her gasp. "It doesn't matter," she whispered, too scared to speak louder.

He stepped even closer. "It is the only thing that matters. Tell me who did this to you, or I will raze the entire fucking town to the ground." His face was inches from hers as his rage enveloped her, and she closed her eyes to separate herself from him.

"Look at me," he demanded. "I am not one to make empty threats."

Her lashes fluttered as her eyes opened. "His name was Ronny, and he's dead."

His chest heaved once before he stepped back. "The next time someone lays a finger on you, their death belongs to me."

The panic melted from her body, and her mind cleared. "Why?"

"Because no one hurts you but me," he murmured as he stepped into her space once more. A shadow slithered up her side and caressed her cheek. "Your pain belongs to me." The shadow left her face and grazed over her breasts on its way to the apex of her thighs. Her body trembled with anticipation, but the shadow stopped. "As does your pleasure."

He watched her as he walked backward before turning to leave, and Rory stood shaking against the wall. "What was that?" she whispered into the empty room.

He was mercurial, and it was confusing as hell. She'd been so taken aback, she forgot to confront him about the file on her sister. She knew it was proof he was guilty, but there was still a small seed of doubt that hoped it was something else. *Why was she trying to make excuses for him?*

She didn't know herself anymore.

Caius stepped into the garden and released his all-consuming rage. Shadows skittered away from him as he walked, and he knew if he didn't get away from her, he would lock her in his quarters to ensure no one came near her again.

He froze mid-stride as pieces of a puzzle slid into place.

His nightmares. He'd had one about drowning the night he found Rory soaked to the bone in the hallway. That was two days ago—the same day the inmate was executed by the lake. "It can't be," he whispered.

If what he suspected was true, it would explain everything, including his obsessive protectiveness. *How did he not realize it before?*

He could be wrong. There was only one way to be sure, but he already knew the answer.

Rory was his eternal mate.

He stalked back to the kitchens and threw open the door. Rory rose from the ground with a screech as she breathed hard.

"I *knew* you did it on purpose," she accused. "It's not funny."

He ignored her and strode across the room. "What do you see when you look at me?"

"An asshole," she replied. Her answer was immediate, and he frowned.

"That was rude," he muttered. "What do I look like to you?"

She planted her hands on her hips defiantly. "Are you fishing for compliments?"

He growled in frustration and looked around. Grabbing

a red bowl from the counter, he held it in front of her. "What color is this?"

Her eyes flicked from the bowl to his face, and anger colored her cheeks. "You *are* an asshole," she seethed.

"What color is the fucking bowl?" he thundered.

She flinched and looked at the bowl again. "Grey."

"Fuck," he swore, dropping the bowl to the ground. "What color are my eyes?" he whispered. The pleading in his voice should have embarrassed him, but it didn't.

She looked away, and the red in her cheeks turned from anger to embarrassment. Her voice was so quiet, he barely heard her when she said, "Gold."

Caius grabbed the counter for stabilization as his knees nearly gave out. He turned, rubbing a hand over his mouth as he walked to the sink to splash water on his face. A steady rhythm shook his ribcage as his heart beat harder than ever before.

"How old are you?" he croaked.

Rory fidgeted, and he could almost taste her confusion. "Twenty-five."

His head hung over the sink, and he closed his eyes.

"Caius?" she said with uncertainty. "What's going on?"

He turned to her and drank her in. She was beautiful, wild, and *his*. On shaky legs, he ate up the distance between them and reached his hand out. He hesitated before placing his palm against the smooth skin of her face and watched her realm explode.

When Caius' hand touched Rory's face, a jolt knocked her off her feet, but he caught her before she hit the ground. She screamed as she fell, and when she looked around, an overwhelming sense of dread and awe coursed through her.

"Wha... how?" Her eyes roamed everywhere and the more she saw, the faster her breaths came until her limbs were tingling and heavy. "What did you do?" she choked out.

Caius pulled her into his lap, and had it not been for the chaos running through her, she would have pushed him away. He looked down at her and murmured, "What color is the bowl?"

Tears pricked the corners of her eyes as they found the bowl still lying on the ground. "Red."

Caius opened the door to Rory's room with her cradled in his arms. She welcomed his help because her legs refused to work, and her eyes were engrossed in the scenery.

Bright orange flames lighting the hallway, red and gold ornate rugs lining the floors, bronze doorknobs, and brown wooden doors.

Caius placed her on her bed, and she ran a hand over the bright yellow comforter. Looking around her room, she noted that her furniture was grey, but the rug in her room was a deeper shade of yellow that complimented her bedding.

The king was silent, and she turned to him with wide eyes. "Thank you."

His brows creased. "Why are you thanking me?"

How could he be humble when he just changed her life for the better? "You did this somehow. Did you know?" she asked. "Did you know I had grey-scale sight that you could have fixed?" If his answer was yes, she was too enamored with her surroundings to be upset.

"I didn't." He rubbed a hand through his hair. "You should have told me."

"Why would I tell you?" she retorted.

His eyes were sad. "I would have fixed it sooner."

She saw him in a new light as she regarded him carefully. There was more to the king than she thought. "You brought me food."

For the first time since meeting him, he looked uncomfortable. "I do not let my inmates want for anything."

Yet another show of kindness from the notorious king. It confused her. "Thank you."

He opened her door with a final glance back. "You're welcome."

"Wait," she called after him. He paused and looked at her over his shoulder. "I broke into your office."

He turned fully with a wry smile. "Is that so?"

"And your desk," she added. "Why do you have a file on my sister?" Her voice broke as she fought tears.

"I wanted to know why you accused me of her murder," he answered simply. "I sent an enforcer for a copy of the emergency report. It said you saw it happen." His eyes softened, and she resented his pity.

"I saw you murder her," she protested, but her voice lost its edge. Had she been wrong, or was her gratitude taking over logic?

"I am sure you did, Miss Raven. You should sleep." With that, he left her.

CHAPTER 22

"She's my *Aeternum*," Caius said as he slammed open Samyaza's door. "Did you know?"

The *Angel's* shirt disappeared from his torso and reappeared in his hand. "I suspected."

Caius fought the urge to rip off Sam's wings. "Why didn't you tell me?"

An *Aeternum* was a *Royal's* eternal mate.

"I didn't know for sure," Sam said as his pants were magically replaced by pajama bottoms. "Had I told you my suspicions, and they were wrong, you would have been devastated."

It was true. When Adila locked Caius in Vincula, he feared he would never meet his *Aeternum*. Once born, it was guaranteed the *Royal* would meet their mate by the time the *Aeternum* was twenty-five. He didn't know if the rule still applied to him since he was banished from Erdikoa, and no one knew what happened if an *aeternum* died before meeting the *royal*. It's never happened before.

"I refused to disappoint you after all you have been through," Sam replied.

"You could have found out. All you had to do was ask if she could see color!" Caius boomed, unable to control his rage. "It was that simple, Sam, and you just, what? Decided I didn't deserve her?"

Sam was across the room in a flash and shoved Caius against the wall. "Never question my loyalty to you again. Grey-scale sight is not exclusive to *Aeternums*, and I knew you would touch her, eventually."

Aeternums were born with grey-scale sight, and when they met their destined *Royal*, they saw them in color. Once they touched, the *Aeternum's* grey-scale sight lifted, confirming the bond.

Caius slumped against the wall. "My nightmares were getting worse," he said, his voice strained. "I should have known."

Only they weren't nightmares. When a mate was in danger, the other received a vision. It was to help them protect one another. Caius' life had never been in danger, sparing Rory the horror of one.

As Caius knew all too well, visions were as close to being there as one could get without being present. The mate sees the event as it happens through their mate's eyes, though often times it was blurry.

Sam laid his massive hand on Caius' shoulder. "You had no way of knowing, but now that you do, what are you going to do about it?"

Caius could use his friend's support, but he already knew what Sam would say. "I'm not telling her."

Sam's hand dropped. "It is not like you to be stupid."

Caius glared at his friend. "She hates me, and until that

no longer holds true, there is no point in telling her." Another thought occurred to him. "Why didn't you tell me the executed inmate attacked Rory?"

"His death was reported to me," Sam replied. "His throat was ripped out of his body and lying on his chest. I did not want you doing something stupid, and he was already dead. It did not matter."

"Her safety matters," Caius growled. "Do not keep things from me again."

Sam's voice was hard when he said, "Control your temper, and I won't."

~

Rory trailed Max through the gardens as he worked, touching every colorful flower she could. Seeing the colors of souls was nothing compared to seeing the colors of the realms.

"Max, what'd you do to land yourself here?"

The old man continued pruning the bush he was working on. "Broke a bastard's legs with my shovel." His tone was unsettlingly casual.

Rory squatted beside him and pulled at a few weeds. "Why?"

"My wife's leg was mangled in a vehicle accident. Even with a cane, she walked with a limp." He sat back and wiped his hands on his pants. "A young man not much older than you walked by our house." He looked at Rory's surprised face. "We lived in the *Munin* compound." *That made sense.* Most people lived in apartments, and the houses were all on the outskirts of town, primarily in the compounds.

Rory's eyes were saucers. Max didn't seem antisocial, nor did she ever expect a *Munin* to be violent.

"He called my wife a name I will never repeat. Our front yard was small, and it didn't take many steps to get to him. I swung my shovel and broke his legs, so he'd know what it felt like to be in my wife's shoes. I leaned over him and told him something for only his ears to ensure he never spoke about her again." He shrugged. "I've been here for three years. My time will be up next month."

Rory tried to unpack his confession. "What did you say?"

"That I would slam my shovel into his prized jewels if he so much as looked in her direction." He returned to his work. "And I meant it."

Rory coughed to hide her laugh, and she saw his lips twitch. "And you're almost out of here? That's great news!" She deflated, the weight of his departure growing by the minute. "I'm sure your wife misses you."

He nodded. "I miss her every day. If I didn't lose my memory, I would check in on that mother of yours." He looked up with kind eyes. "You are good, Rory, and she deserves to know that."

Rory patted his arm, unable to form words. Instead, she reached forward and plucked more weeds. They worked in a comfortable silence until a loud whistle pierced the air.

They both turned to find Asher and Bellina winding their way along the path with big smiles on their faces. "I told Asher your sight was fixed, and he insisted on coming to see for himself," Bellina said as they approached.

Rory stood and wiped her hands on her pants before offering a hand to Max. "You can't see through my eyes," she teased.

"No, but I can quiz you. What color is this?" Asher asked, pointing to his green shirt.

She tinkered out a laugh. "Green. Happy now?"

He picked her up in a bear hug. "Congratulations! Bellina said the king fixed it?" Rory grinned widely. He reminded her of Keith.

"Yes. I'm as surprised as you are," she replied. "Had I known he possessed the ability, I would have announced my grey-scale sight the moment I landed in the throne room."

Bellina placed a hand on Rory's arm. "We're going out to celebrate."

Rory's stomach flipped. She'd avoided the town since her attack, especially since news of Ronny's death spread, but Bellina looked happy, and Rory couldn't help but give in. "Sounds good."

Asher smiled, and Rory's gaze caught on his hair. Her mouth parted in awe as she stepped forward and ran her hands through it. "Auburn," she whispered. "It's beautiful."

She would never know Asher's reply because he was ripped back and slammed to the ground. Rory and Bellina screamed, and Max pulled them both back.

Everyone looked around for the attacker, but no one was there. The garden was completely abandoned and there were no retreating footsteps to be heard. Rory ran to Asher and kneeled beside him. "Are you okay?"

He was gulping for air between coughs as he rolled over onto his stomach. Pushing up to his knees, his head swiveled to search the gardens. "Someone grabbed me," he stammered. "I felt their hands on me."

"There was no one there," Bellina insisted, and her voice was bordering on hysterical, but Rory was calm as she watched shadows swirl and dissolve.

She knew exactly who did it, and her eyes scanned the garden for the king.

That evening, Rory, Bellina, and Max stepped through the palace gates to meet Cat, Tallent, and Kit. They were going out for dinner and drinks, and Rory was excited to see them in person.

They were walking down the sidewalk, talking excitedly, when a man stepped in front of them. It took her a moment to place him, but then she recognized him from the throne room. *Bruce Stewart*, Rory remembered.

"Are you Aurora Raven? The Butcher?" he asked.

Lo appeared out of thin air, surging forward from the shadows, and growled. Asher jumped back and glared at the cat before turning his attention back to the man.

Bruce backed up and held his hands up, eyeing the beast wearily. "I mean no harm." He looked back at Rory. "Are you?"

"I am." How did he not know? She was certain the inmates would have filled him in, warning him to avoid her.

The man's eyes shined, and he took a step forward with his arms spread wide. Lo released a vicious growl and pounced on his chest as Asher tugged Rory back and Max stepped in front of Bellina. Rory huffed. While she appreciated their protectiveness, she could defend herself.

"I was going to hug her," Bruce cried. "I swear! She saved my daughter!" Lo's lips pulled over her teeth in a lethal snarl.

"Wait!" Rory yelled. "Lo, don't hurt him, please."

Lo stood over him and refused to let him up, and Rory walked around to peer down at the man.

"Your daughter?" she asked.

He nodded vigorously. "Her name is Sera. A man, one of your victims, tried to rape her, but you stopped him. She recognized your face on the news."

Rory's hand flew to her mouth. She always wondered what happened to those she saved, but for obvious reasons, could never seek them out. People surrounded them now to watch the spectacle.

"Lo, let him up," Rory commanded.

The panther huffed and backed up. She planted herself at Rory's side and watched Bruce's every move. He stood, stepped away from the giant cat, and held out his hand. "I wanted to thank you. My wife died when Sera was a child, and she's all I have left." Rory shook his hand as he continued, "I did what I could to get here, to thank you. She wanted me to thank you for her, too."

"You came to Vincula on purpose?" someone in the crowd asked incredulously.

Bruce turned. "She is a hero," he told them, pointing at Rory. He turned back to her. "Sera tells whoever will listen. She is determined to clear your name."

"I don't know what to say," Rory babbled, too shocked to form coherent thoughts.

Bruce shook his head. "If you need anything while I'm here, it's yours. My family will forever be indebted to you."

It was Rory's turn to shake her head. "That's unnecessary, but thank you."

She turned to her friends and motioned with her head to leave. Her emotions were all over the place, and she needed to be away from prying eyes. Asher ushered her through the crowd as they watched her.

She glanced back at Bruce. He reminded her why her crimes were something she should be proud of.

As the group waited for Tallent, Cat, and Kit at the bar, Max looked down at Lo sitting next to Rory's chair and chuckled. "Feisty little thing, aren't you?"

The cat nipped at his hand and rubbed against Rory's leg. She hadn't told her friends about the attack at the lake, and since Lo didn't plan on leaving her side, she needed to.

"I think I know why she won't leave," Rory stated. The others looked at her expectantly. "I was at the lake a few nights ago, and Ronny attacked me. Lo killed him."

Bellina gasped, Max looked unbothered, and Asher's tan skin turned white. "What?" Bellina screeched. She looked at Lo. "I thought he was executed for breaking the law?"

The day after Lauren questioned Rory, Samyaza called a town meeting and informed everyone of Ronny's death, stating he was executed. He never said where Ronny was found. Rory knew he was mauled by Lo, and it struck her as odd.

The panther swished her tail. "Everyone thinks you wouldn't hurt a fly," Asher accused.

Rory looked pointedly at Asher. "I told you she was vicious."

"Why are you so calm?" Asher asked Max.

The old man shrugged. "I'm not surprised."

Bellina leaned forward and lowered her voice. "Why would the commander lie?"

"He didn't," Max said, glancing at Lo. "He attacked Rory, and he died because of it. They never said at whose hand."

Lo stepped toward Max and licked his pant leg, and he shook his leg at her. The others busted up laughing, and Bellina looked at Lo appreciatively. "I didn't know you had it in you."

Lo yawned and laid her head on her front paws. Max's blasé expression turned serious. "You don't need to go anywhere alone outside of the palace."

Rory knew that, and she hated the fact. "This is the first time I've been to town since."

"Don't leave the palace without one of us," Bellina said, pointing between her and Max.

"I would say call me if you need me to walk you, but we don't have phones," Asher lamented.

"I won't leave the palace alone," she promised. "Now, can we enjoy our night?"

As if on cue, Cat popped up beside them with Tallent in tow. "Kit will be here in a half hour." She looked at their glasses. "Where's mine?"

Tallent steered her toward the bar. "You can get your own drink." He waved at the table. "We'll be right back."

Nina sidled up next to Tallent and Cat at the bar and smiled politely. Something she said made Tallent laugh, and Cat shook her head. Nina's face was beautiful when she smiled. *Would Rory still be Nina's enemy if she wasn't The Butcher who caught Caius' attention?*

Nina spotted her staring, and the woman's stance transformed, promising violence. Something about Nina had gone from nasty to downright sinister, and it sent chills down Rory's spine.

Shaking off the unease, Rory turned back to the table with a smile and raised her glass. "To my no longer fucked up vision."

CHAPTER 23

Once again, Rory was dying. Nina so graciously switched Rory to the evening shift and put her on toilet duty. Gracie explained where she would go, and that she was to clean every toilet except those occupied by staff, per Nina's orders. Every other room, including those of the legion, was cleaned by the staff.

The palace was enormous, and Nina said Rory couldn't stop until every toilet was clean. She would scrub all night and into the next day, and she considered slamming her hand in a door to get out of it.

Rory decided to start on the top floor and work her way down, but as she stepped onto the final landing, she regretted her decision. Her legs were jelly, and it would have been wiser to start from the bottom and work her way up, taking breaks on each floor. It was too late now.

Her mouth parted in awe as she looked around the top floor. Instead of a group of hallways, it was a large lobby. Velvet couches lined some walls, and tables with various games such as chess sat around the room with chairs.

There was one door at the back, and she hurried across the room and pulled it open. She was greeted by a wide hallway with a single door at the end. It must be the bathroom for the game room, she guessed. She knocked softly to ensure she didn't walk in on someone taking a shit, and when there was no answer, she turned the knob and stepped inside.

She cursed under her breath, looking around the massive room that was definitely *not* a bathroom. It was decorated with black furniture, and instead of looking old-fashioned and ostentatious like the rest of the palace, it was modern, with clean lines.

She gasped when she realized the room had power, like the sky room. Essence lights adorned the ceiling and an essence screen hung on the wall.

It must be Caius' room. She opened the first door on the side wall to a closet full of finely tailored clothes. His scent filled the air, and she took a deep breath like a stalker. The door clicked softly as she closed it, and when she opened the other door beside it, she died of a heart attack, she was sure of it.

In front of her, lounging in a black porcelain tub, was Caius. Steam curled around him, and his broad back rested against the back of the tub.

Strands of his hair fell into his face as his arms rested on the sides. Despite her entrance, he seemed unbothered.

"If you wanted to see me naked, Miss Raven, all you had to do was ask." He stood, and Rory let her eyes trail down his naked form, and her blood heated at the sight. *He was huge.*

"What are you doing here?" he asked as he reached for a towel.

"Toilets," she croaked. "Nina told me to do every room in the palace."

His skin glistened as droplets of water ran down his chest. "Stop gawking, Miss Raven."

Her eyes snapped to his, and her shock turned into annoyance. "Excuse me, Your Grace. I didn't expect to see a penis today."

He moved closer, and for a moment, his eyes reflected what she felt on the inside. "It's night. What exactly did you expect to find in the palace bedrooms?"

Her fist tightened around the bucket handle. "Your girlfriend is the one who moved me to the night shift."

The corner of his mouth lifted with amusement. "Is that so?"

The realization hit her that Nina did this on purpose. She knew people would be pissed Rory was barging in late at night to scrub their toilets. "That bitch," she hissed under her breath.

A beautiful smile spread across the king's face. "Yes, Nina is a vicious little thing, isn't she?"

"Would you like me to still clean your toilet, *Your Grace*?"

"Of course," he said with a flourish toward the toilet. "I wouldn't miss another opportunity to see you at my feet."

She bit her tongue to hold in a retort. Gone was the tender man who cradled her in his arms after giving her a realm full of color. The memory made her hesitate. "Were you telling the truth about Cora's file?"

He stood at the sink, squeezing toothpaste onto his toothbrush. "My answer doesn't matter. You will believe what you wish."

"I need to hear it," she insisted. *Why was she so desperate to believe him innocent?* She was losing it.

His eyes met hers in the mirror. "Yes, Rory. I was telling the truth."

She nodded and turned to the task at hand. As she cleaned his toilet, she dreamed of creative ways to punish Nina.

Caius stood close enough for her to smell the soap on his skin. "Are you jealous of Nina?"

Rory set her jaw. "No."

He crouched behind her, and his lips pressed against her ear. "Liar." She heard that word often lately.

Goosebumps traveled the length of her arms, and her breathing picked up speed. "Don't presume to know what I am feeling."

He moved her hair to the side and placed a kiss on her neck that made her bite back a groan. "Jealousy looks good on you, Miss Raven."

She was painfully aware he was in nothing but a towel. She'd only have to reach back...

He stood and backed away, and she closed her eyes, trying to force her libido to calm the fuck down. Throwing her cleaning supplies into the bucket, she stood to leave, but his hand caught her arm.

She looked at him over her shoulder, and a flash of uncertainty flickered across his features. "You're done working for the night."

Her face was blank, but not for lack of effort. "Are you trying to give Nina another reason to hate me?"

He sauntered past her to his room and said, "You won't be seeing much of Nina anymore."

Rory's brows pinched together as she trailed behind him. "Is her contract almost up?"

He opened a drawer and pulled out a pair of silk pajama pants. "Unfortunately, no."

"Unfortunately?" she parroted. "I thought you'd be happy to keep your plaything."

He dropped his towel and stood in all his naked glory. Her eyes found the appendage she skimmed over earlier, and her tongue darted out to wet her lips.

"I have a new toy to play with," he said, breaking her trance.

His eyes seared into her, the insinuation clear.

"You seem the type to break your toys," she murmured. He wouldn't break her.

After donning his pants, he moved toward her, his blonde hair dripping water onto his chest. "I am."

A shiver ran down her spine as he walked away. "You will report to my office at eight o'clock tomorrow morning." He turned down his comforter. "Starting now, you work for me."

There was no hiding her bewildered expression. "I already work for you."

He gave her a wry smile. "Miss Raven, starting tomorrow, you are my personal assistant. I no longer wish to do menial paperwork."

Her mouth opened and closed like a fish. Did she hear him correctly? Reaching up, she pinched her arm. A slight shock of pain pricked her skin.

"You're not dreaming," he said, reading her thoughts.

"You don't need an assistant," she sputtered, losing control of the situation. There was no paperwork to be done, and they both knew it.

"I didn't say I needed one," he replied. "You're dismissed."

Rory walked into Caius' office a minute after eight the next morning. "You're late, Miss Raven."

Caius watched Rory glance at the clock on the wall and scowl. "One minute does not count as being late."

He took in her hideous maid uniform and beckoned her closer with his hand. "What are you wearing?"

She looked down. "My uniform. Unless you wanted me to wear casual clothes or the dress you ripped, this is all I have."

He preferred the sinful dress from the ball. "This is unacceptable." He stood. "You're going to town to get a work appropriate wardrobe."

She folded her arms across her chest. "I'm out of credits for the month."

He ignored her and motioned for her to follow him out of his office and into the throne room. "I wouldn't make someone pay for their own work clothes, but thank you for reminding me how little you think of me."

He heard her mouth snap shut as she walked after him. Sam met them in the foyer and fell in line beside them. "You have an arrival today," the *Angel* reminded him.

Caius came to an abrupt halt and pinched the bridge of his nose. He'd forgotten. What he wanted was to watch Rory model tight skirts for him, not greet an inmate. "I need you to take Rory clothes shopping," he replied.

Sam looked ready to throttle him. "What about me makes you think that is a good idea?"

"I can go by myself," Rory protested. "I *am* an adult."

Caius ignored her. "Where is Lauren?"

"Right here," Lauren said from the far entrance of the room. "What can I do for you, Your Grace?"

He almost rolled his eyes at her formal greeting. He'd known her as long as he'd known Sam, and they were long past formalities. "Take Rory to town. She needs a wardrobe befitting her new position."

"Do you not trust me to buy clothes on my own?" Rory asked incredulously from behind him. "No offense," she said, looking at Lauren wearily.

"Full offense taken," the *Angel* deadpanned.

"It's for your protection," Caius told her as his eyes glanced at her neck, remembering the bruises that colored her delicate skin. "She needs business attire. Preferably skirts and blouses."

"I am not wearing skirts every day," Rory informed him haughtily.

Caius turned to her and gestured to her dress. "You already do." He gave his attention back to Lauren. "She'll need enough outfits for at least two weeks and however many pairs of shoes to match."

Rory scoffed and shook her head. "Who needs fourteen outfits? They do our laundry twice a week!"

He ignored her and motioned for Sam to follow him back to his office. Rory's protests fell on deaf ears, and he smiled to himself as she trailed Lauren out of the room.

"You have an assistant now?" Sam chuckled. "Since when do you need an assistant?"

"Since I need to protect her," he replied. "She was attacked once, and I won't risk it happening again."

"If you'd stop being a prick to her, she might end up

liking you," Sam said as he pulled an entire banana out of his pocket.

"How did you fit a banana in your pants?"

"My pants already carry something much larger." Sam grinned as he peeled the fruit and took a large bite.

Caius pushed open the door to his office and realized he forgot to lock it again. It didn't matter because no one would steal from their king, but it was a habit that lent him comfort.

He paused and shook his head with a wry laugh. Rory admitted to breaking into his office. *Guess I'm not as forgetful after all,* he thought.

A small knock echoed through the room, and Caius looked at Sam. "Did the arrival come early?" They were always notified before a trial to prepare for a possible new arrival. Trials happened at the same time of day, and they still had another hour.

Sam shook his head. "Not that I've heard."

Caius called on a shadow to open the door, and Nina stood on the other side. She was the last person he wanted to start his day with. "What is it?"

She stepped inside, and her eyes flared slightly at the sight of Sam. "One of the staff shirked their duties and disappeared."

Caius sat behind his desk, pretending to look at papers. "Are they sick or hurt?"

"They weren't in their room, Your Grace." Her face was smug, and Caius was immediately suspicious.

He already knew what her answer would be, but he asked anyway. "Who was it?"

"Aurora Raven." She was positively giddy, and he took a deep breath.

"I told her to stop last night." He pinned Nina with a scathing look. "She is no longer your concern."

The maid perked up. "She's gone?"

"She works for me now," Caius replied. "Now, if you will excuse us, we have matters to discuss that do not concern you."

Nina's rage was palpable. "Excuse me? What does that mean?"

Sam stood to his full six-foot-six height and stalked across the room. "It means there is no need for you to speak to her again. Leave."

Nina flinched and looked to Caius for help, but he ignored her as he looked over his fake papers. "You heard him, Nina. Leave."

After the woman left, Sam said, "She needs to be moved out of the palace."

Caius sighed and set his pen down. "I know. I'll have Rory arrange it tomorrow."

Sam released a booming laugh. "Already trying to woo her, I see."

Caius lifted a shoulder and sat back. "She can't hate me forever."

"If she thinks you murdered her sister, yes, she can."

"I need something tangible to convince her it wasn't me," Caius said, twisting one of the rings on his hand.

"We both know it was Gedeon," Sam replied. "The question is why?"

Rory admired her ass in the red pencil skirt in the dressing room as Lauren huffed from the other side of the door. "Let me see, or I'm coming in."

Rory opened the door and swept a hand over her body. "What do you think?"

Lauren twirled her finger in a circle, and Rory turned around. "Are you trying to get the king to fuck you?"

Rory jerked around. "What? He told me to get skirts!"

"I'm kidding," the *Angel* replied. Her expression said she wasn't kidding.

Rory grabbed Lauren by the arm, tugged her into the room, and shut the door. "Are you trying to get me labeled as the king's whore?"

Lauren laughed loudly and shook her head. "You are not a weak little lamb. What they think of you is irrelevant unless you believe it, little butcher."

Rory stared after her and could almost see Cora's sweet lamb form frolicking around her. Had she really lost sight of what was important that fast? There was a chance Caius was Bane, despite what he said.

"For fuck's sake," she muttered and grabbed at the zipper on the back of the skirt.

The truth was the only thing that mattered, and once she had it, she would either kill the Umbra King, or...

Or what?

CHAPTER 24

Rory walked through the door of Caius' office bright and early the next morning, wearing a black silk blouse tucked into a tight, red skirt. The clack of her high heels on the marble floor made her feel powerful.

Caius was not yet sitting behind his desk thinking of new ways to annoy her, and she rummaged through it again.

She tugged on the drawer that once held Cora's file, and it slid open easily, revealing a note inside.

It is not polite to go through someone's things, Miss Raven.
Perhaps you need to be punished.

"Asshole," she mumbled.

"What was that?" Caius' deep voice asked as he closed the door behind him.

She told him to piss off with her eyes and closed the desk. "Where is my sister's file?"

"Good morning to you, too," he replied and opened one of the file cabinets behind her. "Here."

He held out the envelope with Cora's emergency report, and she tentatively took it. "Why are you giving this to me?"

He rolled up the sleeves of his black dress shirt and sat down behind his large desk. "You already know what it says. Why do you want it?"

She set the file on top of the filing cabinet and careened around the desk to sit in the chair opposite the king. "I don't want you to have it."

He stared at her for a moment before pulling out a handful of files from another drawer in his desk. "According to you, I was there. I should already know what is in that file as well."

"If it wasn't you, then who was it?" she demanded. "I saw you, Caius."

His lips parted. "Say it again."

Did he suddenly lose his hearing? "What?"

"My name," he clarified. "Say it again. It will be good practice for when you scream it later."

A deep blush stained her cheeks, and she momentarily lost her train of thought. "Answer the question."

The rings on his hand glinted as he drummed them against the wood. "It wasn't me. I've been locked in Vincula for almost five-hundred years, and if I broke the magic holding me here, your sister wouldn't be the person I aimed to kill."

She leaned forward in her chair. "I *saw* you."

He huffed out a laugh and shook his head. "You may have seen my face, but you didn't see *me*." He leaned back and clasped his hands in his lap. "The emergency report of your arrest says the video surveillance showed a very large man answering the door to Mr. Witlow's apartment when you arrived. It also says they found several bottles of shapeshifting potions in his apartment, as well as an entire closet full of different sized clothes, yet no one else lived there, nor was anyone recorded leaving the apartment. Besides you, that is."

She knew where this was going. "How would someone be able to shapeshift into you if no one but Samyaza and your siblings know what you look like?" she challenged. "Everyone else's memories are wiped clean."

"Why is it easier for you to believe I broke out of my contract just to kill your sister?" His voice was filled with indignation.

The seed of doubt bloomed. "I don't know," she admitted.

"If you stopped hating me for things I didn't do, then this arrangement could be fun, Miss Raven."

She was embarrassed and angry because what he said made sense. Why would he come to Erdikoa to kill a fifteen-year-old lamb shifter, and if he'd broken the magic holding him here, why doesn't he ever leave?

Being back at square one made her want to pound her fists against a wall. She took a deep breath and stared him down. "You hate me for my crimes. It was only fair I hated you for yours."

"Think what you wish," he said as he stood. "Go through these and write the dates of their departure."

Rory grabbed the files from Caius and opened the top folder. It was Max's contract. "What is this?"

"The inmates that are leaving this month. I need you to

write the dates and their jobs, then make arrangements with their supervisors. The day before an inmate leaves, we arrange for them to have the day off to say their goodbyes," he explained. "Leaving your family behind in Vincula is no easier than leaving behind your family in Erdikoa."

Rory looked down at the files again, and a pang of sadness hit her square in the chest. She would never see Max again. Flipping through the rest of the files, she saw Bruce's name, and when she came to Asher's file, the air whooshed out of her lungs.

Two friends gone in a matter of weeks.

Her throat tightened. "Where do I sit to organize these?"

He pointed to a desk across the room. "Enjoy." He walked out and left her to stew in her misery.

The work Caius assigned Rory took all of an hour to figure out. She needed to contact the employers, but other than that, she had nothing to do. As she debated wandering around the palace to find the king, a knock sounded at the main door she forgot existed.

Apart from her first day, she'd yet to use the main entrance to his office, and he never used it either. She opened the door to find Nina on the other side. The look of contempt on the maid's face brought a satisfied smile to Rory's.

"Caius isn't here. Can I take a message?" Rory asked sweetly.

Nina's fair skin turned red, matching her hair, and she shoved her way past Rory into the office. "Nina, if you don't have an appointment, you need to leave."

Nina whirled on Rory. "You think you're better than me because you're working for Caius?" Her cackle made Rory's ears bleed. "He only wants to make sure you don't kill anyone else. If you think there's another reason, you are delusional."

Rory walked to her desk and sat down. "Says the woman who chases him around like a rabid dog."

Nina advanced, and Rory hoped she attacked. She wanted to make the woman bleed.

"Caius loves me," Nina declared, and Rory's head popped back, making Nina smile. "That's right. He takes me on dates and showers me with his affection. Watch the way you speak to your future queen."

At that, Rory lost it. She was laughing so hard tears were streaming down her face, and as hard as she tried, she couldn't stop. "You really have lost it!" she squealed around a laugh. "Oh aether, I thought you were pissed he discarded you as his plaything, but you really think he'll take you as his bride, don't you?" She started laughing again.

The door flew open with a bang, and Caius stormed in. "What are you doing here, Nina?"

She whimpered. "I came to see if you wanted to have dinner tonight."

He laughed humorlessly and grabbed her gently by the arm. Once at the door, he said, "Leave."

The door shut in Nina's face, and Rory hid a smug smile, but it didn't last long because Caius was in front of her in a flash. He braced his arms on either side of her chair. "Why are you taunting her?"

Rory tried to roll her chair away from him, but he held her in place. "Call off your bitch, and I won't have to." Her voice was calmer than she felt. He was defending Nina, and it threw Rory for a loop. "She shows up wherever I am, not the other way around."

He stood and retreated to his reading nook. "If she comes here again, ask her to have a seat and wait for me."

Everything in Rory screamed at her to flip her desk over. He wanted her to indulge that horrible excuse of a person? There wasn't a chance in the seven rings of hell that would happen. He could fire her for all she cared.

"I need to leave," she responded as she rose from her seat.

"I haven't dismissed you," he said smoothly. "Sit."

Rory bit her tongue and tried as hard as she could to set his shirt on fire with her eyes. Holding up the paper, she said, "I need to contact these employers. Is that not what you told me to do?"

Without looking up, he nodded once. "Go. Then take the rest of the day off to cool down. I can taste your anger." His eyes sliced her way. "And while tasting you sounds exquisite, your anger doesn't hold the same intrigue."

She stomped from the room and slammed the door on her way out as she cursed Caius under her breath. He made her mad enough to kill, but horny enough to rip his clothes off all at once. She needed to get laid.

Two of the inmates were employed within the palace, but the other three were located in town. A phone would have made things easier, but Rory needed to distance herself from Caius anyway.

When Asher first told her he worked at the butcher shop, she thought he was joking, but for once in his life, he was serious. She avoided visiting him at work because she didn't know how she would react. Would her blood lust come back?

Nina was the only person here who pulled that darkness out of her, and she couldn't help but wonder if it was because the woman's soul was as close to black as one could get without actually being black. Not that Rory could see it, but perhaps her own soul could sense it.

Taking a deep breath, she pushed through the door, and a bell tinkered overhead. Rory didn't understand why they needed a butcher shop because the meat was already processed in Erdikoa. There was no butchering going on, and it seemed pointless to have an extra shop when they could sell it at the grocery store.

Asher appeared through a swinging door and grinned as he leaned on the counter. "I knew you'd come home one day."

She narrowed her eyes. "Was that a serial killer joke?"

"And a good one, too." He winked. "Are you ordering cuts of meat for Lo?"

Rory shook her head. "I'm here to speak to your boss." His brows rose. "You didn't tell me you were leaving this soon," she accused. His last day was in a couple of weeks, right before Max's.

Asher's shoulders fell. "What good would it have done?" His voice was somber, and she passed the counter to wrap her arms around his middle.

"You might not remember us, but we'll remember you," she promised him.

He squeezed her before releasing her and put his hands in his back pockets. "We get an entire day together," he reminded her. "When friends request off work for some-one's last day, they are never denied." He grimaced. "I forgot about Nina. She would take pleasure in denying yours. I'll request off whatever day you have off that week."

Rory gave him a cheeky grin. "I don't work for Nina anymore."

Asher choked out a laugh. "Shit, did you kill her?"

Rory shoved him lightly. "No, I didn't kill her. Caius reassigned me."

Asher scratched the light stubble on his jaw. "It's Caius now?"

"I'm his personal assistant."

Asher's eyes bugged out of his head. "Are you the new Nina?"

This time she pushed him hard. "I will hang you from one of these hooks if you ever say that again."

He held his hands up and pinched his lips together as his shoulders shook with silent laughter. "Grow up," Rory grumbled. "I don't know why he moved me."

"The king will give you the day off. If anyone understands how hard losing people is, it's him."

CHAPTER 25

Rory grabbed her alarm clock and snuck up the stairway to the sky room. It'd been two months since she found it, and she'd only been there a handful of times. Once she was more familiar with Caius' routine and what time he arrived at his office on average, she could start sleeping here every night and slipping through the secret passage to get to work.

As much as she loved to sleep in with her new job, she would set her alarm for her regular shift tonight to avoid other staff when she snuck back to her room. If she passed anyone, she hoped they wouldn't think twice about seeing her in her old uniform as she came and went from this room.

Losing those few hours was worth it—she needed the room right now. Her confusion over Caius, her sadness over losing Max and Asher, and her despair over never finding Cora's soul was destroying her.

Her thoughts gave her pause. Did her brain believe Caius once and for all?

She would think about that later. After laying her dress

on a chair, she set her alarm clock on the nightstand and shucked off her dress to reveal her shift underneath.

The bed felt like clouds when she lay down, and a long sigh escaped her as she stared at the starry night sky. It wasn't long before she drifted to sleep, but when someone sat on her, she squeaked like a dog toy.

The person jumped, and the lights on the walls immediately flared to life. When Rory's stomach was back in place after plummeting to the ground, she saw Caius standing over her.

"What are you doing here?" he demanded. "How did you get in here?"

Rory's chest was still heaving, and once she could focus, she rolled her eyes. "I'm sure you have heard of doors before."

His hands fisted at his sides. "The door was locked. How did you get in here?"

She looked at her fingernails, studiously avoiding eye contact. "I picked the lock."

"You shouldn't be here," he rumbled, making his displeasure known.

She remained quiet and crossed the room, grabbed her uniform, and slipped her arm through the sleeve.

"Wait," he called after her, releasing a long, exhausted sigh. "You can stay."

She hesitated. "Why?"

He said nothing suggestive, like she expected. "Because it's late, and you shouldn't roam the halls alone."

His words were thoughtful, and she didn't know what to make of it. "What is this place?"

His fingers began unbuttoning his shirt, and Rory swallowed at the sight. His hands moved gracefully as they worked, and until that moment, she didn't know hands could be sexy.

"It was Atarah's room when she visited," he replied, and threw his shirt over the chair next to Rory's discarded dress. He motioned to the ceiling. "She loved Vincula, but the lack of sunlight made her not want to stay long. Whatever the sky looks like in Erdikoa is reflected on the screens." He smiled to himself. "She hated the regular guest quarters."

Rory looked up and smiled. "I miss the Erdikoa sky, too. It reminds me of the people I love back home."

"Like the *Aatxe*?" he asked crossly, setting his rings on the dressing table.

She eyed him suspiciously. "Yes. His name is Dume."

"Was he your boyfriend?" Caius' movements became jerky as he removed his pants and stood in nothing but his tight boxer briefs.

His dick was perfectly outlined, and she was transfixed by it. "Uh, no, he is—what are you doing?"

"I'm getting ready for bed, Miss Raven," Caius said, bemused.

"I'm not sleeping with you." Her voice held more conviction than she felt.

He looked annoyed. "If you're sleeping in this bed, I assure you, you are." That signature smirk returned, and she hated that she loved it. "We can fuck too, if that's what you want."

It seemed his dirty mouth returned as well.

Sleeping beside him was harmless, as long as he didn't touch her. If he tried, she would break his fingers. *Maybe.*

"Dume is my best friend. My sister and I met him in grade one. He is like a brother to me." She no longer knew if that was true, and it stung. Her eyes watered, and she blinked rapidly.

She didn't normally cry, but this stupid realm turned her into a mopey child. She'd like to see anyone cut off from their family and not cry. It was hard.

Caius' thumb wiped a lone tear from her cheek, and her lips parted at the tender gesture. "I lost my siblings too."

"Did you kill Atarah?" she whispered. If he didn't kill Cora, it's possible he was punished for another crime of which he was innocent.

She watched sadness blanket him when he said, "No." Rory's shoulders sagged with relief.

Why was she happy when he had been nothing but horrible to her? The number of internal questions she'd asked herself since arriving in Vincula disturbed her. Identity crisis at its finest, she guessed.

"What made you change your mind about me?" She walked around the bed and climbed in opposite him as though it were the most natural thing in the realms.

He turned on his side to face her and propped himself up on his elbow. "When Sam looked into your mother, he met your friends. Did you know people are defending you? They say you saved them."

"I didn't know when I arrived, but Bruce said as much. I questioned whether he was telling the truth, but..." Her voice broke. "But it means more to me than I thought it would."

"Bruce?" His body tensed.

"He's a new arrival. The man sentenced to one month; he committed a crime bad enough to get him sent here to thank me. A woman I saved was his daughter." She thought for a moment. "Why would asking an *Aatxe* to arrest him while holding an unloaded gun send him here?"

Caius thought for a moment. "Any form of assault or attempted assault is judged by Adila."

Rory propped herself up, too. "But wouldn't she see his intentions weren't malicious?"

"Maybe she gave him what he wanted," Caius mused.

"Maybe that's why she sent me here, too." Rory lay back down. "When I walked into the judgment chambers, I was prepared to die."

"I'm glad she did." The look on his face suggested the words weren't supposed to slip out, and he lay down to stare at the sky.

She watched him closely, trying to figure him out. He was a walking contradiction. "Why?"

His mouth tipped in a half smile. "Whom would I torture if you weren't here?"

She chuckled and lay back with him. "Why do you come here?" she murmured. "You could have screens installed in your quarters, if you wished."

"I miss my sister. Every day, I miss her." His voice was quiet, and her heart went out to him.

Her hand twitched, wanting to reach for his. "I miss my sister, too."

They fell into a comfortable silence that soon turned into a comfortable slumber.

Rory's alarm clock startled her from a serene sleep, and she swatted at the nightstand next to her, only the clock wasn't there. She looked sideways and saw Caius sit up and glare at the clock on his own nightstand.

Hitting the bell, he picked up the clock and stared at it. "Why is this set for three?"

"So I could leave before the staff woke," she said sheepishly.

He twisted the dial, placed the clock back on the nightstand, and lay back down. "Go to sleep, Miss Raven. The sun will wake you. If anyone says anything to you, I'll take care of it."

Smiling to herself, she plopped down on her pillow and drifted to sleep.

When the sun rose, Caius was gone.

Rory arrived at work early, dressed in a white blouse and black skirt that hung loosely around her hips and hit a couple of inches above her knees. In place of her heels were flats, and she looked like a cute grade school teacher.

Walking around the palace and through town in her heels killed her feet, and she couldn't bring herself to wear them today. Instead of sitting at her desk, she walked around the room to inspect the books lining the many shelves.

She wasn't a reader, but Cora was. Her twin's favorite books always had adventures where young heroines saved the entire realm and defeated evil. Rory teased her endlessly for always having her nose in a book, but now she would give anything to sit quietly with her sister as she read.

"Do you like to read?" Caius asked as he walked into the room.

She glanced over her shoulder before turning back to the shelves. "I don't, but my sister liked adventure books."

Caius stood directly behind her, and his breath grazed

the top of her head. He lightly grabbed her elbow and led her to another section, pulling down a book from a high shelf. "This was my favorite as a child."

She read the title and turned to him. "Cora had this book, too. She must have read it a million times."

He smiled. "She had good taste."

"I didn't realize it was that old," Rory said mindlessly.

Caius glared before he crossed the room to his own desk. "I need you to secure Nina's new living arrangements today. Most of the inmates live downtown in the inmate apartments. The manager who runs the housing is a legion officer named Linda. She will assign the apartment and give you the information you need. Nina's inmate number needs to be updated to her new apartment number. Linda can handle that as well," he said before looking up. "And pick up lunch for us on your way back."

Rory hoped she was the one to deliver the news to Nina. The look on the woman's face would keep Rory on a high for an entire week. "What do you want for lunch?"

He rattled off his order, and Rory moved to her desk to write it down. "And Miss Raven?" She stopped with her hand on the doorknob. "No personal visits."

There was the asshole she was used to. "Wouldn't dream of it, Your Grace."

Caius decided making Rory wear skirts was a terrible idea. He wanted nothing more than to spread her out on his desk and ravage what she was hiding under the billowy fabric.

He adjusted his cock in his pants. A part of him thought she was coming around, slowly deciding he wasn't a vile creature who went around murdering women, but it could still be an act.

Her hatred used to be strong, but an activated bond was stronger.

Then there was the matter of his feelings for her. A part of him still wondered if some of her victims were innocent, and the other part knew they weren't. He didn't love her, not yet, but one day he would. The need to protect her would become so strong, resisting would be futile.

"Damn you, *Seraphim*." The *Aeternum* was said to be a *Royal's* perfect match and the bond only enhanced what was in their souls. By that logic, it didn't force them to love each other; it made their souls connect with their counterparts, and their hearts did the rest.

He chuckled. Maybe their souls *were* perfectly matched. The need for vengeance fueled them both. The thought gave him pause, reminding him of his greater purpose. He would certainly be sentenced to death when he killed Gedeon.

If the bond was solidified, he didn't know if he'd be able to follow through and leave Rory forever.

He couldn't allow his brother's evil to stay within the realms, and Caius knew Adila wouldn't spare him a second time. A pit of despair opened in his chest, knowing what he had to do.

His connection to Rory couldn't grow, and keeping her hatred for him alive was the only way to do that. Would the *Seraphim* damn him to hell when he was executed for his crime, or would they allow him in the *aether*?

Would they permit him to meet his Aeternum in the afterlife?

It didn't matter. He would do what needed to be done. He only needed to avoid her for a little while longer until his sentence was over. Shadows darkened the room as his anger at his own stupidity intensified.

He couldn't risk her safety by putting her back on kitchen duty. His fist came down on his desk, cracking it down the middle. *How dare Adila send her here?* She knew what Rory was to him, he was sure of it, and she knew what Caius intended to do. Did she find it entertaining to torture him?

"*Fuck!*" he thundered into the empty room as he knocked over anything he could reach. Damn his siblings for putting him in this position, and damn him for allowing things to get this far. The chance at happiness blinded him, but he wouldn't make that mistake again.

The door swung open, and Rory stood in the doorway, looking at the destruction. "What...?"

"Clean this up," he said, fixing his sleeves. Treating her like his maid when it was not her position made bile rise in his throat.

Surveying the room, she scoffed. "I'm not cleaning up your temper tantrum."

He stalked across the room and held out his hand. She shoved his lunch toward him, and he motioned for her to get started. "You will clean this up, or I'll have you shadow Nina until her sentence is complete." His voice was lazy, but his body was coiled tightly.

Her skin flushed with anger, and the familiar loathing returned to her eyes. He didn't wait for her retort as he stepped around her, slamming the door on his way out.

CHAPTER 26

Rory was shaking with rage as she picked up the books strewn about the office. Caius needed to pull out whatever stick was up his ass.

The large stack of books she held tipped over, and she screamed, kicking at the heap on the floor.

"What did those books do to deserve your anger?" Samyaza asked as he waltzed into the room. He stopped and looked down when a lamp crunched beneath his foot. "What did he do?"

"Ironic you knew it was the king," she muttered as she bent over to pick up the books. "He was fine, nice even. I left for lunch and when I came back, the office was destroyed. He snatched his lunch and told me to clean up."

Sam cursed under his breath and gathered the shards of the broken lamp. Rory should tell him he didn't have to help, but she didn't want to spend all night picking up the wreckage.

"Caius is dealing with some life altering news," Sam said as he picked up shards of glass. "Please, give him grace."

Life altering news? Interesting, but not good enough. "Are you shitting me?"

Sam's brows furrowed. "Shitting you? That is disgusting. No, I am not *shitting* you."

"Why should I be the one to cater to him?" she asked as she shoved books onto the shelves harder than necessary. "We all go through tough situations; it's the nature of life. Doesn't mean we get to be twats to everyone."

He didn't bat an eye at her name calling.

"You do not understand," he replied, gathering books. "I am asking you to be patient with him."

Rory snorted. "You can take my patience and shove it up his ass." Right next to the stick.

"You are impossible," he said as he turned to Caius' broken desk.

"And you are bigger than a mountain troll, but you don't see me pointing it out," she returned.

He glared at her and surveyed the desk before picking it up, spilling the contents everywhere. The wood splintered in two, and Sam caught both pieces. Rory was amazed at his strength and agility. He was not of these realms.

"Why didn't you take everything out first?" she griped, pointing at the files and pens on the ground. "You're going to break something."

He gave her a flat stare and held up one half of the large desk. "If you are not strong enough to move the desk, you do not get a say in how it is done."

She hurled a book across the room and nailed him on the butt. He turned slowly, and she wondered if he would rip her head off. Literally. "Did you throw a book at me?"

She crossed her arms. "Yes."

He shook his head and continued toward the door.

"It's not fair to ask me to be understanding of someone treating me like dirt, and I'll throw this entire room's worth of books at you if you suggest otherwise again," she called after him.

He gave her a crooked smile that momentarily stunned her. "Finish picking up the books, and I will take care of Caius."

Sam burst into Caius' room like a bull chasing red. "What did you do?" he boomed.

Caius already knew what he was referring to. "What I had to do."

"You had to destroy your office and force Rory to clean it up?"

Caius checked Sam's ears to see if they were emitting steam.

Sam hadn't been this upset in a very long time, and Caius closed the book he was reading. "We need to keep our distance, and if she wants to throttle me, it will be easier."

"Why?" Sam asked indignantly. "Why are you fighting this so hard?"

"Because," Caius shouted as he stood, letting all of his frustrations out on his friend. "If I lose myself in her, I won't be able to kill Gedeon." He closed his eyes to steady his breathing. "I cannot allow Atarah's death to go unpunished. His soul is the blackest of them all, and he rules an entire realm."

Sam's wings flared slightly. "You can still have your retribution, with Rory at your side. Speak with Adila when your contract is up and handle the situation like a king."

"And chance Gedeon interfering?" Caius laughed bitterly. "If he catches wind, he will do everything in his power to stop me, and you know that as well as I do."

"What good does it do to push her away?" Sam's voice was filled with disappointment.

"Because if I had her, *truly* had her, I wouldn't let anything separate me from her, including death," he replied. "My agenda is the most important thing in the realms to me, and I refuse to let her change that. I'd like to think Adila would spare me for ridding the realms of Gedeon. But I also never imagined she would lock me away for a crime I didn't commit."

Sam shook his head, and the look on his face punched Caius in the gut. "You are a fool." He stopped on his way out the door. "Do not treat her like she is beneath you. She is your equal, and while you may not want her, she deserves to be treated as such."

Caius stared miserably at the door. He wanted Rory, but he didn't *want* to want her. Sam was right. Treating her the way he did was not the answer, but being around her wasn't an option, either.

"And then that fuckwad told me to clean it up!" Rory exclaimed, as her hands motioned wildly. "Can you believe that?"

She sat at a table with Bellina, Asher, Cat, Tallent, and Kit. They listened to her entire rant about King Twat, as she now referred to him, but they'd yet to respond. Her name calling was childish, but she didn't care.

Until they exploded with laughter. "It's not funny!" Rory protested.

"Yes, it is," Cat replied as she giggled into her drink. "He either wants to sleep with you, or he *really* despises you."

"Next time, put his books back with the spines facing the inside of the bookcase," Kit suggested. "He'll never read again."

Bellina was quiet as she watched Rory. "What?" Rory asked her.

"Why would he give you a job, be nice to you, and then be a jerk?" she wondered. "It doesn't make sense."

"Nothing about the king's actions makes sense," Asher said, before chugging the rest of his beer. "He killed his sister, but we know he's not the nightmare they say he is. He humiliated Rory in front of everyone and then bought her a new wardrobe. The man is an enigma."

Tallent was quiet during the exchange until he finally set down his drink with an indiscernible look and asked, "He moved Nina out of the palace for you, didn't he?"

Rumors spread about Nina's housing reassignment, and Rory tapped her glass. "I don't know if it was because of me, or because she kept showing up wherever he was, begging for his dick."

Asher snorted beer through his nose and all over the table. "*Seraphim*, Rory. Warn a guy before you talk about the king's goods."

The table erupted with laughter again. "What are you going to do?" Kit asked.

Rory banged her head against the table. "What can I do? Deal with his moodiness, I guess." She lifted her head. "He told me the first time we met that by the time I was done here, I would wish Adila had sent me to hell instead. This place feels like hell sometimes."

"Don't be dramatic," Cat scolded. "Orcus rules hell, and the king rules a prison. One of those things is not like the other."

"Did you know Orcus is a *Seraph*, too?" Kit asked everyone, taking them by surprise.

Everyone turned to her. "That's not in the history books," Tallent replied. "How could you possibly know that?"

Kit threw back the rest of her drink. "Yes, it is. They don't teach much about him in grade school other than the basics, but there are ancient texts from the first days. My parents are historians. It's why I became obsessed with reading."

Seraphim were beings who ruled the aether and created realms as they pleased. They were terrifying creatures with two large wings like *Angels*, small wings covering their faces like a mask, and wings covering their legs. The *Seraphim* responsible for Erdikoa and Vincula created everything here and disappeared. What was the point?

There were only a handful of original paintings of *Seraphim* in existence from the early days, all in The Capital, but prints were available in Erdikoa.

Orcus was the ruler of hell, and Rory assumed since he ruled a realm, he was a type of *Royal*.

Kit nodded. "*Seraphim* live in the aether like mystics live here, only they're all powerful and have no single ruler. Different *Seraphim* create different realms. The closest analogy I can think of is that they are the parents, and we are their children."

"What does this have to do with Orcus?" Asher butted in.

Cat popped him in the back of the head. "Let her finish."

"Orcus and another group of *Seraphim* created their own realms, including hell," Kit continued.

"Wait," Asher interrupted again. "If the other *Seraphim* created hell, why are souls from our realms sent there, too?"

"Will you stop interrupting?" Bellina chided. "You are so annoying sometimes." Asher feigned outrage, but another look from Bellina had him straightening.

"When the other group of *Seraphim* created their first realm and its inhabitants, some souls were born black," Kit explained. "They didn't want them in the aether, so they created hell. Orcus was an arrogant jackass who wanted to rule over others, and he volunteered to be the keeper of hell.

"From there, when other *Seraphim* created new realms, it was agreed upon that hell would be a catch-all for the wicked." Kit stopped to take a breath. The story was long, and Rory was having difficulty following. "Something happened, but I'm not sure what. It was never explicitly mentioned in the texts, but Orcus' sister Lympha and four other *Seraphim* named Aestas, Autumnus, Heims, and Ver locked him in hell. Lympha died in the fight."

Cat glanced at Rory. "Told you the king wasn't as bad as Orcus."

"Well, they *did* both kill their sisters," Bellina pointed out. "Maybe they aren't so different after all."

"Caius didn't kill his sister," Rory said defensively before she could think better of it.

Everyone stared at her wide-eyed. "How would you know that?" Tallent asked. "And you call him Caius?"

Rory fidgeted in her seat as she wiped a bead of sweat from the side of her glass. "He said he didn't."

"And you believed him." Asher deadpanned.

"Why would he lie?" Rory met his judgmental stare. "What could he gain from lying?" They all fell into a contemplative silence.

"Well, I'll be damned," Max said as he approached the table. "Never thought I'd see the day you all were quiet."

"The king didn't kill his sister," Cat chirped as though they were discussing what drapes to buy for her apartment.

Max slid into a seat next to Rory. "I figured as much."

Of course he did. Max somehow knew everything, and Rory wondered if he was actually a *Sibyl* before coming to Vincula. It would make sense his mind wasn't a mess since a mystic's abilities were taken from them once here.

She snuck a glance at his mark. Nope, definitely a *Munin*.

He didn't elaborate on his statement, and no one asked. Something Rory noticed was that Max's word was taken as truth. The old man didn't say much, but when he did, they listened.

"I'm going to miss you," she said, nudging Max's shoulder with hers. "You too, Asher."

The table fell silent again until Cat said, "Way to be a buzzkill, butcher girl."

They all chuckled, but it held none of the amusement from before. "We need to send you guys off with a bang," Cat said. "We can throw a party at my apartment!"

"I bet we could host it at the palace," Rory supplied. "I can ask Caius. As much as he hates me, he has a soft spot for everyone else."

Kit tipped her glass. "I vote for the palace."

"Me too," Bellina said. "Especially since you'll miss the Plenilune ball," she said to Asher. "It's the day you leave."

Asher threw back the rest of his drink. No one had gone for a refill yet, and Rory waved down a server. While they waited, Asher said, "I won't remember it anyway."

"You guys really know how to ruin the mood," Cat muttered, making everyone laugh again.

CHAPTER 27

Rory's days were the same. Showing up to work, reading a list of things to do that Caius left on her desk, and running whatever menial errands he asked of her. She never saw him, as he seemed to avoid her.

She shoved it all behind her. Tomorrow was Asher's going away party, and Rory spent half her day making plans for it.

She'd left Caius a note requesting the use of one of the many banquet rooms that went unused. There were never any visitors, and the large rooms seemed pointless. It's possible they were used before he was convicted of murdering his sister.

She needed to speak with the head cook about food for Asher's party and the Plenilune ball next week, and she rushed out of the office, hoping to finish early enough to find Bellina before dinner.

Caius' notes always instructed her to buy herself lunch every day, and dinner still appeared on her bed every evening. His behavior made little sense, and it drove her crazy.

She now used the main door to the office because it led into a hallway to get around the palace instead of having to cross the enormous throne room, and when she rounded the corner to descend the stairs toward the kitchen, she was shoved, hard.

The force knocked the wind out of her before she ever hit the stairs, and once she did, she screamed out in pain and terror. The momentum was too much, and she couldn't stop herself as the sharp edges of the stairs delivered blow after blow.

Something cracked, and eventually, she hit the landing below in a bloody heap.

Warm, sticky blood covered various parts of her body, and she gingerly touched her face. When she pulled her hand back, it was red and shaking. Her vision spotted, and an excruciating pain in her ribs made it hard to breathe.

She tried to roll over on her side to expel whatever was in her throat, crying out with the movement. When she coughed to clear her airway, blood splattered on the rug beneath her.

Pictures crashed to the ground as shadows slammed against the walls with the king's arrival. He was calling her name, she thought, but everything was fading in and out.

There was yelling, but it sounded garbled. She was floating now, and as she rose, she tried to cry out, but it was interrupted by more coughing. More blood.

Someone cursed as she bounced in their arms, but she never found out where they were going because the realm faded away.

～

"SOMEONE BRING A DOCTOR TO ROOM 21030, NOW!" Caius roared through the halls as he cradled Rory in his arms. The hospital was in town, and he didn't know if she would make it that far. There was a doctor on staff at the palace, but it housed no official infirmary.

Shadows were crashing through the halls with his unchecked emotions, and it was all he could do to keep from bringing the entire palace to the ground. Her room was closer than his, and when he arrived, shadows blew the door off its hinges.

His hands shook as he gently laid her on the bed to survey her injuries. Blood covered her face, the bottom of her leg was bent at an odd angle, and her breaths were shallow.

Running a hand through her bloodied hair, he whispered, "Rory? Can you hear me?" He knew he shouldn't have left her alone. It was only a week, and already she was lying lifelessly in front of him. He'd been a fool. "I need you to wake up, baby."

He'd never felt more helpless in his entire life. His eyes closed as he focused on releasing the shadows. When they were back where they belonged, he looked at his *Aeternum's* lifeless body and ran a hand through his own hair.

The doctor hurried through the broken door and approached the bed. "Are you hurt, Your Grace?"

He was going to fire the doctor for being an idiot. "Do I look hurt? *Help her,*" he snapped.

The doctor motioned to Caius' head. "Your hair is smeared with blood."

Caius looked at the hand he ran through his hair, the same hand that ran through Rory's.

"I'm fine. She fell down the stairs," he said as worry crept into his voice. His chest burned with the possibility of her dying. She was supposed to live a full life without him, not die because he foolishly left her alone.

"Your Grace, I need to examine her," the doctor said cautiously.

Caius stepped around the bed to the other side and kneeled, taking Rory's hand in his. "Don't leave me," he quietly begged.

A maid assisted the doctor while another stood by the door. Caius looked at her and said, "Go find the commander and bring him here immediately."

The doctor worked quietly while Caius stared at Rory's face, silently willing her to wake up. Samyaza's imposing form stepped through the door and inspected the room. "What happened?"

Caius turned. "I don't know. A vision knocked me to the ground as the stairs battered me until it was over. I ran to the stairs as fast as I could and found her on the third-floor landing."

Sam stared at Rory with a flash of fear on his face, and Caius gripped her hand tighter. The doctor turned to Sam. "She needs healing potions from the hospital as soon as possible. Her internal bleeding is filling her abdomen, and her broken rib punctured a lung."

Without thinking, Caius ran for the door, but Sam stopped him. "I'll go. Stay with her."

"She needs a potion for a concussion and broken bones as well," the doctor continued. "I mean no disrespect, commander, but hurry."

Sam nodded and left. "If she gets the potions in time, she will be fine, Your Grace. The worst of her injuries will heal within a few hours, and tomorrow, you can send for potions to take care of her surface level injuries."

Caius nodded, never taking his eyes off Rory. "Thank you. Please stay until Sam returns."

The doctor gave a curt nod and stepped into the hallway. "I'll be out here if you need me."

Caius didn't know how much time passed before Sam returned, but it felt like an eternity. The doctor made quick work of rubbing different potions on different parts of Rory's body.

He held her knee and foot in each hand and looked at Caius. "Do you have a weak stomach, Your Grace?"

Caius paid him no mind as he shook his head and watched Rory's chest rise and fall.

The doctor pushed and pulled on her leg, and a loud crack filled the air. The maid assisting him fainted at the sound, and Sam scooped her up, handing her to Lauren, who Caius hadn't realized was in the hall.

Once Rory's leg was set, the doctor rubbed another potion on the area.

He grabbed another bottle and shook it. "I need her to drink this for her internal bleeding, but you need to hold her up. I have to do a miniscule amount at a time so it will be absorbed by her tongue instead of entering her lungs."

Caius stood, and with the doctor's help, sat Rory up. He slid in behind her, both of his legs on either side, and laid her against his chest.

"Hold her mouth open," the doctor instructed.

Bit by bit, the potion dripped onto her tongue until it was gone. Sam stood quietly in the doorway, and Caius' heart tried to rip its way out of his chest.

"What now?" he asked.

"Now, we wait," the doctor said grimly. "There is nothing more I can do. The potions are already working." He gestured to her leg. "Send for me when she wakes up."

Normally, Caius would never allow someone to give him orders, but the doctor was the only one who could save her. He could tell Caius to fuck off if he wanted.

"I'll be back, brother," Sam said before he disappeared.

Caius settled against the headboard with Rory on his chest and closed his eyes. She took those stairs every day, and even though her *Fey* ability was gone, she was a graceful woman.

He knew deep in his gut someone did this to her, and *Seraphim* help them when he found out who.

Caius heard yelling from the hallway, and his arms tensed around her.

"Let me in there, or I will shove those horns up your ass!" a woman's voice threatened.

The *Aatxe* standing guard rumbled something in return and he walked past the doorway with Rory's friend in tow.

"Wait," Caius called out. The *Aatxe* halted. "She can come in."

The woman whose name Caius couldn't recall stepped into the room with one last glare over her shoulder at the retreating guard. When she turned back to Rory, her hands flew to her mouth as she crossed the room.

"What is your name?" Caius asked.

She sniffled, and tears filled her eyes. "Bellina. I'm a seamstress here."

"You killed your wife's abusive father," Caius recalled, and she nodded.

Bellina rushed to the bathroom and came back with a damp towel. "What happened?"

As she began wiping the blood from Rory's face, Caius internally slapped himself for not thinking of doing the same. "I found her at the bottom of the stairs."

Bellina gasped. "Did someone push her?"

"We don't know." He clenched and unclenched his jaw repeatedly to keep from screaming at the *Seraphim* for allowing this to happen.

"She wouldn't fall," Bellina insisted. "People have had it out for her since she arrived, thanks to you." The seamstress looked ready to rip Caius' head from his body, and he didn't blame her.

He couldn't change the past. Lauren reappeared in the doorway, and Caius beckoned her closer. "Pack up her belongings. It's no longer safe for her to stay in the staff quarters."

"I'll help," Bellina volunteered.

They both moved quietly around the room as they pulled her things from her drawers, packed her toiletries, and set them in a neat pile near the door.

"Leave us," Caius instructed. When the room was vacant, he leaned his head back, closed his eyes, and fell asleep.

Caius walked through the empty halls of his palace, looking for something. No, not something. Someone. A sense of urgency overcame him, and he moved faster, throwing open door after door.

He approached room 21030, pushed it open, and skidded to a halt when he saw Rory sitting on her bed.

Her mouth pulled into a wry smile. "What are you doing here?"

Memories came flooding back—she was hurt. They must be in the mate soulscape. Once two mated souls were both of age, they sometimes shared a soulscape, though they had no memory of it when they woke. Once the bond solidified, they only met in the soulscape when separated, and they remembered it in vivid detail. It was said to help connect their souls. He assumed they were meeting now because she needed him.

"You need to wake up, Rory," he pleaded.

Her head tilted to the side as she regarded him. "I am awake."

"You're dreaming," he insisted. "Please wake up." His words were growing more frantic. He had to make her understand.

She moved away. "What has gotten into you?"

He kneeled in front of her and grabbed her shoulders. "Baby, you need to wake up."

A crease formed between her brows. "What's wrong? I'm fine here."

Desperation clawed at his chest. "There was an accident, and you're unconscious. You need to wake up." He had to make her understand.

Her hand touched her hair and pulled away, covered in blood. She screamed and stood, knocking Caius over.

Feeling her head again, she looked at him. "I need to wake up."

CHAPTER 28

Rory gasped as her eyes flew open and her pillow moved up and down beneath her. *Wait, that wasn't right.*

She tried to sit up and groaned. Did a bear shifter step on her?

Everything came rushing back. The stairs. The shove. The pain. The voice asking her to hold on.

"Rory?" a deep voice said, vibrating her back.

She tilted her head enough to see golden eyes watching her. Caius' face was screwed up with worry, and when she whispered his name, it fell with relief.

"Where am I?" she croaked, looking around the best she could.

"Your room," he replied coarsely. "Do you remember what happened?"

She tried to swallow, but her throat was dry. "I need water."

"Guard!" Caius barked, making Rory groan and grab her head. "Sorry," he said, placing a kiss on the top of her hair, almost making her choke, despite having no spit to choke on.

A member of the legion stepped through her doorway, which no longer had a door. "Yes, Your Grace?"

"Bring water and fetch the doctor," he ordered, before lowering his voice. "Rory, I know you're hurting, but I need you to tell me what happened."

She closed her eyes, immediately reliving the fall. Her eyes flew open and sweat beaded her brow. "Someone pushed me down the stairs."

Caius' entire body went taut. "Who?"

The guard returned with two glasses, a pitcher of water, and the doctor. He poured Rory a glass, and she drank it in one gulp.

"I'm glad to see you awake, Miss Raven," the doctor said. "I need to examine you, if that's okay?"

She nodded, pushed herself up, and immediately wished she were dead. Everything hurt. How was she supposed to beat the shit out of whoever did this to her if she couldn't move?

After being poked and prodded, the doctor deemed her healthy, told her to take the potions Caius gave her, and left. "How many credits do we get at the pharmacy?" Rory asked. She hoped a lot.

When he didn't answer, she turned herself around on the bed to look at him. He only stared. "You will have whatever you want. Credit limits no longer apply to you."

Her mouth fell open. "Did you push me, and this is some type of penance?"

She was only half-joking.

"Did you see who did this to you?" he asked in lieu of a response.

She shook her head as much as she could. "I was in a hurry to arrange the food for Asher's party and the ball." She stopped. "Can you give approval for Bellina to finish the arrangements for Asher's party tomorrow? I'm not sure I can walk down the hall, let alone take the stairs."

Caius continued to stare at her incredulously. "You think so little of me that I would deny you anything right now? You almost died, Rory. I watched you slip away in my arms. You could order Sam to make arrangements if you wanted, and I wouldn't care."

Her stomach flip-flopped at his words. "You made me clean your office."

"I will destroy it again so you can watch me clean it, but first, I need to know if you saw who pushed you." His hand lifted as if to touch her before he thought better of it.

"I didn't see who it was," she admitted. "I was in too much pain to look up."

His nostrils flared slightly. "I'm moving you into Atarah's room."

She gaped at him again. "Why?"

He huffed out a humorless laugh. "Someone tried to kill you. Again." It wasn't an answer, but it was all he gave.

"You will enter and exit through my office. There's a hidden hallway," he continued. "You are not to wander the halls alone."

"You can't tell me what to do," she said, cutting him off.

His brows rose. "Actually, I can."

"You sound like Dume," she muttered under her breath.

"Rory!" Bellina screamed frantically from the doorway, with Max and Asher on her heels.

Bellina tried to throw her arms around Rory's shoulders, but a wall of shadows stopped her. She started swatting them away. "Rory's sore," Caius warned. "Don't touch her." When he said the last line, his eyes were on Asher.

"Aether," was all Asher said as he looked Rory up and down. "Someone pushed you?"

She nodded weakly. "Bellina, can you speak to the kitchen about food for tomorrow night?"

Asher looked offended. "Are you kidding? Fuck my party, Rory." He turned to Bellina. "Cancel everything."

"That's unnecessary," Rory protested. "I can sit on a couch in the room we're using. They're fancy."

Caius' face darkened. "You need to rest."

"Yeah," Asher chimed in. "Can you even walk?"

Rory opened her mouth to defend herself but stopped. Could she? "That's what I thought," he said, sounding like the fifty-one-year-old he was.

"Shut up, Ash," Bellina snapped playfully.

Max stood quietly by the door. "Can't say hi?" Rory teased.

Chuckling, he said, "I figured those two were talking enough for all of us." He crossed the cramped room and lightly touched Rory's shoulder. "I'm glad you're okay, kiddo."

Bellina's eyes ticked from Rory to Caius with an unspoken question, and Rory turned to the king. "Would you mind giving us some privacy?"

"Yes, I would," he replied immediately. "Someone tried to kill you today. I'm not letting you out of my sight until we find out who."

"I'll give you three guesses," Asher bit out. "We all know Nina was involved."

Bellina smacked his arm. "You don't know that." She turned back to Caius. "But it's probably true."

"Nina was at her apartment all afternoon," Sam said, making them all jump. His head looked around the corner of the doorway. "I checked." He disappeared again.

Rory gulped. She knew people hated her, but enough to kill her? She'd hoped it ended with Ronny. "The list of people who hate me should start a club," she joked. "They can get members' jackets, so they're easily identified."

Max shook his head. "This is no laughing matter. They will try again."

Rory straightened. It was unlike Max to scold anyone, and it made her nerves fray.

"Okay," she conceded. "But can we still have Asher's party?"

She glanced at Caius. "I won't leave their sides."

He looked at Asher. "You won't leave mine either." He slid off the bed and motioned toward the broken door. "Rory needs to rest. I'll escort her to the party tomorrow, and you can see her then."

The three bid Rory goodbye and left, and Sam, who Rory forgot was in the hall, stepped through the door, grabbed all of her things piled on the floor, and exited.

"Who packed my things?"

Caius bent over and scooped her up. "Lauren and Bellina."

"Put me down," she demanded. "Where are you taking me, anyway?"

He maneuvered her through the door and said, "To your new room."

Caius knew he was being irrational, just like he knew his actions were in direct contrast with his prior declaration, but she wouldn't die on his watch.

Once she settled into her new room and he arranged protection for her, he would keep her at a distance. His erratic behavior over her fall was proof she was changing his priorities.

That couldn't happen.

She stopped fighting him about halfway down the hall, presumably too sore to put up much of a fight, and when he arrived in his office, the bookcase was already moved aside thanks to Sam.

He moved through the hallway on muscle memory as he stole glances at the woman in his arms. Even with her face swollen and bruised, she was beautiful.

"Stop looking at me like that," she grumbled. "I know I look like death warmed over."

His laugh shook them both. "Tell people you went a few rounds with Lauren. You wouldn't be the first person she put in the hospital."

Rory snorted and winced. "Everything hurts."

Sam held up a woman's skirt out in front of him. "Where does this go?"

"You don't have to unpack my things." Rory wiggled in Caius' arms again. "I can do it myself."

Sam shrugged, folded the skirt, and stuck it in a drawer before grabbing another article of clothing.

She puffed out a gust of air. "You two are impossible."

Caius set her on the bed, and when her head hit the pillow, her body melted against the sheets.

Satisfied, Caius addressed Sam, "Have a contractor from town seal off the staircase to this room."

"What?" Rory half-shouted. "How will my friends visit?"

"They won't," Sam and Caius said at the same time.

"Then take me back to my room."

"You can visit Bellina in her room when you are better," Caius assured her. "Asher is leaving the day after tomorrow, and Max is leaving the week after that."

Rory's shoulders slumped against the mattress. "Does it always feel like this?" she asked them. "Knowing your friends won't remember you?"

Caius ran a hand through his hair, and bits of crusted blood fell out. He needed a shower, which reminded him that Rory did, too. Looking at her blood matted hair made him grimace at the soiled sheets.

He pushed his hands under her body and lifted her once more.

"Hey!" she shrieked. "What are you doing?" She looked at Sam. "What is wrong with him?"

"You need a bath," Caius replied. "You have blood in your hair."

Sam pointed at her. "Under your fingernails too." He put away the garment in his hand and walked into the closet, returning with fresh sheets. "I will meet you in your office after I change the bed," he said to Caius.

"You are not bathing me," Rory growled at the king. "I don't even want you touching me."

"I will dunk you in the bath fully clothed if that's what you wish, but you *are* bathing," he informed her.

The clothes she wore were covered in blood and torn in places where the doctor had to examine her and add potions. Caius set her on the side of the tub and turned on the water, adjusting the temperature.

"Clothes on or off?" he asked her.

"Off, but my bra and panties stay on." She stood on shaky legs, and Caius unzipped her skirt to work it down her hips. Normally this would turn him on, but all he could focus on was not hurting her, and the bruises that tainted her skin made him murderous.

Once undressed, he lowered her into the warm water, grabbed a washcloth, and squirted soap onto the soft fabric.

When he tried to clean her arm, she pulled back. "What do you think you're doing?"

He blinked and looked at the cloth in his hands. "This is called bathing."

She plucked the cloth from his hands and shooed him away. "I don't need you to wash me. I'll call you when I'm ready to get out."

He opened his mouth to protest, but she held up a hand. "This is not a discussion."

Amused and a little disappointed she wouldn't accept his help, he walked back to the bedroom, but left the bathroom door open.

He could hear the water splashing and little grunts through the open door, and he forced himself to stay put.

"I need your help," Rory said reluctantly after a few minutes.

He stood by the bathtub within seconds. "What can I do?"

She motioned to her hair. "Can you wash my hair?"

He nodded, wanting nothing more. After she was better, he would distance himself. If that's what he told himself over and over, eventually, he would believe it.

"Sit up," he instructed, before stepping into his room for

a pitcher. When he returned, he filled it with bathwater, but she grabbed his wrist.

"The water is disgusting. Let me drain it, and you can use fresh water from the faucet."

When the plug was pulled, he waited for the fresh water to warm up before filling the pitcher again. "Lean your head back." Slowly, he poured water over her hair, refilling the pitcher when necessary until the strands were saturated.

He lathered the shampoo in his hands before rubbing it into her hair. After covering her head from root to tip, he massaged her scalp and relished in the soft moans she made. After shampooing twice, he added conditioner and did more of the same.

Seeing her shoulders relax at his touch had his blood heating, and if he didn't leave soon, he would ask to feast between her legs.

He helped her from the bathtub, handed her a towel and shift, and stepped from the room. When she emerged, she walked faster than before, the hot water having eased some of her aches.

"A guard will be stationed at every entrance to this room, and you are not to leave until someone trustworthy comes to fetch you."

She glared at him again but gave no argument. He helped her into bed, turned out the lights, and slipped behind the bookcase to his office.

As he walked down the long hallway, he reminded himself that he couldn't let himself fall into her.

CHAPTER 29

Rory asked Bellina to grab her a sundress from the shop in town to wear to Asher's party that night. Leggings were a bitch to put on, and loose dresses seemed like the easiest option.

Her face was bruised and swollen, and her lip looked like it went ten rounds with Lo's fangs. Bellina blew through the door with multiple shopping bags on her arms and smiled. "We have plenty of options."

Rory blanched. "You didn't use all your credits, did you?"

The smirk on Bellina's face made Rory immediately suspicious. "The king told the store clerk you have unlimited credits."

Rory scoffed with indignation. "I'm going to kill him."

Bellina waved her off. "Let him buy you things. If it weren't for him, you would've never been a target to begin with."

She had a point. Rory peeked into the bags and pulled out different dresses. Nestled at the bottom of one bag was a long, soft, cotton dress. It was red, and Rory marveled at the color.

"I'll wear this one," she announced.

Bellina looked over and snatched the dress. "This is for the ball tomorrow. Fancy dresses are harder to get on, so I got you a soft cotton one."

Rory sighed and reached back into the bags, settling on a pretty blue dress that hung comfortably on her frame.

"Why didn't they use a potion on your bruises and cuts?" Bellina asked. "Don't they have potions for sore muscles?"

"I don't know. I have a pain-relieving potion that helps. They were worried about keeping me alive, and I guess vain potions were the farthest from their minds."

"I won't have time today or tomorrow, but in a few days, I'll ask the pharmacy. We may not have them in Vincula," Bellina said as she put away the other dresses. "We're setting up for Asher's party in half an hour. I'll come back to get you when we're done."

· Rory waved as her friend left and made a mental note to speak to Caius about credits when she saw him next. Giving her free rein for whatever she wanted would put a bigger target on her back, and she'd rather not spend the next five-hundred years tumbling down stairs.

She should be more traumatized that someone tried to kill her, but fighting her fair share of men before murdering them desensitized her. All day she stared at the bookcase, waiting for Caius to walk through, but he'd yet to show, and when it opened after Bellina left, she hoped it was him.

But it wasn't. Lauren and Sam sauntered through the door holding flowers and pizza.

Sam set the vase on her dresser and said, "You need to get better."

Rory started to flip him off but remembered the last time she did and decided better of it. "I believe the phrase you are looking for is, 'Get better soon.'"

"No, I said what I meant," he replied as he stared at the chairs like they personally offended him.

She looked between him and his new enemy. "Did my furniture do something to you?"

Lauren patted him on the shoulder as she set the pizza on a small two-person breakfast table in the corner. "He's pouting because he can't sit anywhere with those gaudy wings."

"Oh," Rory said, examining his wings. "What do you sit on, then?"

His wings disappeared, and Rory rubbed her eyes to make sure she wasn't imagining things.

"Benches or chairs with a low back," he replied. "And before you ask, no, it doesn't hurt to lie on my back, and yes, my bed is huge."

Rory pressed her lips together to stop from laughing as she lifted the lid to the pizza box and leaned over to smell it. "Never have I been so happy to see food. I'm starving."

Lauren kicked off her shoes and plopped down on the bed. "I bet. Eat up."

"Where did your wings go?" Rory asked Sam and shoved a piece of pizza into her mouth.

He grabbed a book from a shelf and sat in one of the plush chairs. "I can shape shift."

Rory stood staring at him, unsure if he was kidding, but his lack of wings would suggest he told the truth. "Like a shifter? Is this your normal form?" She motioned to his large body. "Or are the wings your normal form?"

His nose was already buried in his book. "I prefer my wings." That didn't answer her question.

"Because they make you look horrifying?" Rory joked. Half joked, anyway.

Lauren burst out laughing from the bed and sat up. "More like a giant bird."

Sam set the book down with a grunt. "You two are not as funny as you think you are."

The girls looked at each other and busted up laughing. "Thank you for bringing me food." Rory moved to sit on the bed beside Lauren. "I feel like an inmate."

"Technically, you are," Lauren pointed out, and Rory bumped her shoulder, immediately regretting it.

"Ow," she hissed, rubbing her shoulder.

Sam's eyes were zeroed in on her shoulder. "Do you have any pain relief potion?"

Rory motioned to the bathroom. "I try not to take it more than necessary. I don't want to run out too fast."

"Here we go," Lauren mumbled under her breath, and Rory looked at her inquisitively.

Before she could reply, Sam stood and stomped to her bathroom, only to return with the potion. "Open your mouth."

He had the dropper filled and ready, and when he hovered it over Rory's mouth, she pulled back and swatted his hand away. "I said I don't need any."

"Just take it," Lauren muttered. "You activated mother hen mode."

Sam reached down and poked Rory's shoulder, hard.

"Ow! Why'd you do that?" When he lost his wings, did he lose his mind?

"You're in pain," he replied and held up the dropper. "Open your mouth, or I will make you."

Her jaw dropped at his brashness, and before she realized what she'd done, he dropped the potion on her tongue. It was bitter, and she gagged; she hated taking potions and had since she was a little girl. Cora never minded them, but Rory would hide.

Sam grinned and put the potion back in the bathroom. "Caius made it clear you had access to anything you need. There is no need to hoard your potion."

She glared at the oversized dove. "It's disgusting. I hate taking potions, even if I have a lifetime supply."

Sam returned and took a seat. "Don't be childish."

As if reading her mind, Lauren handed her a pillow, and Rory launched it across the room.

"Stop throwing things at me," Sam warned. "You do not want me to throw them back."

Lauren leaned over and whispered, "He's not bluffing."

Rory tried not to laugh again but failed. "Are you two excited about the ball tomorrow?"

Lauren leaned back on her hands and glanced at Sam. "Sure."

Sam shifted in his chair and avoided looking at her. "Are you two not allowed at the ball or something? Why do you look like that?"

"This is how my face looks," Lauren replied at the same time Sam said, "You aren't allowed to go."

"*What?*" Rory looked between them. "You can't tell me whether I can or can't go to the ball."

"We could," Sam reminded her. "But we wouldn't. Caius is another story."

"I'm going," she stated, leaving no room for argument. "I worked the last ball, and I won't miss this one, too."

Sam stayed silent, and Lauren rose from the bed. "We'll let you eat. Tell the guard if you need anything else." She grabbed Sam's arm and pulled him up. He grumbled as he extracted his arm from her grip and called on his wings.

They left Rory staring after them, fuming at the nerve of Caius. Bellina opened the door, already dressed for Asher's party, and motioned to Rory's shift. "Why aren't you dressed yet? I can't do your hair and makeup if you're not dressed."

Rory grinned, her annoyance pushed aside, and she and Bellina fell into easy chatter as they got her ready.

Tonight, nothing would dampen her mood.

When Rory walked into the banquet room, Asher spotted her immediately and jogged over. The room was huge, and had he waited for her to come to him, they'd be there all night. His arms spread wide to wrap around her, but a shadow caught his arm.

Rory and Bellina jumped as the shadow dissolved, and annoyance soon replaced Rory's shock. Swiveling her head from side to side, she looked for the king, but came up short.

"Where is he?" she asked mindlessly.

Asher cleared his throat, and when she turned back to him, he pointed at himself. "This is my party, and I demand all your attention." His boyish grin made her laugh, and she carefully wrapped her arms around his middle.

"That's more like it." He smiled down at her and steered

them to their other friends. Bellina got there first, chatting animatedly with Tallent.

Cat whistled. "Damn, you look bad."

"Cat," Kit hissed. "What is wrong with you?"

Cat and Kit started arguing, and Max gave Rory a single nod. "Glad to see you up and around."

"Thanks, Max." She removed herself from under Asher's arm and patted the old man on the shoulder. "I don't think I'll be helping in the gardens any time soon."

He chuckled and pulled on his suspenders he'd paired with a bow tie. "You can take over when I'm gone."

The chatter in their group died down, and they all remembered why they were there. "Shit, Ash. We're going to miss you," Kit said solemnly.

Asher swallowed and nodded, and when he spoke, his voice cracked. "I've been waiting for this day for decades. I should be happy."

"But you're not," Bellina pointed out. She ran a soothing hand down his arm. "You'll be free, and you'll get to see your family."

"I've been here for a long time, Bell. I don't know what I'm walking into."

"I don't know what it was like thirty years ago, or I'd tell you the differences," Rory said. "But you can rest well, knowing the notorious Butcher is off the streets."

His smile was tight, and when he looked at her, his eyes shone. "I hope word gets around how great you are."

"It will," a man's voice said from behind them. "Sera and I will make sure of that." Bruce stood a respectful distance away and tipped his head at Rory. "I only regret that I won't remember meeting you." He looked at Asher before turning to leave. "Take care out there."

When he was out of earshot, Cat asked around a mouthful of food, "Why'd you invite the new guy?"

Asher scratched his jaw and looked in Bruce's direction. "He seems like a good guy, and he's come in to work on our plumbing at the shop."

"Where did you live in Erdikoa?" Rory asked Asher.

"Right outside of The Capital with my parents," he replied. "Hopefully, they're still alive. I'll go see them first. Once I find a job, I'll get my own place."

"What do you want to do?" Bellina asked.

"I haven't given it much thought," he admitted. "What's the point when I won't remember, anyway?"

The longer Rory was here, the more she understood the only true punishment to be found in Vincula was knowing you would lose a chunk of your memories. Some, like herself, would be here an entire lifetime and have no recollection.

It terrified her, and by the look on Asher's face, it terrified him, too.

After a few hours of mingling, laughing, and drinking a little too much, Rory's body felt the effects of being out too long. Everything ached, and she hoped Bellina found potions at the pharmacy to heal her smaller injuries.

"It's time for you to leave, Miss Raven," Caius' voice said over her shoulder.

Those around her stopped talking and watched the king as he placed a hand on her lower back to guide her. She hadn't seen him in days, and her irritation flared.

"I don't want to leave yet," she fibbed, determined not to let him control her more than necessary.

Shadows curled around her arm opposite Caius and assisted him in leading her away. "Wait," she protested. "I need to tell Asher bye."

Caius' eyes hardened as they ticked to Asher before he nodded once. Rory hugged Asher's neck, and he wound his arms loosely around her middle. "I'll miss you enough for both of us," she whispered in his ear, and he nodded into her shoulder.

"I may not remember you," he whispered back. "But when I see your face or hear your name, my soul will know you're good."

She pulled back and swiped a tear from her cheek.

Caius' hand found her back once more and directed her to the exit. "Did you fuck him?"

Rory's eyes narrowed. "How is that any of your business?"

"Everything involving you is my business," he replied smoothly. "Answer the question."

"If I said yes, what would you do?" she asked, raising her brows.

He fisted the back of her dress and pulled her closer, his lips brushing against her ear as they walked. "I would fuck you until the only name you remembered was mine. Do not tease me, Miss Raven."

She stopped. "I haven't seen you in days and before that, you were an asshole. What gives you the right to say those things to me?"

He was silent as he watched her, and shadows swirled across the ground as his intensity grew. "Are you saying you don't think about it? That it's not what your body has craved since the moment we met?"

The words were confident, and the look on his face never

wavered. She hated he was right, hated that his words made her wetter than she'd ever been. What was it about him? Why did she believe his declaration of not killing either of their sisters? Why was she asking herself so many questions again? She annoyed herself.

Like the names of colors, her soul just *knew*. Her body wanted him despite the way he treated her, and it made her grit her teeth.

"I cannot control my body's reactions, but I can control my actions. You will never touch me again," she seethed, angry with herself more than anything.

The bastard smirked. "Haven't you learned? I know when you're lying."

She wanted to stomp her foot and demand he believe her. "Your words are honey, but your actions reek of shit because you are full of it. No woman wants a man who treats her like an insignificant ant, not even if he is a king."

With all the dignity she could muster, she threw open the door to his office, pissed it was the only entrance she could use to the sky room. She left him standing in the hall, and to her disappointment, he let her.

Caius watched Rory leave with her head held high, and while her words were harsh, her determination to resist him made his cock harden against his zipper. His feisty little mate with a savagely dangerous streak was no longer someone he could resist.

When she was hurt, his entire existence narrowed to her and only her. Sam's words ran through his mind on repeat, and for the first time, he considered approaching his sister for help about Gedeon.

When his brother framed him for Atarah's murder, Adila refused to allow him to defend himself, but what if he could make her listen this time around?

The morning of Atarah's murder, Caius was in Erdikoa, hungover from the night before.

His brother went out with them, and when Caius woke up the next day, it was almost lunchtime. The woman he'd fucked in the bar's bathroom was nowhere to be seen, despite him usually bringing his women back to his room for more.

He had no recollection of the end of the night.

His head was killing him, and after drinking a pitcher of water and showering away his hangover, he donned his signature black button-up shirt, black pants, and silver rings.

He left his room in search of his brother to ask him what happened and saw Gedeon standing at the end of the long hallway dressed in the same outfit as Caius.

Caius remembered thinking it was odd because where he was all dark colors and silver accents like his palace, Gedeon was the golden child, dressed in light colors and gold.

Caius followed him, and by the time he rounded the corner and entered the only door in the hallway, which led to the throne room, his heart plummeted. Atarah lay on the ground with a dagger in her heart, and her dead, glassy eyes looked back at him.

Caius raced across the room and fell to his knees to feel for a pulse, knowing he would find none. One hand wrapped around the dagger and the other braced on her chest as he pulled the weapon out and inspected it.

His vision tunneled when he realized it was his dagger their father gifted him when he came of age, and as he climbed to his feet, a maid stepped into the room and screamed. When his eyes met hers, she turned and ran, and when the Lux Palace legion ran into the room and caught him red-handed, he knew he'd been set up.

And he knew Gedeon was to blame.

He couldn't let his brother get away with killing Atarah and framing him.

Caius finding his *Aeternum* complicated things, but maybe it didn't have to. If he could make Adila understand, he could have his cake and eat it too.

At least, he hoped. But revenge was a powerful motivator, more so than fear or greed, and if Adila wouldn't hear him out, he would send Gedeon to hell himself.

Even if it meant going with him.

CHAPTER 30

Lauren stepped through the office entrance to the sky room and held out a piece of paper to Rory. She grabbed it from the woman who was becoming her friend and scanned the words written in haste.

Rory,
The oversized buzzard won't let me in. I guess your royal
boyfriend hasn't changed his mind about letting you attend
the ball. Tell him to fuck off for me. The bird, too. I'll be back
tomorrow, and if the brute doesn't let me in, I will light his
wings on fire.
-Bellina

Rory both laughed and huffed with frustration. "Tell me again why the mighty king is keeping me locked in this sunny cage?"

Lauren shook her head. "Because he thinks you are a fragile bird."

"I'm not a bird." She tucked the paper into the book Caius had left beside the bed. "I'm a *Seraphim*-damned serial killer, and I am two seconds away from murdering him next."

Lauren threw her head back with a laugh. "A fragile bird you are not." Her voice took a serious turn. "Let him fuss over you in his own way, at least while you're still recovering. If he's still hovering when you're back to normal, I'll help you kill him myself."

Rory eyed Lauren suspiciously. The *Angel* knew something about the king Rory didn't, and if there was anything she hated more than being coddled, it was being left in the dark.

"The plus side of the ball being tonight is that there is no one in town, and your warden has given Sam and me the okay to take you out for dinner," Lauren told her. "Get dressed. Sweats and a t-shirt will do since no one will see you."

"He'll allow me to walk through town but not down the stairs to the ball?" she asked incredulously.

"It isn't the walking he's worried about," Lauren corrected. "It's the people. Someone tried to kill you, and while I think it's unfair to keep you from the celebration, his worries are valid."

Rory grumbled as she changed out of her pajamas. She had comfortable sleep shorts and tank tops brought in from town, and since she didn't leave her room all day, she never changed.

She slipped on the long, soft dress Bellina bought for the ball and left her hair down. She forewent the makeup because she hated taking it off at night.

"I said sweats and a t-shirt," Lauren said, looking Rory up and down.

"Bellina bought this dress for tonight, and I'm going to wear it." She refused to let it go to waste, and next Plenilune, she would get a more appropriate dress for the ball.

She sighed long and loud. "Lead the way, jailer."

Lauren flipped her hair over her shoulder and opened the door. "You say that like I'm not actually your jailer."

Sam grinned from the doorway. "She's no more an inmate than you or I."

His words piqued Rory's interest because they were the farthest thing from the truth, and Sam didn't lie. She studied the *Angel* carefully, and he lifted a blonde brow. "Why are you staring at me?"

She chuckled. He was incapable of lying because he was blind to all social cues. "I was admiring your flowing locks. What products do you use?"

Lauren barked out a laugh and looked at Sam knowingly. "Don't say a word," he warned, but it only made her grin wider.

"Smell his hair," she said to Rory.

Rory hesitated for a second before turning to Sam. "Let me smell your hair." She reached for a handful, but he pawed her hand away.

"You are not smelling my hair," he replied, and shot Lauren a warning glare.

"He uses strawberry mango scented conditioner for dry hair," she said in a sing-song voice, and once Rory was over the shock of it all, she bent over laughing so hard her eyes watered, ignoring the pain.

Sam crossed his massive arms and glared at Rory, who

had her hands on her knees trying to catch her breath, and Lauren, who was grinning like a cat. "We are going to be late," he said as he led them into the hallway.

Lauren motioned for Rory to follow as they both tried to hold in their laughter.

"Do they have potions at the pharmacy to heal my bruises and sore muscles?" Rory asked them as they walked through town.

"No," Sam said a little too quickly, and Rory narrowed her eyes at him. He was lying, meaning he *could* lie, he was just terrible at it.

"You're lying," she accused, and turned to Lauren. "Tell me the truth, or I'll be as difficult as mystically possible."

Lauren's lips pressed together as she side-eyed Sam, who shook his head. With a sigh, she said, "Yes."

Rory stopped and stared at the two. "What the fuck? Why can't I have some? I have—" She held up her hands for finger quotes. "Unlimited credits, remember?"

"That is not our business to tell," Sam said curtly.

"What does that mean?" Rory demanded. "Whose business is it?" Before she finished her sentence, she knew the answer. "Caius."

Lauren and Sam were quiet, and Rory stalked off. "I'm going to the pharmacy, and if you try to stop me, I will break everything I can get my hands on." Rory didn't know what her own threat meant. Windows? Decorations? Bones? She spewed the first thing that came to mind, but she would keep her promise somehow.

They didn't stop her, and when she pushed on the door,

it didn't budge. She whipped around and stared at them. "Open it."

Sam shrugged with a smug look on his face. "Can't. Everything is closed for the ball."

Rory's anger rose until she thought her head would explode, and she looked around, smiling, when she spotted a small sign advertising the specials of the café next door.

She grabbed it, against the protests of her muscles, and swung it as hard as she could against the glass door. Lauren jumped forward to stop her, but she was too late.

The glass shattered, and Rory used the sign to knock enough away to step through.

"For aether's sake," Sam said. "What is wrong with you?"

She lifted her hand above her head and gave him the universal sign for *fuck you*.

Moving her head side to side as she walked up and down the aisles, she spotted the healing section. "Bruises," she read aloud and grabbed the bottle from the shelf. Ignoring the exasperated sighs of the others, she popped the lid and drained the bottle, not bothering to read the directions.

Gagging, she tossed the empty bottle to Sam, who begrudgingly caught it. She found one for surface wounds, chugged it, and tossed it to a pissed off Sam as she walked farther down the aisle. "Aha!" she said with a wicked grin as she grabbed a potion for muscle aches and drank it dry.

Without another word, she walked around them and toward the door as the potions worked their magic. Within minutes, her bruises faded, her cuts healed, and her body moved freely.

"We're going back to the palace," she informed them, leaving no room for argument.

Rory was too mad to go to the ball and slammed the door to her room open, but when she stormed inside, her steps faltered. Aside from the full moon and stars lighting up the ceiling, there was music playing from a small radio, and against the far wall sat a table with champagne, wine, and finger foods.

Caius, who was fixing his hair, stopped at the sound of her dramatic entrance, and his eyes ate her alive. When they made their way to her face, his mouth pulled into a half smile. "You are beautiful when you're mad." He crossed the room to where she stood. "I knew the ball was important to you, so I made you your own."

She closed her mouth, but before she could say anything, Bellina, Max, Kit, Tallent, and Cat strolled through the door. "Are we late?" Cat asked. "You said six o'clock."

Caius' eyes moved to Sam and Lauren, who stood silently to the side. "You're on time. Rory is early."

Sam shook his head once and scratched his jaw. "I didn't give them a choice," Rory snapped, remembering why she was mad. She ignored the twinge in her chest at the thoughtfulness of the king. "Why did you keep the healing potions from me?"

Caius stepped back, but his gaze never left hers. "I think the rest of you should leave."

To Rory's surprise, they gave no argument as they slipped into the hallway and shut the bookshelf. "Well?" she demanded. "Did you enjoy seeing me in pain?"

Hurt flitted across his face. "Is that what you think?"

"What other reason could you possibly have?" she yelled, no longer able to rein in her temper. The potions had kicked in, and she felt no physical pain.

His face morphed to mirror hers, but where she lost

control of her anger, he was unnervingly calm. "Had you taken the pain potion as prescribed, you wouldn't have been in pain as long as you took it easy, and I needed you to stay put."

Stay put? "What kind of bullshit is that? I'm not a bird to be kept in a cage." She was furious. "Were you tired of seeing me minding my business around the palace and decided to lock me away?"

He laughed humorlessly. "Someone tried to kill you, Rory, or did you forget?" He closed the distance between them. "You will put yourself in danger time and again, and I can't allow that to happen."

His words shocked her, but the last part pissed her off. "You don't have the power to *allow* me to do anything."

The muscle in his jaw ticked. "Fine. I can't *watch* you do that."

"Can't, or don't want to?" she shot back, still angry.

"I can't," he said softly. "I would set this entire realm ablaze to keep you safe, and if you think I'm bluffing, you haven't been paying attention."

"Let's not jump to mass murder," she said, holding a hand up. "I can take care of myself, and I promise you, I will look behind me before I bolt down a set of stairs again."

His nonchalant shrug set her teeth on edge. "I meant what I said. You aren't safe here, and it's my fault. Let me protect you."

"No," she said flatly. "Why the sudden change of heart?"

He stepped closer without answering. "Dance with me."

Her confusion was palpable. "Did you hit your head?"

"Dance with me, Aurora," he said, his voice low.

Hearing him call her by her full name again made her

feel things she didn't want to acknowledge. It was only a month ago she was planning to seduce and murder him, and when he chased her through the gardens, something shifted between them.

Something they both tried to fight and failed miserably. She knew she could fall into him as easily as she forgave him. It wasn't like her, and bit by bit she felt as though she was losing herself and finding herself all at once.

"Did I lose you?" he asked, breaking through her thoughts. His words had a double meaning, and they both knew it.

Instead of answering, she draped her arms around his neck, and he splayed one hand on her back, pulling her close enough to taste her breath, and every place their bodies touched burned in the best way.

As they swayed to the music, barely moving from their spot, he pulled her even closer and bent his head to rest on hers. No words were exchanged, not even as his hand moved lower and rested at the bottom of her spine.

"Do you want this?" he murmured, and she detected a hint of apprehension in his voice.

"No," she whispered, and he tensed in her arms. "And yes."

She felt him relax, and after placing a gentle kiss on her hair, he said, "It was inevitable. Your soul calls to mine and mine to yours. We couldn't fight this if we tried."

She pulled her head back and met his intense gaze. "You speak as though we are soulmates. I don't love you, Caius, and if you love me, you fall in love too quickly."

His throaty laugh made her stomach clench, and when his eyes returned to hers, they danced with amusement. "I don't love you, but I want you. One way or another, you will be mine."

Her brows drew together. "You're speaking in riddles."

He pulled her close again. "I know."

She laid her head on his shoulder and let the music take her away. It was the least chaotic her life had been in some time, and she worried he was luring her into a false sense of calm.

She could feel his heart beating hard against his chest, and shadows curled through the air, moving against her skin in a sensual caress, and with each brush of nothingness, her body reacted.

The hand holding hers ran achingly slow down her arm to her side, skimming the side of her breast on its way to her hip. Her body craved him, and she pushed back, moving her hand to his chest.

The heat in his eyes made her breath hitch. "You're quiet."

"Do you miss my voice, Miss Raven?" he asked in a low timbre, making her shiver. He leaned forward and pressed his lips to her ear. "I don't think you could handle what is running through my mind."

Her pussy throbbed, and she turned slightly, making her lips brush his cheek. "Maybe I can."

He dropped his head to the crook of her neck and placed a feather-light kiss on her bare skin. "I'm wondering what your skin tastes like." His warm tongue moved against her pulse. "Better than I imagined."

Her breathing picked up, and she would have been embarrassed if she wasn't turned on as he continued, "I'm remembering you in the garden as your knees gave out, and my name crossed your lips."

His finger slipped under one of her cotton straps and slipped it off her shoulder. "I want to know what your pussy looks like when it's wet and craving my touch." She adjusted her stance, needing the friction. "Will your nipple pebble in my mouth, or is it already hard?"

He removed her other strap and tugged lightly. Her breasts were small and unable to hold up her loose top, and when it fell to her waist, Caius looked down and licked his lips. "Already hard, I see."

"Touch me," she begged, hating how much control he had over her. His thumb grazed the peak of her breast, and she moved closer for more contact.

"But what I can't stop thinking about," he said in a husky voice. "Is your mouth."

With that, his hands grabbed the sides of her neck and tilted her head as he descended on her. She expected the kiss to be rough, but it was slow and sensual, and one of his hands slid to the back of her head, threading through her hair as the other on her throat squeezed ever so slightly.

His tongue was smooth as it moved with hers, and when he nipped at her bottom lip, a long moan escaped her. "There's the sound I love," he crooned, smiling against her lips.

He stepped back, motioning to her dress. "This has to go." When the words left his mouth, shadows pulled the fabric to the ground, exposing her panties and sandals.

His eyes roamed her nearly naked form. "Come here," he ordered, and while her self-respect demanded she resist, her body obeyed.

He kneeled in front of her to remove her sandals, and when he looked up at her, he grabbed the sides of her panties to ease them down. She smirked down at the king and said, "I enjoy seeing you on your knees, Your Grace."

A low chuckle rumbled through his chest as he stood and moved to her dresser. When he returned, he held out a shift and signaled for her to hold her hands up. Her brows shot to her hairline as he slipped the nightgown over her head. Was this some sort of fantasy of his?

His fingers worked at the buttons on his shirt, and after he shrugged it off, he removed the rest of his clothes, save for his boxer briefs. Grabbing the corner of the bedding, he pulled it back and gestured for her to climb in. "Lie down."

Once again, she obeyed. After tucking her in, he crawled in beside her, tucked her into his side, and sent a shadow to turn out the lights.

The music still played, and she waited for him to move his hand lower, but he only pulled her closer. "What are we doing?" she asked, trying to twist to see his face.

He kissed the back of her neck and said, "Sleeping."

"The fuck we are," she growled. Her body wriggled in his hold as she tried to sit up, but his arms tightened. "You can't work me up and then tell me to *sleep*."

She felt his smile against her neck and the erection against her ass, but he didn't reply.

Reaching her arm back, she clutched his dick, making him jump. "I would love nothing more than to fuck you until you walk with a limp, but only this morning you were limping for a completely different reason."

"I took a million different potions," she protested. "There's no pain anywhere in my body, unless you count the ache between my thighs."

He laughed as his hand moved south. When he reached

the bottom of her shift, his fingers moved like silk up her bare thigh, and she swore if he stopped, she would die.

His voice was rich when he whispered against her hair, "Is this what you want, Miss Raven?"

"Yes," she breathed.

His finger reached her clit but surpassed it to slide through her arousal. He dug his head into her neck and made an animalistic sound. "Fuck, you're soaked."

She moved against his hand, wanting him to touch her more, and he obliged by moving his fingers through her folds to circle her clit. His touch was feather light as he rubbed lazy circles, and she moved her hips for more pressure.

His other arm snaked under her, pinning her arms as his hand flattened across her hip to keep her still, and she whined. "I need more."

"You need to rest," he replied in a dark voice. "But you said your pussy ached, and I can't have that."

His fingers moved to her entrance, and one plunged inside while the heel of his palm ground against her clit, making her body jolt. Torturously slow, his finger moved in and out, curling toward her stomach to hit the sensitive spot there.

"Shit," she panted as she tried to move her hips to no avail.

"Tell me," Caius murmured. "When I stroke your sweet little cunt with my hand, do you wish it was my tongue or my dick in its place?"

Her nipples begged to be touched, and her clit demanded more pressure, but she could pacify neither in his hold. "What makes you think I don't want your hand?"

He inserted another finger, and she gasped. Like the night in the gardens, this was torture. Her body hummed with need, and the buildup was so slow it was hard to stay still. She wanted to go in every direction, and her skin needed to be touched everywhere.

She was alight with anticipation as his fingers dragged in and out, his palm rubbed up and down her clit in the softest of ways, and his breath fanned across her face.

"No one likes the fingers best," he answered with another smile. "The fingers remind your body of what it can have, but only deliver a fraction of what you need."

He added a third finger, and she bucked. His fingers were large, and they stretched her as much as an average man would, only they curved. "Fuck," she moaned.

"Which is it?" he asked again. "Tell me what you want, and I'll give it to you."

His strokes picked up, and she almost cried with relief. "I want to come," she begged. "I don't care how."

He hummed against her hair. "I do." His movements slowed again.

"No," she whimpered. "Inside of me," she stammered through the torment. It didn't hurt, but it was indescribable.

"Mmm," he hummed again. "I can be inside you in a variety of ways. I'm inside you right now." He pulled his index finger out and pushed his middle two fingers in as far as they would go, making her cry out.

She panted hard, and words evaded her. Not being able to move was frustrating; not being able to touch her breasts was frustrating; everything about the situation was frustrating, but she never wanted him to stop.

"Your..." she tried to say what she craved but couldn't get the words out.

"My what, Miss Raven?" His fingers delved deep as they pumped.

"Cock," she rushed. "I need it inside me *now.*"

"I want to *fuck* you," he said, emphasizing his meaning. "But I can't do that when you are recovering."

She shook her head. "I'm fine."

His fingers retracted from her body, and his other hand loosened its hold. Rory breathed a sigh of relief mixed with exasperation and immediately shot one hand to her breast and the other to her clit.

"None of that," Caius reprimanded as shadows grabbed her arms and pulled them above her head. He rolled his body to hover over hers as his eyes roamed over her shift. He sat back, grabbed the neckline of her dress, and ripped it down the middle.

"I'll go slowly this once," he said. "But rest assured, the next time I have you naked, I will fuck you like the savage you are."

Her eyes moved from his chest to his face, and it became clear. He knew who she was, completely, and he wanted her anyway. It was her biggest fear that those important to her would recoil at her true nature. She had friends, but they would never understand.

All she could do was nod, and something passed between them. Tonight, something would shift more than ever, and they both knew there was no turning back.

He lowered himself and aligned with her entrance. When he slid in, she stretched as they both moaned.

"Fuck," Caius said hoarsely as Rory lifted her hips to meet his. He moved, and the feel of him inside her, on top of her, *with* her was a feeling like no other.

She reached for her breasts again, needing to give them the attention they'd demanded, but the shadows held fast.

"Tell me," he commanded. "Tell me what you want."

"I want you to touch me," she whimpered.

"Where, Rory?"

Her name on his lips had her eyes turning to his again. Taunting her with the formal name was one thing, but hearing him call her by her familiar name was something else entirely. "Everywhere."

His mouth pulled into a half grin. "Use your words."

"My nipples," she said finally. "I need you to touch my nipples." She felt foolish when the words left her mouth, but she was rewarded with his hot tongue pulling her breast into his mouth.

The feeling of his mouth running across the sensitive skin was what she wanted, but she needed more. When he switched to the other side, she tossed her head back.

He was still moving in and out of her with long strokes when she said, "My clit. I need to touch my clit."

He smiled against her skin and looked up. "Very good." One of his large hands trailed down her stomach until it was where she wanted it. His thrusts came faster, working in tandem with his thumb.

Rory's chest was heaving. "On top," she said, stumbling over her words. "I want to ride you."

"You're a fast learner," he praised, and she preened, loving what his words did to her. She was an independent woman, but here, with him, she was different.

He rolled them over and held her hips as she sat on her knees. "If you need me deeper, tell me."

Nodding, she sank down, and her hands braced on his chest as he filled her, inch by glorious inch. It was cliché for an immortal king to be hung like a horse, but then again, he *was* blessed by the *Seraphim*.

Using her knees, she moved up and down. Feeling him drag against her inner muscles as he bottomed out was unreal. Again and again, his skin moved against hers. Up and down she went, but as her body caught fire with the first signs of an orgasm, she switched to moving back and forth, rubbing her clit against his pelvic bone.

"That's it, baby," he rasped as his golden eyes watched her. His hands never left her hips when he thrust upward, driving deeper.

"Caius," she moaned as she moved faster and he thrust harder, all reservations of treating her with fragility gone. He moved deep inside, and her breasts bounced with each thrust.

Her nipples were diamonds, and her stomach quivered as they moved faster. Her pussy began to spasm, and he cursed as his head pressed against the pillows. She felt his cock pulse, the sensation sending her over the edge.

Rory's cries echoed through the large room as her body turned to jelly, and she lost the strength to hold herself up. Caius sat up, and she wrapped her arms around his neck for support as he moved her hips for her.

She was sensitive, and to feel him moving inside her still was euphoric.

He claimed her mouth, and as his body tightened, he buried his head into her neck and bit down, causing her to release a silent scream. His cum pumped forever as his cock released.

When they both stilled, he lifted her, slid her off his shaft, and set her on the floor.

Placing a kiss on her stomach, he stood and took her face in his hands. "You are beautiful when you come."

"Don't think you can tell me what to do outside of this bed," she warned, making him smile.

"I wouldn't dream of it." She gave him a pointed look, and he added, "Anymore."

She gave his cheek two pats and sauntered to the bathroom to clean up. When the water to the shower was warm, she peeked into the bedroom and crooked a finger at the king. "Come here."

CHAPTER 31

Caius lay on his back, staring at the Erdikoa sky. He knew sleeping with Rory would do him in, and now the bond was a tangible thing between them, like an invisible rope tying them to one another.

He rolled his head to the side and watched her sleep. She would feel it, but the chances of her knowing what it was were slim to none. Sleeping with her before telling her what it would mean was something he swore he wouldn't do.

"Shit," he cursed under his breath. Telling her was his first priority. She deserved to know what was happening between them.

Telling her as soon as she said good morning was best, but he considered having Sam there as a buffer. Rory was terrifying in her own right.

Movement next to him broke him from his thoughts, and when Rory turned over with a tired smile, his chest constricted. "We need to talk," he blurted out. *Damnit.*

A frown pulled at her sleepy smile, and once she processed his words, she bolted upright.

"What the fuck, Caius?" she hissed. "If you tell me this was a mistake or one of your sick games, I'm leaving the palace."

He sat up too and held up his hands. "Not at all. The opposite, actually, but it might piss you off." He was nervous.

She scrubbed her hands over her face. "You're not making sense."

Running a hand through his hair, he stood and grabbed his pants, pulling them on.

"You son of a bitch," she seethed as she grabbed a pillow and hurled it at him. "Say what you have to say."

"I'm only dressing in the event you kick me out," he said calmly.

"Is that supposed to make me feel better?" She scoffed. "Spit it out."

"You're my *Aeternum*," he informed her.

Her eyes flared. "Is that some kind of sex slave?"

He closed his eyes at her ridiculous assumptions. She still thought so little of him, which made this worse. "An *Aeternum* is a *Royal's* eternal mate."

She blinked. "Come again?"

His arm threaded through the sleeve of his shirt to shrug it on. "You're my mate." He met her wide gaze. "Our souls were made for one another."

Her silence was worse than yelling, and he finished buttoning his shirt before tucking it into his pants. "Last night when we had sex it, uh..." The next words choked out of him. "It solidified the bond."

Rocks moved more than she did. The shoes he'd worn were half under the bed, and he was leery to turn his back to her to grab them. "I didn't want to have sex with you until I explained the repercussions, but I—"

"Trapped me," she accused, cutting him off. Her stoic expression shifted slightly but gave away nothing.

"No," he hurried. "No. I wasn't thinking clearly." He hesitated. "But yes. I would never force you to marry me, but now that the bond is in place, your soul will need mine, and mine will need yours."

"What else?" she demanded, her voice holding authority that made his pants tighten uncomfortably. *There's my girl who might kill me,* he thought.

"If you are away from me for too long, you will dream of me every time we are asleep at the same time." He swallowed. "We'll meet in our soulscape. You can never truly escape me nor I you."

"What is a soulscape?" she asked, her voice leaning more toward curiosity than anger.

He sighed and sat in a chair. "It's a place where our souls meet when we're asleep at the same time. We've been in the soulscape before, but we don't remember. They start when we are both of age." He rested his elbows on his knees and looked at her. "But now that the bond is solidified, we'll remember the soulscape vividly as though we met in person."

"This is what you meant," she surmised. "When you said we would love each other." She scrambled from the bed. "Why didn't you tell me then?"

Nothing scared the Umbra King, but her rejection did. "I didn't think it was time," he answered honestly.

She nodded. "You're right. Telling me after attaching me to you for life was a much better option." Her eyes promised a painful death.

"It wasn't supposed to happen this way," he said through gritted teeth, standing. "And if you remember correctly, you begged me to fuck you." He was towering over her now. "You are beautiful and sexy, and you were so wet for me, pleading for me to be inside you." Her chest was heaving as they stood toe to toe. "I lose myself with you, and I lost myself last night."

"You're blaming me?" she yelled.

He backed up. "No. Not at all. I blame *myself*, but I don't want you thinking I did this to trap you on purpose." He crossed the room and opened the door. "If you think I would force you to be with me, then you don't know me at all. It was a mistake."

She sucked in a sharp breath, and something akin to hurt crossed her face.

"Not being with you," he amended. "I would fuck you every hour of the day if I could, and I want nothing more than to fall in love with you. But I regret forgetting myself." He stepped through the door and paused. "My contract is up shortly, and I will stay in Erdikoa until yours is too if that's what you want; and in the soulscape, I will leave you be. This bond does not make you love me, but your soul *was* made to love mine, and it will want to."

Caius closed the door and took the long hallway to his office in search of Sam. He needed to have a drink with his oldest friend and forget the look on Rory's face.

∾

Rory gawked at the bookcase. "Fuck that."

She jogged to the door and jabbed the button. "Caius, you prick, get back here!"

He halted his retreat and turned around. "What can I help you with, Miss Raven?"

"Don't '*Miss Raven*' me," she fumed. "Get back in here and talk to me."

"What more is there to say?" he asked, and while his words were confident, there was a flicker of something else in his eyes.

"You talked *at* me. I deserve to say my piece and have my questions answered. Get back in here."

He ran a hand through his unkempt hair and trekked back to her room, pushing the button to close the door once they were both inside. "What questions do you have?"

"What did you mean?" she asked, lowering her voice from the shrill yell it had been. "When you said our souls were made for each other, what did you mean?"

He sighed and sat at the small table, gesturing for her to do the same. Once she was sitting in front of him, he leaned back and drummed his fingers on the wood. "Exactly what I said. When a *Royal* is born, they are born with an incomplete soul."

"You only have half a soul?" She huffed out a laugh. "That explains a lot."

He scowled at her. "I have a whole soul." His eyebrows drew together as he searched for the right words. "It's like a blank puzzle. All the pieces are there, but the picture is missing. The picture makes it better and complete."

What he said made sense. Kind of. "And I'm a picture without a puzzle? That doesn't seem so bad. There are tons of pictures without puzzles."

He pinched the bridge of his nose, and she fought a smile. "I am a book without a story, and you are a story without a book."

"There are a lot of stor—"

"Damnit, Rory." He was around the table and caging her in before she could blink. "You can give yourself an orgasm." He leaned his head down so his lips brushed her ear, something she'd come to love. "But I can make you scream." *That* she understood. "You were made for me, and I was made for you, whether you like it or not."

He pushed off her chair and moved away from her. "I will not force myself on you, but what I say is the truth. Take it or leave it."

She crossed her legs and cursed herself for not putting panties on before charging after him. The wetness between her legs would likely show on the seat if she stood. Damn him and his filthy mouth.

She cleared her throat and lifted her chin. "What now?"

Surprise flickered across his face. "What do you mean?"

She hiked a shoulder. "What do we do now? How would this normally play out?"

It caught him off guard, and she smirked. "You don't know, do you?"

"My parents and my father's siblings were already married when my siblings and I were born. Gedeon and Adila have not yet met their *Aeternums*, nor had Atarah. I've never seen it play out," he admitted.

They stared at each other, neither knowing what to say. "Well," Rory said at last. "I suggest you get very good at wining and dining me if you want me to love you."

He lifted his eyes to hers. They darkened as his pupils pushed out the gold. "And fucking you." His arrogant smirk returned, and she found she'd missed it.

Standing, she nonchalantly checked the chair and ran her hand down the back of her shift before turning to him with an appraising look. "We both know you've mastered that."

She left him standing in her room and shut herself in the bathroom. If she was being courted, she needed to look damn good.

When Rory emerged from her shower, Caius was gone, but in his place was Bellina.

The seamstress took a bite of the pastry in her hand and smiled. "Good morning. Why does it smell like sex in here?"

Rory kept a blank expression. "I don't know what you're talking about."

"Bullshit," Bellina shot back. "Here." She held out a second pastry, and Rory plucked it from her friend's hand.

"It was the king," Bellina said with confidence. "I knew you two would get together, eventually."

Rory clenched her towel tighter and sat beside Bellina. "You won't believe the shit storm that was this morning."

Bellina swallowed the last of her food. "Tell me everything."

Rory covered her face and lay back on the bed. "Apparently, I'm Caius' eternal mate."

Her friend stared at her like she'd grown a second head. "What?"

"You heard me," Rory replied. "He called it..."

"*Aeternum*," Bellina finished for her. She looked at Rory like she saw her in a new light. "I read about them once in an old fairy tale book. I thought it was made up."

Rory threw her arm across her eyes. "I thought Samyaza was made up, and we've all seen him peacocking around the palace."

"That's rude," a baritone voice said from the open doorway, making Bellina and Rory jump.

"Everyone in this palace needs to wear a bell," Rory snapped, making Sam grin. "Have you ever knocked a day in your ancient life?"

Sam waltzed across the room, put away his wings, and sat down. "The door was open."

"Oops," Bellina said sheepishly.

Rory sprang into a sitting position. "Sam, what do you know about *Aeternums*?" The *Angel* froze, and Rory narrowed her eyes. "You knew."

He scratched his jaw, the scruff making the movement audible. "Yes."

"And?" Bellina asked impatiently.

"*And*," he said tersely. "There is nothing else to tell. She is his eternal mate, and once they sleep together, the bond will strengthen." Rory squirmed, and Sam flashed a smug smile. "When you marry, you will become a *Royal*."

Bellina's jaw hit the floor. "As in, an *actual Royal*? Immortality and all?"

Sam nodded as Rory flinched. "Why do you look as if you will faint?" he asked her.

She motioned wildly. "Immortal? Do you know how long that is?"

He gave her a look that told her he knew exactly how long it was. "You are already set to live another five-hundred years at least," he pointed out. "Why are a few hundred more unsettling?"

"Wait," Bellina said, holding up a hand. "You said she would be immortal."

"She will," he replied. "She will only be able to die by a knife to the heart or decapitation, and she will not age until the new Umbra King or Queen takes the throne."

Rory and Bellina stared at him, and Rory was more

confused now than when the conversation started. "Explain it to me like I'm a child," she said to the giant turkey.

He mumbled something under his breath before obliging. "When the Lux King or Queen finds their *Aeternum*, they will have three children. One will possess the power of light to rule Erdikoa; one will possess the power of darkness to rule Vincula, and one will possess the gift of judgment to become the Scales of Justice. Once they are born, they take the throne at twenty-five years of age, and the current rulers step down."

"What happens to the parents when they step down?" Bellina queried.

"They lose their memories of ever having ruled and receive new memories. They remember their children but think they work in The Capital. It allows their children to still visit them," he explained.

"And when their kids don't age?" Bellina challenged. "This sounds made up."

Sam looked ready to flick her across the room. "They take a shapeshifting potion to make them look older."

"I would lose my memories?" Rory almost cried. How cruel to narrowly escape losing her memories in Vincula, only to lose all of her memories when a new ruler took the throne in Vincula.

"No," Sam said, confusing her. "Only the Lux rulers because their children will already be grown. You and Caius will step down and move out of The Capital to live normal lives, aging like normal and able to have children if you wish."

"Had I known I was getting a history lesson today, I would have brought a pen and paper," Bellina groaned.

"He said he wouldn't make me," Rory forced out, trying

not to freak out. "He said he'd keep his distance, even in the soulscape."

Sam's face turned grim, and Bellina threw her hands up. "What is a soulscape?"

"Is that what you want?" Sam asked, ignoring Bellina.

Rory shrugged helplessly. "I don't know. We agreed to date, but there's no guarantee we'll like each other enough to get married forever." She smoothed a hand down her towel. "Can *Royals* get divorced?"

Sam shook his head. Whether to answer her or because he wanted to throttle her was up for debate.

"When is your first *'date'*?" Bellina asked with a gleam in her eye. "We need to go shopping."

"He didn't ask me out on a date," she replied. "I told him to wine and dine me."

"And sixty-nine," Bellina added, shimmying her shoulders.

"For aether's sake," Sam grumbled as he stood. "I will leave you ladies to it."

"Bye, Sam!" Bellina called after him, wiggling her fingers before turning back to Rory. "Was he any good?"

Laughter bubbled out of Rory at her friend's abrupt change of subject. "The best I've ever had," she confirmed.

Bellina wrinkled her nose. "You've obviously never been with a woman."

Rory snickered and stood to grab clothes. "You were right about shopping. I don't know if or when he'll take me somewhere." She paused. "He doesn't seem the type to take women on dates."

Bellina rose from the bed. "He doesn't, but he took Nina out to dinner."

Rory's jaw locked at the memory of Nina and Caius

together. "If he tries to take me to the same restaurant, I'm not marrying him."

"Feed him to Lo," Bellina suggested. "She likes you."

"Asher is going to..." Rory's voice trailed off, and her chest ached.

Bellina rubbed a hand down Rory's back. "I'm not used to him being gone, either."

"Max leaves next," Rory lamented. "At least I still have you for a bit longer."

Bellina looked thoughtful. "When you marry Caius, does your contract end? And being a *Royal* means you won't lose your memory when you leave."

Rory stilled. *Did it?* She could see her parents, and maybe her friends would speak to her if she were a *Royal*.

"I don't know," she answered. "I'll let you know when I find out."

CHAPTER 32

Caius was nervous, an unfamiliar feeling he experienced often as of late.

"Get out of your head," Sam said as he approached the pond where Caius stood.

"She thought I killed her sister, and while she says she no longer believes it, a small part of her might." There was no reason for her to believe him.

Sam stood beside him with his wings tucked tightly. "Dissolve her doubt."

He said it like it was the easiest task in the realms. "She said my actions didn't match my words." Shadows swirled with his anxiety, and Sam kicked at them.

"That was before yesterday," Sam pointed out.

Caius tried to show her he cared by throwing her the ball and inviting her friends, but when she blew in like a tornado ready to blast him to bits, everything was ruined. Until it wasn't.

Sex with her was unlike any he'd experienced, and now

that the bond was nearly complete, he wanted nothing more than to be near her.

"What if you don't like her?" Sam asked, breaking his thoughts.

Caius turned to his friend. "Repeat that."

"What if you don't like her?" Sam repeated, making Caius laugh. "I am serious. You are worried she will not like you once you get to know each other better, but what if it is the other way around?"

"I know her," Caius told him.

"Perhaps." Sam stood stoically beside him, letting him stew.

"You were sure we would marry, and now you aren't?" Caius shook his head.

"I still believe you will marry," Sam corrected. "But you don't, and thinking you will be the one to let her down is preposterous. Do not feel sorry for yourself."

Caius sighed and looked to the aether. "You're a terrible motivator."

Sam's deep laugh surrounded them. "She said you were to court her." His wings flared slightly. "You have never courted a woman in your life."

Caius' brows drew together. "Yes, I have. I courted women into my bed all the time."

"That is not *courting*, and if you think it is, you will fail." Sam spread his wings and took to the skies.

"Fuck you!" Caius yelled, and Sam's laugh echoed like thunder as he disappeared, presumably to the other realm.

Caius needed something to relieve his stress, and he knew just the thing.

∾

"You're the king's what?" Tallent asked as their group sat around a tall table at the bar.

"His *Aeternum*," Kit said, clearly irritated. "How you guys made it through life without knowing the basic history of our realms is beyond me."

"Not everyone grew up with history experts," Rory snarked. "I don't like to read, anyway."

"The education system needs a reboot," Kit said and threw back a shot.

Cat's hand raised. "I knew."

Bellina choked on her beer. "There is no way you knew what an *Aeternum* was."

Cat pulled her shoulders back. "I'm not an idiot, and I love reading. I wanted to be a teacher."

Everyone stared at her. "You would have killed your students," Tallent informed her. "You nearly killed your brother for messing with your hair."

Cat shrugged. "He deserved it, and I stand by that." She paused. "He was going to use it for an illegal potion."

Everyone was quiet at her admission, and Rory saw her in a new light. "You should have shot him in both legs," she said, making Cat smile.

"This means you'll be our queen," Kit said, getting the conversation back on track. "Do we get special treatment?"

Rory rolled her eyes at her friend. "I will not be your queen."

"Yes, you will," Cat returned. "Did you not know marrying a king makes you a queen?" She squinted at Rory. "Do you know how to read at all?"

Rory threw a balled-up bar napkin at her. "I know how to read." The thought of being a queen made her pits sweat. She fanned her underarms, and Bellina patted her shoulder. "Think of it this way: Nina is going to flip out when she sees you on the throne."

"I bet you can pass between realms," Cat added. "Your sentence would be over."

"You don't know that," Tallent argued. "The king is still bound."

"Not for much longer," Bellina reminded them. "His contract is up in a month or so, isn't it?"

Rory's hope moved like a rollercoaster at the prospect of leaving, and she needed to ask Caius when the time was right.

"Evil bitch incoming," Cat muttered under her breath.

The group turned toward the door, and the women groaned. Nina walked in with the men Rory saw her with in the hallway a while back, and when they saw her, they shot daggers in her direction.

"Sometimes I wonder if she follows me," she whispered. "Everywhere I go, there she is."

"To be fair, the town isn't that large. Do you think she's the one who pushed you?" Tallent asked, glancing back.

Rory took a drink. "I don't think so. Whoever pushed me was strong, and Nina's arms are like limp noodles."

The group busted up laughing, but Rory didn't find it funny. Someone tried to kill her. She needed to spar with someone to brush up on her skills. Next time, she would be ready.

Even though there was nothing she could have done to fight off being shoved from behind, it couldn't hurt to prepare herself.

Bellina bumped her shoulder. "If she tries anything, we'll all beat her ass. Caius may even kill her."

"You think he would?" Rory mused.

"Of course he would," Kit said with a snort. "I don't think you understand the *Aeternum* bond. You would kill for him, too. Especially once you're married."

"*If* we're married," Rory corrected, and Kit shook her head. "Are there any books on *Aeternums* in Vincula's library?"

"I'll look," Kit promised.

Cat was uncharacteristically quiet, and it didn't go unnoticed by Tallent. "What are you thinking about?" he asked her suspiciously.

She looked at Rory thoughtfully. "If someone is trying to kill you, it'd be wise to marry the king as soon as possible. You *will* love him, Rory. It is not damning yourself to a life of misery."

Rory's knuckles turned white as she gripped her glass. "I wish everyone would stop telling me whom I will love. How is that fair?"

Bellina ran a soothing hand down Rory's back. She did that often, her maternal instinct coming out when her friends were upset.

Kit sighed. "You really don't understand."

"Then tell me," Rory snapped.

Kit narrowed her eyes. "The *Aeternum* bond doesn't force you to love him. You would love him anyway, given the opportunity. Your souls were created by the *Seraphim* at the same time, but yours was sent when he needed you most. You're soulmates, and I can't believe I have to explain this."

"Then why is there a bond at all?" Bellina asked. "Why not let nature take its course?"

"The bond connects them like..." Kit searched for the right words. "Like a safety device. They can tell when the other is in danger, and they will always find one another. It connects their souls."

Cat slammed her glass down with a smack. "I can't wait for all of Erdikoa to know The Butcher is the new Prison Queen. Fitting."

Bellina and Rory parted ways at the door to the throne room. She needed to speak with Caius about reopening the outside entrance to her room. It felt ridiculous, taking a secret tunnel.

Not wanting other staff to see her walk into his office, she often took the back entrance behind the dais. When she closed the door to the throne room behind her, the room was dark, and her soft-soled slippers made no sound as she crossed the room.

In the dim lighting, she saw Caius exit the door behind his throne and pound down the stairs toward the door leading to hallways and stairwells. He was only wearing athletic shorts, and her heart skipped at the sight of his muscular back as he pulled on a t-shirt.

She'd only ever seen him in slacks and a dress shirt or pajamas. He looked damn good. She still needed time to process how she was feeling, and instead of calling out to him, she let him leave.

She opened the door to his office, and ice doused her insides. Nina slid off Caius' desk as she buttoned her dress, and when she saw Rory, a smug smile pulled at her lips as she stepped into her shoes and sauntered to the exit.

"You didn't really think you could keep him, did you?" the redhead asked and opened the door with a wicked laugh.

Rory's chest cleaved in two, and white-hot rage filled the canyon. He'd played her. It made her question if she was really even his mate.

She couldn't make heads or tails of it, nor did she understand his motivation for wooing her.

"That jerk!" Screams ripped from her throat as she swiped everything off his desk and smashed anything breakable she could get her hands on.

Next were the books, the ones she worked hard on putting back. They sailed across the room as fast as she could throw them.

Fuck him, and fuck Nina.

Chairs were flipped over, and her last parting shot was opening the drawers to the contracts, ripping them out, and throwing them around like confetti. "Have fun reorganizing those, *Your Grace.*"

As she stood in the middle of the rubble, her shoulders sagged. The staff would clean this, not him, and immediately guilt overcame her. She was too pissed to pick it up now, but she would sneak back once she calmed down to get to work.

Turning on her heel, she marched out of the office toward her old room. If he thought she was sleeping in a room he gifted her after this, he was out of his mind.

When she turned the corner to the staff quarters, she caught Nina in the hallway with the same men. The men didn't work in the palace, or Rory would have seen them. Well, maybe not. The staff was huge, but seeing the three together made unease snake down her spine.

There was a good possibility one of them pushed her, and being alone with them felt like a bad idea. She reversed before they spotted her and snuck back up the stairwell.

Where would she go now? Max and Bellina's rooms were both in the staff quarters, and she didn't know if Max was even home. He hadn't joined them at the bar, and she suspected he was preparing for his departure.

He insisted they not have a party and instead wanted to say a quick goodbye. It made Rory sad.

A few staff greeted her as she snuck through the hallways. Since Bruce's arrival, some treated her better. Others did not. Bruce was due to leave soon, too, and she made a note to seek him out before he left.

Not knowing where else to go, she wandered to the legion quarters and sought Lauren's room. When she knocked, Lauren opened the door with a wide smile, but it dropped at the look on Rory's face.

"What happened?" she asked as she moved aside.

Rory followed her inside and plopped down in a chair. "Caius screwed Nina today."

Lauren's cheeks flushed. "That's not possible."

Rory laughed humorlessly. "It is. He came out of his office shirtless. He didn't see me, and when I walked into his office, Nina was buttoning her dress and bragging about it." She looked miserably at Lauren. "He can rot in hell, and so can she."

Lauren rubbed her forehead. "It must be a misunderstanding. He wouldn't do that."

Rory laid her head back on the chair. "Whatever you say. I'm not staying in the sky room, and when I tried to go to my old room, Nina and two men were whispering in the hall."

"Did they say something to you?" Lauren asked, grabbing her boots.

Rory held out her hand. "No. Calm down." Lauren shot her a look. "I don't recognize the men, but I've seen her conspiring with them a few times. I'm just paranoid."

"Do not underestimate Nina's hate for you," Lauren cautioned. "Stay away from her. She is a manipulative con artist who wants the king."

"She can have him," Rory spat. "He'll never touch me again."

Lauren sat down and rubbed her forehead again. "You're wrong. I don't know what happened, but I have known Caius for a long time, and I know you're wrong."

The conviction with which she spoke caught Rory by surprise. With no other option but to return to the sky room, she stood with a sigh. "Thanks, Lauren. I'll see you around."

"I'm serious about Nina," Lauren called after her. "Stay away from her."

That wouldn't be an issue. The last thing Rory wanted was to see her or the king ever again.

Caius stared wide-eyed at his office. "Damnit, Nina." He'd gone for a run, and when he returned, Nina was perched on his desk with her top undone. It was time to assign her a new job out of the palace. All he'd wanted was to see Rory, and he was met with his biggest mistake instead.

He'd left her in his office to find his head of employment and speak to them about finding Nina a job in town. Leaving her alone with his things was a mistake, and he needed to lock his office every time he left. He'd give Rory a key, and no one else.

Rory burst through his office door, and the tension from Nina's tantrum left at the sight of her. An easy smile pulled at his lips. "Hello, Miss Raven. Did you miss me already?"

The snarl he received in return took him off guard, and he made to grab her as she stormed past, but she slapped his hand away. "Don't touch me." She looked around ruefully. "And don't make the staff clean this. I'll do it."

He looked around, bewildered. "You did this?"

Ignoring him, she continued on to her room, but he threw up a wall of shadows.

"*YOU STUPID FUCKING ASSHOLES! GET OUT OF MY WAY!*" she screamed at the wall. Caius would have laughed if everything wasn't falling apart.

"Rory..."

"Don't," she snapped. "You don't get to call me that."

His mind reeled, trying to remember what he'd done to piss her off. "I don't understand."

She turned dead eyes to him, all the anger gone. It was worse than her rage. "I saw you leaving," she informed him. "Shirtless. Imagine my surprise when I walked into this room to find Nina getting dressed, too."

He tried and failed to control his own building rage. The shadows twisted into the air, and she slapped at them. "Call off your dogs."

"Listen to me," he said in a voice so lethal it would send the bravest of mystics scattering. "I didn't touch Nina. When I returned from my run, she was waiting for me. I told her to get dressed and leave, and I left to have her reassigned."

Rory's mask cracked with a flash of uncertainty, and Caius approached her. "Believe me," he pleaded.

The wheels in her mind turned, and when she looked

back to him, she said two words that gave him hope. "Prove it."

"Come with me," he said, taking her hand.

He marched her through the palace to the staff quarters, blowing open doors with his shadows. "Where is Nina?" he growled to various staff in their rooms.

"She doesn't live here anymore, Your Grace," a maid stammered.

"I am aware," he returned. "But she was in the palace recently. Someone must have seen her."

"She was in the staff quarters earlier," Rory supplied. "With two men."

Caius turned back to the staff gathered in the hall. "Where is she?"

"She left, Your Grace," a man said. "I saw her, Felix, and Vince leave not long ago."

Felix and Vince. He needed to check the files to find out who these men were.

Guiding Rory through the palace, he looked at her as they walked. "How easily you believed the worst of me."

Rory stared straight ahead, her face never betraying her emotions. "I don't know you, Caius."

He gave her hand a light squeeze. "You will."

When they entered Nina's apartment building, he stopped by Linda's office and asked her to call Nina down.

"The king is here for you," the woman's voice said as she made her way back to the front with Nina on her heels.

Another voice echoed through the hall. "The king?" Nina sounded excited. "You didn't give me time to freshen up."

. The woman made a gruff sound. "I don't think it will be necessary."

When Nina rounded the corner of the hall, the excitement drained from her face at the sight of Caius' anger and Rory's presence. "Nina," Caius clipped.

Her eyes darted between Rory and him. "Yes, Your Grace?"

"If you ever lead my *mate* to believe you and I had relations again, I will send you to hell," he snarled as he took a threatening step forward. "Understood?" Rory's spine straightened when he claimed her, and he fought to keep his attention on Nina.

Whether or not Rory wanted to admit it, they were mates, and he would be damned if anyone treated her as anything less than the queen she was.

Nina's face leached of color. "Mate?" She shook her head wildly. "No. No, that's not right. She's been bothering you, and I was *helping*. It was the only way to keep her away from you." She reached for him, but a shadow grabbed her wrist. "You're too kind to tell her yourself," she tried again. Her face was stricken. "You would keep her by your side? A ruthless murderer? What about what we had?"

Before Caius and Nina had a physical relationship, he made it abundantly clear it was purely physical and nothing else. He didn't know why Nina was acting this way.

Her lip wobbled, and she fled, crying, down the hall.

"What was that?" Rory muttered under her breath.

"That," Linda said, "was a delusional girl coming unraveled." She waved and stepped back into the manager's office.

Caius said nothing as he and Rory left, and once on the street, Rory grabbed his arm. "I'm sorry."

"I've given you no reason to trust me," he replied. "But I will."

As they walked through the town, he resisted the urge to grab her hand. He held it on their way to the apartments, but it was more so to drag her. "What did you do in your free time?" he asked her. "Before coming to Vincula."

Without hesitation, she said, "Hang out with my mom and friends." A bit of sadness tinged her voice. How much she missed them was hard to see. He'd always petitioned for inmates to be allowed visitors, but Gedeon denied his request every time.

They weren't allowed letters or phone calls because no one in Erdikoa save for the *Royals* and *Angels* could know anything about the prison realm. Visitors, however, would forget the moment they left. Loved ones were good for the soul, and even the morally grey deserved that.

"What else?" he pressed.

She eyed him. "Most of my time was spent looking for my sister's killer and the *Merrow* who stole her soul. I found the *Merrow*, but he said her soul was with Bane."

He remembered her calling him Bane. "I think I know who killed your sister."

She halted in the middle of the sidewalk. "What?"

"I don't know why, but there is only one explanation why you saw me murder Cora," he explained. She said nothing as she waited for him to continue. "My brother, Gedeon."

Her brows drew together, and her mouth moved, but nothing came out.

"I don't know why he did it, but it had to be him," Caius went on. "There's no other explanation."

"How? My sister and I look alike, but you can still tell the difference," she challenged. "I may not have been able to see colors, but I wasn't blind."

"We're identical twins," he said, causing her to shake her head as if to expel the information. "The Lux *Royals* only ever have three children, but identical twins were once the same embryo that split in half. You couldn't tell the difference between us if you tried."

"That's how he framed you," she realized. He saw the moment her brain put everything together because her features turned from that of shock to one of steel resolve. "When we marry, will my sentence end?"

He didn't know what he expected her to say, but that wasn't it. "No. I can extend a contract, but I can't dissolve them."

"I need you to do something for me," she said with a voice of iron. Everything about her transformed into the woman who appeared on his throne room floor months ago.

"Anything," he replied, wondering if he would regret it.

"When your contract is up, find my sister's soul, and kill him." The fire in her eyes burned brightly. "And before he takes his last breath, let him know I will dance on his grave."

Caius stared at this woman hell-bent on retribution, not caring about salvation so long as she avenged her sister. In that moment, he understood the true meaning of being mates. Her motivations mirrored his own, and he knew, without a doubt, if the roles were reversed, she would hang Gedeon from her hook and watch him bleed for them both.

He pushed a stray hair out of her face. "With pleasure."

Rory slipped her hand into his, and together, they walked toward the palace.

"The gym," she said out of nowhere.

He huffed out a laugh. "What? Are you telling me I'm out of shape, Miss Raven?"

She bit her lip to keep from laughing. "I liked going to the gym."

It didn't surprise him. She wasn't shapely, but her body was lean and toned. "There is a gym in town. Have you been?"

Her hand tightened around his. "I haven't tried. The dining hall is not something I wish to relive."

He hated everyone in the entire realm for treating her this way, and when her throne was built and she sat upon it, he would relish in their fear and awe.

"You can use mine," he offered.

Her lips parted slightly. "You have your own gym?"

He gave her a cheeky grin. "I am king."

"Will you show me?" she asked. "I need to start training in case someone tries to attack me again."

He squeezed her hand. She was right. Her independence and pride meant he wouldn't be able to stay with her every second of the day, nor would she allow a guard. She needed to be able to defend herself. "Sam, Lauren, and I will teach you self-defense."

She bristled, offended. "I know self-defense. My abilities were taken, including my strength and speed, and I need to reacclimate to my new body."

"Who trained you?" If it was a boyfriend, Caius would train her ten times better.

Her eyes grew sad, as they always did when someone from her past life was brought up. Caius would do anything to take that pain away. "Dume, my *Aatxe* friend."

He nodded. "We'll make sure you fend off anyone who tries to hurt you," he promised.

"Thanks." She looked at him with a small smile, and he couldn't help but kiss her on the forehead.

CHAPTER 33

ERDIKOA

Dume, Keith, Kordie, and Sera sat in a corner booth in Whiplash, waiting for Sam. After their first meeting, Sera charged into Whiplash one day, looking for them, and demanded they help her clear Rory's name.

From there, she became a fly, always buzzing around with her bossy attitude, and it drove Dume crazy.

"Where did this guy come from?" Sera asked the group. "I mean, he showed up out of nowhere, demanding information about Rory, and you guys just gave it to him?"

Dume scrubbed a hand down his face. "He said it was to help her."

"What Dume is trying to say is that the guy is terrifying. He's bigger than my truck," Keith chimed in.

Kordie pushed Keith's head playfully. "He's not that big." Keith winked at Kordie and leaned forward to whisper something in her ear, making her blush.

The two were closer than before, and Dume suspected

they were sleeping together at the least, if not in a full-blown relationship.

"Get a room or join the conversation," Sera scolded the two, and they broke apart.

"You're terrifying, too," Keith told the small redhead, and Dume swore something akin to pride shone on her face.

"Good evening," Sam said robotically, appearing from nowhere. How did someone that big move around undetected?

"What kind of mystic did you say you were?" Dume asked him.

"I didn't." Sam sat down beside Sera, and Dume had the urge to make her switch seats. "Who are you?" the giant asked Sera.

"Sera," she said, holding her chin high. "Rory saved me." That was all she said, offering this stranger nothing more, and Sam appraised her before nodding.

"Have you found anything else?" Sam asked, directing his question at Dume.

"Two more victims came forward," Sera answered before Dume could open his mouth. "That's six out of thirteen. Seven if you count me."

Sam's eyes went from Sera to Dume, and Dume saw him fight a smirk. *Smug asshole.* "And what of her mother? Do you still care for her?"

Kordie shook her head. "We are taking care of her the best we can, but she's been... acting out."

Sam leaned back and draped his arm along the booth behind Sera, and Dume's eyes tried to saw it off. "What do you mean 'acting out'?"

Keith rubbed the back of his neck. "Her babbling has gotten worse. She's had a few good days since Rory left, and each one, she tries to leave, saying she has to save Rory."

Sam remained impassive. "She has seen something."

"Before Rory left, she spouted a prophecy," Keith said. "Rory was freaked out by it."

"What was the prophecy?" Sam asked, sitting forward.

"*Two were one, and one is yours. Do not let him fool you. His darkness is poison. Only the golden child can save you,*" Dume recited like an oath. It was still scribbled on Lenora's walls, and he labored over the meaning and how it related to his best friend.

Sam flagged down a server and asked for a pen and paper, jotted down the prophecy, and folded it into his pocket. "Thank you. I will check back for updates." He stood.

"That's it?" Sera asked, scooting out of the booth to stand. "What about Rory? I thought you were going to help her."

Sam towered over Sera, and when he looked down at her, his eyes shone with humor. "Don't worry, little one. I am not one to lie."

Sera told him to fuck off with her expression and sat back down. "Good day, then." She dismissed him as though he were no one, and Dume covered his mouth to smother a laugh.

"I like her," Sam said with a tip of his head before leaving.

"Can you control that mouth of yours before you get yourself killed?" Dume grumped.

"Just because you fear the brute doesn't mean I do," she quipped, making Kordie and Keith laugh.

"What do we do now?" Keith asked.

"We keep looking," Dume replied. "Sera's protests at the enforcer's station and outside The Capital walls are garnering attention. If there are more, they will come forward."

Sera was fierce in her own right and demanded to be heard. Dume had to keep a low profile, but Kordie and Keith attended her rallies, and the turnout was slowly growing as more victims came forward.

"We'll clear her name," Kordie said with conviction. "I just wish she were here to see it."

"My father will tell her what we're doing," Sera assured them. "She'll know she has fighters on the outside."

CHAPTER 34

VINCULA

Rory pounded the pads on Caius' hands, half expecting her arms to fall off. They'd been in the gym for hours, and while she liked Caius' commanding attitude in the sack, she hated it everywhere else, especially in training.

"Good girl," he crooned, taunting her.

She purposefully swung above the pads to knock the smile right off his face, but he blocked it with a laugh. Dropping her gloves, she bent over and put her hands on her knees. Out of shape was an understatement.

"You're not out of shape," Caius said, grabbing them bottles of water.

"Is mind reading a *Royal* ability?" she asked. It would explain how he always knew she was lying.

"I wish," he replied. "Your thoughts are written all over your face."

They both hit the gym showers, and when Rory emerged, Caius' hair dripped down his face.

Her legs ached as she sat down and grabbed a bottle of water. "It sure feels like I'm out of shape."

"You're not used to being weak," he replied, sitting beside her with his feet planted in front of him and his elbows draped loosely around his knees.

As much as his teasing irritated her, he was right. "Where is Sam?" He wouldn't be such an ass during training. She hoped.

"Erdikoa."

She perked up. "Did he check on my mother?" It was foolish to think his trips to Erdikoa were about her, but he checked on Lenora the last time he'd gone.

"We'll find out when he gets back," Caius replied and pulled his shirt over his head.

Still wet from his shower, he was the sexiest man she'd ever seen, and her mouth salivated at the sight. He used his shirt to dry his hair, and she wondered why he didn't just use a towel.

"You can touch me, Miss Raven," he teased in a sensual tone that made her core heat. "I'd prefer if you did." She licked her suddenly dry lips.

His athletic shorts hid nothing as his erection grew, and her fingers ached to run the length of it. She didn't think, just acted, leaning forward, and when he moved his arms, she crawled between his legs.

"How do you want me to touch you?" she purred. "Use your words."

He bit his lip, and his strong jawline begged to be licked, and that was precisely what she did. He groaned, and his dick poked her stomach through his shorts.

When she was at his neck she whispered, "Tell me, Caius. What do you want?"

He grabbed her wet hair and tilted her head back. "I want these," he said, running his tongue along her lips. "Wrapped around my cock. I want my head to hit your throat so hard you gag, and when you think you can't take me any deeper, you will. I want to watch your throat bob as you swallow every drop of cum I give you." He kissed her, tightening his hold on her hair. "That's what I want."

She didn't like giving head, but his words made her wet. He was going to get the best blow job of his life, and then he was going to fuck her as a reward.

She crawled backward and sat back on her heels to pull his shorts down, freeing his impressive length. Once they were tossed aside, she fisted his shaft as his eyes watched her like a hawk.

"Lick it, Miss Raven," he drawled. "Show me what that sharp tongue can do."

She ran her tongue over the tip with her eyes glued to his as he sucked in a sharp breath. With a smile and her ass in the air, she sucked the tip like a lollipop. He made sounds that shot through her and urged her on.

She sat back on her heels again, and Caius' lust filled gaze followed the movement. She pulled open the waistband of her shorts, swiped her hand through her arousal, and returned to his cock, wrapping her wet hand around his girth.

"For fuck's sake," Caius moaned as she dragged her hand up and down with a twisting motion while sucking his head. "Do you have any idea how sexy that is?"

She picked up the pace, and before long, his hand grabbed her hair. "Swallow me," he instructed, and she did.

Moving her hand to his balls, she relaxed her throat and took him all. There was no way she could keep from gagging, and her eyes watered, but still she moved him in and out of her mouth.

"Fuck, Rory," he growled as his head fell back. He pushed her head down and fucked her mouth. Abruptly, he pulled her off him. "Take off your shorts."

She scrambled to stand, shimmied her shorts to the ground, and stood in front of him. He lay back on the ground and beckoned her closer. "You will finish your job, while seated here," he said, motioning to his face before grabbing her thighs to pull her down.

She faced his cock and seated herself on his warm mouth, both of her legs braced on either side of his head.

"Ride me, Miss Raven."

Taking him as far into her mouth as she could, she worked him, but when Caius tugged her down to feast, she cried out, feeling a sense of déjà vu.

Her hips moved, and she had to focus on pleasuring him, too. He moaned against her pussy and lifted his hips as she picked up speed, and the faster she went, the harder he ate. Teeth scraped against her clit as his nose swiped across her sensitive skin.

She was practically screaming around his cock, and when her muscles clenched, she moved faster. "Caius," she panted. "Oh, fuck."

She came hard, and as she rode out her climax, she neglected him, but he didn't seem to mind, because he flipped her over and had her pinned to the ground in seconds.

"Lift your leg." He grabbed her left knee and draped it over his shoulder while simultaneously wrapping her right leg around his waist seconds before slamming into her.

They both moaned, and he rammed harder than she'd

ever experienced. She swore he hit her cervix as he pounded. Her clit was swollen and sensitive from her first orgasm, and she could feel another building.

"You're stunning," he rasped through labored breaths.

His thrusts split her open, and her leg tightened around his waist, trying to pull him closer. She held herself in place on the ground the best she could as she pushed her hips to meet his.

She would never tire of the feel of him moving inside her. They were both close, and she felt his dick begin to pulse. He grunted as he came, and as he rode it out, she sparked and followed. It wasn't as explosive as her first one, but it was enough. Her pussy milked him, and his chest heaved.

Their freshly washed bodies were covered in a new layer of sweat, and when he pulled out, he smiled. "I guess we're both out of shape, but you did good, baby." He leaned forward and kissed her, dissolving her into a puddle of goo.

Once they were both dressed, he picked up her gym bag and slung it over his shoulder. "Max leaves tomorrow."

Her eyes burned. "He does."

Caius gently touched her arm to stop her. "Are you okay?"

She averted her gaze with a slight nod. "I will be. We're meeting him tonight for a quick goodbye. He didn't want to make a big production out of it."

Caius' hand moved to the back of her neck and pulled her to him. Kissing the top of her head, he put his arm around her and led her to the door. "I have an idea."

"Where are we going?"

"Where I go when I feel like shit," he replied.

Intrigued, she went without argument but couldn't help but ask, "What makes you feel like shit?"

"I miss my family, too," he said ruefully.

Empathy flowed through her as she followed him through the gardens, past the pond, and down a hidden trail. As many times as she'd been here, she had never noticed it. They came out on the other side of the trail into a long field marked with lines and two arrowball nets on each side.

Arrowball nets sat atop large, forked poles, split down the middle, with a net between each pole vertically, and a horizontal net cresting the top. Caius jogged to a building behind the nearest net, opened the door, and emerged with three arrowballs.

The name arrowball was misleading because it wasn't a ball at all. It was slender and shaped like the tip of an arrow, and when thrown, it eventually circled back to the thrower.

It was what made arrowball so hard. They passed it down the field by throwing it to their teammates, but if they didn't throw it hard enough and they didn't catch it soon enough, it circled back and not only did they lose ground, but they might also lose the ball. The key was to get it into the net, but again, if they didn't time it right, it would circle back before hitting the net.

Rory saw an arrowball circle back out of a net after it was already in. The team didn't get the point, and the stadium went crazy. The two vertical nets were three points each, and the net on top was worth five points. It was high up, and hard to make. They had to throw the ball from far back to angle it right.

She wasn't much for sports but watching an arrowball game in person while drinking beer with friends was fun. "You play arrowball?" She didn't think kings played sports.

His smile was a mile wide. "I played in grade school."

Rory jogged across the field to where he stood. "I didn't know *Royals* went to grade school."

He dropped the balls, removed his shirt, and wiped his forehead. "How do you think we learned to read and write?"

She paused for a beat. "Tutors."

He picked up a ball and motioned for her to go downfield. "There was a school right outside The Capital we went to under aliases. We even had a house and fake parents we pretended to live with."

Rory's mouth ticked up. "I bet the ladies stumbled over themselves to get to you," she teased. "Even without being a *Royal*."

He waggled his eyebrows. "You will stumble, too."

She shook her head lightly, laughing, and he barked out directions as she moved down the field. He pulled back, twisting his upper body, and let the ball fly. When he did, he took off running toward Rory, and her pulse picked up as she tried to gauge where to run.

The ball was low, but not low enough for her to reach, and she jumped, making a grab for it, but she missed it right before it circled back. "No!" she screamed as her feet hit the ground.

Caius jumped, his vertical impressive, and his abs and obliques flexed as his arm reached above him and snatched the ball from the air. Watching him in action was like watching an artist create a masterpiece. His body was made for this.

Still, she hated losing, and when he turned to her with his winning smile, she attacked, making his smile grow. He picked her up and threw her over his shoulder as she squealed and beat playfully against his back. "You apologize right now," he teased. A sting on her ass was accompanied by a loud slap, and she bucked.

"Did you just spank me?" she asked in disbelief.

He spanked her again. "I did. Cheaters will not be tolerated, Miss Raven."

She wriggled in his hold, and despite herself, she giggled like a schoolgirl. "Do you promise to be good?" he asked, his deep voice rumbling against her thighs.

She bit back a smile. "Yes, Daddy."

His body went tight, and his grip bit into her legs. "Watch what you say to me, unless you're ready for the repercussions."

He slid her down the front of him, every part of her touching his torso, and when her feet hit the ground, his hands cupped the side of her neck and jaw as he leaned in for a kiss.

The kiss started slowly, but soon turned desperate, and when he pulled on her bottom lip with his teeth, she moaned into his mouth. He pulled back and pressed his forehead to hers.

"Do you feel better?" he asked quietly.

She lifted on her toes to brush a light kiss against his lips. "Yes. Thank you."

He backpedaled until he reached the arrowball, bent down to grab it, and pointed at her. "Anything for you. Don't ever forget that. Now, go long."

She laughed and took off running, her heart feeling lighter and happier than it had in a very long time.

CHAPTER 35

Rory sat at the bar surrounded by her friends for Max's last night in Vincula. They were sad, but everyone knew how much Max missed his wife, and knowing he would be reunited with her consoled them all.

Asher would have raised his glass and said something stupid to make them laugh, but he wasn't here. Rory held hers up instead. "Here's to hoping they don't put me on garden duty."

Max chuckled as the others looked on in confusion. "Hear, hear," Max agreed and clinked his glass to hers.

"Here's to hoping we understand the next joke," Cat added and lifted her glass.

They chatted back and forth, but Max stayed quiet. He always did, but tonight felt different. There was a deep sadness in his eyes, and Rory reached under the table to grab his hand. "Don't worry about forgetting us," she whispered. "We're all on borrowed time, anyway."

His old eyes bore into hers. "Sometimes, when people borrow something, they don't want to give it back."

Her heart ached for him, for all of them, including herself. It was likely she wouldn't lose her memories if she married Caius, but knowing they'd forget her *hurt*.

"That's called stealing," Cat piped up from across the table.

Max huffed out a laugh, blinked away his unshed tears, and squeezed Rory's hand before letting it go.

Before letting them all go.

A couple of hours later, Rory, Max, and Bellina walked through the palace gates, and after one more round of teary goodbyes, they went their separate ways. Bellina and Max headed to the staff quarters, and Rory turned toward her room on the opposite side of the palace.

When she turned down the hall to the throne room, a meaty hand clamped over her mouth and hauled her back into one of the large banquet rooms. She struggled against his hold as her anxiety peaked. Remembering her training with Dume and Caius, she stomped on his foot while simultaneously elbowing him in the stomach.

He grunted and pushed back, and she used the distraction to break his hold. She needed to run but didn't want to turn her back to him, so she backpedaled deeper into the room, searching for another exit.

"Little butcher bitch wants to play?" the man asked, and as he moved closer, she recognized him as one of Nina's henchmen. *Vince or Felix*, she recalled.

"Stay away from me," she warned.

His raucous laugh made her flinch, and the glint in his eye could have come from Orcus himself. The man moved fast, faster than she'd thought possible for his size, and when he was close enough, he swung.

She deflected the blow, her entire body rattling with the contact, but her muscle memory kicked in, and she held her own. Round and round they went; him attacking, her evading until he landed an uppercut to her jaw, and she swore a tooth cracked. Her movements were slowing, but she had to keep going.

Another man, the missing part of the duo, barreled through the door, and dread seeped into her bones.

One man she could take, but two was impossible. Her boot slammed into the first man's jaw, snapping his head back. The other man ran across the room, and Rory sprinted away. The exhaustion from fighting the first man slowed her down, and pain shot through her when she was yanked backward by her hair.

She flipped around and began fighting the second man, the first where she'd left him, catching his breath. A crash sounded, and Lauren ran through the door, straight for Rory. Rory nearly folded with relief, and when the man fighting her turned and saw Lauren, he didn't have time to scream.

Lauren snarled and transformed into a lethal panther mid stride, knocking him to the ground, and with one bite, she clamped down on the back of his neck and ripped his spinal cord from his body.

Rory screamed and fell to the floor as the panther transformed back into Lauren, but not the Lauren she knew. In her place was an *Angel* with bloodied wings and white fire in her eyes. She looked possessed, and when she turned to the other man, who was trying to crawl away, she took measured steps across the room as the bones dangling from her hand whispered like a wind chime.

Before she reached him, the wall between the room and the hallway blew to bits as shadows blasted through the stone. Rory screamed and covered her head, but no debris touched the ground. It hovered in the air, balanced on shadows as Caius stormed into the room, and Rory saw what the tall tales depicted.

There stood the King of Monsters, and his golden eyes blazed as shadows branched across his skin like roots. His expression was deadly, and when he saw the other man struggling on the ground, he became darkness itself as he moved across the room.

A shadow lifted the man into the air, and Lauren stood back, letting Caius have his kill.

"You dare touch your queen?" he snarled in the deepest voice Rory had ever heard.

"Q-queen?" the man stammered.

Before he could say another word, Caius grabbed the man's jaw and ripped it from his face, tossing it on the ground as a strangled cry emitted from the man's throat. "You will never speak of her again," the king told him. "Tell Orcus hello for me."

The man's head snapped with a resounding crack, and his body fell in a heap on the floor.

Lauren dropped the bloodied bones in her hand and ran back to Rory. It was then Caius turned, and when he saw her, he ran, shadows flying erratically in every direction.

Rory trembled, wanting to back away as Lauren approached her, but she didn't. She knew the *Angel* wouldn't hurt her.

"Don't pass out on me," Lauren said as she helped Rory to her feet. "Are you hurt?"

"I—I think I lost a tooth," she said absentmindedly, searching the floor for it.

Lauren wrenched open Rory's jaw and looked around. "Just one. Nothing a potion can't fix."

Rory stood motionless, taking in the gore of it all. "I · knew you weren't a house cat."

Lauren threw her head back and clapped as she laughed. "You're fine. We need to ge—"

Darkness encased them in a shadowy coffin, cutting her off as Caius pulled Rory into his arms. "I saw him," he rasped into her hair. "I didn't think I'd get here in time."

She held him, needing him to calm her nerves as much as he needed her to calm his. "I hope you like holes because I lost a tooth," she mumbled into his shirt.

He pulled back and pried her mouth open as Lauren had done, and Rory swatted his hands away. "Lauren said she'd get me a potion."

Caius' eyes returned to normal, and the vein-like shadows receded from his skin. "Why did you look like that?" she asked cautiously.

He smoothed her hair out of her face where it'd come loose from her ponytail. "I have a temper."

She ran her finger along his jaw where the dark lines once marred his skin. "Did you lose control?"

"I don't lose control," he said smoothly. "But I intend on killing anyone who hurts you."

"Not if I get to them first," Lauren said, making them both turn. She was inspecting her blood-covered nails. "Which I did."

Caius' arm banded around Rory's waist. "I owe you my life," he said, dipping his head respectfully.

"*You* didn't almost die," Rory protested. "I did." Being able to joke after almost dying had to be a good sign. They say trauma makes people funnier.

She would likely throw up later to make up for it.

"What happened?" Caius asked Lauren.

Lauren placed her hands on her hips, and for the first time since meeting her, she looked guilty. "I was trailing her, as you asked."

"Excuse me?" Rory cut in, breaking Caius' hold.

He didn't look sorry. "Go on."

Rory tabled the conversation for later, but she *would* come back to it.

"An enforcer stopped me in the foyer to ask about a disturbance," Lauren went on. "By the time I broke away, I jogged to the throne room, knowing she would use the dais door, when I heard the struggle."

"And then she turned into a cat," Rory accused, offended no one had told her.

"Panther," Caius and Lauren said in unison.

Rory pointed at Lauren. "You let me pet you." Another thought occurred to her. "You saved me from Ronny."

Lauren flipped her hair over her shoulder. "I did. He deserved it."

Rory narrowed her eyes. "Then why did you give me the third degree about his death?"

"Why are you giving me the third degree now? I saved you. You're welcome, by the way," Lauren returned, popping a brow.

Rory crossed to Lauren and wrapped her arms around

her neck. "Thank you. I will bring you all the big juicy steaks you want."

Caius' hand covered his mouth, and Lauren mouthed something over Rory's shoulder. "Make sure they're fatty cuts." She gently extracted herself from Rory's arms. "I need to bathe. Try not to die while I'm gone," she called over her shoulder as she left.

"That's not funny," Caius said gruffly before addressing Rory. "You need to bathe, too."

"That felt rude," she muttered under her breath, suddenly tired as she followed him to her room. When they stepped into the hallway, the still suspended debris crashed to the ground, and Rory jumped at the sound. "Can I have all the healing potions this time?"

"Yes. After your fall, I had the palace doctor set up a fully stocked infirmary. I'll send for him."

"No," Rory rushed. "I don't want to be poked and prodded. I'm okay, just banged up and toothless." She puffed out her chest. "I actually kicked his ass. If he hadn't been triple my size, I wouldn't have needed Lauren's help."

Caius beamed with pride. "That's my girl."

A joke about not being anyone's girl was on the tip of her tongue, but she swallowed it. She was his girl, and they both knew it. "I'd still like potions tonight. Just basic bruises, cuts, and muscle aches." She paused. "And a tooth regrowing one. Does that exist?"

"The first three I can get tonight." He eyed her mouth as if he could see through it. "You'll need to see the dentist tomorrow for the correct tooth potion."

"Thanks," she replied. "What did you mean when you said you saw him? Back in the banquet room."

"It's the bond. When one of us is in danger, the other

has a vision." He gave her a half smile. "I've had them for a couple of years, but I thought they were nightmares."

"You've been dreaming about me for years and said nothing?" she asked, her voice raising an octave.

He exhaled. "No. I don't see you in danger. I see through your eyes. The same would happen for you if I were in danger, but I'm a *Royal* locked in my own realm, and the odds of that happening are not high."

"Not for long," she reminded him as they approached his office. His hand stalled on the doorknob, and his knuckles turned ghostly. "Caius?"

Hand still on the door, he turned to look at her. "I promise to avenge our sisters, but if I fail, you mustn't ever tell anyone what you are to me. If Gedeon finds out, he will torture you out of spite."

Rory nodded numbly. "Okay, but don't talk like that. If you think you're going to lose, you will."

Caius pushed open the door and stepped inside, surveying the room. Rory tried to follow him, but he held up a hand. "I need to make sure no one is in here."

"I doubt there would be two assassination attempts in one night," she said, ducking under his arm.

He gave her an annoyed look and closed the door behind them, turning the lock before checking the other door. "I don't think I'll lose, but I won't underestimate my brother."

"Before we head up, will you send for the potions while I shower?" she asked, slumping against the bookcase leading to her room.

"I'll get the potions, you get showered, and then we'll both get in bed," he said, pulling on a rope in the corner of the office, ringing for a maid.

When Rory stepped out of the shower, she felt like a

new woman. She wasn't bloody like Lauren, save for her mouth and a small cut by her eye, but nothing made her feel better than washing the day away.

Caius waltzed in with a basket, and the sight was so odd, Rory couldn't help but laugh. He gave her a wry smile and set the basket on the table to unload. "Take these," he instructed as he handed her three potions. "I brought food and juice."

After shooting down the potions and gagging, she peeked over his shoulder and squealed when she saw a donut. She had it halfway to her mouth when he snatched it from her hand. "That's mine."

She tried to get it back, but he held it in the air. "You're missing a tooth."

He was right, but donuts were soft. "Why did you bring food if I can't have any?"

He reached into the basket and pulled out a bowl. "I brought you applesauce."

"Applesauce?" It was thoughtful, and she knew that, but if she had to watch him eat a donut in front of her while she ate pulverized apples, she would lose it.

He chose that exact time to bite into the donut with a wide grin. "Delicious."

She jumped at him and grabbed blindly for the donut, but he moved out of the way, spewing crumbs as he laughed. He shoved another bite into his mouth, but before he could hold it above his head again, she swiped it from his hand and tore into it with her teeth.

His chewing slowed as his face darkened at the sight of her ravaging the pastry. "Do you shove everything into your mouth with that much enthusiasm?"

She antagonized him as she chewed slowly, careful not to use her side with the missing tooth. "You know I do."

"Careful, Miss Raven," he warned.

She took a step back and shoved the rest of the donut in her mouth. "Or what?" Bits of food fell from her mouth in a very unappealing fashion.

Caius watched her every move as though chewing food was the sexiest thing alive. "You almost died today, and I'd rather not heal you only to break your back."

Everything in her flushed hot, and his expression revealed the truth in his words. "The potions worked fast." She stuck a finger in her mouth and slowly licked the sugary glaze from its tip.

He followed every flick of her tongue, and when he rubbed his thumb across his bottom lip, she knew she had him. The truth was, she needed to forget what had transpired today.

Yes, she'd held her own, but if Lauren and Caius hadn't shown up when they did, the outcome would have been different.

Caius shook himself and turned from her. "Tempting me will only make your punishment worse when the time comes."

Rory deflated. She could press him, but she was tired too, and if he wouldn't fuck her stress away, then she would sleep it away. The cool air hit her still damp skin, and she shivered before walking to turn out the bathroom light.

Caius followed close behind. "Why are you shaking?"

She straightened the products in the shower, used her towel to wipe down the glass doors, and tossed it in the hamper before turning back to him. "I'm cold."

He frowned and scanned her clinically. "Wait here."

"No." She trailed behind him and closed the bathroom door behind her. It freaked her out to leave doors open when she slept. Waking up to a person sized gaping hole in the wall was not her idea of a good time.

"You're impossible," he grunted and opened the dresser she never used. "Put these on."

A bundle of fabric hit her in the chest, and upon inspection, they appeared to be a pair of his sweatpants and a t-shirt. "You own sweatpants?"

He tilted his head to look at the ceiling, muttering to himself. "Yes. Put them on. As much as I love seeing you in that scrap of silk," he said, gesturing to her shift. "It's not practical to sleep in all the time."

"It was this or a set of flannels," she pointed out. "It's too hot in the staff quarters to sleep in flannels."

Caius' lips lifted into a bemused smile. "You know there are different styles of pajamas in town, don't you?"

If she weren't hopping on one leg to pull on the warm pants that smelled like him, she would have told him to go screw himself. "I used my credits on sleep shorts, but they're no warmer than a shift."

"You don't have credits," he replied, exasperated. "You can buy every set of pajamas in every size and color."

The pants slipped from her hips because she was shaped like an ice pop stick, and she tugged them back up. "Stop doing that."

Large hands grabbed the fabric around her waist and cinched it closed. "Hold this," he instructed and disappeared into the bathroom, only to return with a ponytail holder. Grabbing the bunch of fabric from her, he secured it with the tie.

"They make these with drawstrings, you know?" she said, inspecting his work.

The shift slipped over her arms in one fell swoop before he pulled the shirt over her head. "I buy my clothes to fit." He placed a kiss on her forehead. "I don't need ropes in my clothes; only my bedroom."

Rory turned his chin to look at her. "Funny. Next time, bring them over to play."

Lips brushed her ear. "You are not getting me naked tonight, Miss Raven. Crawl in bed, or I will put you there myself."

Sighing, she slipped under the blankets and waited for him to join her. After showering and changing into sweats, he slid in beside her and folded his arms beneath his head.

"I almost lost you today." He'd been holding back his emotions for her sake, she knew, and as much as she didn't like to be coddled or have attention brought to a situation she'd rather forget, he needed to unload.

"But you didn't. You gave me protection I was too stubborn to accept." She was on her side with one arm under her head, and the other reached for him, settling on his chest. "Thank you."

"It's my job to protect you," he said, swallowing hard. "I almost failed."

"It's not your job," she murmured. "That responsibility lies on no one but me."

He rolled his head to look at her. "You're wrong. As my mate, I was made to protect you, and you me. Would you let me die?"

"No." Her answer was instantaneous. She could no more let him die than herself. It wasn't love; it was instinct— one she would follow without question.

His hand grabbed hers, stopping its descent. "Careful." Lacing his fingers with hers, he murmured, "Tell me about Cora."

Rory's stomach tightened, and she swallowed her emotions before exhaling. "She was good. If she did anything considered mean, it was in defense of someone else, usually me." Tears pricked Rory's eyes. "One time, she heard me crying in the bathroom, but I wouldn't let her in." She laughed at the memory. "She shifted into her lamb and kicked the door in with her back hooves."

Caius' expression softened with a crooked smile. "That sounds like something you would do."

Rory's laugh was light. "She shifted back and wrapped me in her arms, asking no questions. I never liked to be pressed, and she knew that. We sat in the bathroom for an hour, and when I was finished crying, she said, '*Never lock me out again.*'"

A soft sob ripped from Rory's throat, and Caius pulled her close, rubbing soothing circles down her back. "She sounds exactly how I imagined your twin would be."

Rory shook her head against his chest. "She didn't deserve to die before me. She would be ashamed to see what I've become."

"If she was the person you say, she could never be ashamed of you." He lifted her chin with his finger. "Despite what you think, you are good in your own way. Everyone does bad things. Yes, some are worse than others and deserve a fate worse than death, but most are only trying to navigate life and all it throws at them. Never discount yourself for your flaws."

Her lower lip trembled as she swallowed another sob.

"How can you know? I did terrible things. *Terrible*, and I deserve a fate worse than death."

"You are stuck with me for eternity," he teased. "That is punishment enough."

She sniffled with a wry smile. "You're not so bad, Umbra King." Laying her head back down, she said, "Tell me about Atarah."

His arm tightened slightly, and his heart pounded harder against her cheek. "She was something else. Good doesn't describe her. When I took the throne, we began discussing reform for Vincula."

"What else could this place need?" Rory mused. "Some inmates prefer it to Erdikoa."

"Things can always be better. Visitation, for one. Allowing pre-approved friends and family members to visit or, at the very least, allowing inmates to bring pictures of loved ones from home."

She shifted closer to him. "Why can't they do that already?"

"We weren't sure. The visitors are a safety concern. There would need to be a protocol in place to ensure they bring nothing in or that they wouldn't stir up trouble. We were brainstorming on ways to make it work. As far as the pictures, I can't say."

Rory stayed quiet, giving him the time he needed to continue. "Gedeon murdered her before we could put our plans in motion."

"And you're sure he killed her?" she asked cautiously. It was a sensitive subject, and she understood the conviction. She'd been wrong about Caius, but not wrong about what she saw. *Identical twins.* She still couldn't believe it.

Even though his face was the one she saw, she no longer saw Cora's lifeless body when she looked at him. There were subtle differences she hadn't noticed before. Gedeon wasn't in color, and the way Caius carried himself and the lack of cruelty on his face. Caius' hair is shorter than Gedeon's, and the Umbra King wouldn't be caught dead in the light suit his brother wore.

Since getting to know him better, she knew he could no sooner put a knife in her sister's heart than he could in hers. She hoped he brought her Gedeon's head on a spike.

"Yes. Gedeon's soul is black, and it suffocated me growing up, but I never told our parents." He huffed out a false laugh. "I was trying to protect him."

"How did no one else feel it?" she asked.

"*Royals* cannot see souls as *Fey* do, except for the Scales of Justice. Even then, Adila can't see the souls of other *Royals*; only the accused." He shifted under her. "I couldn't see all souls, only black ones, and in their presence, I felt weighed down. No one knew, and I was too afraid to tell anyone because I thought something was wrong with me." He glanced down at her. "It makes sense now."

She chewed her lip, trying to make sense of the way he was staring at her. "What do you mean?"

"As I learned when I was older, *Royals* display a bit of their *Aeternum's* abilities."

"It's my fault," she whispered. "I wish you'd been able to see the beautiful souls instead. They're a sight to behold. I was obsessed when my abilities manifested and could see colors for the first time."

Her breath stalled. *Her grey-scale sight.* She shot up and twisted to look at Caius. "Cora had grey-scale sight."

His head moved slightly before he sat up, too, coming to the same conclusion she had. "She was Gedeon's *Aeternum*."

He scrubbed a hand across his jaw and cursed as he threw the blankets back and paced the length of the room.

"Why would he kill her? Isn't he supposed to protect her?" Rory asked incredulously.

Silence stretched between them before Caius stopped, his face lighting up with understanding. "He wants to stay in power."

"He wants to stay in power?" Rory parroted. "What does that have to do with Cora?"

Caius cursed. "If she is his *Aeternum,* and he trapped her soul, he would never have children, thus he would never give up the throne. Neither would Adila and I, for that matter. That son of a bitch."

"No," Rory gasped. "He can't mean to keep her soul in a jar for all eternity. That's *cruel.*"

Caius' face was grim. "He murdered his own sister and *Aeternum.* Cruel does not begin to describe him." He sat on the edge of the bed, looking tired.

Rory reached for him, needing something to anchor her, and his hand landed on top of hers. "We'll free her soul," he swore. "Even if he kills me before I kill him, I'll find her first and set her free."

She crawled into his lap and laid her head against his shoulder, glad when he wrapped his arms around her. There they sat, much like she and Cora had so long ago, and comforted each other until they fell asleep.

CHAPTER 36

Caius stood in the kitchens and shoved as much sugary food in his mouth as he could. After Rory fell asleep, he snuck off to clear his mind. When Gedeon killed Atarah, Caius wasn't surprised her power passed to his brother because there was no one else for it to pass to.

The Lux rulers could only have three children, and when his mother got pregnant with her fourth, everyone was shocked. Caius and Gedeon were technically one when conceived, and identical twins were a rarity in the realms.

When the twins were born, everyone assumed Gedeon would be the Umbra King since he was born first, making him the second born, and Caius would be the Scales of Justice.

But when the twins turned six, Gedeon had no abilities other than that of a *Fey*, minus the soul seer ability, and Caius could control shadows. When Adila turned six, her abilities to see souls manifested, and as she aged, the seed of justice grew.

Gedeon always felt jilted, and by killing Atarah, he took

the highest-ranking position among the three. His selfishness was unmatched, but to kill his own *Aeternum* was more than Caius could comprehend.

"You haven't been down here in a while," Sam said from the dark.

Caius shoved a spoonful of cake in his mouth, chewed, and swallowed. "When did you get back?"

Sam tucked his wings to weave around the kitchen island. "About an hour ago. I came to grab a fresh pitcher of water,"

"A night maid could have gotten that for you," Caius pointed out.

Sam walked to the sink to fill the pitcher in his hand. "No need to bother them when I can do it myself." Once the pitcher was full, he shut off the water and turned. "What's on your mind?"

Caius set down his dish and leaned against the counter with his arms folded across his bare chest. "I think Gedeon killed Rory's sister."

Sam mirrored his movements, leaning back. "I figured as much. There is no other reason she would have seen you in Erdikoa only a decade ago."

"Cora also had grey-scale sight." He met Sam's stare, and understanding passed between them.

"And you think she was Gedeon's *Aeternum*," Sam concluded.

Caius sighed and ran a hand through his unruly hair. "I do, and I think he did it to prevent himself from losing the throne. He intends to rule forever."

"We can't allow that," Sam said, stating the obvious. "Adila cannot ignore this."

"She won't kill our brother," Caius replied ruefully. "I'll have to do it, but I need her blessing first."

Sam's brows rose. "You have never cared for her blessing before. What changed?"

"I can't leave Rory." When Caius looked at his friend, the *Angel* was smiling like an idiot. "This isn't funny."

Sam pushed off the counter. "I'm not laughing." His hand clamped down on Caius' shoulder. "I am happy for you, brother. It is good to see you in love."

Caius shrugged him off. "I don't love her."

Sam looked bemused. "Are you sure about that?"

Not anymore.

"Both attacks are linked to Nina," Lauren said from the bookshelf she leaned against in Caius' office. "She needs to be dealt with."

Sam shook his head. "We have no proof. On the off chance there are other powers at play, we cannot send her to hell on a hunch."

"It's not a hunch," Rory protested. She couldn't believe her ears. "When Ronny attacked me, it was because of what I said to Nina, and the other two men were always with her."

Caius lounged in his chair with his chin in his hand. "Sam's right, but I want her watched around the clock."

"Are you kidding me?" Rory asked, rounding on the king. "How is letting her go unpunished protecting me?"

Caius' eyes sharpened, and she swore Lauren and Sam held their breath. "My priority is always you," he said with a glacial calm. "We can't damn a woman who has never stepped out of line until you arrived based on subjective evidence. I know she's behind this," he continued. "But if there is even the slightest chance she's not, I can't send her to hell."

Rory's fingers flexed with the urge to break something. "You were ready to burn the entire damned realm once, and now you hesitate?"

"Would you like me to commit mass murder, Miss Raven?" He sat forward. "Sam would have never let me do that, anyway. Please, trust me."

Her jaw tensed. "Fine, but if she comes near me, I'll kill her myself."

Caius' lips twitched. "I expect nothing less."

"I'll take care of Nina's detail," Lauren said, getting the conversation back on track.

"And I will be Rory's," Caius added, his voice daring Rory to object.

She knew fighting him was futile, even if she could beat the shit out of Nina on her own. There was also no telling who else did Nina's dirty work. "Fine. I hope you like beer."

Caius looked taken aback. "What?"

"Beer," Rory said again. "We're going out with my friends tonight."

The king closed his eyes, mumbling under his breath, and she inflated with satisfaction. "Be ready to go at seven. If you'll excuse me, I'm going to get lunch." She glanced at Caius. "Coming?"

He pushed his chair back and stood. "I need to speak with Sam before we leave."

"I'll report back after Nina's detail is settled," Lauren said before leaving.

Sam walked forward and said, "More victims have come forward to vouch for The Butcher."

"What?" Rory gasped. She'd forgotten he went to Erdikoa. "Did you speak with Dume?"

Caius looked annoyed at the mention of her friend, but even more so when Sam nodded. "As well as Kordie, Keith, and Sera."

Rory searched her memory. "I don't think I know Sera."

"She is a woman you saved," the commander replied. "She is a feisty one."

"Bruce's daughter," Rory recalled, snapping her fingers. "He said her name was Sera."

"Have the enforcer departments made any statements?" Caius asked.

Sam shook his head. "Not to my knowledge." For the first time since arriving in Vincula, Sam looked uneasy.

"What else?" Rory asked, on high alert.

"Your friends still take care of your mother, but she has been difficult," Sam replied carefully. "They do not know why."

"What does that mean?" Rory demanded on the verge of hysteria.

Sam's eyes darted to Caius before returning to her. "On her lucid days, she tries to escape, going on about saving you. Keith said it was a prophecy."

Rory's body was numb. She caused this. "It's too late," she croaked. "My darkness sent me here, and my mother will be dead before I return. She doesn't understand."

"What prophecy?" Caius asked with a sense of urgency, surprising Sam and Rory both.

"*Two were one, and one is yours. Do not let him fool you. His darkness is poison. Only the golden child can save you,*" Rory recited. "It was something she said not long before I was arrested. I don't understand the rest, but the darkness reference was obvious."

"*Two were one, and one is yours,*" Caius said, barely above a whisper.

All three seemed to realize the meaning at once, because they all moved. Rory's knees almost buckled with shock. "You," she said, pointing at Caius. "*'Two were one, and one is yours.'* She means you." Identical twins, once a single embryo, split in two. "You really are my mate."

Caius looked offended. "You doubted me?"

"No," she lied.

Caius circled back to his desk and sat down, grabbing a pen and pad. "Say the prophecy again." He scribbled as Rory repeated each line. Once finished, he tapped his pen against the pad as he read the words before looking up. "You won't have one second alone for the next five-hundred years, maybe longer."

Rory narrowed her eyes. "It is only one possibility of an infinite number of futures. Just because a section of it is true doesn't mean all of it is."

"I don't care," he clipped, putting the pen and pad away. Standing, he rolled up the sleeves of his shirt and approached her with an outstretched arm. "Shall we?"

Rory looked at Sam for backup, but he only gave her a toothy smile.

"Where would you like to eat?" Caius asked casually.

Giving up, she grabbed his hand. "The sandwich shop next to the bakery."

He leaned over and kissed her forehead, warming her insides. "Good choice."

. . .

Rory's face curled in disgust as she watched the deli worker make Caius' sandwich. "Ketchup and lettuce?" She was going to hurl.

"Many people eat ketchup and lettuce on burgers," he replied smoothly, taking his sandwich from the worker.

"You're eating a turkey sandwich!" she exclaimed.

He waited for her to get her food and led them to a small table in the back. She was used to the stares by now. Word had gotten around about her relationship with the king, and while she hated prying eyes, it was better than the sneers she used to endure.

"Why does the type of meat matter?" he asked, pulling out her chair.

She thanked him and placed a napkin on her lap. "It just does."

He watched her unwrap her sandwich and take a huge bite. "You take that sandwich almost as well as you take my cock."

She sputtered, and for a split second, she knew she would die of either embarrassment or asphyxiation. He smirked and took a bite of his own food. "You can't say that in public," she whisper-yelled.

He took a sip of water and smiled. "I can say whatever I want."

Her boot found his shin under the table, and he grimaced with the impact. "Save it for the bedroom, Miss Raven." The table of women next to her stopped talking, and Rory begged the ground to swallow her whole.

"You look a bit flustered." Caius observed, making her cheeks burn brighter.

She ripped into her sandwich with her teeth and chewed mechanically while glaring at the villain across from her.

"If you eat too fast, your stomach will hurt," Caius warned. "And we have plans tonight with your friends."

She choked down her too-big bite. "Have you ever been to the bar in town?"

The chair beneath him groaned as he shifted. "A few times with Sam, but we prefer to drink in the palace."

"Why not put a bar in the palace for you and the staff?" she suggested. "Everyone there is used to being around you regularly, and it might not be as uncomfortable for you."

His fingers toyed with the wrapper of his sandwich. "I like that idea."

She stopped chewing. "You do?"

"It's a good idea," he replied. "And you *are* queen. You could put a bar in the middle of the lake if you so wished."

A woman beside them spewed her drink across the table, and Rory threw a napkin at Caius. "I am not the queen," she announced loud enough for the woman to hear.

Caius turned to the woman. "She will be."

"You haven't asked me to marry you," she said sharply. "To be queen, we must be married."

"Is that what you want?" he asked, folding his napkin. She set herself up. *Damnit.* "If a proposal is what you want, I will get down on one knee here and now."

He rose, and she leaned forward to push him back down. "Stop being ridiculous."

His expression turned grave. "The sooner we marry, the sooner you will become immortal. Your essence will return, and you will be faster and stronger."

"That is not a reason to get married," she said, shaking her head. "If you want to marry me, earn it, but more importantly, mean it."

She never wanted to get married in the first place, but

even she couldn't deny her growing feelings toward the king. It was scary and new. Going from hating someone and wanting to murder them to whatever they were now was surreal.

"When you realize you love me, I will drop to one knee wherever we are," he murmured for only her to hear.

She shook her head. "It won't matter if I love you or not. I refuse to marry someone who doesn't love me back."

His lip tugged to the side. "I will fall first, Miss Raven, and we both know it."

Her lungs took it upon themselves to stop working, and when her breath returned, she used it to change the subject. "Is everything you own black?" she asked, gesturing to his shirt.

If the question surprised him, he didn't show it. "My pants were grey last night."

"Sweatpants to bed don't count," she quipped. "Even your athletic clothes are black. Why don't you like color?"

Rory became obsessed with colorful clothing once she could see it. While a lot of her comfortable clothes were still black, she liked to buy dresses and blouses in brilliant colors.

"I like black." He popped a chip into his mouth and chewed thoughtfully. "I can wear the grey sweatpants tonight if you'd like."

She thought of his dick outlined in his sweats. "No." She didn't want anyone enjoying the view but her.

He winked and grabbed another chip. "You should wear that dress from the first Plenilune. It's my favorite."

"You destroyed that dress," she reminded him.

"I only made the split higher." His smile was hellish, and she knew he was thinking of the gardens.

Heat bloomed low in her gut. "I'd rather not parade around with my vagina hanging out."

Something caressed her leg, and she yelped, glancing under the table. A shadow curled around her, and Caius leaned on his elbows. "I like to show off what's mine."

Her lips parted. "Most men don't want their women dressed scandalously."

"Most men want to control women." He pushed his chair back and stood. "If you want to walk through the realm naked, you will do so, and I will admire you the entire way."

Before he could pull out her chair, she stood, needing to move before she led him into a side alley to blow him.

Caius sat in the corner of their room reading and waiting for Rory to finish getting ready for their outing. He moved his things from his quarters to the sky room because going back and forth wasn't logical.

There was a secret entrance from the sky room to his quarters, making going back and forth easier, but he didn't want to be one room over. He wanted to be *here*.

She stepped out wearing a bright blue top, jeans, and heels. Her long hair was pulled back in a sleek ponytail, and her makeup accentuated her eye color and cheekbones.

"You look beautiful," he said, meaning every word. He couldn't build a better woman if he tried.

"I know." She did a slow turn to show him every angle. "Thank you."

He chuckled quietly and crossed the room to stand

beside her. "Whom are we meeting tonight?" he asked as they headed out.

"Bellina, Cat, Kit, and Tallent." She ticked them off on her fingers. "You met them at Asher's going away party, I think."

He knew them. Not personally, but he had Lauren look into everyone Rory surrounded herself with. "Do they know I'm coming?"

"I haven't seen Bellina since this morning, so no, but it will be fine." She slid her eyes to him. "I hope you have tough skin, because as soon as Cat is comfortable around you, you'll wish you hadn't come."

"I do like my women feisty," he purred, and she pulled back, jealousy flashing in her eyes, and his face split into a wide grin. "Is something wrong?"

Her cheeks pinked. "Yes," she snapped, but the look on her face said she didn't mean to say it out loud.

He studied her tight features. "Don't filter yourself with me."

The words hung in the air as she made an internal decision before finally releasing a long exhale and stopping in the middle of the courtyard. "The only woman you should like anything about *in that way* is me." She stared him down, letting him know she meant every word. "I don't care if you're joking, it's disrespectful, and I don't like it."

Vulnerability clouded her eyes, and he reached for her hand. "Always tell me how you feel. We're in this together for the long haul. Even if you decide not to be my wife, you are still here for five-hundred years. If we can't be ourselves with those closest to us, then whom can we be ourselves with?"

The uncertainty left, and there stood the woman who

made him love feisty women in the first place. "Like I said, I don't like it. Don't do it again, or I will cut your balls off."

Instinctively, his hand flew to his crotch, and Rory burst out laughing. "You're so violent," he tsked.

"I sewed people's hands to their shoulders, and you're surprised I'm a little aggressive?" she asked, laughing.

Still hand in hand, they walked through the dark night with only the streetlamps illuminating the sidewalks. "Why can't you power the entire realm with your essence?" Rory asked him.

Caius' brows rose. "It would drain me. I'm powerful, but if I were to power the entire realm all day and night, I would be powerless, like the inmates."

"Are your shadows that important?" She glanced at him with a small smile to let him know she was teasing, but it still left a weight in his stomach.

"I've considered it, but if there was an uprising, I would be powerless to stop it." He adjusted the collar on his shirt. "The lack of technology is nice."

"Says the man who has essence powered quarters."

"Our room is essence powered too." He reminded her. "I believe you are a hypocrite, Miss Raven."

Her steps faltered. "*Our* room?"

He turned to her. "Yes. What else would you call sharing the same space?" He regarded her carefully. "I can move my things back to my quarters if it makes you uncomfortable."

She squeezed his hand. "No, stay."

He drank her in, wondering why the *Seraphim* deemed him worthy of someone like her. "Always," he said, pulling her in for a kiss.

His tongue caressed the seam of her lips, asking for

entrance she immediately granted, and his hands tilted her head to deepen the kiss.

Her fists bunched the fabric of his shirt, and he felt his heart hang over the edge. He was ready to fall, and as he kissed his future wife, he knew it wouldn't be long.

When they pulled apart, they were both breathing hard, and Rory's lips were swollen. "Your lipstick is smeared," he murmured.

Her thumb swiped the area around his mouth. "So is yours." He grabbed her hand and placed a kiss on her palm. "We'll clean up when we get there."

"Absolutely not," she said, laughing as she tugged her hand from his. The intimate moment was over. She produced a mirror and tissue from her small purse, and Caius wondered what else was in there. It wasn't very large, and there wasn't anything she needed to carry other than her inmate card.

After cleaning herself, she used the tissue to tidy up around his mouth. "There." She held out her hand for him to grab. "We're late."

The bar was busy, but inmates cleared a path when he walked in. It felt ridiculous to be king sometimes. Rory's friends waved them over to a large table, already littered with empty glasses.

"You're late," the girl with dark, curly hair said. She turned to Caius with an almost giddy smile. "I'm Cat."

He shook her hand. "Please, call me Caius. Nice to see you again." Her eyes lit up, and she opened her mouth to say something else, but was interrupted.

"I'm Tallent," the man said tightly, refusing to hold out his hand, and it took Caius by surprise.

Caius tipped his head. "Nice to see you again."

"I'm Kit," the taller woman said as she threw back a shot. "Nice to meet you, Your Grace."

"Where's Bellina?" Rory asked, looking around.

"She's late, too," Cat snipped. "We thought you were together."

Rory continued to survey the room, but eventually sat down. "If she's not here within the hour, I'm going to look for her."

Kit zeroed in on Rory. "You're anxious. Is there a reason to be worried about her?"

She shook her head. "No, it's nothing. She's never been late before, is all."

"She's been late a time or two," Tallent reassured her. "She'll show."

Bellina didn't show, and Rory stayed perched on her stool, watching the door. "I'm sorry guys, but if I don't find Bellina and know she's okay, I won't be able to think about anything else."

"Why are you worried?" Cat asked. "She's an adult. Maybe she was tired after work."

"Or maybe she's at the bottom of a set of stairs," Rory countered, making the table fall silent. "Or being beaten by two giant men."

Rory stormed out, and Caius turned to the others. "I want you three to go home. She's right, someone is trying to hurt her, and they might try to hurt her through you."

He left, not waiting to hear their replies, and caught up

with Rory before she stepped through the door. "Where do you want to check first?" he asked.

She grabbed the sides of her head. "I don't know. She was coming to meet us. Anywhere between here and her room."

"Keep an eye out, and stay close to me," Caius told her as they set off toward the palace.

There was no trace of Bellina in town, and when they hit the landing for the staff quarters, Rory was so tightly wound she could have sprung into Erdikoa. She knocked on Bellina's door, but there was no answer, and Caius watched her anxiety grow.

Instead of knocking again, Rory opened the door, and Caius pulled her back. "Please don't barge into dark rooms unprepared," he said, grabbing a torch off the wall.

The room was pitch black, and when the flame lit the small space, Rory cried out and ran across the room before Caius could grab her.

Bellina was on the floor with her hands and feet bound. A gag covered her mouth, and she was beaten black and blue.

Caius stepped into the hall and called for an enforcer to fetch the doctor and Samyaza. Bellina was out cold, and Rory worked furiously at the rope digging into her friend's wrists.

She was crying, and Caius knew images of her sister were assaulting her. He bent down and stilled her hands. "I'm faster. Take the torch and light the lamp."

He called on the shadows to make quick work of the ropes, and within less than a minute, Bellina was free. Rory pulled her into her lap, and Caius fetched water and a rag from the bathroom.

Sam barged through the doorway like a hellhound, and when he stepped into the small room, his wings vanished. "What happened?"

Rory stopped whispering to Bellina and looked up. "Where's the doctor? She needs potions."

"He's on his way," Sam assured her and turned to Caius. "What happened?"

Caius set the water next to Rory and handed her the rag, instructing her to clean some of the blood from Bellina's face. "We don't know. She was to meet us for drinks, but when she didn't show, Rory thought something was wrong."

Sam looked around the room in commander mode. "What is that?" he asked, pointing to the bedside table.

Caius twisted to see a small paper. Standing, he grabbed it and read the note. *Aether, this was bad.*

"What does it say?" Rory asked from the floor.

He tried to think of a reason not to read it, anything that would keep her from hearing these words, but he knew her. She wouldn't stop until she read it herself because she wasn't a porcelain doll to be handled with care. She was the beast who stomped on dolls for fun.

"Do not marry the king, or everyone you love will die, including your family in Erdikoa. This is your last warning."

Rory's face was stricken before it filled with rage. "Nina did this."

"She couldn't have," Sam replied. "Lauren has been watching her all day."

"Then she made someone else do it!" Rory yelled. She turned to Caius. "We have to do something."

He knew she was right. "We'll bring her in for questioning tomorrow."

The doctor rushed in with a bag of potions and got to work on Bellina. He said she had a minor concussion, but was otherwise fine, and Rory refused to leave her side.

Caius grabbed the extra potions from the doctor to give Bellina when she woke up and approached the commander. "Sam, carry her to our room."

Caius grabbed Rory's shoulder and stopped her from trailing the *Angel*. "We'll catch whoever is behind this. Someone in the palace had to have seen something."

Rory's features hardened. "I learned a long time ago not to wait on someone else to exact justice. I'll take care of it myself."

"Then I will help you," he promised.

CHAPTER 37

Bellina's memory was foggy when she woke, even after taking the potions provided by the doctor. She looked fine once they kicked in, but Rory could tell she was shaken.

Rory was shaken. Seeing her friend lying unconscious was like watching Cora through the window all over again.

"I'm going to sleep in my room," Bellina said, standing. "I want to be in my own bed."

"It's not safe. You should stay here," Rory insisted. Caius had Bellina brought to the sky room and gave the two women space for the night. He was thoughtful, and every time she was around him, another layer was revealed.

Bellina tried for casualness but failed miserably. "I want to be in my room."

"Wait," Rory tried again. "At least let me get you a lock for the inside."

"Locks aren't allowed," Bellina reminded her. "I appreciate what you're doing, and I know you feel responsible, but you're not. You can't blame other people's actions on yourself." She sighed. "The black hole in my memory is more unsettling than waking up broken, and I just want to be in my room to see if it will jog my memory. Alone."

Rory nodded. "I understand. I'll send someone down with a lock as soon as possible."

Bellina gave her a small smile and slipped through the sliding bookcase where Sam stood.

"Sam!" Rory called, as the shelf closed.

He stuck his boulder-sized hand out to stop it and poked his head in. "Have a lock installed inside of Bellina's room, please."

He smirked. "Yes, Your Grace."

The title didn't bother her this time, and that scared her. She looked at the bookshelf on the opposite end of the room that led to Caius' quarters and released a long breath.

She meandered through the hallway to Caius' room, and with each step toward him, her anxiety eased a fraction. He sent word last night to put enforcers with Kit, Tallent, and Cat, and now that she knew Bellina would have a lock, a weight lifted from her shoulders.

Not bothering to knock, she pushed the button to open the door to Caius' room, and when she stepped inside, her body lit like a match. A towel hung low on his hips, and tiny water droplets fell from the tips of his blonde hair.

She didn't know what it was about his inability to dry his hair, but damn, was it attractive.

His mouth lifted when he saw her, and the clothes in his hands dropped to the floor. "Please tell me I don't need these."

Her laugh was genuine as she went up on her toes to place a kiss on his cheek. She'd seen him that morning when he came in to check on Bellina and bring them breakfast, but seeing him now made her realize she missed him last night.

"I came to see if you wanted to take a nap with me." She had slept little the night before, and judging by the dark circles under his eyes, he hadn't slept either.

In reply, he grabbed a pair of boxer briefs to put on and turned down the comforter. Grateful, she joined him in bed and moved closer, needing to feel him. "Thank you."

He kissed the top of her head. "Are you okay?"

Nodding, she burrowed farther under the blankets. "I will be."

"Tell me about your mother," he said, banding his arm around her. "You only talk about her when you're sad. Tell me something happy."

Rory swallowed past the knot in her throat and called upon her favorite moments. "She danced when she cooked." She laughed lightly. "It was terrible, but she loved cooking, and it was like her body couldn't contain the joy within her. My sister and I would join when we were younger."

She felt his smile against her hair. "Will you dance?"

"When?" she asked, not understanding his question.

"If you have children. Will you dance in the kitchen?" His voice was airy, and she wondered if he was picturing their children dancing with her.

"If I decide to have them, yes. I'd want them to remember me happy." She'd never given much thought to having a family, but now it seemed... nice. *Not that having children was the only way to be happy.* But if she had them, she wouldn't hate it.

"When we did something we weren't supposed to, she never yelled. We had to sit down at the kitchen table and explain our reasoning for our actions. She listened without interrupting, and when we finished, she said her piece. She was kind, like Cora, and it showed in everything she did."

"You're kind, too," Caius added.

She stayed quiet, knowing kind wasn't the right word to describe her.

He nudged her. "You are. After you destroyed my office, you insisted on cleaning it yourself. You organized a huge going away party for your friend, and you helped Max in the gardens." His fingers stroked her arm. "Only a person with kindness thinks of others."

Seeing herself through another's eyes was strange because, until now, she hadn't thought of those actions as anything special. "When is your release exactly?" she asked, tilting her head to look at him.

His heart picked up speed beneath her cheek. "A little over a week."

She shot up. "Why didn't you tell me it was that soon?"

"Because I'm not leaving you," he replied. "I'm not like the others. My memories are not erased, and I can move between realms as I please."

She knew that, but it didn't make it any better. "You're planning to confront your brother. That's a big deal."

"It won't be immediate." It was then she saw the worry lines etched in his face. Killing his twin wouldn't be easy; it was unfathomable to her. They were two sides of the same coin, and when Cora died, so did a piece of Rory.

"I'll meet with Adila and see if she can sentence him to hell," he continued.

"And if she doesn't?" Rory's voice shook. Gedeon deserved hell. Adila must understand that.

Caius was quiet, and she dreaded his next words. "Then I will do as promised and kill him."

It was what she wanted, but at what cost? What if Gedeon killed him first, and when did she change her mind from wanting retribution over everything, to wanting Caius' safety above all else?

"Come back to me," was her response, because it was all she cared about now.

He turned to her. "I can't guarantee that."

"You have to." Fear crept over her, and she wanted nothing more than to lock him in Vincula for another five-hundred years. "When I'm free, we can make Adila understand, or we can deal with him together."

He tilted his head to look at the ceiling. "Please don't ask this of me. I have spent five-hundred years planning."

"You would leave me so easily? After all your proclamations of our future together?" Dread consumed her, no longer tamable. Was this what love felt like, this all-consuming need to be with someone?

It felt fast, but in hindsight, it wasn't. It'd been about three months since they first met, and the bond was always there, pulling them together, and who knew how many soulscapes they'd met in over the years. They didn't remember them, but their souls did.

"Leaving you will be the hardest thing I will ever do, but I thought you'd understand that our sisters deserve this. Your sister's soul is trapped, and she deserves to ascend into the aether."

"Don't," she whispered. "Don't throw her in my face. We will find her." She swallowed hard. "But if Adila refuses to help, we will find her *together*. You have waited five-hundred years. What is five hundred more?"

The silence that filled the air was heavy, and she prayed he would reconsider. She lay back down and pulled herself as close to him as possible, and before she drifted to sleep, he murmured, "I will always come back to you."

~

The next day, Rory sat in the office with Lauren, Sam, and Caius, discussing the possibility of Nina being involved in Bellina's assault and the attempts on Rory's life.

"Who else could it be?" Rory asked, throwing her hands up. This was exhausting.

"She was in her apartment all night," Lauren informed them. "It's possible she convinced someone else to do it, but she hasn't corresponded with anyone outside of her new job at the hobby store. Caius' last visit seemed to have shaken her."

"We need to find out who attacked Bellina and make them tell us who put them up to it," Sam said. "Lauren can get anything out of anyone."

Lauren's mouth spread into a feline grin. "Gladly."

"How do we do that?" Rory asked, determined to put this to rest as soon as possible.

Caius shifted in his chair. "We have enforcers questioning the staff with hopes someone saw who entered Bellina's room or other suspicious persons."

Lauren began pacing. "How did they wipe Bellina's memory? Her concussion wasn't that bad, and once healed, her memory should have come back."

They pondered the observation, and Rory remembered something Kordie told her once. *Never accept food or drinks from anyone. Some harmless potions mixed together can be dangerous.*

"They mixed potions," she guessed. "An alchemist friend back home told me regular potions can be mixed to make dangerous ones."

"Sam, bring every alchemist in for questioning," Caius

told his commander. "Lauren, stay with Nina." He paused, cursing. "Nina is an alchemist. Question her first. Meanwhile, Rory and I will speak with the palace doctor to see if there is an antidote to reverse memory potions. We'll have it imported from Erdikoa if needed."

They broke apart with a plan in place. Rory wanted to check in on Bellina, who insisted on returning to work, and when Rory walked into the seamstress quarters of the palace with the king, everyone stopped to stare.

"Please return to work," Caius said, addressing their audience. Rory held in a laugh at the expressions on their faces as they ducked their heads and started snipping and sewing furiously.

Bellina looked up with a smile. "To what do I owe this pleasure?" Her cheery tone was forced, and Rory's stomach hurt, knowing it was her fault.

Rory perched on the edge of Bellina's workstation while Caius stood with his hands in his pockets. "We just stopped in to say hi."

Bellina pointed her scissors accusingly. "You're checking up on me."

Rory lifted a shoulder. "Guilty. How are you feeling?"

She sighed. "I feel fine. The potions made me feel as good as new."

That wasn't what Rory meant, and they both knew it, but her friend needed time. Rory understood. She didn't like discussing her attacks, but now that she was on the other side of it, wanting to comfort her friend, she understood why people asked.

"I can ask everyone to dinner tonight," Rory offered. "They want to see you."

Bellina smiled, and it seemed genuine this time. "I appreciate everything you're doing, but I want to work and rest for a while. I'll let you know when I'm ready."

Rory nodded. "Okay. I'm here when you need me."

"Thanks. You two have fun," Bellina said smugly, a bit of her old teasing self seeping into her words as she looked between Rory and the king.

Rory waved her off as they left, and Caius tugged lightly on her ponytail to get her attention. "Are you okay?"

"Yes." She took one last look at Bellina before they stepped into the hallway. "Being friends with me did that to her, and she didn't deserve it."

Nothing he said would make Rory feel better, and he knew it, because he knew her. "We need to get going," he said, placing his hand on her lower back. "The doctor is expecting us."

Caius chuckled as Rory practically bounced out of the doctor's quarters. He knew of a few potions that reversed memory potions and assured them it wouldn't hurt Bellina to take them all.

"I'll send Sam to Erdikoa to fetch the potions as soon as possible," Caius said as they walked back to their room to change into gym clothes. He wanted Rory to train now more than ever.

They stood in the middle of the gym as Rory did pull ups while Caius supported her legs. Her bare stomach was on display between her bra and shorts, and it glistened with sweat. Remembering their last gym session, he stopped to adjust himself.

When Rory finished her set, she released the bar, landing gracefully on the ground. "I want to spar."

"I would annihilate you." Caius waved his hands over his body. "Immortal strength, remember?"

She planted her hands on her hips. "Exactly. If I can hold my own against you, I can beat anyone without mystical abilities. Besides, I can take potions to heal whatever injuries you cause."

"Fine," he grunted.

They moved to opposite sides of the mat and counted down. Circling each other, they analyzed the other for weaknesses. She dropped her arm, and he took his chance, jabbing at her jaw and stopping short before contact.

"You let your guard down," he said and grabbed her arm. "Keep it up to cover your face at all times."

"And you pulled your punch." Her agitation was cute. "If you refuse to fight me, I can't learn."

He opened his palms. "I won't hit you." He lifted his shirt to wipe the sweat from his brow. "Ask Lauren. I doubt she has reservations about hitting anyone."

Rory shuddered. "She is vicious. I thought watching her rip a throat out was bad, but it had nothing on the spinal cord."

Caius agreed. Lauren did nothing halfway; if she was going to kill you, she would make it a show. "What do you want for dinner tonight?"

She made a show of tapping her finger on her chin as she thought. "Burgers. We can pick it up to go; I don't feel like dealing with your explicit behavior in public again."

He licked his lips and raked his eyes down her body

appreciatively. "I would rather be explicit in private, anyway."

"Feed me, and maybe you'll get lucky," she said as she sauntered to the door.

He would buy as many burgers as the shop could make.

Caius and Rory sat at the table in their room, eating. "Good call on the burgers," he said, taking a bite.

She grinned with a giant bite in her mouth. "I didn't know Vincula had burgers until you left one in my room."

The memory of her face when she told him she'd been sneaking food made his chest tighten. To think she endured cruelty because he'd been quick to judge her made him physically ill.

He set his burger down. "I'm sorry for everything."

Her brows pinched together. "For what?"

"For humiliating you and putting a target on your back. I don't treat my inmates that way, and I should have looked into you more before making a snap judgment."

"Thank you," she replied. "I was still plotting to kill you then, so it was a pretty sound decision on your part."

"My little butcher," he crooned.

"Have you ever loved an inmate before?" she asked, making him pause mid-bite.

"I've never loved anyone before," he replied. "Except my family and friends. Would you be jealous, Miss Raven?"

She pointedly ignored his question. "In five-hundred years, you've loved no one?"

"No, I haven't," he said truthfully.

"Then how do you know you'll love me?" Her eyes

conveyed her uncertainty, and hope took seed within him. *Was she falling for him the way he was falling for her?*

He pushed his plate aside and rested his elbows on the table. "How could I not?"

She tucked a loose hair behind her ear and stared at her food. "I've never loved anyone either." She looked up. "But if I were going to love anyone, it would be you."

"Oh, you will love me, Aurora, because how could you not?" He smiled to put her at ease, and she rewarded him with a small laugh.

"Are you planning a celebration for the end of your contract?" She changed subjects quickly, and his head spun.

"No. I'm not leaving," he reminded her.

She set down her potato sticks. "It's still something to celebrate. Five-hundred years stuck in the same place is a long time."

"I love my realm," Caius replied easily. "Do I miss visiting Erdikoa? Yes, but were it not for my score to settle with Gedeon, I wouldn't mind being stuck here for eternity. It's beautiful, and mostly, the people are pleasant. I have my friends, and if my siblings wanted, they could visit. That's what I miss the most. My sisters."

"I miss my family, too," she said solemnly, and he wanted to rip the realms apart to wipe the sadness from her eyes. It killed him she was here for crimes that saved people.

Was she wrong? *Yes.* Did she deserve half a millennium? *No.*

He cleared his throat and prayed he could make his idea come true. "Once I am released, I will try to arrange a visit."

Her face brightened. "You can do that?"

"I don't know," he admitted. "I would need to clear it with Adila and Gedeon." He was thoughtful. "Gedeon doesn't know that I know he killed Atarah for sure. I always assumed he did, but really, there's no way for him to know because I never confronted him. I could play it off like I'm glad to see him, and it's possible he would grant my request."

Rory fidgeted with her napkin. "I want nothing from him."

Caius didn't blame her. "At the very least, I will visit them regularly and bring back pictures and reports."

A small smile tugged at her lips. "Thank you."

They talked about everything they could think of until the Erdikoa sun went down, and that night as they lay in bed blanketed in post-coital bliss, Caius fell for Aurora Raven.

CHAPTER 38

A few days later, Sam walked into Caius' office with a bag of potions and a grim look on his face.

"Welcome back," Rory said in greeting, leery of his demeanor. He seemed off, and dread seeped into her bones. "Were you able to find the potions?"

"I was," he replied vaguely as he set the bag on Caius' desk.

"Then why do you look like someone clipped your wings?" Caius asked carefully.

Sam's eyes sliced to Rory, and his already grim face darkened. "It's your mother."

Rory grabbed the arms of her chair. "What's wrong with her? Is she okay?"

Caius was quiet, and his eyes were trained on her as Sam cleared his throat. "Her outbursts are worse. She calls for you constantly and is becoming a danger to herself." He hesitated. "If your friends cannot get her under control soon, she'll either land in jail or they'll be forced to put her in a Crown sanctioned facility for *Sibyls.*"

Rory's realm crumbled away, and a tear slipped down her cheek. "No. No, they can't." She looked around, lost. "This is my fault. She's looking for me, and I—I did this to her."

No one bothered telling her otherwise because it was the truth. "There is still a chance she'll settle down when she realizes you won't be coming back," Caius tried to reassure her.

Rory shook her head. "She's stubborn, even when her mind is scrambled. She'll never stop looking for me." She pressed a fist to her mouth to collect herself. "What of my father?"

"He quit his job and found a night job to stay with her during the day, and your friends take turns staying with her at night," Sam replied. "I will do what I can to keep her out of a facility, but there will come a time when it is out of my hands. I am sorry, Rory."

With her head in her hands, she cried harder than she ever had before. Cora's death was not her fault, but her mother's outbursts were. Rory was lifted in the air as Caius cradled her in his arms and carried her to their room.

The next day, a knock on the door roused Rory from sleep, and when Caius opened it, Tallent stood on the other side. He looked surprised to see the king. "I came to see Rory and ask after Bellina," he said cordially.

Caius clapped Tallent on the shoulder with a nod and let him in. "Will you stay with her while I check on Bellina? She was to take a few potions this morning, and we were to meet in half an hour."

"Yes, Your Grace," Tallent replied before turning to Rory. "If that's okay with you?"

She nodded weakly, and Caius walked over to kiss her goodbye. "I'll be back as soon as I can. Let Tallent know if you need anything, and don't leave this room alone."

Another nod was all she could manage. Her throat was raw from crying, and her eyes were swollen beyond recognition. When Caius was gone, Tallent nodded to the bathroom and excused himself, and when he was returned, he sat on the edge of the bed. The silence stretched between them before he reached over and patted her leg in silent support. What was there to say?

Eventually, his voice broke through the quiet. "We miss you, kid." He gave her shin a light squeeze and withdrew his hand. "The girls have been asking about you, and since I had the day off, I volunteered to come check on you."

She pushed herself to a sitting position and grabbed the glass of water from beside the bed to wet her throat. "Thank you," she said after taking a drink. "Bellina is shaken up, but physically she's fine. Except for the hole in her memory, I mean."

Tallent's throat bobbed. "Good." His eyes traced her face. "Is there another reason you've been crying? You look like you went another round with the stairs." His mouth tipped in a teasing smile, and she tinkered out a small laugh.

"I received bad news about my mother." Her eyes burned, and she fought the tears down. "When Bellina feels up to it, we should get dinner and drinks."

Tallent sighed again. "That would be nice, but unfortunately, you won't be able to make it."

Caius stood at the end of Bellina's bed, waiting to see if the memory potions would kick in.

He'd arrived early since Tallent showed up to see Rory, and after the first potion didn't work, Bellina tried the second.

"We will give this one a few more minutes before trying the third," the doctor told them, and Bellina nodded.

She wavered a little and grabbed her head with her eyes closed. "I—I think it's working."

Caius' arms dropped to his sides. "Take your time."

She scrunched her face, and her head twitched. "I remember running into Tallent in the hallway." She shook her head. "He said he needed to speak with me about Rory and asked if we could talk in my room."

Caius' ears rang. "What else?"

Bellina gasped, and her tearful eyes flew open. "It was Tallent." Her mouth opened and closed as her body shook. "He—he held me down and forced a potion down my throat, and he..." She choked on a sob. "He did this."

Caius didn't stay to hear the rest, and Bellina's sobs chased him as he raced back to Rory.

～

"What?" Rory asked, confused.

Tallent stood and placed his hands on his hips, hanging his head. "You couldn't leave Nina alone, could you?" She couldn't make sense of what he was saying. "She only wanted happiness, you know, and you took that from her. You *humiliated* her."

His scornful laugh grated her ears. Something about him had changed.

"She was crushed when she heard the lies you spouted about being the king's mate." Tallent's face hardened with hate. "As if the king would be mated to someone like you."

She flinched, and her pulse skyrocketed as she scrambled backward off the bed. "Why are you doing this? Nina was terrible to me from the start." He moved, and she stepped back, cursing Caius for barricading the main entrance to their room. "You were supposed to be my friend. How can you take her side?" She gasped in horror. "Did you hurt Bellina?"

"It had to be me," he said simply. "Nina is a work of art, and you know how much I love art." His smile was deranged, and she set her feet, ready to fight. "I've always admired her beauty, and when she started working at the hobby store, I realized how wrong I'd been about her. And you."

Rory shook her head frantically. "No, Tallent, she manipulated you. That's what she does. You don't want to do this."

His head tilted to the side. "Yes, I do."

He lunged for her, and she jumped out of the way to run for the bookshelf, cursing the stupid thing for having a button instead of a knob. Tallent grabbed her by the hair and ripped her backward, making a scream tear from her throat. She was cutting her hair as soon as possible.

She turned on her heel, shoving her palm into his elbow, hyper-extending it, and he howled with pain as he released her hair. Fighting was her only option, and she prayed Tallent had no training.

Not waiting for him to attack, she charged at him and drove her foot into his knee, causing him to double over. He righted himself, and the look on his face made her gasp. He was completely mad, and her heart broke for the friend she thought she had.

He swung wildly, but she ducked and delivered a brutal right jab that snapped his head back, followed by a left jab to the throat. Grabbing his good arm, she flipped him over her shoulder, straddled him, and began punching his temple, his eye, his cheek, his mouth, and anything she could connect with. He'd betrayed her, and he'd *hurt* Bellina.

The bookshelf door blew off its hinges, and shadows filled the room, but she didn't stop. Strong hands pulled her from the ground, and she struggled against their hold. "*It was him!*" she screamed, trying to get back to Tallent, to punish him for what he'd done.

The shadows receded, and Caius' arms held her steady as she struggled. "Look at him, Rory," Caius said against her. "*Look* at him."

She stopped moving and glanced at the bloodied heap on the floor. The side of Tallent's skull was partially caved in, and his eyes were glassed over. Her chest heaved as she stared. "He hurt Bellina," she rasped. "He attacked me." She was coming down from her hysteria, and the icy calm of The Butcher took over. Damning the guilty was familiar; it was home.

"Let me go," she commanded, and Caius obliged, noticing the change in her. She crouched beside Tallent. "If I had my hooks, I would display you for the town to see." Standing, she stood and turned to Caius. "Find Nina. She will pay for what she has done."

Examining the knuckles on her right hand, she sighed. Potions would be needed to heal her broken bones.

Caius didn't question her. "We'll find her *together* once we clean up this mess. You have my word."

She gave a single nod and left to shower. "Remove the barricade on our main door, or I will do it myself."

Caius' lips twitched. "Yes, Your Grace."

CHAPTER 39

Nina sat in front of her dressing table, combing her hair a little rougher than necessary. What was it with these men? Not one of them could manage to finish the jobs she'd given them. She sighed and pulled open the drawer to check her potion supply.

When she was in Erdikoa, she often helped her mother make illegal potions to sell in the underground market. Their specialty was concocting *unsavory* potions made from normal, everyday potions.

She and her mother would spend hours in her mother's workshop, mixing different things and trying them out on random volunteers. It was a stroke of luck Nina was also born an alchemist, and she shadowed under her mother from the time she was old enough to walk. Luckily, the potions in the pharmacy were already made, and mixing them didn't need magic. The spells fused on their own.

Few alchemists were as talented mixologists as Nina and her mother. Even if they found her out, she knew Caius wouldn't send her to hell. He loved her, no matter what the little butcher bitch said.

A stronger potion was needed to work on stronger men. Her current mind-bending potion wasn't potent and only worked on the weak. She found men who looked at her with desire, spoke with them to see how gullible they were, and when she found the perfect candidates, she would lick the potion from her finger, kiss them, then immediately lick her other finger containing the antidote.

With regular doses, they were putty in her hands, wanting nothing more than to do her bidding. She was meant to be queen, and before Aurora came along, she was well on her way.

She'd tried the potion on Caius once, but it hadn't worked. He was too powerful. Finding a way to make her potion stronger would be her next course of action.

Just then, she heard the door to her apartment fly open, and before she could stand to investigate, Lauren, an imposing member of the legion, stepped into her bedroom with murder in her eyes.

CHAPTER 40

Rory stood beside Caius on the dais, flanked by Sam and other enforcers as Lauren dragged Nina in by the arm. "What is the meaning of this?" the red head demanded. "I have done nothing wrong!"

Rory's fingernails dug into her palms as she fought the urge to launch herself at the vile woman, and once Nina stood at the foot of the dais, looking at them with as much hate as she could muster, Rory smiled.

"Hello, Nina," she cooed.

"Don't talk to me, butcher bitch," the woman spat, clearly lacking any self-preservation. Nina turned to Caius, the picture of a damsel in distress. "Your Grace, whatever she said is a lie. Since she arrived, she has been terrible to me, spreading terrible rumors. I only tried to protect myself, for I feared for my life."

She cried big crocodile tears, and Rory had to give it to her—she was good, and had Rory not seen her evil firsthand, she might have believed her.

"You are charged with conspiring against a fellow inmate

and the future Umbra Queen," Caius boomed, his voice echoing in the large room.

Nina recoiled and looked between Rory and the king. "No, I didn't. I was only protecting myself," she cried. "*She conspired to kill me!*"

"And now you lie to your king." His smile was merciless. "Your sentence is death."

He turned to Rory, giving her the go ahead, and her own mouth curled into a wicked smile. Seeing Nina's face as she descended the steps of the dais gave her great satisfaction.

Nina fought against Lauren's hold, and another member of the legion took her other arm to hold her steady. When Rory stood in front of the woman, she looked deep into her eyes and held out her palm.

Sam placed a black dagger in her hand, and she looked away from Nina to inspect it. When she turned back, Nina thrashed, trying to tug her arms free. "No! You can't do this!"

She struggled harder, and Rory grabbed the top of her hair to hold her in place. "Tell Orcus hello for me," she purred, repeating Caius' words. She sliced the dagger across Nina's neck and watched as the blood poured out. When Nina's gurgles finally stopped, her body slumped forward.

Turning to Caius, Rory held up the dagger. "Can I keep this?" The ghost of a smile played on his lips.

"You can keep her head if you wish."

This was why they were made for each other. He understood her savagery, admired it even.

As she stood facing the king with the sound of Nina's lifeless body being dragged across the marble floor, she knew she loved him.

He had been wrong.

She was the first to fall.

That night, Caius stood in the doorway to the bathroom, watching Rory through the glass door of the shower. Seeing her strength today was exhilarating, and it confirmed how great of a queen she would be, if given the chance.

Her eyes were still swollen, but not from her fight. Tallent didn't land a hit because she had been ready. They'd gotten the best of her once, and she wouldn't allow it again. No, her face was swollen from crying over the news of her mother, and Caius had agonized over it all day.

He couldn't let Rory suffer, and she would, knowing the state her mother was in. He would petition Adila to bring Lenora here, but allowing an innocent into Vincula was unheard of.

If Lenora came in Vincula, her abilities would disappear as her essence was siphoned to power Erdikoa, alleviating her madness. It could work, if only his sister would agree. If Adila had to clear it with Gedeon, it was a no, but just maybe she would grant him this without going through their brother.

"Are you going to stare all night, or are you going to join me?" Rory said without looking at him, and he chuckled as he shed his clothes.

He stepped in behind her and moved her hair over her shoulder to kiss her neck as the water pelted them both. "You were beautiful today," he murmured against her skin.

She turned, wrapped her arms around his neck, and lifted on her toes to kiss him. Their tongues danced together, gliding smoothly as they gave in to their need for each other.

His hands explored her slick body, and his own heated in return. She moaned into his mouth, and he pulled back to wrap a hand around her throat. "I won't be gentle," he warned. He was predatory after watching her in action today, and he needed to fuck her hard.

She grabbed his cock and squeezed. "I won't be either."

He flipped her around and ran his fingers through her arousal. "You will scream for me, louder than you ever have."

"Fuck me hard enough, and I might," she said, shooting him a taunting smile over her shoulder.

He pulled his fingers back, aligned his cock, and thrust into her, the momentum slamming her against the wall. His hand flew up to protect her face from hitting the tile, and she arched her back in response.

One hand dug into her hip, and the other snaked under her arm to grab her neck and pull her back. He squeezed the sides of her throat as he rammed into her again, and her head lolled back.

"Fuck," she moaned and pushed her hips back against his.

"Louder," he commanded.

Her hand moved down her stomach to the apex of her thighs, and he licked the shell of her slightly pointed ear. "Play with your clit for me, baby."

Her fingers worked circles as he thrust into her until her breaths came in pants. "I can't hear you." He pulled back and stopped with only the tip in.

She whimpered and pushed back. "Caius." Her hand reached blindly behind her, but he removed his hand from her hip and batted it away.

"Scream for me, or you won't like the outcome." He

slammed into her as hard as he could, and she cried out. "*Louder.*"

With every thrust, her moans and cries rose. "Good girl. *Louder.*"

The hand on her clit moved in time with his hips, and before long, he felt her smooth inner walls squeeze. He moved faster, until his balls drew up, and she exploded with a scream so loud, the shower door shook. Her pussy milked his dick, and he came harder than he ever had before.

They tried to catch their breath as the water rained down on them, and when he pulled out, she stepped out and looked over her shoulder. "Is that all?"

He pounced and ripped the towel from her hands with a growl. "You'll pay for that smart mouth."

Picking her up, he stalked to the bed and threw her down as she yelped and propped herself up on her elbows. The smile on her face was a challenge, and he wanted to swallow it with his own.

Shadows darted to her arms and legs and pulled them wide, and he delighted at the alarm on her face. "Is this okay?" he asked. If it made her uncomfortable, he would stop, but aether, he hoped he didn't have to.

"A little bondage doesn't faze me, Your Grace." Her words held an underlying challenge.

"If you change your mind, use a safe word of your choosing," he replied.

"King," she said coyly. "My safe word is king." *This woman.*

Positioning himself between her legs, he grabbed her hips, and when he seated himself inside her, she gasped. The angle was deep, and she felt amazing. It would take all of his focus to keep from coming in three pumps.

Shadows caressed her bare skin and covered her breasts, pulling a moan from her perfect lips. He moved slowly, and she wiggled against the restraints. When her eyes found his, they were hazy as another moan escaped her.

"Remember, Miss Raven, you brought this on yourself."

She threw her head back as a shadow vibrated over her clit, making her jerk against the shadowy restraints. "Caius," she breathed as her legs tried to draw up.

He moved at a leisurely pace, enjoying the sight of her body twitching beneath him. She screamed his name and arched off the bed as her body trembled and squeezed around him.

He closed his eyes and breathed through his nose to keep from blowing, and when he regained control, the shadow on her clit dissolved. "I..." she trailed off, rolling her head from side to side. "I can't..."

Caius watched his cock slide in and out of her, and when he picked up the pace, she gasped. He grinned as he pulled another shadow to her clit, making it vibrate in a pattern of pulses, stopping when she came close to exploding.

She thrashed and cried out, begging him to stop, but until he heard the safe word, she was at his mercy. "Caius," she sobbed.

Her legs tried to pull from his grasp, but he held on. Watching her convulse with another impending climax was too much, and when she came, he would come with her.

Placing his hand on her lower stomach, he looked up. "Look at me."

She opened her hazy eyes, and when her grey met his gold, he smiled and pushed down, making that inner sensitive spot brush against his dick. Her eyes widened, and she threw her head back with another scream.

She squeezed around him as she came, covering him in her cum. It sent him over the edge, and he fell forward as he filled her with hot streams of his own. The shadows disappeared as he slowed his pumps, and they rode out the waves of their releases together.

His pelvis brushed against her sensitive clit, and she shook her head. "King! For aether's sake, *king!*"

"You did good, baby," he crooned as he pulled out and grabbed a towel. After cleaning her off, he picked her up and moved them both under the covers. "I would tell you not to speak to me that way again, but I quite enjoyed seeing you at my mercy."

She replied with a sleepy chuckle, and together, they drifted off to sleep.

Early the next morning, soft cries pulled Caius from sleep, and he sat up, looking around. Rory was nowhere to be found, and a soft light shone from under the bathroom door. As he walked closer, he realized they were coming from inside, and he quietly turned the doorknob, only to find it locked.

He knocked softly and called through the wood, "Rory, baby, are you okay?"

He heard sniffles before she croaked, "I'm fine. Go back to sleep."

Worry seeped into his bones, and he tried the door again. "Let me in, Rory."

"I said go back to sleep."

He stepped back and kicked the door in, and the sight before him made him falter. She was curled into a ball on the floor, and when she saw him, she cried harder. Rushing to her side, he scooped her into his arms, sat down, and rocked her slowly.

They sat like that for what felt like hours until her cries died down. "I'm a murderer. How is it fair that I am happy when my mother is suffering because of me?" Her red, puffy face turned to his. "The guilt will haunt me for the rest of my life."

Caius swallowed hard as his heart broke for the woman he loved. There was nothing he could do to console her, and he knew that, but damn it if he hated that she didn't trust him with her tears.

He said the only thing that came to mind, "Never lock me out again. I will always make your tears my own. We're in this together."

He might not have the right words, but a plan formed in his mind. Placing a kiss on her head, he picked her up and carried her back to bed.

Rory sat around a table at the bar with Kit, Bellina, and Cat. The air was somber, the hurt of Tallent's betrayal and death hanging over them.

"I'm sorry," Rory said for the hundredth time. "He was trying to kill me, and after what he did to Bellina, I couldn't let him hurt anyone else."

Even though he betrayed them in the worst way, they mourned the friend they thought he was.

"Don't be sorry," Cat said, reaching across the table to grab her hand. "Any of us would have done the same."

"I only wish you could've hung him from a hook, the

double-crossing bastard," Kit said, throwing back another shot. The woman could drink like a fish. "He deserved that and more."

Bellina's eyes watered. She'd been quiet, and Rory knew she needed time to heal. "I wouldn't feel safe if he was still here. You did for me what I did for my wife, and I don't regret my actions. You shouldn't regret yours.

"And fuck Nina, too," Cat added. "That bitch had it coming, and if Tallent was weak enough to fall for her tricks, he had it coming, too."

"Cheers to The Butcher," Bellina said, holding her glass high. "For doing what she does best and ridding the realms of evil. May they rest unpeacefully in hell."

CHAPTER 41

Rory crawled into bed, exhausted from the day. To celebrate Caius' last day of incarceration, they stayed together, doing whatever he wanted. He'd wanted to play arrowball and eat at their favorite spots in town, mostly. He even asked to meet her friends for a few drinks.

He crawled in beside her, quieter than usual, and she assumed he was nervous and excited for the next day, which was understandable.

"What are you thinking about?" she asked.

He reached out and caressed her cheek. "You. How perfect you are, and how much being apart from you will hurt more than anything in the realms."

Tension seeped into her shoulders. "You said you wouldn't go after Gedeon until we could do it together."

His eyes moved over her face until they met hers. "I'm not going after Gedeon."

She felt the truth in his words and relaxed. He must have meant when he would visit Erdikoa because their souls needed to be together. Wasn't that what he'd told her?

"We'll meet in the soulscape until you come back," she reminded him.

He leaned forward and kissed her forehead. "We'll always have the soulscape."

Rory woke with a start, and when she felt the bed beside her, all she found was air. The clock read a little past eleven-thirty at night. She fell asleep on Caius' chest, and now he was gone. Where was he?

Her body craved him beside her, especially after they'd made love earlier in the night. The phrase 'made love' always made her cringe, but now she understood. She knew in her heart that's what they did.

Because she loved him, and he loved her. Even if they hadn't told each other, they both knew. She was going to tell him tomorrow so the day would be filled with happy memories all around.

She didn't know how the process worked for him. For the others, they vanished from their beds or wherever they were at midnight, but with him being king, she assumed he would stay until he wanted to leave.

Apprehension filled her from head to toe, and all she wanted to do was find him. Even though they spent time together over the last few days, a lot of it was devoted to her friends, who were having a hard time with Tallent's betrayal.

They were all shocked, of course, and none of them knew if he had an infatuation with Nina before she started working with him, or if she convinced him to betray his friends in such a short amount of time.

Rory preferred the former, because knowing he could be swayed so easily felt worse. The town was rattled to hear the news of Nina and Tallent's treachery, but what really shook them were the rumors about Rory taking the throne.

The thought made her grin, and she decided she wouldn't wait until tomorrow. When she found Caius, she would tell him how she felt. His favorite book sat on the nightstand, and she swiped it. Sometimes when he couldn't sleep, he liked to read or sneak sweets from the kitchen.

When she slipped through the door to the office, she halted.

Sam, Lauren, and Caius stood around his desk, and Sam and Lauren were arguing with him.

"What's going on?" she asked tentatively. Whatever was happening was serious.

Caius' head snapped in her direction, and anguish filled his face. "Rory," he rasped. "You should be in bed."

She willed her voice to strengthen. "Tell me what's wrong."

He hung his head while Sam and Lauren glared at the king. "Caius?" Rory tried again.

His fingers were curled around a piece of paper, and without looking at her, he scribbled something along the bottom. "What is that?" she tried again. No one would answer her, and she was on the verge of a panic attack. Her fingers filled with pinpricks and grew heavy as her breathing picked up speed.

"I've taken over your contract," Caius said, his voice full of emotion.

His words made little sense, and she looked at Sam and Lauren for clarification, but they refused to meet her gaze. "Took over my contract? I don't understand."

She was at his side now, gazing over his arm to see the

papers he held. The top sheet was a contract, and she saw both of their names listed on the top.

"What is this?" She tucked his book under her arm, tore the paper from his hands, and scanned the document.

It said her contract transferred to him. She would be released tomorrow, and he would serve another five-hundred years.

"What? Why would you do this?" She was touched by his selflessness, but she couldn't allow him to give up his freedom. He'd waited too long for it.

His eyes glistened with unshed tears. "Your mother needs you, and I can't watch you blame yourself for her condition."

She shook her head, grasping for whatever piece of the puzzle she was missing. Then it clicked, and the floor fell out from under her. Her memory would wipe clean, meaning she would forget Vincula, her friends, and *him*. "Why would you do this?" she repeated, raising her voice. "You said you can't change contracts."

She'd never seen such pain in his golden eyes. "I can't dissolve contracts, and I didn't. I switched them."

Rory's mind raced, and she shook her head again. "Please don't do this, Caius."

"It's already done," Sam said with a voice of steel as he glared at the king. "It cannot be undone."

"Undo it!" she screamed as she ripped the document to shreds. Her hand clasped around his arm, making him look at her. "I love you, Caius. I love you. You can't do this."

Tears slipped from his eyes. "I can't keep you here in misery. I wouldn't be able to live with myself."

"No!" she sobbed as she beat her hand against his chest, the other still clutching the book. "You promised. You promised to get down on one knee when I said it. I'm saying it. I love you, and I am begging you not to do this."

He grabbed her hand and brought it to his mouth. "Don't you see? I have been on my knees from the moment you landed in my throne room."

She shook her head and backed out of his hold, turning to the *Angels*. "How could you let him do this? *How?*" she screamed. Her realm was falling apart at the hand of the man she loved, and tomorrow, she wouldn't even know it.

"Do you not love me?" she choked out. "Is that it?"

The horror on his face matched her own, and she crumbled from the weight of it. "I love you more than anything, and I always will."

"I will find my way back to you," she vowed.

"We'll always have the soulscape," he whispered. "It will only be a dream to you, and you won't remember me, even there, but I'll be there waiting."

She choked out another sob and reached for him, but her vision went black.

Caius stared at the spot where Rory once stood, grief destroying his insides. His only reprieve was their soulscape, and the *Angels'* promises to check in on her frequently.

"You should have married her first," Sam thundered. His best friend was pissed, and rightfully so, but it had to be done.

"Had I married her, she would've been on Gedeon's radar," Caius yelled back. "I am no fool. Do not think I didn't weigh every option. You didn't see the guilt that weighed on her every day after hearing of her mother, but I did." He lowered his voice. "She won't know what I've done because she won't remember me."

The pieces of his heart were scattered on the floor next to the contract Rory destroyed.

"You said you would ask Adila to send her mother here," Lauren said in a crisp voice. She was never one to yell, and when she stared at him with vast disappointment, he had to look away.

"She said no before I told her who the mystic was or why," Caius replied. He had a phone in his quarters that connected to his siblings. Adila shut him down immediately, without question.

"We have an arrival scheduled in the morning," Sam said. "I suggest you sleep, *Your Grace.*"

Caius pulled up to his full height and pinned the two *Angels* with a dangerous look. "Do not patronize me. It is done, and I will punish myself far worse than either of you can. If you want to do right by her, protect her."

He'd known once their bond snapped in place, he would put her above all else, even his need for revenge, and if he could go back, he would choose to love her every time. Turning on his heel, he left them standing in his office. He was a king, and while his heart was in Erdikoa, his responsibilities were here.

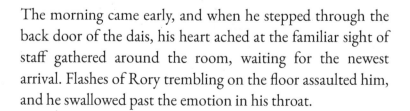

The morning came early, and when he stepped through the back door of the dais, his heart ached at the familiar sight of staff gathered around the room, waiting for the newest arrival. Flashes of Rory trembling on the floor assaulted him, and he swallowed past the emotion in his throat.

Taking a seat on his throne, he waited, willing his sister to be swift. Either an inmate would show, along with an enforcer, or only the enforcer would appear with news of the condemned going to hell.

Minutes passed before an older woman stumbled to the floor at the end of the aisle, and an enforcer appeared along the side wall. Caius sighed, rose from his throne, and descended the stairs. He'd only taken a few steps when the woman scrambled to her feet, frantically looking around.

"Where is she?" She was yelling, and Caius walked faster. "*Where is she?*" the woman demanded again, speaking to no one and everyone at once.

The woman spotted him as he continued his path toward her, and her eyes widened. "You sent her already, didn't you?" she asked, covering her mouth. Now her voice filled with pain, and she met him halfway, pounding her fists into his chest, much like Rory had done. "*You gave her to him! You gave her to him!*" She swung with impressive strength for a woman her age as she swore and screamed. "*How could you?!*"

The woman sobbed and slumped to the floor, and Caius looked at Sam and the accompanying enforcer with bewildered eyes. He motioned for the enforcer to bring the woman's contract, never taking his eyes off her as she wept at his feet.

His eyes scanned the document, and his knees nearly buckled.

Lenora Raven.

Sibyl.

Sentenced to one year for attempted armed robbery of a bank.

The contract fluttered to the floor as he stumbled back a

step. "You're Rory's mother." His voice was barely a whisper as shock overtook him.

She looked up through her tears. "And you are a *fool*. She was safe with you, and you sent her into his arms."

His?

"Whose arms?" Caius demanded as his voice shook with emotion.

Lenora looked at him with such torment, he felt the weight of it like a tangible thing. "The Lux King."

The air whooshed from Caius' lungs. "He doesn't know about her," he said, trying to convince himself more than anyone.

Lenora released a humorless laugh. "I have seen it, just as I have seen you."

She was a *Sibyl*, and the prophecy written on a paper in his desk drawer proved what she said was true.

He tried to save Rory, and instead, he sent his mate into Gedeon's waiting arms.

EPILOGUE

ERDIKOA

Rory tumbled to the ground, the cold from the concrete floor seeping into the hand holding her up. She looked around the tiny room, trying to figure out where she was. The last thing she remembered was the Scales of Justice sentencing her to five-hundred years in Vincula, then everything went black.

Was she in a holding cell in the prison realm? In her other hand, she clutched a book for dear life, and upon further inspection, she was surprised to see it was one of Cora's favorites from when they were kids.

She didn't remember bringing this with her to The Capital.

Sitting back on her heels, she surveyed the small room and covered her mouth to muffle a scream. Everything was in color. Plush red chairs lined one wall, and a brown wooden table sat between them. She shook as her brain tried to process what she was seeing.

The door to the room flew open, and Rory scrambled to her feet. A woman with white streaked hair stepped inside and looked at Rory with a tinge of sadness.

"Hello, Aurora Raven. Welcome back to Erdikoa."

"Welcome back?" Rory squeaked. "It's been five-hundred years?"

The woman shook her head. "Somehow, your sentence ended early. It's been three months."

Rory's jaw dropped to the ground, elated to be home but terrified to see her friends and family again.

Would they hate her? Either way, it was a miracle.

Read the conclusion to Caius and Rory's story in
Aeternum
Vincula Realm Book II

ABOUT THE AUTHOR

"Why is no one having a good time? I specifically requested it."

—*Raymond Holt*

LET'S CONNECT!

Newsletter

I rarely send out newsletters unless it's to announce book releases, giveaways, or free books/content.
<u>SIGH UP NOW</u>

TikTok
@<u>jah.hdj.books</u>
Instagram
@<u>jah.hdj.books</u>
<u>Discord</u>
Members of my Discord get sneak peeks and first dibs on ARCs (among other things).
Facebook Group
Same perks as Discord
Website
<u>www.jamieapplegatehunter.com</u>

ALSO BY JAMIE APPLEGATE HUNTER

<u>Vincula Realm Duology</u>

The Umbra King

Aeternum

<u>Standalones</u>

Silenced Fate

ACKNOWLEDGMENTS

I want to thank my husband for being my biggest hype man. He does what he can to make sure I have plenty of uninterrupted writing time, including wrangling our feisty daughter, taking our son wherever he needs to go, and fetching me coffee when I need it. He constantly asks me how my books are doing and brags about me to anyone he meets.

I want to thank one of my best friends and editor, Erica. She messaged me to tell me how much she enjoyed The Compeer, and now, we talk every day about life and books. When I found out she was an editor, I hired her without question. Thank you for listening to my textcasts.

I want to thank my alpha and beta readers. Without y'all, this book would suck big donkey balls, and we all know it.

Last, but not least, I want to thank everyone on BookTok for reading my debut series and giving me the confidence to continue writing.

CONTENT WARNINGS

Not suitable for those under 18 years of age.

Graphic violence and death, torture, mature language, explicit sexual situations, death of a loved one, murder, memory loss, and brief mention of sexual assault

Made in the USA
Columbia, SC
30 July 2024

39677089R00252